I0603918

welcome!
browse, sit awhile or borrow.
but, please
RETURN TO:

Also From the Author

- *A Lad From Sardinia* The Adventures of Morgan Harmony

   A High Seas Adventure In The Mediterranean Sea
   In the 1600's. Story set in prose poetry.

- *Poetpourri* A Labyrinth of Wandering Thought

   A Collection of Short Stories, Poems and Prose Poetry
   From the Ridiculous to the Sublime.

- *A Ranger's Tale* Jacks' Vendetta

   An Old West adventure revolving around the fledgling
   band of Texas Rangers in pursuit of the Jacks' gang.

- *Cowboy Justice* On The Border

   A fictional account of an Arizona lawman who
   joins a vigilante group to rid the influx of illicit drugs and entry
   by undocumented migrants along the southern U.S. border.

- *A Cry For Justice* (continuing the fight against corruption)

   Trafficking and drug-running are ugly, ongoing problems, not just
   in Arizona, but in every state--and now, as a couple, Frank and his
   bride feel a shared obligation to follow the desperate cry for help
   wherever and whenever it presents.

The Reunion
a Case of Revocable Trust

A GUMSHOE & FOX
CRIME STORY

By

Myron Ferdig

This book
is a work of fiction.

Names, characters, events, places or incidents are the product of the author's imagination or are used fictitiously.

Any resemblance to actual persons, living or dead, or events or locales is entirely coincidental.

The Reunion
a Case of Revocable Trust

A GUMSHOE & FOX

CRIME STORY

ONE

I looked at my cell phone/watch--It was only 5:48 p.m. *I could use a drink.*

Class of 1999 was, on the whole, a noisy flock. As I meandered away from the crowded cacophony of almost-forty-year-olds undulating, writhing flesh in their sundry attempts for purchase of a square foot of parquet flooring--or perhaps a pound of flesh--I felt several pairs of eyes on my backside. The open bar was crowded as well . . . Perhaps outside . . .

I reached my hand between suit jackets, slacks and dresses, trying not to be arrested for groping, and came away with an open bottle of *Chivas Regal*, not my favorite, but any port in a storm as they say . . . I used to know who *they* were . . . I pulled it away from the bar, midst "Heys!" and "Where you going with that?" from my fellow graduates and headed for the nearest exit.

Outside was hardly better. Small groups and couples had scrounged chairs and benches from the ballroom and were now lounging in the balmy July evening, catching up on the past twenty years--their successes, failures, children, divorces, travels, on and on . . .

As I searched for familiar faces, I made my way to the observation deck, two decks above the ballroom, found the hatchway door to a cylindrical shaft . . . more of a tube . . . complete with a short ladder. I had no reason to stop and chat; hell, I didn't remember any of these people. Twenty busy years, indeed!

A quick few steps upward found me on the flying bridge, then another few steps to the ship's railing; and there I sat watching the last few remnants of a Saturday sun in July 2019. I felt the breeze from the Malibu, the rise and fall of the Pacific swells against the giant vessel, wondering why the hell I had come to this reunion.

Strange, isn't it, I thought. *Most of the fellows I recognized enough to shake their hands here this evening--among them the jocks--and I actually only recognized them from name labels . . . Matt Wallis, Barry Franks, Allen Bergstrum (and maybe a few more)-- were bullies, and I was a favorite target; most of the gals--Patti Brown, Gerri Kitchens, Roberta Cordero among them--shunned me twenty years ago as a bookworm or some even as a nerdy know-it-all.*

Thinking back, I could never see myself as a know-it-all. I can't remember ever trying to show up any of my classmates. I probably weighed 135 pounds soaking wet, with my nose always in a book. My grades were always near the top of the class, but I made no big deal about it. I kept to myself back then. That's one trait I still prefer.

A bit different this evening. I had to inwardly smile to myself . . . no wonder I had a few pairs of eyes on my "six". I had changed quite a bit.

* * *

Memories of my early school years took over and flooded through my mind as I prepared to take a swig of Chivas--it was worth a giggle or two. Let me take you back in time a score or more years. I was brought up as an only child in a happy, Christian home.

I was a bookworm, and not only that, but a little bit of a twerp as well. I had no spurt in height as most of my fellow classmates enjoyed. As I grew into puberty, I was, I suppose, like any typical bright-eyed kid, hormones beginning to suggest I was no longer a child, eyes as big as saucers when I caught glimpses of female anatomy that should have been covered with at least a strip of cloth.

I stayed at 5'1" from twelve years until almost fourteen years. Then in my fourteenth summer I spurted up to 5'6", and by sixteen I reached 5'7" and weighed one hundred thirty-two pounds . . . and the jocks and their counterparts--the female clique--were murderous with their taunting and teasing. Today of course, it would be called bullying, then it was just good, clean fun. *Yeah, Right!*

My grades were at the top, I kept to myself, was slated to deliver the Valedictory Address but for circumstances I will describe a bit later. I suppose Sherri Foote took that spot. She would have done an exemplary job.

Dating? Seldom. My free time was spent on the water: surfing, fishing, or perhaps, sailing with the folks. Sure, I dated--several times in fact with Sherri Foote-- fewer times with other young ladies, but as memory serves, always with proper decorum and respect.

I remember taking Sherri to the senior prom. I remember walking her to her door; when I hesitated, she asked me if I wanted to kiss her goodnight. I kissed her cheek and walked away . . . so, yes, I suppose the jocks were right . . . I was a nerd, spending most of my time studying, reading, fishing, sailing or surfing.

There was one incident . . . I'll unpack it here as it relates to much leading to our twenty year reunion . . .

In our junior year, I was just walking out of the cafeteria during lunch hour when I was surrounded by five or six girls--the popular crowd. One of them, Patti Brown, challenged me with, "Alan, you should take Roxy out. She'll be good to you." She pushed a laughing Roxanne DeVry toward me, "Won't you, Roxy?" Now, Roxanne was a very pretty girl in our class, but she was known to be extremely loose; had probably screwed every boy on campus--except me. Roxanne looked at me and said, "I don't know if I would or not . . . how big is your dick, Alan?"

Of course, the circle around me, including Roxy, broke into fits of laughter. Sherri was walking by at the time and stopped to watch. My face turned purple with embarrassment, I retorted with the only thing I could think of "You'll never know," and walked away.

Roxy's question became the most repeated snicker on campus. For the remainder of that year and all through my senior year it was voiced within my hearing scores of times, usually not to my face, but as an aside.

If Sherri was around, she would take my arm, and reprimand the offender . . . she was, in short, my guardian angel. But most of the time I dealt with the crude language myself. In fact, toward the end of the year, I told Sherri to please butt out; I would handle Roxanne myself. That seemed to upset her. She turned on her heel. We never spoke again.

Which brings us up to the present . . . the reunion.

* * *

And again I ask myself, *Why are you here, Alan?* Preparing to take a first swig from my liberated bottle, I heard a metallic click, followed by a rustling sound. I set the bottle down and listened. Nothing. I started once again to raise the bottle, but I heard another metallic click, like perhaps, the latch on the hatchway door. Finally, a definite footstep on the ladder rung. I set the bottle down yet again. Someone was preparing to join me on the bridge? *Crap! No peace for the . . .*

"Alan! Alan, are you up there? Alan?"

. . . female voice, I think. Couldn't recognize it . . . but after twenty years?

"It's Roxanne. Remember me? Roxy DeVry."

A scrambled, vague series of bits and bytes began to gel in my brain. *Oh, sure, I remember you, Roxanne DeVry . . . The "how big is your dick?" Roxanne!* I thought. Strange voice though . . .

I shook my head, rose to my feet--expecting to walk across the bridge to the tubular shaft, reach down, assist my old, slut of a classmate up the ladder rungs. Instead, I was just in time to hear a muffled, gurgling sound, then a heavy *thump!*

No more words. Just a *thump.* Then, one last click as the latch closed.

* * *

It became clear something unusual had just happened. I hadn't recognized Roxanne's voice, but as I used my lighted cellphone and peered into the laddered shaft below I could make out a yellow flowery pair of legs, a matching long flowery jacket--more of a tunic-- and long, wavy red hair, all in a crumpled heap at the bottom.

She was definitely dead. I descended. I was not about to turn her over to get a look at her face; this was not my crime scene. I simply assumed I was looking at a very dead Roxanne DeVry.

Again I thought, *I could use a drink* . . . but I took a couple of pictures and called 911 instead. A growing halo of crimson was oozing around the lifeless figure below--a slightly darker shade of red. I was able to push the hatchway door open, hop over the heap on the floor and back to the observation deck.

TWO

Inspector Morris arrived twenty minutes later . . . maybe 5'9", sixty-ish, sandy-graying hair, the beginning of a paunch, pants creased, Windsor knot perfectly tied, all business. His assistant, Bradley Swazer—or something like that--looked to be still in high school, 6' easy, nonchalant, not nearly as tidy, and I sized him up immediately as a cocky know-it-all.

The third and fourth members of the *visiting squad* were CSI types, complete with their bags of crime scene tools. Non-identical twins, no doubt. More 'no nonsense' types--both forty-ish, one stout, the other anorexic, both women looked tired.

They met me on the observation deck without fanfare--as I had asked. So far as I knew, no one was aware of the murder except me . . . and the killer.

I couldn't bring myself to crawl or tiptoe back over the dead red head for the *Chivas Regal*, so I sat on a lounge chair and soberly waited for the cops.

I led the foursome to the hatchway door and opened it. No surprises there; she was still dead—throat obviously cut from ear to ear, blood everywhere.

Back in the lounge chairs. Questions. All but one of which came from Morris:

"Who was she? What's her relationship to you? Why was she here? Did you invite her up? How long have you known her? Who are you? Why were you up here?"

"Where did you put the knife?" Bradley asked.

That last question pissed me off, but I kept my cool . . . and calmly went through everything I knew, thought I knew, and surmised had gone on earlier this evening:

"Her name was Roxanne DeVry when we went to school together. I don't know what she calls herself after twenty years . . . I should say, called herself, because, whoever she was, she didn't make it up that ladder.

We had probably shared a couple of classes together."

I cleared my throat, thinking of that incident of twenty years past, and carried on, "I hardly dated, and certainly Roxy and I never dated; she had the reputation on campus as a slut, we were not in the same social or academic circles and definitely went our separate ways. I do know our graduating class boasted 455 graduates; I didn't keep in touch with any of them.

In fact, I lost my mom on May 27 of 1999. Her commercial flight crashed in the Himalayas ten days before graduation day. I demanded that I travel to the crash scene with Pop to search for survivors, got a special visa and was gone for almost the full month of

June. So, whatever school friends I had disappeared into the fog of June, 1999."

Morris held his hand up, answered his phone, mumbled, "I see. Thanks." Turned back to me and said, "Continue."

"I immediately joined the Air Force, after four years became a member of AFOSI (Office of Special Investigations) and served in that capacity until I retired just three months ago, after twenty years. With my special training, my plan is to become a private detective, and I've filled those prerequisites. Would you believe, Sir, I received my license to practice and *carry* in California just last Wednesday?

A couple-three weeks ago a mailed notice came from Patti Wellings -- used to be Brown -- reminding all graduates from the class of '99 to come to the 20th reunion aboard the cruise ship.

She put a personal note on a corner of the invite saying, 'Please come, Alan; we'll have a great time.'

My first thought was, *how did she know my address?* Then I thought, *why not go*? Might even drum up some business . . . you know, cheating on partners, teen gone missing, that kind of thing . . . so I brought some business cards, even handed out a couple dozen earlier this evening.

But I'm not too much for socializing, so I went looking for a peaceful, quiet spot to view the sunset on my own. Come to think of it, as I walked over to the bar, I had the eerie feeling someone or *someones* were watching me--maybe because of my doling out those business cards, I don't know.

Anyway, I'm just settling in, haven't even taken a swig of Chivas when I hear this gal say, 'Alan, are you up there?' So I get up, hear a noise, go to the ladder, look down and call you. And no, I have not had a drink in over an hour! And no, I did not have a knife! And no, I did not kill her! And yes! I could use a drink."

THREE

The body was removed. A team of officers was called in to take information from every one of the more than three hundred attendees. Word circulated of a female's death, but as yet it was simply listed as: unknown female found dead; cause of death unknown.

Inspector Morris asked me to join him at a table in the center of the ballroom. He jotted down a note on a pad he kept in his jacket pocket, then asked me to grab the band's mic (the band was on a break anyway) and make an announcement, exactly as he had written. Without pre-reading it, I agreed. "Hi folks. Alan Garrett here. Remember I told a few of you earlier, I just applied for and qualified as a private eye. I haven't set up shop yet, but I find myself in the middle of an investigation here tonight. This party started around 4 p.m. today and we've had a lot of fun; some have left for the day, some are bagged and gone to get some rest in a rented stateroom, some in the restaurant on the next deck, and some are still here. Please look around. Anyone in your circle of friends, especially a lady, who should be here and is not, anyone out of place, perhaps an estranged husband, or complete stranger, any peculiarities you have noticed, please walk over," I pointed, "and let the gentlemen and me know. I'll be at that table as well." Inspector Morris waved to the folks.

"Oh! And please, no one leave before supplying contact information for the fellows with badges walking around with clipboards. If you have a schedule that must be kept--babysitter, that kind of thing, you search one of them out, answer some questions, and you can be on your way. Enjoy the rest of your evening folks. Thanks."

I walked back toward my seat amid a few "Atta boy, Alans," and "WooHoos," and "We got ourselves a private Dick!" With that remark came scattered, crude snickering. There were five or six people already circling Inspector Morris before I got there; I dragged a couple of extra chairs with me. Hell, I didn't remember any of these people. The few I do remember aren't here, with three or four exceptions.

* * *

Patti Wellings hurried to take the seat next to me. She had a faint, but definite medicinal odor about her, masked by a lovely, expensive perfume. "You don't remember me, do you, Alan?"
"Not at all, Ma'am. Sorry."
Patti continued, "No matter. To be honest I don't remember you either. I'm Patti. Patti Brown. The Alan Garrett I knew was about 5'8 or 9", and a shy kid. You're certainly not shy, and you must be 6'2" at least."

It was true. I had grown almost five inches in my first year in the Air Force, surprising everyone in my squadron. At the same time, I had developed an assurance never   before realized. Several higher-ups noticed my abilities as well as my new-found comportment, and the rest is history . . . but I digress . . .

"Now, Mr. Alan Garrett, I have made some rather interesting observations this evening." Patti began to itemize her thoughts--some interesting, some not worth documenting--but they were Patti's, and they were observations; I filled a sheet of paper with her ideas, then I handed her a sheaf of paper and listened while she continued to talk as she wrote. This was going to be a long evening, and I could use a drink. But I smiled.

Inspector Morris and his sidekick, Swazer were at the table, interviewing and note-taking others as well, while the fifteen or so city cops were taking down names, addresses and phone numbers of everyone still at the reunion. "Someone needs to go into bathrooms, staterooms, and on the different decks to bring anyone else down to the ballroom for questioning," Morris, sitting opposite me at the circular table, announced.

"Before you get involved with your next, uh, *customer*, Alan, why don't you run up to the observation deck. Take Ms Wellings, there, with you. She can peek in the ladies' rooms while you the men's; then the stateroom deck, restaurant, then get yourselves back here, pronto. Advise everyone. Crew members, everyone!"

Not the way I would handle this! But . . . I handed the sheaf of Patti's writings to Morris. Patti and I took the ship's elevator to the observation deck. Again I noticed the strange odor, like a cross between a linament I had smelled in Veterans' hospitals and a weak household bleach, masked nicely by her lovely perfume. I was just beginning to remember Patti as part of that inner high school clique when she turned to me with a pained expression on her face. "I need to speak with you alone, Alan. I have your card. May I call you tomorrow? It's important," she pleaded.

FOUR

Two or three gents were in the men's room, a few couples in the lounge area and I caught a couple as they were climbing the stairs from a lower deck. I scuttled their plans with the news of the death and encouraged them to head for the ballroom.

Patti was obviously having similar success, as a bevy of ladies exited the powder room on their way downstairs, midst a hubbub of excited chatter.   After a longing look at the exit leading to the flying bridge where my recently procured Chivas Regal stood-- *probably being guzzled down right now by the two CSIs on scene in that narrow hatchway*--I smiled a *Damn!* smile as I waited for my new partner to exit the ladies' so that we might continue to the staterooms.

The entire observation deck had emptied. I shrugged my shoulders; Patti had left without me. *Probably thought I had already descended the stairs to the staterooms.*

I continued down the stairway and began knocking on doors. Five people were on the floor: two fellows in the men's room, a ship's cleaner who hadn't yet heard the word, and one couple in a rented stateroom. They begged me to keep their liaison private; they had come with other than present company.

Shaking my head, I laughed, let them know my occupation, advised them to take separate avenues downstairs, and handed each a business card. I asked the cleaner to check the ladies' bath for occupants. There were none.

I rejoined Morris and Swazer at our table. The newcomers were brought up to date by their classmates, and had given their information to the clipboard cops. Morris handed me another note to recite to the entire group.

"Hello! Yeah, it's me again . . ." I was interrupted by several voices shouting over each other . . .

"Hey, Mr. Private Dick Garrett, the word is that Roxanne DeVry was found dead. Is that right?"

"Yeah," another asked loudly. "Is it her or not?"

"Can't be Roxy," another shouted. "Roxy's dead."

I held my arms out to settle the crowd down.

"You may be right, but the police have means to identify her. They have gathered your information. Anybody here we missed? No? Okay, now let me give you Inspector Morris' contact information. Enter this on your smart phone or grab a pen and some paper. You may think of something to add to your previous thoughts and I know he'd like to hear."

I gave them name, rank and serial number, so to speak, of Morris.

"Now," I continued, "cops are going to leave. Let's enjoy the rest of the evening. The band is ready to come back to this podium. I know you are all anxious to get back to dancing and doing whatever it is we do at a twenty-year get-together. Thanks for your attention and for your cooperation."

Morris gave me a thumbs up, motioned for me to join him at the door, and stood to leave, his entourage with him. Suddenly a male voice in the crowd yelled out, "Hey, Alan! Where's my wife?"

I had started to walk from the podium, but I reached back and grabbed the mic. "Who asked that? Please stand."

A well-dressed gentleman, I'd guess in his late thirties, quite tall, athletic build, mustache, slight graying at the temple, stood and repeated the question. "Where is my wife, Mr. Private Eye? Patti Wellings. You went upstairs together; but only you returned!"

Tom Wellings! I hadn't seen him in twenty years. Older, heavier, sadder, but not a doubt about it. Tom Wellings for sure.

FIVE

The packed room became a renewed beehive, filled this time with suppressed panic. Patti Wellings missing! The echo caromed off every wall. Inspector Morris called Mr. Wellings to our table. I remained frozen at the mic trying to wrap my mind around this new situation. Had Patti not returned to the ballroom a few minutes ago? Apparently not.

I had to say something to put the crowd at ease. My mind sorted through possible courses of action. Within milliseconds I used my most calming voice, asked everyone to please remain in the ballroom, then I spoke very clearly into the mic. "Bradley Swazer, please join me at the elevator." Morris nodded his head. Swazer stood and joined me.

* * *

Morris was sitting with Tom Wellings when Swazer called in the news.

Patti's body was found in the ladies' room on the observation deck, throat cut from ear to ear. No knife found.

* * *

Except for a lifted eyebrow, Morris remained expressionless at the news, but Mr. Wellings took one look at him and suspected the report would be devastating. He remained stoic throughout, even as the inspector confirmed what he already knew. Morris watched as a tear rolled down the man's left cheek.

While Swazer was on the phone, I ran to the hatchway door to fetch the CSI ladies to the new crime scene before they could leave for the lab. Unfortunately, I was probably ten minutes too late. Their bodies were still quite warm.

The band packed up and disappeared. A new CSI team was called on-scene, along with two more detectives. Shortly after, a bus showed up to take the dead to the morgue.

The inspector held back the few people who had yet to be interviewed and bid all the other attendees a good night, assuring them--with the confirmation of the vessel's officers--that all attendees would have some kind of refund for the early inconvenience.

So the ballroom, by 9:30 p.m. had shrunk from more than three hundred to a mere twenty-one: two new CSI's, two new investigators, Inspector Morris, Bradley Swazer, fourteen guests who had recently descended from the upper decks, and me.

We left two street cops outside with members of the cruise ship to escort those whom we had finished questioning. We moved our party upstairs to the observation deck for a final round of questioning.

We were finished within an hour. Nothing new was determined. But the shocking news to the class of 1999 was that four vile murders had been committed tonight: two CSI investigators, and two of our 1999 classmates: Patti Wellings and Roxanne DeVry.

While that came as a shock, there was one even more shocking bit of news to Morris, Swazer and me. A few of the graduates sucked in their breaths before gushing forth: Roxanne DeVry could not have been a victim tonight. Roxanne DeVry had been brutally murdered twenty years ago on a senior outing in a coastal state park. Her throat had been cut from ear to ear while alone in her berth, aboard a small cabin cruiser a group had rented for the afternoon. Her assailant has never been caught.

* * *

Inspector Morris wasn't finished with me yet, and for good reason. After all, I was his best suspect for all the murders.

> A. *I had hurried all the guests downstairs and was the last person on the observation deck where Patti Wellings was last known to be.*
> B. *I had called in the first act of violence--the unknown redhead, presumed to be Roxanne DeVry.*
> C. *I had also found the two dead CSIs, so consequently a good suspect. I could have done the two ladies in just   before proceeding downstairs.*

It was 10:19 p.m. I could use a drink! But Morris surprised me.

"Garrett!" he barked at me, after the last of his team was ushered out into the night air. "Garrett, I'm heading home. It's been a fun evening. I'm supposed to be attending a birthday party tomorrow. You sticking around Manhattan Beach for the next little while? I have a question or two to ask you."

"I live there. I'm looking for a small office to hang a shingle, Sir. I'm going nowhere."

"Next Monday morning, say 10:15?"

"Park Street, Hermosa? Same place it's always been, right?" I accepted his offer and walked through the open door.

"Right. See you."

I fumbled for Pop's car keys, watching the inspector's tail lights fade into the darkness.

SIX

Twenty-eight minutes later I stood in front of a cork-board, sipping from a snifter of *Martell Cordon Bleu*, talking to four dead women.

I had printed photos of the four murdered females; two of whom were classmates from twenty years ago, two who just happened to be in the wrong place at the wrong time. Now they were in front of me with thumb tacks stuck through their foreheads . . . Except for Roxanne. Hers was a faceless mop of red hair. I plunged the pin into the top of her skull.

I paused and looked out through the arched-top picture window at the endless Pacific, with its white-tipped roiling surf still visible against the darkness.

From here I could see the pole lamps lighting yellow circles the full length of the almost one-thousand-foot Manhattan Beach Pier, providing hop-scotch markers for the giants that came out to play at night . . . at least, that's what my mother told me when I was in knee-pants.

The bungalow Pop had signed over to me is right off the strand on 11th street, just two blocks from the pier. It was a modest two bedroom, one bath, quite similar to others on the street, but it was mine. When we first moved in those many years ago Mom named it *Pop's Place*; that name stuck. Even to the present day we hardly ever say we're going home--we're heading to *Pop's*. The firemen held meetings or played many a card game there.

As a boy, I remember the pier had to be restored due to part of the structure breaking away, but it still amazes me how, through all the poundings taken, it has survived over the many decades.

I had spent many an evening as a teen, walking the length of that concrete pier--at times with my fishing gear, at times just enjoying the sea breeze and dreaming.

I turned back to the ladies.

"Yes, Pop is still alive. He's roaming around upstairs somewhere. Perhaps already in bed, but I doubt it. He's probably watching a late night movie. If we're really quiet he won't come down, but if we get rowdy he'll be down those stairs quick as a wink.

Mom is no longer with us, I'm afraid. Horrible plane crash. She was only forty-three."

I paused, looked at Patti, thinking she and I should probably have had our talk in the elevator, then looked at the mop of hair that was Roxanne (or whomever), "Mom was just a little older than we are now, ladies."

I poured myself another couple of ounces of cognac, stepped back to the window and peered through the antique brass telescope--an old Griffith.

"You know, ladies, if we could just look through one of these things and get a close-up of time as well as distance, we'd have a handle on so many things, like the son-of-a-bitch that did this to you. And if I had my way, we'd have him underground in a hurry."

Turning back to the cork board, I saluted the four figures with my glass. "I'm going to do my best, but it may take a little time."

Tough night, I told myself. *Different, for sure.* I drained the snifter, trudged to my bedroom, hung my pants on a pants' hanger, took a quick shower, turned out the lights and fell on top of the sheets.

SEVEN

Pop was first up. He was staring at the cork board, coffee in hand, when I walked into the study. There was another steaming cup waiting for me on a glass-topped coffee table.

"Is this what happens at a high school reunion, Alan? Must have been a real blast!"

"First case, Pop. Problem is, I'm right in the middle of it. Might get a bit sticky before it gets better; but I have a good feeling about the inspector on the case."

"Did you know these two?" he asked, pointing at the young ones. "They look like part of the party. The others look like they were there on business."

"You're a good detective, Pop. Four for four."

I filled him in on the highlights of the previous evening. He nodded, made an occasional comment.

"I hardly knew a soul, Pop, and hardly anyone knew me. That's what twenty years and a growth spurt does for you I suppose. I'll be going out for a few hours."

"Breakfast?"

"Naw. I'll pick something up."

"Need the car?"

"No. I need the exercise."

"Okay, Alan. I'm here if you need me."

* * *

There are several bicycle rentals down along the pier. I rented a bike for the day. I wanted to stay in my neighborhood, get a little exercise and see what might be available to rent. All I needed was a small office.

There were a few *for lease* signs. Two were particularly interesting: one on the corner of Highland and Manhattan Beach Boulevard, and the other in an office building near Polliwog Park. I took down a few phone numbers. Perhaps I can nail something down Monday.

After a quick meal at the Rockn' Fish on the Boulevard, I headed for the library. I hoped they still had a twenty year retrieval system.

The librarian, Bertie, was very helpful. In fact, she remembered the tragic cabin cruiser incident. I was able to print off four separate accounts of the murder, as well as her personal recollections.

"The whole school went berserk. It happened a week before graduation, and there was no other topic of conversation, right up to the passing out of the diplomas."

I rolled up the printed articles, jotted down the few names Bertie had given me, including her own, thanked her and cycled back to the bicycle rental. Then I walked up the hill to the bungalow to have another chat with the ladies.

EIGHT

Monday morning right on time, I met with Inspector Morris. After cordialities we sat in his small office; I glanced around as I accepted an offered cup of coffee. One small window let morning light in, the walls were adorned with photos of a handful of officers killed in the line of duty, some going back as far as 1923, but most in recent years.

In addition, I noted one complete wall of framed news articles with photos of good deeds of the cops on the street, and one complete wall covered with photos of car wrecks . . . interesting appointments indeed. Morris watched as I made my observations, then broke the silence.

"Who told you the lady in the hatchway was Roxanne DeVry?" was his opening volley.

"She did, Sir. Or at least that's what the gal told me from the bottom of the shaft. By the time I looked into the hole, she was on the floor, dead." I took a sip of coffee and watched a frowning Morris shake his head.

"Hmph," Morris rubbed the side of his nose

with his finger. "You should understand, we have several problems with that movie. We both know Roxanne died twenty years ago by similar means, we have no connecting tissue to relate the two murders, we don't even know who this new lady is yet, but I can assure you of one thing, Mr. Garrett, you didn't kill her . . . at least not Saturday night."

"I knew that, Sir, but thank you for coming to the same conclusion. May I ask how?" I stood and returned with a carafe to refill both cups.

"Certainly." The look on Morris' face was almost expressionless. A trait I admired. Only a trace of emotion flashed across his eyes and a slight eye twitch. The eye twitch I associated with weariness, the look was definitely anger. He lifted his cup for another one of many refills. I could only guess how many.

"The lady was already dead--in fact, frozen for some time. Her face unrecognizable, her teeth and fingers missing. Oh! and she had been eviscerated and lay on the floor in two pieces. She had been perfectly placed to appear in one piece. The blood was a 'nice touch' --poured on the floor under her . . . the blood wasn't even human.

You, Garrett, were supposed to be scared shitless! regress to that 5'8" weakling, and piss your pants as you ran screaming to the ballroom. And in the meantime, it was a great way to finally get rid of a body that had been dead for perhaps months or even years."

I sat back down with a jolt, speechless. I managed a "Wha" . . . and finally, "have you ever had anything similar happen on your, uh, beat?"

"Never, and I'm no longer on a beat . . ."

"Wrong word. Sorry. Your *watch*!"

"Okay, Alan, let's just say you're the bad guy. Do you have a scenario that fits? Let's just say that this really is Roxanne and go from there. Let's just forget the Roxanne that died twenty years ago."

Where to start? Knowing that my first victim was frozen made it harder to imagine the killer's [my] methodology, because the first image was so tattooed on my brain.

"I guess, Inspector, I bring Roxanne to the reunion, see her gawking at someone else, catch her following him, and in a fit of rage, I follow and kill her, figuring to have the murder blamed on that innocent guy up top.

Then, coming out the door to rejoin my fellow graduates, I meet the eyes of that other lady, Mrs. Wellings. Now I'm in trouble. She will put two and two together and identify me. Now I have to find a good place to kill her, too. So when she goes upstairs, I excuse myself from my party's table and duck out. I find her and kill her in the ladies' room. Problem is one of the police ladies spots me coming out of the ladies' room, so I follow her to the hatch door, kill them both, then go on with the festivities."

"Any holes in that theory?" Morris asked.

"Sure. Bloody clothes, knives, timing and I had left the ballroom twice, just before the murders happened. Big holes, Sir."

"They are big holes aren't they? Now add the frozen Jane Doe. Oh, but she's in two pieces, subtract out the jealous rage which clearly was not the case . . . at least straight up jealous rage . . . Hmmm, could have been jealousy of a different sort, though, Alan."

"Like what, Sir?"

"Like this little punk-assed wimp who runs from anyone that wants to kick sand in his face; twenty years later he comes back to a school reunion as Charles Atlas. Women drooling, point him out to their hubbies; hubbies suddenly recognize him as their bully toy and hate his guts. That kind of jealousy, Alan."

I rolled my eyes at him, "Really, Inspector? Fellas jealous of me? I find that very hard . . ."

"Garrett! Don't tell me you haven't thought you've made an impression on quite a few people, with your change of, shall we say, geography. Heads turned last Saturday night."

Morris pulled a black and white photo from his desk drawer and shoved it across at me. Then he added a second photo, full color, of me from yesterday-- standing in front of a bike rack. The difference, admittedly, was dramatic.

"You're good, Morris!" I smiled, thumping on the one from yesterday. "That's me. Now, where did you get that black and white?"

The black and white was a Polaroid, enlarged to approximately 5" x 4" with the date August, 1998 clearly printed on the top--the last picture of Pop, Mom and me together, taken on the beach. Me, with my treasured item--7'2" surf board, shark teeth on the front . . . under the Manhattan Beach pier. You couldn't see it from the picture, but it was yellow and red with that open shark mouth. The board stood at least 15" above my head.

"Your pop," Morris smiled. "We had a nice chat. I like him."

"I'm sorta fond of him myself," I grinned. "So you did a little checking on me, huh?"

"Yeah, but the 5" growth spurt is verified by the snapshot, and when you gathered the news clippings from the librarian I drew a line through your name," Morris laughed.

"Alright, Inspector, now that introductions are properly over, I'd like to help you on this case."

"You know I can't pencil you in on police details, Garrett; but I can give you copies of everything we took from the guests Saturday night. That should give you enough reading material to finish off the *Cordon Bleu*."

"Does that include names and addresses?"

"I said *everything*."

"Thanks. Appreciated. By the way, whose blood was seeping out from under the redhead in the tube?"

Morris picked up his phone and asked that the entire Reunion file be put on a thumb drive and brought to his office. He stood.

"Another coffee?" he asked, turning and raising an eyebrow.

"No. I'm good."

A female cop knocked, entered and handed Morris a thumb drive. When she left, Morris handed it to me.

"It wasn't a *who*, Garrett. It was a what." He took a swig from his fresh cup. "Someone perhaps sending a message to someone . . . Forensics has determined that blood came from a canine."

NINE

12:30 p.m. I called Pop to see if he wanted to join me for lunch at a quiet little place we used to go to when I was a kid. He agreed. We met at the *Ocean View*. I was a bit surprised that I was asked if I had a reservation, but I guess the times, they are a-changin'. *Did I say a quiet little place*?

"So, did you see your Inspector Morris?"

"Yes, Pop. I saw my Inspector Morris. He showed me the picture you gave him. Here. I brought the original back.

I'm thinking about setting up shop in this area, Pop. You know a few people down here. Still have any pull at all?"

"I might for the right price."

"I'll spring for lunch," I answered.

"Okay, let's see your list. If I know you, you have five or six locations picked out."

Roland, or *Pop* as everyone came to call him, was a firefighter. Started with Ojai, then he and Mom moved to Manhattan Beach in 1982 to be closer to Los Angeles International Airport. I have really only known

Manhattan Beach as home. I was still in diapers when we moved.

Mom (given name-Sarah) was an attorney for an investment firm. She often flew to assist in negotiations and signings. At times they flew commercial, at times charter. The flight that ended her life was the victim of a torrential storm with one hundred forty-one passengers plus an eleven-person crew.

Pop retired three years ago after forty-one years as a fireman--four in Ojai, and thirty-seven here. I say all this because Pop knows a lot of folks in this town and is friends with most of them. And some of them still remember Sarah, my mom.

I showed him my list. Had it numbered by preference.

He put a line through my number three and five--one was a firetrap, the other *run by a tight-fisted rascal that would take you to court if you drop a piece of popcorn on the sidewalk in front or if a client wore jeans or drove a Nissan Cube.*

"Your first location is the best one if it's still available. Old Man Grinnell still owns it last I heard. If you want to call him after lunch we'll go take a look at it."

We did just that By afternoon, I was looking at my new digs. A block off the water and one hundred dollars less than he was trying get for it on a five year lease.

"Thank you for your service to our country, young man. I'm not up on all the cyber-terrorism we hear about, but I've had my personal accounts hacked, so I'm fairly confident you were fighting to keep our country free from being infiltrated-- either personally or electronically."

"Oh, yes, Sir. We have thwarted scores, even hundreds of attempts to damage or destroy our way of life. A lot of good people keep this country safe."

With that, Grinnell included three parking spots. At no extra charge. He normally charged seventy-five dollars for each one.

Then he waived the front-end money and the last month's rent. Told Pop he'd just come to our house and burn it down if I skipped. Only one problem--the place sat empty. Grinnell couldn't get in touch with the last tenant, who still had belongings inside. We struck a deal for the first of September and signed a contract.

Then finally, Grinnell gave me my first assignment . . . if I were to accept.

Skip-tracer. Four cases. Not very glamorous, but it would help steady my sea-legs in the field of private investigation as well as give credence to my business role in the community. Skip-tracing is honest investigation. Not exactly anti-terrorism stuff for which I am thoroughly trained. I snapped at it.

Pop and I went back to *Pop's.*

* * *

All afternoon I sat at my computer with, I assumed, the four ladies watching intently.

I created a file from the library news clippings regarding the real Roxanne DeVry. Pertinent information, though sketchy, told me the death occurred on May 30, 1999, just ten days before graduation. The boat had been rented by a group of twelve graduates for a half day, piloted by a resort staff member.

Nothing appeared out of the ordinary until someone questioned why Roxanne hadn't come out of her berth to sit with the other eleven and enjoy the cruise. Betty-Anne McConnell went to check and came back with the dire news.

Charles White, Ocean Vista P.D. officer in charge of the investigation, found no trace evidence; the crime was never solved. Still listed as a cold case. (Note to self: *see if Officer White still works out of Ocean Vista.*)

There was a list of the eleven students and the pilot; the reporters said it wasn't a clear cut, easily solvable crime because the cabin cruiser was moored well within swimmable distance from the shore. In fact, one report went on to say that some students were seen diving off the deck while others swam to the craft from shore.

* * *

Next came files from the thumb drive I had received from Morris. I pored over the various thoughts and recollections of guests who had come to the table, including those of Patti Wellings.

Some of the more interesting I re-read orally to the four ladies, but--no response, not even a raised eyebrow. I determined they would be of little use in this stage of fact-finding . . . a bit too premature. Perhaps as clues became more clear cut, I thought.

The long list of names, addresses and phone numbers/e-mails I would follow up later.

* * *

Grinnell sent over PDF files on the four skips. *This is good,* I thought. A change of pace. I created four new document files and marked the folder, SKIPS. I'll look at those later as well.

* * *

I turned back to the best of the *interesting* notes from the reunion.

"Pay close attention ladies. I'm going to re-read these few once again. I would like a reaction.

<u>Rachel Block</u>: *"A lady in a uniform boarded just ahead of me with oversized checkered luggage. She slowed, causing me to bump into the suitcase. We exchanged 'pardon me's' . . . she explained that a couple was awaiting her arrival, then hurried on. I remember laughing to myself that the case was unusually large.*

Then I returned to my car to get something I'd forgotten and I saw one of the ship's male attendants in the same type of uniform--a younger man, walking up the gangplank dragging the same patterned suitcase. I made a mental note of it.

I don't know whose luggage they were carrying, but someone obviously thought they were here for a ten-day cruise. They must have rented a suite. Never saw those porters again."

<u>Barry Franks</u>: *"I can't believe Alan Garrett. Doesn't look a damn thing like he used to. Not sure he's who he says he is. Anyone can grab a name tag. Something to check into."* (one of many guests making similar comments)

<u>Patti Wellings</u>: *"My ex-husband, Tom, thought I had a crush on Alan, because I made sure to invite him. Some of my girlfriends, Gina and a few others, saw Alan about a month ago in a department store. Some of them followed him home. Verified it was really Alan. I saw Tom about 5:30 p.m. this evening for the first time in weeks. He watched my every move like he was really jealous, rented a stateroom here--without me--I noticed he changed shirt and tie after only an hour or so."*

<u>Matt Wallis</u>: *"I expected to see my high school sweetheart Sharon Etts here tonight but she never showed. We just talked on the phone last month; she assured me she was coming. In fact, she was to be here with a couple of friends."*

<u>Jeremy Brownaire</u>: *"I hopped from table to table. At one table I was just walking by, looked down and told a guy he had something red on his shoes. He had a name tag on but I didn't notice. Used a Kleenex or napkin and wiped it off. He thanked me, said it was red wine, but I think he was drinking a mixed drink. I think it may have been blood--might have been steak sauce. Too thick for wine."*

"So what do you think, Ladies?" I looked up from the notes and asked the four. "Anyone? Yeah, that's what I'm thinking, too. Not a lot to go on, but some. Some, right? And that's a start."

Was this whole thing done in a fit of jealousy? No! It had to be planned. Two large pieces of luggage could bring in two halves of our Jane Doe--a.k.a. Roxanne DeVry.

I cracked a fresh Martell, poured two fingers, took a sip, leaned back in my chair, closed my eyes . . . but sleep was the last thing on my mind.

I fell asleep in my chair, thinking, *time to call a few people and line up a few interviews. This case won't be a slam dunk.*

TEN

Tuesday morning I put all the reunion names in alphabetical order and started on the list. I decided my Roxanne must be a local frozen lady, stored within perhaps at most a twenty-five mile radius of the reunion ship.

There were six names right in the school's hometown and eleven more within my target circle. It came as no surprise that two of the eleven were residents of Ocean Vista. Perhaps today would bring a few more unanswered questions to light, especially if Charles White is still around.

Pop tossed me his set of car keys. I was still car shopping.

I made three phone calls before heading out: the first to Ocean Vista Police Department to see if Mr. White was still working in that town. He had retired, but was still living there. Then I called the attendees from the Ocean Vista area. One couple, the Krups--Jerry and Molly--was not available; but my call to the Madison's met with success--Ted was home. I made arrangements to see him for lunch at a local coffee shop. He owned a business right around the corner. Winnie was a school teacher; she was gone for the day.

I was on the road by 8:15 a.m. and at the Ocean Vista Police Department at precisely 8:42 a.m. Traffic was always heavy during an August rush-hour morning, but this morning I was particularly impressed by the number of twenty-year-old kids driving either a Beamer, a Maserati, a Porsche or maybe even a Tesla.

Things have sure changed in this new century. I had a 1978 Toyota Corolla wagon my senior year with, as I remember, more than 180,000 miles on it. But I babied that thing, and it carried my board, so it was all good. I think I paid $500.00 for it.

But then, thinking about it, my parents-- especially Mom, taught me to add to a bank savings account that I had started at ten years old. It was at the point, now, where I could just about live my life out, just on the interest.

Which reminds me, I thought, *I should put a living trust together.* That's when the argument started. *Who would be the appropriate beneficiary? I had none but Pop.* So I acquiesced with a promise: *Someday . . . soon.*

Desk Sergeant Leah Rey called a phone number, then gave me the phone.

"What's this about?" White asked.

I told him. He gave me his home address. I was there in ten minutes.

"Helluva case, Garrett," White said as we sat in his den. "But what brings you out here after twenty years?"

"Last Saturday was the school's twenty year reunion. There were some unfortunate deaths, some throats cut, and one upsetting similarity."

I filled White in on the Jane Doe, the strange voice identifying her as Roxanne DeVry, the frozen, eviscerated body. White listened intently until I got to the body being eviscerated. Then he stiffened.

"Yes? Did I say something that twigs your memory?" I asked.

"Yes, you did. Some parts of our file were sealed from the media on a *need to know* basis. Being eviscerated was *nobody's* need to know. We didn't even tell her father."

"You mean . . ."

"Yes, partly. Everything was missing except for her womb with the fetus. The rest of the entrails were stuffed, along with a thick plastic sheet, into a trash bag and simply tossed overboard weighted down with rocks. What was left was washed up to shore two weeks later."

"Roxanne was pregnant!" I voiced it as an exclamation, not a question. Well, she didn't commit suicide! That was not even close to being debatable!

"Three or four months. She had no mother," White was saying. "Her father worked long hours; she was a pretty little thing, but as you probably know had a reputation for being loose as hell!"

Did I ever! I kept my mouth shut.

"Word among the boys we interviewed was that maybe as many as twenty visited her berth. Kids were diving off the cruiser; kids on the shore were diving out to it when they heard the word."

"Did you interview girls?"

"Oh, yes, in fact. I was getting to that. We interviewed at least ten young men; they all said they didn't even know Roxanne was on board, or they hadn't visited her cabin.

Finally, one young lad was so ashamed of himself he admitted he had visited her. But he said he had been urged--actually dared by certain girls. We had interviewed a few girls already, but now we included that question in our interviews. The stony faces softened, and they all admitted to their part in the debauchery."

"Who was the last person to enter the berth? Who found the body?"

"The owner and pilot of the craft. They entered to make sure everyone was accounted for.

My team was called. We found the usual murder scene clues and semen, but we were overwhelmed by the list of suspects, both males and females. The incident was sealed, with the exception of community service for those who admitted to being involved. The father committed suicide within a week. It was assumed he was the father of the baby, but nobody knows for sure."

"Whew!" I breathed out. "Man! I don't suppose you kept a journal of the students you interviewed?"

"From twenty years ago?" the seventy year old gave me a sly look and winked. "I just may have a binder somewhere in the cavern. Just remember it's all sealed. If I find it missing, you stole it."

He looked at his wall clock while walking into his small office. Books and bound journals covered three of the four walls. "It's after 11:00 a.m.
Garrett. Care for a drink?"

"No thanks, Sir. Anything else that may be of help?"

"Look through this." He handed me two spiral bound Rediform steno pads marked May 1999 and June 1999, which he had obviously pulled off the shelf while I was on my way to his home.

A slight, gray-haired lady joined him at the door as we shook hands; she handed him a tomato juice with a celery stalk in it, and looked a bit disappointed that I smiled and shook my head at a second one she held in her other hand. They bid me a good morning.

ELEVEN

I would love to have read the steno pads from cover to cover right then and there, but I needed to see Ted Madison for lunch. *May just be a waste of time, but I'm committed now,* I told myself.

I found the cafe a bit early, sat in a window seat and wondered what nearby business Ted owned. Ted was another fellow graduate I didn't remember at all . . . come to think of it, I remembered only those that hassled me, and a few brainiacs that I respected for their intelligence--namely, Sherri Foote, Greg Bronson and Steve Mitsui.

Ted came in, spotted me, smiled. I stood, we shook hands.

"Quite the evening the other night, huh, Alan?" he said by way of greeting. "I wonder if the committee will reschedule a follow-up get-together at a different venue."

"Hello, Ted. Thanks for meeting with me. Yes, it was strange to say the least."

"I understand you're the one who found her. Who was it? Winnie and I filled out the information the cops asked for, then we left, along with a few other couples."

The waiter came around with water and menus. We ordered, then Ted continued, "Not interested in murders at a party, you know? Did you find out who it was? Someone said it was Patti Wellings, but that can't be. She was at the table next to us."

I waited until Ted was taking a drink from his water, then, watching him closely, I said, "Roxanne DeVry."

Ted sat bolt upright, almost spitting out the water. "What?" he gasped.

I nodded, "And Patti Wellings."

"You're kidding! Patti? She's dead?"

"And two Police forensic officers as well, Ted. I noticed you looked shocked when I mentioned Roxanne. Why?"

"I'm sure you know about Roxanne. She was killed at our party twenty years ago. Remember? That couldn't have been her on Saturday night. It just couldn't have been!"

"Yes, I did hear about how she died. I wasn't there twenty years ago, I was in Asia. I didn't know the girl well--only talked with her once . . . but, just like not knowing you, I didn't know her either. I guess in a class of over four hundred fifty kids, we all had our own circles. I've heard some wild tales about her recently."

Our lunch was served. Between bites I learned Ted owned the nursery around the corner, mostly native California plants. Winnie was a high school history teacher--volunteering to teach this summer at a different town in the district. She wouldn't be home until after 4:00 p.m.

"You said you heard the dead person was Patti Wellings. How did you hear, Ted? And while I'm at it, one more question, if I may. Did you not hear about the two other ladies that had their lives snuffed out?"

"Your questions are beginning to sound more like grilling, Alan. Like the police of twenty years ago. They grilled everyone at that beach party regarding the Roxanne incident. I *was* there. Minnie was from Northern California, but I was there. I have one of your cards, but I doubt I will ever use your P.I. services." Ted started to rise. I motioned for him to please stay seated.

"I didn't mean to annoy you, Ted. There are just certain similarities in the two cases, and as I understand it, the case of twenty years ago is still unsolved. Were you aware that the real Roxanne was disemboweled and pregnant?"

"What? No! Are you saying that Jane Doe Saturday was disemboweled to end a pregnancy? Who was she, really?"

"Don't know yet. But the blood all around the body was fake as well, Ted. Our Jane Doe had been dead for some time."

No sense in belaboring the situation any longer. We were both a bit tight-lipped. That was fine. I can't blame him. We walked to his nursery, where I bought a California Penstemons and a stone bird bath, shook his hand, thanked him for his time, then before heading to *Pop's* I called the Krups once again. Still no answer. I headed to *Pop's*.

TWELVE

I think better with a snifter of Martell, so I stifled my desire to run through White's notes until I could read them aloud to my ladies.

Pop and I found the perfect spot for the mound of red Penstemons, he grabbed a shovel and planted it while I set up the bird bath and filled it. It made a nice statement in the southwest corner of our yard.

"Perfect marriage. Your mother would have loved the birdbath. She spent hours in the evenings watching the doves fly in, ."

"Care for a drink, Pop? I'm going to read some classified notes from twenty years ago, and I need to clear my head." I smiled and winked at him.

"May I listen in, or is it a private reading?"

"I'll have to ask the ladies, but I personally see no problems."

I removed the day's clothes, ran a cold, wet wash cloth over my arms, neck and hair, donned a fresh tee-shirt and sweat pants, passed a brush through my hair;

Pop met me in the study. The ladies were assembled as before on the cork board.

I poured two cognacs, handed one to Pop. Sat in my chair, White's note pad in hand. Interesting, I mused, there were a couple of bits of paper on the coiled wire. Must have started to write a thought and changed his mind. It happens quite often. I've done it.

I began to read:

- Charles White- May 30, 1999 -- 2 p.m.

P.1 Called on scene of homicide of young seventeen year old female. Victim identified as Roxanne DeVry.

Body on bed in berth #3 of cabin cruiser, Gone Fishin, owned by Regina Leone. Body had been mutilated, partly eviscerated, throat cut, womb with fetus still intact, bed saturated with semen -- signifying multiple sexual partners. Also in evidence was salt water, indicating some partners not initially aboard craft.

Twelve members of the senior class had initially rented the craft for the four hour period from 10 a.m. to 2 p.m. Payment was made weeks in advance to Ms Leone.

P.3 Those registered as legitimate renters

Among the males : Terrance P., Tommy A., Barry F., Matt W., Ted M., Anthony G.

Among the females : Roberta C., Trudy W., Gina B., Carol E., Ruby S., Gerri K.

Noted: the deceased was not on the roster.

Questioning of those aboard inconclusive. Mixed stories: Boys accused girls of daring them to perform. Some stories included several 'watchers' while act was being performed. Many on board denied being aware of the activity. Some said boys from shore swam to the craft and committed the rapes.

All those on the roster were under age. (18)

...Then a post script... See June 4 entry

I looked up at Pop from the note pad. Took a sip from my snifter, then turned to the ladies, especially Jane Doe and shook my head.

"What do you think, Pop? Roxanne wasn't even supposed to be on that boat. Sounds like she was invited to perform."

"Then shame, jealousy, hate and finally murder, filled with brutal savagery." Pop summed up.

"Maybe," I agreed, "but it doesn't answer Saturday night, not unless," . . . I turned back to Jane Doe. "You're not Roxanne, are you?"

Time to read White's June 4 entry. I took another sip of cognac and flipped a few pages.

Charles White June 4, 1999 -- 12:50 p.m.

P.1   Forensics report: subject deceased as a result of blood loss -- throat slit -- razor. Stomach contents also removed -- razor. Womb with lifeless male fetus remains. Subject's blood test as well as skin and organs show visible Kaposi's sarcoma--a confirmation of her being HIV positive--with full blown, irreversible aids. Fetus also victim of aids in womb.

Recommend testing be done for all male students who may have come into contact with Miss Roxanne DeVry. School officials to make announcement tomorrow. All male students known to have been on the craft will be personally encouraged to be tested.

I finished off my two fingers of Martel, then added two more. Pop joined me with his own refill. We sat in silence for perhaps two minutes. Finally, I broke the silence.

"Jane--Roxanne, whoever you are, I'm so sorry you ended up at our reunion. I'm so sorry someone treated you with such disdain and venom. I'll find out who did this to you."

"What's this *Kaposi's sarcoma* she had, Alan?"

"It means her disease has become very obvious to everyone who takes a good look. It takes months, maybe even years, but her parents or teachers should have noticed, and taken her to a doctor."

I walked to the print of the faceless mop of hair, turned it over, and taking my black felt marker I drew a big smiley face on the reverse side, complete with two laughing eyes. I tacked the print back on the cork board.

THIRTEEN

Spent the rest of the afternoon shopping for necessary items, but I couldn't get *Smiley Face* off my mind.

Notes to self: *Call Morris--ask*

> *1. if Jane Doe(Smiley Face) had AIDS?*
> *2. if they could approximate how long her body had been preserved?*
> *3. if they could test and conclude if she was pregnant when she died?*

When I got to *Pop's* there was a message on my voice mail. Old Man Grinnell had another skip job for me. He said it would be an email attachment. *Sure. Why not?* . . .

I called four more attendees of Saturday's reunion. Two were available for a visit tomorrow. At this rate I'd need to stop borrowing Pop's car . . . get my own set of wheels.

Might start looking tomorrow. Get myself a Corvette, run with the twenty-year-old punks, maybe do some wheelies on the Boulevard, drive halfway through a storefront . . . *yeah, man! . . . bunch of brainless punks!*

* * *

Rachel Block was expecting me when I arrived at 9:30 a.m. the following morning. Tall lady--5'6" or maybe 7". Nice features, strawberry blond hair, poised. She led me through the two story California Adobe Style home to a lovely back garden. She bid me sit, motioning to vintage lounge chairs grouped around a long, carved, wooden table within a mandevilla-covered Pergola.

Beyond was a lovely grand-piano-shaped pool. The entire back garden was enclosed with 8' shrubs, giving it complete privacy. I sat and looked around. A man could become very envious of Ms Block.

Rachel disappeared, only to reappear a few moments later with a coffee carafe and fresh-baked cookies on a silver tray. I stood, took the tray from her, set it on the table. Sat down again. She sat next to me, perhaps a bit too close.

She spoke first, "So, you're a private detective. I was going to major in law enforcement right out of the gate. My uncle was a cop. Then I met and married a cop and quickly changed my mind. Became a psychologist instead. Six more years of schooling."

"So where's your hubby today, Ms Block?"

"Rachel. Call me Rachel. I'm going to call you Alan, Alan. Chris and I were married seven years, no kids, he was killed in a traffic stop shooting. Just down went the driver's window, up came a gun, and Bam! Bam! The perps were never caught. City and Department took really good care of me. We had a good insurance policy. End of story.

Different way of life. Every day is a new nail biter. So, you came here to ask me about two big pieces of luggage pushed to the elevator by two different people, right?"

"Exactly. Inspector Morris shared some notes with me. Your input caught my attention. You said the cases matched. I know you said you couldn't describe them, but you also said you had looked around and didn't see them sitting anywhere. Perhaps you could describe them to an illustrator. Would you try for me?"

"If you come back for a dinner sometime."

"Beg your pardon?"

"Oh, come on, Alan. I'm a woman, you're a man. I like company. You're single. Make it just a friendly dinner and perhaps a swim after. If you end up belly up in the pool, I didn't do it."

I like this girl. Cute sense of humor . . . I hope.

"Damn! How can I say no? You're on. I'll set it up. When are you available to meet with a sketch artist?"

"Weekday afternoons I'm counseling at a woman's shelter. Any morning is fine. And now about that dinner?"

"Slow down, Rachel. We can start with lunch after the sketch artist and discuss dinner. Besides I need permission from Pop."

"You're a funny man, Alan."

FOURTEEN

Now there's a lady from high school I don't remember, I thought. I left the Block house intrigued, amused, and perplexed . . . but mostly intrigued. Dinner and a swim? Maybe. I'll think about it. *Too late, Alan--you already opened your mouth.*

My second visit was in a half hour. This fellow I remembered from twenty years ago, and recognized on reunion night . . . but Barry Franks shook his head in disbelief when I handed him my business card, so when I called last evening he jumped at the chance to chat with me. I had a two-fold reason to spend some time with him. He was one of the six fellows aboard the *Gone Fishin'* twenty years ago.

I popped into a 7-11, picked up a ginger ale, a 6-pack of Modelo Negra, a bag of salted peanuts and some chips--the best part of the seven essential food groups. *No? I probably misunderstood my fourth grade science teacher.*

Then it was on to see this old classmate of mine. A bit older, but undeniably Barry Franks.

Barry had two chairs on the front porch of his small bungalow. He was sitting in one as I pulled up. He stood, I carried the Modelo under an arm and as we shook hands, he looked up at me still in disbelief.

"You really are Alan Garrett! I came home the other night and had to look you up in my old yearbook, you little wimp!" He gave me a bear hug then sat back down in his chair, motioning for me to sit across from him. I popped a beer and handed it to him, then one for myself.

For the first time I had the chance to really study the man: 5'10", balding, pock marks, sad. Probably not the same person from twenty years ago. He looked his age plus, plus.

We broke the ice with a few back and forth comments 'n questions.

I started. Rattled off a few of my Air Force adventures--following up on several tips of cyber espionage, being instrumental in bringing down a porn ring in Mississippi, including three Air Force officers-- breaking off an engagement at the last moment, and finally coming back to *Pop's* to Manhattan Beach to take on a civilian population with the investigative strategies I'd learned.

All during my ten minutes of narration Barry seemed alive . . . fascinated, enthralled, but when it was his turn his demeanor changed--his energy faded. He had had a scholarship to a recognized university, but dropped out after only one semester. He now worked night security at a public utilities installation, had a few small investments, married, divorced, no children. It was his depressive sadness that most affected me--I had to make it a point to be very direct.

"Why aren't you at the top of your game, Barry? You seem awfully depressed. What on earth happened to you?"

"I screwed up a long time ago, Alan. Thought I was a big man on a lark. Suffered ever since. It's eating me alive, getting worse. It's just a matter of time."

"Whoa, whoa! Barry!"

I didn't mean for him to go from zero to two hundred mph on a single sip of beer.

"Barry, there are folks who can help. The biggest help is probably a shrink or a pastor no matter what your screw-up!

And by the way, I think I know a chunk of what you're talking about."

"How could you know what I'm talking about?" he snorted. "You've been in Quantico or D.C. or stationed someplace overseas for twenty years."

Ignoring that question, I asked, "What do you mean, 'just a matter of time'?"

"I have AIDS, Alan. Not just HIV frickin' positive, but full blown--*just a matter of time*--AIDS. You? Huh! You don't know shit! This is my last month of work. Doc says I'll be too weak to walk the perimeter, let alone stand on my feet much longer. I had to go to that reunion, to see some of my old friends and apologize to a few before I go. I wish I'd seen a few more.

And then to top it off, there you were, Alan Garrett, bigger than life! Imagine the shock to see you there! Like another apology needed saying. But I ain't saying it yet--not until I have proof. So I run home, find the yearbook.

If you hadn't called me, I'd have called you. So I'm saying it now. I'm sorry I treated you so despicably, Alan.

And I was probably the reason so many others in our class did--both guys and gals."

I wasn't prepared for such humility. Maybe I expected something more like, *I was a real asshole at times wasn't I?* but this was genuine and heartfelt. I looked at him in a different light . . . almost forgot why I had arranged the meeting.

"Barry, I forgive you of any schoolish pranks or wrong thinking about or against me; thanks for telling me to my face.

I've taken on a couple of criminal cases since coming back to Manhattan Beach, one involving the death of Roxanne DeVry twenty years ago."

Whatever blood was still showing in Barry's face seemed to drain as I mentioned Roxanne.

"So you *do* know?" Barry asked.

"I know some, some is sealed, but I intend to bring it out from under wraps; and while names are not particularly important, events are.

Before I go any further--are you aware the first dead girl Saturday night was thought, by the police to be Roxanne?"

This time it was Barry's eyes that gave his incredulity away. "No, not at all!" he answered. "That's impossible!"

"Here are some confidential facts not many people know," I continued, "please keep them as such."

I watched his face carefully for any untoward indication, "Our reunion lady had been disemboweled, she was frozen, and she was in two pieces!" I left out the disfigurement of fingers and face and the dog's blood.

"Why?" Barry's eyes were as big as saucers.   "Who could play such a macabre joke, especially since it should be a happy memorial?"

"My thoughts exactly."

We sat in what shade the porch provided for a few moments, opened and *clinked* a second beer, then, after a swallow, Barry broke the silence.

"Roxanne DeVry. Cute girl. Her mother died when she was about ten. You might remember her. She went to Jefferson Middle School, then on to our high school."

"Sort of," I volunteered. Barry continued . . .

"Very well developed . . . early. Became popular, dated a lot, became known as easy. I think every guy on campus banged her--more than once . . . except, maybe you.

That last senior outing . . . we rented the cabin cruiser, Roxanne asked if she could get in on the rental, four of the guys said no, but Turk and I said, *"Let's invite her as a guest."*

"Excuse me--who's Turk?"

"Sorry. Terrance Perle. Turk is in the hospital, or maybe dead by now. He was real bad last I saw him, two weeks ago.

The girls were also split, three against three. Finally, everyone laughed and said we could have an orgy with Roxanne aboard.

So, once aboard, we said, *Roxanne is in berth #3; who's going to start?* The girls goaded us, saying, *You said,* and then one of the girls said, *we need to watch to make sure you go through with it . . .* So I started.

It must have gone on for an hour or two. Roxanne thought it was fun at first, then she got sick and wanted to quit, but it was like a feeding frenzy . . .

girls were cheering, and even taking part in oral and other sexual play; there was lots of drinking. Both guys and girls were barfing over the sides and then right back in the room, some guys were swimming out to the boat and getting in on the action . . . I took three turns, and by the third time Roxanne was unconscious. I dove to shore and didn't go back aboard until 1:45 p.m. to make sure I was there when the owner took a head count.

We all started off the boat at 2:00 p.m. when the owner screamed. When that happened we about trampled over each other getting down the ramp. Cops were there within minutes. We were all questioned. We confessed to the mass rapes, but all denied a part in her murder. A few days later we were told Roxanne had AIDS and we should get tested and treated. That's all I know."

"And you ended up with AIDS from that experience." I finished for him.

"How many fellows do you think took part?" I asked.

"Probably fifteen." Barry admitted.

"How many girls cheered you on?"

"Just four. Not just cheered either. They took part. It started with just Roxanne, but escalated from there. I remember a couple who thought it was just too disgusting, and they stayed out of the action. In fact, they wanted off the boat, but they couldn't swim that far in the salt water."

"Do you remember the four who stayed and took part? Can you write them down for me?"

"Yes. Give me your note pad. I have no problem giving you their names."

"Good seeing you, Barry," I said, as I took the slip of paper. "Last question, your best guess. Who do you think the dead reunion girl is?"

"Alan, I have no idea. It seems strange that the person yelled up that ladder specifically to you, if that's what happened."

"That's what happened, Barry. I'll say a prayer for you, my friend, maybe swing by again."

"I'd like that," he replied.

"Barry, if you need anything; I mean it . . . anything, I'll do my best. Even things like making last arrangements, as strange as it sounds, I can assist with that."

"Already taken care of, Alan. I'm in contact with a few from the old gang. Gina Brand . . . remember her? Gina's business is wills, trusts, that kind of thing-- anyway she was recommended to me. She came by and worked out the estate details with me."

"Excellent, Barry." I said. "I'll keep in touch."
I left the beer and chips.

FIFTEEN

Barry Franks. Tragic ending to a tragic life, I thought, as I pulled Pop's Subaru up the circular drive. *Everything going for him. What was that old hymn . . . People Need the Lord.* Today, more than ever.

Pop met me at the door with a message from Morris: *Have a bit of information to share if interested. Meet me tomorrow 10 a.m.*

"Where, Pop?"

"Didn't say. You're the detective, Son!"

"Thanks, Pop. Uhh, Never mind! I think I know where, but . . ."

I had Morris' private office number. I called.

"Hi. Morris here. . ."

"Hi Inspector. Alan Garr . . ."

" . . . your number, I'll call you back as soon as I can."

I slammed the phone down for effect. *Damn answering machines!* Then I told myself, *that was stupid,* and dialed the number again. Busy! *Of course it's busy, stupid! It's that damn answering machine silently recording your non-message!* I waited a few minutes and called again.

"Hi. Morris here. . ."

"Hi. Tell the Inspector I'm retu . . . "

"Alan. Inspector Morris here. Thanks for getting back to me. I forgot to tell your pop where to meet me tomorrow."

"I have a pretty good idea, Sir. The cruise ship, right?"

"Oh, no. We kept the Old Girl closed down to tourists for the whole day Sunday while my boys did a thorough search for clues. No, meet me at the city morgue. It's around the corner on Balboa. Little white building with a drive on the left side. Take the drive. Park in any of the spots in back, even though they all say reserved."

"I'll be there. By the way, did your boys find any discarded luggage?"

"Luggage, no. But ask me if they found cameras, a couple of yearbooks, pictures, three pairs of undies, and empty bottles galore."

"Did you happen to question staff about their interactions with the guests?"

"Ahh, you're wondering about the luggage that one of the ladies commented about--that Rachel lady. Am I right? Short answer, no . . . but we can talk tomorrow."

Do you have a sketch artist I can borrow for an hour or so?"

"Sure. I'll bring her. What's the occasion?"

"No, don't bring her. Just want to set up an appointment with her. Might help jog a memory or two. You never know. So it's okay?"

"Short answer, yes . . . unless it isn't the incident we are working on, in which case, she can work for you privately. We have her on a retainer for our investigations."

"Morris, why should I spend my money on city business? And it is our case."

"Then you'll share the info, right?"

"You have my word."

"Tomorrow at ten."

* * *

Morris was peeking out the rear door of the morgue when I pulled up and parked. It was 9:57 a.m. He opened it wide to let me enter.

"Like to show you something, Alan."

"I've seen dead people before, Sir. Even dead women." Scenes from the Himalayan crash flashed through my brain. I bit my tongue-- immediately regretted being so flippant. "Sorry, Sir. What do we have?"

The inspector simply waited out my mini-- less-than-humorous volley, then continued, "The two CSIs, well . . ." he grimaced, "they're just dead, but the other two . . . look here."

He pulled the drawer open to reveal a naked Patti Wellings. Her throat had, indeed, been slit, causing her death, but her skin from neck to knees was deeply involved with ulcers, open sores and scar tissue, showing evidence of a long-standing excoriation disorder.

"What do you make of this , Garrett?"

"Not 100% sure, Sir; however, I have some ideas." I bent closer, examining Patti's torso closely. So sad! *What a troubled woman,* I thought. I straightened, turning to the Inspector.

"I noticed at the reunion a definite medicinal odor, much the same as you might smell walking down a hospital corridor. She masked it well with expensive lotions and perfume, but it was there."

"Coroner says it's probably an autoimmune skin disorder called *Pemphigus foliaceus*, which can lead to a very serious infection. I'm thinking hers was out of hand," Morris said, shaking his head. "Read about it, never seen such a serious infection, but there it is if ever there was one."

"Agreed," I nodded, "my guess is shame and guilt."

"Ahh, shame and guilt! Fits my theory as well. How did you reach that conclusion, Alan?"

"Did the lab test her blood for HIV?"

"Well, I'll be damned, Garrett! You really are an investigator! Spill it! How did you get there?"

"Take a look at these names, Inspector." I showed Morris the list of names Barry Franks had given me.

"What's this? You have a list of ladies. There's Ruby, Gina, Patti and Gerri. Should that mean something to me?"

"These are girls on the boat twenty years ago when the real Roxanne was killed. The problem is, Patti Wellings wasn't officially listed as being on that boat.

I've made you a detailed audio of my findings thus far. I sent it to you this morning before coming.

Now," I added, "regarding our Jane Doe, is she here?"

"Yes, young man, she's here," Morris smiled

as he led the way to another pullout drawer.

"Any theories, questions or summations?" he asked, as he exposed a faceless female figure, lying on her back--two body parts had been stitched together at an area above the hips.

The face had been mutilated beyond any recognition and the entire chest cavity was missing. The corpse had a ghastly bloodless pallor about it.

"So, Mr. detective, do you have any ideas, thoughts, conclusions?"

"Not yet. What I have right now are two or three questions for your forensics."

Morris pulled a manila folder from the face of the drawer and handed it to me. "Their findings, Alan. Jane Doe's complete file."

- Subject identity unknown
- Subject frozen. Estimate: 72 hours or more
- Bone volume estimates cadaver thirty to forty years of age--5'2" tall
- Bone tests for pregnancy conclusive -- subject not pregnant
- Bone & tissue tests for HIV inconclusive -- not known at this time

"Well, there goes my theory. I was sure she was the real Roxanne. Now I'm a bit at sea. Back to the drawing board." I shrugged ruefully as I smiled at Morris.

The Inspector slapped me on the shoulder.

"Now, all we need to do is understand why you were targeted as an unwitting participant, why this ghoulish murder took place, find the son-of-a-bitch, and determine how this gruesome crime ties in with the one from twenty years ago."

"I'm off to purchase a set of wheels," I told Morris. "I've been taking advantage of Pop for a couple of months and it's beginning to wear on me; Pop hasn't mentioned it at all, but it could affect his insurance if anything happened with me behind the wheel."

"Did you just change direction of our conversation, Alan? Ever think about driving around in a police cruiser?"

"Not even once," I laughed.

"Change your mind, let me know. Oh! I almost forgot. Here's a business card for the sketch artist."

SIXTEEN

Hormones were working pretty heavily. I had a couple of cars in mind--both convertibles. I'd been looking on line for some time, knew about what I would be willing to shell out.

Left side of the brain said *it's just a set of wheels. Who are you trying to impress?* Right side said, *Come on, Dude, You have the money. You've always wanted a candy apple convertible. Pick one, fork out the loot and drive it away. Just that simple.*

I scoped out a few dealerships for new and used vehicles; spent most of the afternoon. The left side of my brain won today's round. I drove Pop's Subaru wagon to *Pop's*. Nice, sensible ride.

* * *

Carla Balboa was available any morning next week. I made an appointment for Tuesday at 9:30 a.m. at the Manhattan Beach Library. Then I called Rachel Block to confirm the appointment. I told her I had been car shopping all afternoon.

"Looking for something specific?" Ms Block asked?

"Rag top, not necessarily new, but nice. Power this'n that. You know, the usual power toy to impress the ladies," I laughed.

"I may have just the thing. Are we having lunch Tuesday after meeting with your artist?"

"Absolutely!"

"Good. See you."

* * *

I spent the weekend following *skip* trails--about to collar three of them. Two of the three were less than clever at covering their tracks, but the other one took more work. The easiest one was my new leased space. The guy walked away from Grinnell's building for a larger space in Torrance and just simply carried on. Didn't go back to take anything away. Didn't change business name or phone number! Talk about brass! . . . or those other things!

I visited the new site Saturday morning, wearing a wire, handed him my card identifying me as a private investigator, gave him an option to come back and fulfill his obligation for the balance of thirty-six months left of the five year lease, or simply pay six months' rent to me today ($10.5 grand) and be free of the lease obligation.

He shrugged his shoulders and laughed, told me to tell Grinnell to *shove his lease where the sun don't shine*. I informed him that every day he postponed his decision would cost him $150.00. I then walked out. From there I called the Torrance landlord and played the tape for him.

At 2:30 p.m. I got a call from the Torrance asshole. "Come pick up your check!" he screamed at me.

I was there in thirty minutes. "If the check bounces we tack on 25% and call your new landlord once again!"

"It won't bounce! Hey, you hear me, Mack? It won't bounce! Keep the crap I left there. Don't want it!"

"Put that in writing."

Interesting. Now all I need to do is convince Grinnell it was a reasonable offer. I may get in there sooner than August. A good day . . . hormones working just fine.

SEVENTEEN

Sunday.

I spent the morning with Pop. He insisted on preparing breakfast, so, who am I to argue? I might *after* breakfast . . . No, I'm only joking. My pop is an excellent cook/chef whatever you want to call him. I sat at the island, spinning on a swivel chair, drinking coffee and nibbling black grapes.

"Stop eating! You'll spoil your breakfast!" Pop scolded me. "Do I have to get out your mother's switch?"

That was a family joke. She kept a switch in the broom closet, but it never touched my bottom.

During breakfast we caught up on the latest developments in my adventures: recovering money for Old Man Grinnell, the possibility of getting in the space sooner, and more work for my new landlord.

Then Pop brought up his car. "Use it as much as you want, Son. I might want to visit a friend once in a blue moon or take a rare drive, but we can work around that."

"Thanks, Pop. My heart is set on a sporty number; maybe a convertible, candy apple red number, you know, nothing too outlandish. . . Jag, Caddy, McLaren."

"Sure! To change the subject, how is your case coming along?"

"It doesn't make sense, Pop. I start down an avenue, it dead ends. Same with the next and the next. The key is me. But why? Revenge? Jealousy? Hatred? I don't get it, Pop! Why does someone call my name up that hatchway, then leave a frozen, unknown corpse. Disjointed at that, and lying in a pool of fresh dog's blood? Do you have any roads for me to try? I'm open to suggestions."

"Give me a hand with the dishes. I have a couple of suggestions. Put some company on that board, so everyone can look around at everyone else, maybe start a fight or nod in agreement. Pictures are worth a lot. You have pictures? You can think better with pictures."

"Ahh! Yes I do! Thanks, Pop."

I loved Pop's level-headedness. He loved tossing me a dish cloth.

* * *

"I'm going shopping. You need anything?" Pop asked.

"Bottle of Martell."

"You got it. Be back soon."

EIGHTEEN

Monday morning, 7:50 a.m. Pop was waiting with the ladies in my study. He was thumbing through my senior high school yearbook, and studying the twenty-two new photos I had tacked on the cork-board.

Sunday I found the yearbook in a box in my closet. So, using scissors, I had cut out photos of everyone directly or thought to be involved in the horrible events that bridged the twenty years.

Pop had evidently approved of my way of interviewing clients . . . felt no compunction or shame about parroting my methodology and butting into my business. No respect for client confidentiality. Fortunately for Pop, he had a mug of coffee for me.

My first order of the day--call Grinnell. He was beside himself with delight at my success. Invited me to lunch. His office. 1:00 p.m. I accepted.

It was now 8:10 a.m. I frowned at Pop and took over the morning briefing.

"Ladies, I spent time over the weekend looking closer at a few more details. Most of them are from twenty years ago, but it will all come into focus, I promise. Here's what I have so far."

I pointed at the cork-board starting with the twelve who were supposed to be aboard the cabin cruiser as renters.

White had blacked out surnames to protect the privacy of the under-aged students, but it was a simple matter to connect the dots using the yearbook. I was able to match them with very little effort. I made a list of the guys and gals

<u>Guys</u>	<u>Gals</u>
Tommy Acosta	Gina Brand
Barry Franks	Roberta Cordero
Anthony Guerrero	Sharon Etts
Ted Madison	Gerri Kitchens
Terrance Perle	Ruby Salinas
Matt Wallis	Trudy Wells
	Patti Brown Wellings?
	Roxanne DeVry--
	dead--1999

The other pictures I simply lined up in a column with a note of explanation, starting with:

Tom Wellings-- ex-husband of Patti--changed his shirt and tie at reunion--1st hour

Jeremy Brownaire-- saw blood? on shoe

Allen Bergstrum-- a bully 20 yrs ago--   someone said he was on boat

Steve Mitsui-- classmate I respected

Greg Bronson-- classmate I respected

Sherri Foote-- classmate I respected

Bertie-- Librarian--No picture.

Betty-- Anne McConnell---no picture. Exist?

Rachel Block-- saw 2 suitcases carried by crew members--man & woman--
Oooops! wait a minute!
There is no Rachel Block in the yearbook!
Just who is Rachel?

"Ladies, we have a problem or two. Ocean Vista police record shows the six girls shown on my list here, and yet two newspaper reports name a passenger, a Miss Betty-Anne McConnell, saying they were on the deck waiting for Roxanne to come out of *her* berth to sit on the deck with the other eleven.

There *is* no Betty-Anne McConnell in White's report, and neither is she in the yearbook; consequently, there is no photo on the board.

"So," I turned to Pop, then back to the ladies, "who the hell is Betty-Anne McConnell, and why would she mention that berth #3 belonged to Roxanne? And how the hell did Roxanne get aboard the cruiser?"

I wondered if the reporter was fed wrong information, or if it was a misleading, spurious report. Big deal? Maybe, maybe not. Just another rock to turn over.

Neither the ladies nor Pop had any ideas. I jotted all the questions on a note pad and tacked it on the cork-board. I think I need to talk to Bertie, that librarian again. Oh! and a few more questions for our Mr. White as well. Questions regarding Regina Leone, the owner of *Gone Fishin',* and the unknown pilot. And, while I'm at it, I'll return his steno pads.

"Next briefing will be Wednesday morning, ladies. Hopefully, we get closer to solving these cases. Perhaps

I can have a consult with Inspector Morris between now and then."

My coffee, I discovered, was cold. I needed a refill. I walked to the kitchen, Pop following. I filled his, then mine, offered him a donut, took a maple bar for myself.

"Gotta stay fit, Pop. I'll eat a regular meal when I'm with Grinnell."

* * *

A warm handshake met my right hand as the other reached for the two checks I held out in my left. Grinnell looked at the checks, then at me, then back at the checks, shaking his head. I handed him the letter from my Manhattan Beach skip. He stared at it for a couple of seconds.

"Son, you've outdone yourself!" he chuckled. "So, when do you want to move in?" He walked to a pegboard behind the door, pulled a set of keys and handed it to me. "Front and back, two sets, and a key for the Schlage padlock on the rear chain link fence for parking and rear entrance."   "Probably by week's end," I answered his question. "I'll go take a look this afternoon, maybe start to clean it out; keep what I want, trash or sell the rest, paint and move in.

"Grand!" Old Man Grinnell slapped me on the back. "Let's go eat."

There were two small, private offices, one on either side of the front entry of my new digs. The larger of the two was equipped with relatively new office furniture--wood desk and office chair with arms. A couple of stuffed chairs were against the wall. A window presented a good view of the street.

The other office was a storage area . . . stacked with well-used furniture--old desk, old swivel chair, filing cabinet, waste basket, side tables lamps . . . thrift store special stuff.

The main office area was very nice. A counter/desk combination I could use. Four stuffed arm chairs lined up in front of the counter.

I tried out the swiveling, rolling desk chair for size, and examined the business side of the counter. Sliding cabinet drawers hid several feet of shelving, even a couple reams of printing paper.

A good beginning, I thought. *All I need is a library wall, a printer and a TV . . . maybe a police scanner. Wonder if I can lean back and put my feet up on the desk, like Boston Blackie or Philip Marlowe?*

I gave it a try. The chair flipped over backward, landing me on my keister. *Needs some adjusting.*

NINETEEN

I spent a couple more hours there Monday afternoon.

I called a nearby thrift store; the owner was there in fifteen minutes. We put masking tape on every item I wanted to donate. He promised to swing a truck by within the hour to clean the place out so long as I was there to help the driver load. Done deal. By 5:00 p.m. the place was ready for prep and paint. I headed to *Pop's*. I had a 9:30 a.m. appointment tomorrow at the library.

* * *

Rachel Block was sitting on the library steps as I locked Pop's car in the small parking lot and joined her. She was early. I was on time.

"Hey, Alan! Good to see you. Did you call the sketch artist to remind her of our meeting?"

"Don't think I need to," I said, as a gray Chevy Volt pulled into the drive. "I have a question . . . who is Rachel Block? You aren't in the yearbook."

"Yes, I am. You're looking for a retired name. I picked out a different one," she winked and walked on.

We all shook hands and entered. Still shaking my head at the oblique answer from Rachel, I left the ladies to their task, and went to find the librarian.

Bertie was at her desk. After cordialities, I asked her if we could take another look at the articles we had printed off before.

"What are we looking for?" she asked.

"Two of the news clippings didn't jive with the police report," I explained. "I'd like to see the bylines. Who wrote those stories?"

"Let's take a look, Alan."

Bertie pulled up the articles, gave me the reporters' (yes, there were two of them) names . . . one a man, one a woman.

"Now," I asked her, "highly unlikely, but can we check to see if they are still living and where they might be . . . perhaps still at their respective papers?" I jotted down the two reporters' names.

"That would take a 'people search', Alan. I can do a quick check with the newspapers, if that will help."

"Yes, please. By the way, when did you go to our high school?

Bertie seemed to avoid the question. Instead she said "I had the nickname, 'Peanut' for two years, then in the eighth grade I created my own nickname--Bertie. My name is actually Alberta. My married name is Wilson."

All this time, Bertie had been going through the roster of the two concerned news outlets. Neither reporter was still employed at his old post.

"Thanks for your help, Peanut." We laughed.

I went in search of Rachel and Carla. I found them in a quiet corner--not that the place was buzzing with activity. I stood over Carla's shoulder as she made a slight correction on a woman's nose with her pencil. Interesting, I thought, she used a pencil much like we used as little kids in kindergarten. Soft, large lead, easy to smudge or create shadow.

"That just about captures her," Rachel exclaimed, "I'm amazed you could bring her out of me!"

"She looks older than forty," I suggested. "Are you sure?"

"Probably just my interpretation," Carla said. We'll leave her aside for the moment and go on to the fellow." Carla smiled and pulled up another piece of sketch paper, clipping it to her portable easel. Turning to our client, she began. "Round face? Long face? Prominent nose? How far apart were his eyes? Just tell me the first thing that pops into your head, Rachel."

"Well," Rachel began, "we almost bumped into each other on the gangplank.Younger than the woman--by maybe ten or fifteen years. He seemed in a hurry, said he was headed toward the elevator. I'm 5'5", he was much taller than I--perhaps 6'2", had rather darkish hair, mustache, and didn't smile at all, kept looking at his watch. He was frowning. Furrowed brow, deep-set eyes--brown or hazel. Uhh, longish face, I suppose. I . . ."

"That's good!" Carla stopped her. "Let me start there. Give me a minute or two for that outline, then we'll proceed."

A small gathering joined me behind the artist, enjoying what they thought was about to be a cartoon caricaturist at work; most of them disappeared when they saw a realistic image take shape--of a man--not the woman sitting next to the artist. But two or three continued to watch.

"I know that guy!" one of them said to me, even before the face took shape. "That's Mr. Taft."

"Bull!" I snapped at him. "There's no way you can identify someone from an oval-shaped face with furrowed eyebrows."

"I guess you're right," he said apologetically, "but it sure looks like Taft."

I turned back to watch the sketch take form. Hell, it could have been Pop, or any number of guys I knew. *Who the hell is Taft*? I reached around the table and picked up the completed sketch of the female.

"May I?" I asked Carla.

"Certainly, but bring it back for any final changes or alterations."

I took the sketch to 'Peanut' (*Cute name*, I thought) for a copy. "Make two, please. There'll be more, so just put it on my bill."

Carla Balboa, by now, had a face. Deep-set, sad eyes, rather long, Greek-like, chiseled nose, mustache sitting atop thin lips. She was thinning the eyebrows when I took my place behind her.

"Are you sure?" I asked.

There was something about the faces . . . something recognizable. Perhaps I, too, had seen them the reunion night. I said nothing.

Rachel noted the way I had asked. She looked up at me with surprise.

"It's the best I can do," she asserted, as if resigned to a failed attempt.

Ms Balboa handed me the sketch to make copies. She then picked up the sketch of the female, turned to Rachel and said, "Let's take one last look. Any changes, corrections?"

I tucked the copies of the sketches into a folder. The artist presented a bill . . . "My usual fee," she explained unabashedly.

"Carla, I'm quite happy. Thank you for meeting with us!"

I cut her a check. We shook hands all around, Carla left. Rachel and I sat in the library for a few minutes reviewing the session. In the end, she seemed pleased with her efforts, saying it was the best she could do.

"Do I get a copy?" she asked.

"Police business, Ma'am. I keep the original, Morris gets a copy, an extra for the file."

"Oh, come on, Alan. You're being silly."

"Fifty cents each, Ma'am, to recover costs."

She pulled out a buck and handed it to me. I examined it under a light, smiled and stuffed it in my pocket.

"Let's go to lunch!" she said vivaciously. "I know just the place."

"Wait a minute, Lady! This is my treat, my choice!" I had a place already picked out, but she smothered me with her exuberance.

"Alright! But if I'm unhappy, I'll let you know. I might even embarrass you right in the middle of the meal."

"I promise, you'll be delighted! Follow me!"

I jumped into Pop's Subaru and followed the tail lights of her silver Class C Mercedes Benz. No question about it, the lady had bucks!

I'm new at being a private eye, but it didn't take much detective work to figure out where we were having lunch. Her garage remote worked just fine.

I parked in her circular drive, left my swim suit in the trunk.

TWENTY

"Start up the grill, will you please, Alan?" Rachel asked, soon as we walked through the front door. "You know where it is, remember?"

"Uhh, yes, I believe I do," I said, raising an eyebrow. *Bossy little twerp.*

Rachel disappeared as I walked out into her back garden and pulled the cover off the grill. About the time I had the thing started, she had reappeared clad in a very brief two piece swim suit, carrying a pair of mens' trunks and two towels.

"Here, Alan, put these on," she said, tossing the trunks to me, while placing the towels on a lounge chair. "I won't peek. I'm going in the kitchen to grab a pitcher of Calvados, but you'd better hurry; I won't be long."

"Sounds special. What is it?"

"Bitter apple brandy, twice distilled. Tart, very refreshing."

She disappeared again. I lay the trunks on the towels and turned back to the grill.

Rachel returned, shaking her head. "Ahh, so you prefer no trunks? That's fine."

"No, I'll just watch today, Miss Block."

"Miss Block?" she laughed, handing me a full aperitif glass. "Okay, then--to friendship, Mr. Garrett."

We clicked glasses. It was tasty! A palette cleaner, for certain.

"Sure you won't change your mind?" she asked as we had refills. "I'm going back in the kitchen for another five minutes or so."

"I'm positive."

"Okay. Don't leave. I'll be right back."

* * *

The luncheon was delicious. All done to perfection. Rachel placed three foil-wrapped items on her grill, timing each to her satisfaction, then served them on over-sized plates. I was blown away by presentation as well as the taste: *blistered shishito peppers, fried green tomatoes topped with a blend of melted swiss cheese with minced garlic, and finally* (she told me later) *honey ginger cedar-plank salmon.* For dessert she grilled apples with cheddar cheese and honey. Before the dessert we had another glass of the aperitif.

For an hour or more we sat under the Pergola sipping cognac and discussing the murders of 1999 and 2019, and Rachel's own sketches.

"I sure hope they help. I can't think of who they might be."

"Morris is working his angle as well, but I have a good feeling about it. I think I'll beat him to it. This case and the cold case as well."

"Right!" Rachel laughed as she dove into the deep end. She swam the length and back and put her elbows on the pool curb. "Coming in?"

"No, not today. Maybe next time. Thank you for a lovely lunch." I stooped down, gave her a peck on the cheek. "Next time it's my turn, Rachel. I'll let myself out."

"No! You stay right where you are, Alan." she exclaimed with authority, "I have something to show you. Hand me a towel, please."

Instead, I offered a hand. She accepted. I pulled her from the pool, wrapped a towel around her shoulders. A certain look crossed her smiling face, a look I couldn't allow to develop.

"You have something to show me?" I asked, raising an eyebrow. "I mean, something more?"

"Ahh, yes, I forgot! Mr. Garrett!" she smiled. "Follow me."

Back through the house we went to the side door leading to the garage. Next to the Mercedes was a mystery vehicle of some sort. A layer of dust lay atop the canvas covering.

"My late husband's baby." Rachel pointed. "He loved it more than he loved me."

"What is it?" I asked.

"Pull the canvas off, carefully, and have a look."

Under the canvas was a candy-apple red, pristine 2009 Cadillac XLR hardtop convertible.

"Holy cow, Rachel! This is quite a ride!"

"You like it? Hubby didn't even get to drive the nipples off the tires. I think there are only twenty-one hundred and eighty miles on her. She's brand new."

"How many miles? Just over two thousand and it's ten years old?"

"That's right. It's been sitting in my garage for all these years, and I promised myself I would keep it until our reunion year, then get rid of it."

"Do you have a price in mind?"

"Are you interested?"

"I might be, for the right price."

"Let's suppose I don't know what it's worth. I'm just a poor widow that has this red car I want to sell. I don't know anything about it. I don't want to be taken for a ride, I want a fair price. You're an investigator. Figure out a fair price so I won't get screwed. Can you do that for me, Alan?"

"Sure . . . but I prefer 'taken advantage of' to screwed. I'll get right on it. Have a fair price for you by tomorrow. Oh, Rachel, has the vehicle been started in ten years? If not, the fluids will all need to be drained, the lines cleaned, let's say, perhaps new hoses, gas tank and radiator."

"Oh, no doubt," Rachel nodded her head, laughing. "Just come back with a fair price. This is the year I sell it." She pushed the garage door opener. "*Now* I'll let you out."

TWENTY-ONE

Morris was waiting for me at the intake desk as I walked into police headquarters. On the way I imagined myself behind the wheel of a Cadillac XLR, just to see how it would feel. *Hummh, not bad!* "Come on up to the cavern." He led, I followed.

"What have you found out in the last week, Alan?"

"I found an office; I need a painter, a plumber and a small sign."

"You're just a regular Charlie Chan, aren't you, Alan? When are you going to earn your rent money?"

"I visited a few of the attendees on your list, Morris. Still working on a theory. But I have eliminated a couple of people: Barry Franks--he's so weak with HIV, he'll be dead within a few weeks, Terrance Perle is in the same boat--no pun intended, and Ted Madison--he and his wife left right after they answered some questions. Patti Wellings was still alive.

Here are some sketches your Ms Balboa cranked out for us, for Rachel Block actually.

I'm also working on the twenty year old angle. Nothing to report as yet, but interesting questions so far. And you?"

Morris took his time examining the two sketches before he answered. He looked up.

"Huh? Oh yeah, me? We're going through the names methodically, you know, by alphabet. Nothing to report."

"Bullshit, Morris! You must have something to share with me. Did you check up on Jeremy Brownaire's story about the red stuff on the shoe? What was the look on your face when you saw the sketches? What are you hiding?"

"Alright, alright. We questioned the others at the same table. It was blood. The guy, a Mr. Alberts claimed he had a bloody nose. He didn't attend the school but his wife, Betty had. They left shortly after that first series of statements, so again, Ms Wellings was still alive. The Alberts live in Fountain Valley if you desire a follow-up."

"Thanks. I might. And the sketches?"

"Not prepared to speculate. I'll get back to you. Are they mine?"

"Of course."

"I'll bring my *reunion* team in to see if they recall seeing these two. Might spark a memory, and link a name to a picture when they were interviewing and getting names and addresses."

Then in the same breath . . .

"Miss Balboa is single, you know," Morris said, glancing at me."

"Your point, Sir?"

"She's cute, too, don't you think?"

"Aren't you a bit too old for her, Sir? She must be ten years younger than I am; besides, aren't you married?"

"That's all I'm saying, Alan, except, she called me after your sketch session, wanted to know if you are married, divorced, gay or what."

"Do you have a little bow and quiver full of arrows, Inspector?"

"That's all, Garrett. I'll keep in touch."

Still had two things on my agenda before heading to *Pop's*. Now I added a third, thanks to Morris.

Pop had recommended a plumber and a painting contractor. My first call was to the painter. He could bring a crew in immediately. I swung by, dropped off keys, gave him a color scheme and my complete trust. Next was the plumber. He promised to coordinate with the painter, and have a new toilet and wash basin installed before the end of the weekend.

It was after 4:30 p.m. *Should I? Oh, why not?* I thought. I made the call.

"Hello." Feminine voice.

"Hello, Miss Balboa? Alan Garrett here."

Silence for what seemed a minute. Then finally, "Oh, what a surprise, Mr. Garrett. Did you have a question regarding my work?"

"No, as a matter of fact, I was visiting Morris today. He said you had questions regarding, of all people, me. So, I thought, the best person to give you straight answers wasn't Morris, but your subject matter. I mean, why ask for a sketch when you can get a portrait?"

Carla agreed to meet me at the <u>Strand</u> for a cup of coffee Thursday afternoon at 2 p.m. I was hoping it would be sooner but as luck would have it, she was busy most of Wednesday, and had a date Wednesday night. Ahh, well, gives me a day to make an impression.

Other necessary things crept into my mind . . . like: *back to business!* . . . the skips, my murder case, the cabin cruiser . . . I called and made an appointment to see Charles White the next day.

Besides, maybe it was just Morris playing with me. But Carla does intrigue me . . . I knew I was beginning to like the inspector. He had a wry sense of humor. I smiled and headed to *Pop's*. It had been a full day.

* * *

7 a.m. Wednesday. Pop, again handing me a coffee, waiting for a morning review as promised.

I laid out the two sketches for the ladies, then I began. "These two were seen pulling large matching luggage to the elevator. They walked in separately, went up separately. Do any of you recognize either? No? Okay let's go on to another possible clue. Do you remember a fellow who had a nosebleed that night? Or did you know a Betty Albert? No? Okay, well, I'm working on a few other things. I'll keep you in the loop ladies, I promise.

Oh! By the way. I'm working on the value of a 10 year old Cadillac convertible. Any ideas? Pop? You can get in on this." I took a sip of coffee. It was a perfect temperature. "I'll be here for a few minutes if any of you have any questions or ideas."

Pop said, "Son, are you serious about that Cadillac being brand new?"

"Twenty-two hundred miles, Pop. Needs a mechanic to go through it. Sitting, covered in a garage for the past ten years."

"I'll ask my old firehouse mechanic. He has a warehouse full of classic cars; should have a good number for you. Get back to you a little later today."

"Thanks, Pop . . . appreciate it. Can I borrow your car?"

TWENTY-TWO

Charles White seemed pleased to see me as I stood at his doorstep. He invited me in.

"Honey! We have company. That detective, Alan Garrett!"

"Who?" came from another part of the house.

"No. Who's on first!" he yelled back. He turned to me, laughed and shrugged his shoulders. "Been doing that for years," he explained. *Unconventional and humorous*, I thought. I shook my head and laughed with him.

"Returning your note pads, Sir. I have a few more questions if you don't mind."

"Ask away," White replied. "Just remember it was twenty years ago." He led me into his study. I set the steno pads on his desk.

"I interviewed one of the young men. He gave me a girl's name not even on the roster. A Miss Patti Brown ... married name Wellings, now dead."

White's wife came into the room, smiling, setting a tray of home-made peanut butter cookies and a carafe of coffee on the table in front of me.

"This time you will not refuse, or I will have Charles deny entrance to any future visits!" she said with firm decision, but with a twinkle in her eye. She shook my hand. "Catherine," she said.

"Then I am resigned to partake, Madam." I bowed suavely, as would have Errol Flynn, I'm sure.

"I see no further mention of the boat owner or the pilot in your notes. You must have interviewed them, since they found the body."

"Refresh my memory, young man."

"From what I read, you identified the boat and boat owner but you didn't mention the marina or the pilot's name in your report. Do you remember either?"

"Didn't I? What was the boat's name?"

"The *Gone Fishin'*."

"Ahh, yes, *Gone Fishin'*. The owner was Regina Leone and the marina was *The Sandpoint*. Regina still owns the Marina, leases out the tackle shop, and still owns three or four boats there. I think she scuttled the *Gone Fishin'* right after that tragedy.

Don't know what happened to the kid that piloted the boat that day. Can't help you with his name. I should have had it somewhere in my notes. Are you sure I didn't have it there somewhere?"

"No, it's not. A newspaper report said it was piloted by a marina employee, but that's all I have. There is one curious thing in your note pad, though." I took a sip of coffee and continued, "small bits of paper in the wire, indicating a page or pages ripped out."

"Let me see!" White exclaimed, reaching for his pad. While I watched, I bit into a peanut butter cookie, nodding my approval.

"You're right. It looks like a sheet was torn out. Sometimes I ripped out a page myself, but I was careful to pull out all the little bits of paper so I didn't second guess what I may have written or decided to say in a different way. Look here!" the retired cop almost shouted, "another thing I always did was number the pages on each case. In this case there is a page one and a page three. There is no page two. Something is very wrong, Alan. Insofar as another girl on board, my list is accurate, Son."

"Okay, Sir, I believe you, but now at least I have the whereabouts of Regina Leone. Perhaps she can shed some light on who and where that pilot is now. I'll be heading for Sandpoint Marina from here."

"Shall I call her to set up an appointment for you?" White asked.

"Oh, no. I'll just mosey over there, and if she's not there . . . oh, well. If she is there, I'm sure I'll gather some good intel."

My phone rang. I answered. It was Pop. "Just a minute, Pop." I bid the Whites a goodbye.

TWENTY-THREE

"Yeah, Pop. What's going on?"

"Got some figures on the Cadillac for you."

"Shoot!"

"My buddy Walt says the car is virtually new from what we told him. Kelly Blue Book goes right out the window value-wise. He would buy the car for his collection today for twenty-four, then put a few more in it to put it on the road."

"That's great, Pop, thanks. I'm on my way to a marina to follow up on the cabin cruiser personnel. I'll see you tonight."

I called Rachel Block as I jumped into Pop's car and started the engine.

"Hi, Rachel, Alan Garrett here. I told you I'd get back to you today regarding the Caddy. Best estimate including replacing a few things and getting it roadworthy, twenty-eight grand."

"So, you're offering twenty-eight grand, Alan?"

"Rachel, I'm not sure I'm looking for a Caddy. The twenty-eight includes three to four in parts anyway. Beautiful vehicle, though."

"So, when will you know? I realize you have other things on your mind."

"Thanks for the consideration. How about we have lunch Saturday?"

"That's longer than I had in mind . . . but, Saturday it is."

"I'll call when I have a bit of time."

"Aren't you in town?"

"No. I'm down the coast, heading for the Sandpoint Marina."

"Oh!" She said it like I'd punched her in the gut. "What on earth are you doing down there?"

"My job, Rachel. Does going to Sandpoint bother you?"

"Of course not. But you should be driving Highway 1 in a cherry red Cadillac convertible, not a Suburu," she laughed. "Call me, Alan." She hung up.

Okay, I told myself, *you need to make a decision, Alan. You can't let this lady dangle. Yeah, yeah, later!*

By the way, I asked myself, *what was up with her reaction when I mentioned Sandpoint? Don't overthink it, Alan. Okay, but still . . .*

I cranked the engine over and pulled out of the White's driveway. In fifteen minutes I was pulling into Sandpoint, a small, deepwater marina, sheltered by a low-lying stone breakwater. Craft moored here included a few larger yachts, a smattering of outboards, hard-bottomed zodiac types as well as a couple of strange sports-fishing boats, four or five Boston Whalers and even a couple of catamarans. As I drove in I estimated as many as forty vessels.

There was a bait shack on the wooden walk

going down to the three legs of the mooring piers. I headed there. The young fellow inside pointed up the hill to a small white building away from the pier.

"You looking for Ms Leone? She's up there. She's expecting you. You're that private eye, right?"

"Right."

With each 2x12 board of that pier my brain sorted through the reasons someone would announce, beforehand, my coming here. I wasn't trying to catch someone in an illicit romantic liaison or fluster or catch Ms Leone or anyone else in a lie. *But this is a red flag, Alan! I know, I know!* Only three people knew: Pop, the Whites and Rachel Block.

Ms Leone met me at the cottage steps and ushered me into her office.

"I understand, Mr. Garrett, you have some questions for me about that dreadful day almost twenty years ago. I don't know how I can help you, but here I am."

"I was told the cabin cruiser, *Gone Fishin'* was destroyed immediately after the incident."

"Absolutely. I acquired the necessary permits, contracted a fire boat from the city fire department, towed the cabin cruiser out a mile and a half and set it on fire. We, in the city, wanted no more memory of that boat. And yet, here you are." She sounded bitter.

"And yet, here I am," I agreed. "Tell me, who told you I was on my way here?"

"Ahh, Mr. Garrett, I have my own set of private investigators. Just leave it at that."

"Fair enough, Regina. Then you must know my next question." I waited for her to give an answer; she only looked at me blankly.

"No? Okay, I'm hoping you kept a log from that day so I can confirm the passenger list, the pilot and the chaperone on board."

I knew, or thought I knew there was no chaperone; I thought of it just now, and decided to throw it out there.

"From twenty years ago? Why would I keep such records?" she asked incredulously.

"Hotels, motels, gift shops, many others in the hospitality industry keep such records to create a clientele base, send a post card for a re-invite, that sort of thing. I thought perhaps the marina rental business may do the same. So, do you keep such a list?"

She smiled, "Let's go check, Mr. Private Eye." She led me through a hallway to a back room, like a small library. On the shelves were bound ledger books, one for each year, starting at 1991. She pulled 1999 off the shelf and handed it to me.

"Fill your boots, Mr. Gumshoe. Do you need pen and paper?"

"No, I'm fine. *Gumshoe*? Ha! I haven't heard that term since Mike Hammer or Sam Spade. I'd like to think I am a good Gumshoe, Ms Leone."

"Call me Regina. You have already, anyway. And may I call you Alan, Mr. Gumshoe?"

"Actually I prefer Gumshoe without the Mr."

"Gumshoe it is. You need a fedora."

I thumbed through the 1999 ledger until I reached the Sunday, May 30 entry. And there it was--

Just Fishin' --Reserved.

Io a.m. -- 2 p.m.
high school seniors:
Terrance P., Tommy A., Barry F.,

Matt W., Ted M., Anthony G. Roberta C.,
Trudy W., Gina B., Carol E., Ruby S.,
Gerri K.
Fee paid in advance --$800.00 cash
Monday May 17
by Betty-Anne McConnell
Crew Captain: Drew Penn

The last names of the twelve seniors were blacked out as per protocol, but they were the same that I already had. No surprises there, but I found my Betty-Anne McConnell. Also, I now knew the pilot was one Drew Penn.

Holding the ledger in my hand, I looked at Regina. "Did you collect the money from this young Miss McConnell?"

"Yes, she worked for me on commission. She was no young Miss. She had to be an experienced street-smart twenty-five. But she was well-spoken and insisted the seniors were a responsible bunch. She was to go along as chaperone.

I put Drew on the boat. He was young, bright, and going to college in San Diego. I figured he would be comfortable with the kids and set a good example for them."

"Do you know what happened to either of them-- Drew or the lady?"

"Sorry, no I don't. I never saw Drew again."

"Did the police not question Ms McConnell?"

"You mean White? Yes, I'm sure he did. I remember them sitting at a table talking for some time. I think it was because her skirt was up to her thigh. He seemed thorough in his questioning of everyone there.

He's the one who recommended that I never rent out that boat again. I agreed and called the fire department almost immediately. But Drew must have swum away from the boat. As I say, I never saw him again. Huh, Drew Penn. Funny, I'd forgotten all about him . . . ."

"Tell me, Regina, after twenty years, you still remember Betty? How about a sketch artist?"

"Sketch artist, no. How about photos?"

"You have photos?"

"They worked for me. On the ocean. The ocean can be dangerous. So I have photos of everyone who worked for me. I also have a photo of the twelve with Drew and Betty-Anne if you want it."

"I could kiss you, Regina!"

"Don't even think about it, Gumshoe."

I drove to *Pop's* armed with some new, albeit twenty year old information. I pulled over and called Morris. His secretary answered.

"He's not here right now. Would you like to talk with his partner, Bradley Swazer?"

"Sure."

"Hi, Bradley. Alan Garrett from the high school reunion case."

"Yeah, I remember. What gives?"

"I'm swinging by with a couple of photos. If you can run them please, I'd appreciate it. They go back twenty years, but we may get something."

"Sure. Bring them by."

After making copies at the police station, I left the original photos with Bradley, and hustled to *Pop's*.

I tacked the new photos on the cork-board, introduced Drew and Betty-Anne all around, then pulled the Martell off the shelf and poured myself two fat fingers.

My last skip was in Arizona. He had given me his word to get back to me. He didn't. I would have to be a bit tougher. I sat back in my chair, determined to spend the afternoon analyzing my next move.

The phone broke my concentration. The voice was female, unfamiliar.

"Alan Garrett?"

"Speaking."

"Regina Leone says you're looking for me."

TWENTY-FOUR

"Is this Betty-Anne McConnell?"

"Yes. What can I do for you?"

"It's regarding the murder of Roxanne DeVry twenty years ago. Newspaper report says you went to her cabin to see why she hadn't come out to the deck chairs to join the girls topside and found the body. Is that accurate?"

"Not even close!" Betty-Anne gasped. "Where did you get that report?"

"Two of them, actually. Local beach papers. I have names of reporters, but I've located neither, nor do I know if, in fact, either is alive."

"Give me their names. I'll look them up and let you know."

"Ha! You sound like you have nothing better to do."

"I'm serious. That kind of reporting is, even from twenty years ago, just too sloppy. When can we meet? I'll give you the real story--all of it. I was asked twenty years ago to bite my tongue because of the age of the kids involved, but I feel no such compunction today."

"Then we should meet. Where are you? I have a luncheon engagement tomorrow at two here in the beach area. I'm free all day Friday, busy all day Saturday, and nothing on my schedule beyond that. Perhaps we can we fit something in within those parameters?"

"How about tomorrow morning, say 9 o'clock? I live right here in Hawthorne."

I gave her my address.

* * *

Thursday morning, 8:55. Into the drive pulled an older green sedan. A well-dressed woman emerged, carrying a black attaché and a yellow plastic shopping bag with what appeared to be a bulky item inside. She walked with purpose to the front door. I estimated mid to late forties, blonde, 5'5", 140 lbs, pleasant looking.

I opened the door. She stuck her hand out with a smile . . .

"Gumshoe?"

"Sure. Why not?" I shook the hand, and returned the smile. "And you are Betty-Anne."

"Yes, and I brought you a present from Regina Leone," she said, handing me the bag.

My brow furrowed. *Why on earth would Miss Leone send me a present?* The bag said it all: "<u>Village Hat Shop of Redondo Beach</u>." I laughed.   "Methinks I have officially become a genuine *Gumshoe.*" I tried the fedora on for size--perfect!

"She shouldn't have done this you know," I scolded Betty-Anne. "This is not a cheap hat!"

"So, why go cheap? If you make a point, make it right," Betty-Anne came right back. "Pay ten bucks for a hat that'll last three months or pay fifty bucks for one that will last twenty years. Regina wishes you at least twenty more years as a successful Gumshoe; she wants to buy you only one hat."

"Fair enough. Come into my study. Let's hear what you have to say."

Pop was gone for the morning with some retired firefighters, so we had no audience other than the occupants of the cork-board. As Betty-Anne walked by the cork-board she noticed her own picture among the others.

"Your retinue?"

"You're tacked up there. What do you think?" It was a rhetorical question.

I bid Betty-Anne to take a seat across from me on a small loveseat. I leaned back in my chair, and pushed my new fedora back on my head. I felt suddenly like Bogart in the _Maltese Falcon._

(note to self: make sure I buy a hat rack for my new office--and once in place, make sure I practice tossing my hat until it hangs on it every time)

Betty-Anne opened her attaché, pulled out a manila folder and handed it to me. "This, Gumshoe, is exactly what happened. I made copious notes immediately after we landed--even made copies for White. I understand he wanted nothing made public, but he should have kept my eyewitness account in his personal notes."

I, in turn, handed her the two long ago news reports complete with reporters' names . . . we sat in silence and read.

* * *

"Betty-Anne!" I started . . .

"Liz," she interrupted, "call me Liz. I was Betty-Anne in grade school."

"Oh! Sorry. I simply go by the script. So, Liz it is. I started to say this is a damning allegation against several players on that boat."

"Except it is not an allegation, Gumshoe--it's fact! An indictment, really!"

"If you have your facts straight, there's no question, Liz."

"I have my facts straight, Gumshoe."

"You're not going to let up on that Gumshoe thing, are you, Liz?"

"Why? It fits."

"You working?"

"What?"

"Watch my lips, Liz. Are .. you .. working?"

"Of course, I'm working."

"How would you like to work for me, with a reduction in pay, of course?"

"Oh sure. A week, we're done. I'm out of work. Thanks, no thanks."

"Now, there's a vote of confidence. Perhaps you're not aware of my background in the Air Force. I'll have you know I have many military friends in high places as a past AFOSI officer. I've been promised many *spill-over* cases to investigate as time goes on. Tell you what-- come work for me. If it doesn't work after three months, go your way;
I'll give you three months' severance pay."

"When do you need an answer?"

"My office officially opens Monday. I believe in giving an employer reasonable notice. Call me." I gave h e r m y c a r d , a n d w a t c h e d a s s h e p l o p p e d back into her tired-looking green machine.

I sat back in my chair, leaned my head back. The back brim of the fedora lifted the hat completely off my head. *Ha! Gumshoe.* I set it on my desk and finished reading Liz's eye witness account.

I looked at my watch. I still had time to make a few phone calls. Hopefully, I'd get a live one or two on the other end.

I went to Morris' file of attendees at the reunion-- the names, addresses, phone numbers-- they were all there.

I started with Gina Rowling--
maiden name, Brand. No answer. She must be at work. At least, not home. I went on to Gerri Alvarado--
maiden name, Kitchens. Second ring, female voice, "Hello."

"Gerri?"

"Yes?"

"Alan Garrett here. I don't know if the police have followed up on the horrible incident at our reunion, but I'm doing a bit of legwork myself."

"I have nothing to say to you." She hung up.

I decided to try one more. Roberta Burns-- maiden name, Cordero.

Voice mail: *please leave your name and phone number* . . . beep: "Hi, Alan Garrett here. I'm looking for Roberta. Call me." I left my phone number.

Twenty seconds later the phone rang.

"Hello, Alan Garrett. This is Roberta. What's on your mind?"

"I'm working in conjunction with Inspector Morris on the tragedy at our reunion. Wondering if I might swing by or meet with you somewhere to discuss a couple of things."

"Sure, why not. Today?"

"No, but anytime tomorrow. Pick a time, I'll be there. I have your address from the information you gave the inspector."

"9 a.m. sound good?"

"Sure, see you then."

That was painless! I said aloud, staring at my landline phone as I hung up. *No hesitation, no stuttering. Almost as though she expected my call. But then . . . perhaps she did--after all, there is a murder investigation going on, Alan . . . er, Gumshoe.* I laughed.

Needed to freshen up before my luncheon date with Carla Balboa. I was going to walk the short five minutes to The Strand House just down on the beach next to the pier. I looked at my watch--I had twenty minutes.

I ran a brush through my hair . . . *no wait! you're wearing your new hat, remember?* I donned the fedora and started out the door. Pop was reaching for the door knob at the same time.

"Oh, sorry, I . . . Hey! If it isn't Indiana Jones! What's the hurry, Indie?"

"Just on my way to have lunch with that cute sketch artist, Pop."

"You want the car?"

"Not today, but I'll need it tomorrow if that's okay."

"It's all yours, Indie."

"Wrong image, Pop," I laughed as I jogged down the drive. I did a quick pirouette. Wheeling around, I doffed my hat and called out, "It's *Gumshoe!*"

* * *

I had made reservations at a window, and was already seated when Miss Balboa entered. I rose when I saw her. She glanced around and spotted me, smiled and came to the window. In my most gentlemanly way I held the chair for her and slid it in behind her.

"Good afternoon, Miss Balboa."

"Good afternoon to you, Alan. It's Carla, remember? We've already met."

"Of course."

Noting my new accessory on the inside corner of the table, she said, "I like your hat."

Our afternoon was more than I expected. After lunch we walked the length of the pier hand in hand. We sat close to the end and watched surfers attacking the waves.

I gave her my history, including some of my own surfing adventures under and around this same pier, my few weeks experience aiding in the horrific Himalayan tragedy, the almost twenty years in the Air Force-- including fourteen years in investigative service, and tied it all together with my purchase of the family home, which I pointed out to her from where we were sitting.

The afternoon was somewhat warm, but as almost always on the southern California coast, there's a bit of overcast . . . sometimes it burns off by noon, sometimes it never burns off; today was a good day--I wrapped my arm around her shoulders; she leaned into me, with no display of uneasiness.

"Your turn," I said, pushing my Fedora a bit further back on my head.

"Alright," she agreed, not moving her head from my neck. "Born May 1986, Pinole, California. Graduated UC Davis--Commercial Arts, Sculpture in June 2009. Joined two others in a joint consortium of 'painting and sculpting for profit' endeavor, but couldn't pay my personal rent, let alone our storefront lease . . . so in 2016 a friend asked me to move in with him down here in Santa Monica. I did . . . for two weeks. That's when I came to the conclusion that a long distance friendship is better than a full-time fantasy."

"Ahh, yes," I interrupted, "but sometimes you need to experience the one to appreciate the other."

"I would far rather learn by observation than by experimentation."

"So, continue," I encouraged.

"So, I applied as a sculptor for the L.A. Museum. Word got out that I had some talent. I was hired as a free lance artist in the Southland . . . police departments, museums, even morticians to do face rebuilds of loved ones for funerals.

I've done work for L.A., Hawthorne, Hermosa Beach, Thousand Oaks, I could go on and on. I'm now in a good spot. I have clients within the entire Los Angeles basin." She looked up at me, smiling. "I could be working right now, Alan, but decided to play hooky."

We walked back to her car.

"May I see you again?" I asked.

"I'd like that," she said, reaching up and giving me a peck on the cheek.

I took off my fedora and responded with a kiss of my own. "I'll call you next week."

TWENTY-FIVE

I took a stroll up the block to Ocean Drive, jogged left to 12th Street to check on my painting crew. The plumber's van was parked in front as well. I poked my head in.

A radio was blaring out some old-time rock and roll; two painters in traditional garb were busily rolling on new color, one concentrating on the walls, the other was coming behind, with a freshening of the trim.

The old toilet was standing in the hallway near the rear entrance. I couldn't see the plumber, but I knew he was there. Things were moving along. Note to self: *You need a sign . . . should have asked Carla? Maybe . . .* I continued my journey to *Pop's*. Something else was niggling me . . .

* * *

I had information from Morris, White, Rachel Block, Barry Franks, and Betty-Anne. I needed to sit quietly with a Martell and the ladies and compare it all . . . something I had not as yet done. Oh, I had it all running around in my head, but I needed to lay it out in front of me. *I need another cork-board, I thought . . . put that on my list, right up there with the hat rack.*

From the police inquiry files I took a count of the couples that had come to the reunion. There were one hundred twenty-one hetero-couples, six same-sex couples, plus fifty-three singles: forty men, thirteen women.

Of those on the cabin cruiser from twenty years ago, there were three men: Barry Franks-alone, Matt Wallis-alone and Ted Madison (there with his wife, Winnie); then of the ladies only three: Roberta (Cordero) Burns-alone, Gerri (Kitchens) Alvarado-alone, and last, Gina (Brand) Rowling (came to the reunion with her friend, Patti [Brown] Wellings--now unfortunately gone). *Was Patti on that boat as well?* I wondered.

"Ladies," I smiled, "I'm seeing Roberta in the morning, There is a rumor that Ruby died in a car crash, Sharon promised, but didn't show up, and no one knows the whereabouts of Trudy.

Who attended the reunion that was on that boat twenty years ago? I need to revamp my list."

On the '*Just Fishin*'

<u>Guys</u>	<u>Gals</u>
Tommy Acosta	Gina (Brand) Rowling
Barry Franks	Roberta (Cordero) Burns
Anthony Guerrero	Sharon Etts (Disappeared?)
Ted Madison	Gerri (Kitchens) Alvarado
Terrance Perle	Ruby Salinas (died in crash?)
Matt Wallis	Trudy Wells (missing)

At the Reunion

<u>Guys</u>	<u>Gals</u>
Barry Franks(sick,weak)	Gina (Brand) Rowling
Ted Madison(left early)	Gerri (Kitchens) Alvarado
Matt Wallis(alone)	Roberta (Cordero) Burns

I needed some answers. There have been disappearances, car crashes, case notes missing, a cop killer, Regina Leone tipped off. Why? Hopefully, Morris can help. I reached for the cognac and a snifter; poured myself a couple of fingers, took a sip, too late to get answers tonight. Perhaps tomorrow I'd climb a step closer. I sat at my computer and banged out an email with the following requests:

- Background on Rachel Block
    Maiden name, facts surrounding her husband's   death, her family
- Any details [such as addresses] police data bases might share on the whereabouts of the following 1999 graduates:
    Ruby Salinas, Trudy Wells, Sharon Etts.
- Background on the following:
    Regina Leone, Charles White, Drew   Penn.

Of course, I provided a blurb on each person with what information I had and asked Morris for discretion as he sniffed around.

I looked at my email and smiled; Morris will probably read it and explode at my *demands*. Satisfied, I drained the snifter, then sent the message off.

TWENTY-SIX

"Alan," Roberta Cordero Burns began, "you are certainly a different man from that eighteen year old kid of twenty years ago. But then, we've all changed--some for good, some for bad." She smiled a wistful smile as she handed me a coffee.

Roberta lived in the Rolling Hills Estates just off Hawthorne Boulevard, on the Palos Verdes Peninsula. It was 9:03 a.m. Friday morning.

We took turns recounting our years since high school. Roberta had married twice, divorced twice, decided a dog was a better companion--at least for the last six years. Then she began--

"Worst day of my life, Alan. Got caught up in a terrible mob mentality. You're here about the cabin cruiser mass rape and murder aren't you?"

"And how it relates to the reunion killings," I acknowledged. "What do you mean by *mob mentality*?"

"Oh, you know, cheering on, then actually taking part in the disgusting thing. Became an orgy of brainless young hormones."

"Weren't there two adults aboard?" I asked, taking a gulp of coffee.

"There were, but we tied them up with ropes and left them on the top deck."

"How did Roxanne get aboard, Roberta?"

"Two guys brought her out in a speed boat and dropped her off. One of the guys jumped aboard the *Just Fishin'* as well. Two girls on the *Just Fishin'*-- I can't be sure, but I think they were Ruby Salinas and Trudy Wells--got into the speed boat and left with the skipper."

My cell phone rang. I excused myself and stepped to the door. It was Morris.

"What the hell is this litany of requests, Garrett? I'm supposed to use my team to do your private investigations?" The inspector had a bit of merriment in his voice. "I'll see what I can find out, Alan, but don't expect a lot from me. I have a full plate as it is."

"Any help you can provide," I laughed. "If you find nothing, Sir, I completely understand."   We   hung up. I came back, apologized and sat back down with Roberta. She poured another coffee for me, and continued her narrative.

"It was pre-planned by almost all of the boys, and although none of the girls were involved, some of us just looked at it as a playful lark. We'd all looked at porn sites on the net . . . seen this kind of thing going on in college dorms; the guys just figured they'd start early. It got out of hand very soon after. Became an orgy."

"Did anyone on that cabin cruiser *not* take part?"

"No . . . well, just the two girls that left . . . oh! And the two tied up, of course."

"Well, all I can say, Roberta, is that you have certainly opened up to me regarding that outing. I'm also hoping to get your opinion and thoughts surrounding the unfortunate reunion tragedy. Please bear in mind, Roberta, I am investigating a murder; I am not attached to any news media, and will not disclose any sources."

She laughed. "I've just bared my shoddy past and soul to you, Alan. Now you tell me I can breathe easier. Do you mean anything I say going forward, or do you mean everything already said as well as yet, unsaid?"

"Everything," I assured her. "Oh, one more question while we're still on the water. Who were the two guys on the speed boat, and which one boarded the *Just Fishin'* from that speed boat?"

"The driver was Tom Wellings, the other was a kid I'd seen picking up paper and debris at the marina when we first got there. He may have worked there. Don't know him, don't think he went to our school, but he jumped off that boat and joined in immediately."

I glanced at the clock on her mantle. "It's 10:30, Roberta. I don't know what your schedule is, but if you want to knock off for today . . ."

"No! By no means, Alan. I've cleared my schedule. I'm all yours for as long as needed today."

We agreed on the crimes that had been committed--the unknown female, Patti Wellings, the two CSIs-- Then I asked her if she had seen anything at all odd--not previously mentioned.

"Not that I can think of. I got there just before 5:00 p.m. I was right behind Gina and Patti. Another lady, Rachel--I didn't know her--was right behind me. We decided to all sit together. I remember the time because Gina said, *It's after 5,* and Patti said, *Not for another forty seconds. If it's after 5:00 p.m., then it's acceptable for a lady to have a drink.* I remember Tom Wellings, Patti's former husband, came over almost immediately, said he was happy to see someone he knew, and asked if he could sit with us. Patti blew up and said no. He looked disappointed but sat at an adjacent table."

"You sure your timeline is accurate?"

"Yes. Why?"

"I have some notes that differ from yours. Rachel for instance. You say she came in right after you. She says a lady with a suitcase was ahead of her. Did you have a suitcase?"

"No, but there were people pulling wheeled cases up to staterooms. Someone could have been ahead of us. Rachel was flitting quite a bit. Ladies room, drinks, table-hopping, plus dancing. Didn't spend a lot of time with us at our table. None of us did, really."

"Did any in your circle get a stateroom?"

"The only one I knew was Tom. Only because Patti told me."

"Who do you think the first victim was, Roberta? And who killed Patti? Any ideas?"

"I wish I knew, Alan, but I have no clue."

TWENTY-SEVEN

I grabbed a burger and a piece of cheesecake at the Cheesecake Factory on the way to *Pop's* . . . sat outside and watched the surf and seagulls play as I ate. Then, feeling guilty, I had the crew wrap up the identical fare for Pop.

While I sat there I went over some of my notes. I needed to call Regina about the young dude that captained the speedboat to the *Just Fishin'* and stayed.

I needed to call White to see why his list of personnel didn't change based upon Roberta's telling. It looked like White simply copied Regina's original list, making no changes. Did he interview anyone at all? Why so incomplete or sloppy? Or is Roberta lying? *Remember, Gumshoe, twenty years has passed. You can't even remember your fellow students!* Loaded down with questions, I pulled out of the parking lot and spurred Pop's Suburu back to *Pop's Place.*

* * *

Pop smiled when he saw the name on the bag I carried into the house. "For me?" he asked.

"For you. I ate on the road."

"Down at that marina again?"

"No, Pop. I visited one of the reunion ladies who also happened to be on that boat."

"Get any answers?"

"No. Just more questions."

"Anything I can do?"

"Oh, no. I have a few phone calls to make. You just toddle along and enjoy your cheesecake."

"Toddle along?"

"Toddle along, Pop."

"Oh, you'll be sorry you said that," Pop laughed and headed for the stairs.

I knew I would. But that was enough bantering with Pop. I needed to make some phone calls.

My first call was to White. "I wrote what I wrote, Mr. Garrett. There was no other boy on board, and I counted the girls on the boat. All I'm missing is that second page of my notes."

"I have an eye witness account that says otherwise," I responded. "You have only what someone said happened. I'm not saying what you wrote isn't as you saw it, but someone closer to the event saw it differently."

"They were all kids, Garrett. Leave it alone!"

"Thanks for talking with me." I hung up before he had a chance to say another word.

Next I called Regina Leone, went through the same eye-witness account. She seemed surprised when I asked about the young man who worked around the marina, boarded a speedboat and was aboard the *Just Fishin'* for the entire ordeal. She had no idea what I was talking about.

"I have had young fellows and gals cleaning up the marina grounds for twenty-five years. I pay them cash for day work with no payroll, but there was no unaccounted young man on that boat."

Again, I thanked her for her time, and went on to call number three . . . Rachel Block.

"Hi, Rachel, Alan here. Have a question or two for you, and an answer."

"Give me the answer first. I'm dying to know your decision."

"Twenty-four grand straight up. Then I can put in a few more to bring my cost up to twenty-seven or eight and we both are being fair."

"I have a better idea, Alan. How about twenty straight up? Have a mechanic go through it 'til you're perfectly happy, and if it's less than you thought, maybe you can write me a bonus check."

"Deal," I said. "I'm picking you up tomorrow, shall we say 5:30 p.m.? I'll have a mechanic pick the car up at the same time. Does that sound like a plan?"

"Sure. So, what's your question or two?"

"I've talked with a few people in the last couple of days. At the reunion you sat with Patti, Gina and Roberta, right?"

"Yyeesss? Sooo?"

"They all said that they--and you--walked up the gangplank together just minutes before 5:00 p.m. and that they saw no one with a large suitcase. Someone's timeline and story is wrong. Just wanted you to know."

"Ahh, so now that we've struck a deal on the Caddy you can call me a liar."

"Not at all, Rachel. Perhaps I was too blunt. I would just express my need as an investigator to get correct, indisputable timelines from witnesses. Right now I don't have that. If, between now and tomorrow, you would articulate your footsteps, exactly when you saw what, I would appreciate it."

"Yes Sir, Mr. Investigator!" she hung up on me.

I waited the appropriate time before calling back . . . a minute.

"See you at 5:30 p.m.?"

"I suppose so, Mr. Investigator Garrett. I'll have the appropriate bill of sale for the Cadillac drawn up, and your reunion report completed as ordered, typed up, double-spaced, truthful--all to your satisfaction!"

"Rachel, I . . ." She hung up on me . . . again.

* * *

"Going out, Pop!" I yelled up the stairs. "Walking! Keys are on the coffee table!"

I heard an acknowledgement from above. I closed the door quietly and jogged down the drive. A neighbor, Mrs. Mason, called out a hello as I trotted by, so I stopped and spent a moment chatting with her, then continued to my new rental space.

It was locked up. The crew had finished for the day. I unlocked the door for an inspection visit. The inside of the place was perfect. The land-line phone was already in place. I lifted the receiver-- heard the dial tone. It's working! The old style floor lamp and hat rack I had ordered were in place behind the desk . . . note to self: *wear my fedora here next trip so I can practice hanging it on the rack.*

I looked through the documents I had received from the city licensing and regulations department. Based on those regs, I designed what I wanted for the outside of the storefront: a vintage style sign painted on tin, maybe 3' x 2', framed in ornate wrought iron and swinging from a two-sided railroad clock.

The clock will be attached to the building by a wrought iron angle brace, fifteen feet above the sidewalk, making the bottom of the sign at eleven feet above. The vision was clear in my mind. The sign will be simple--just *Private Investigations* and a phone number, all in a style of the '40's or '50's. Perhaps put my name somewhere above the phone.

Should I or shouldn't I? Yeah, why not? I called Carla.

"Carla, Alan here. I need a sign. Interested?"

"Sure. Hello, by the way. Send me a sketch, Alan, I'll start work on it; send you some ideas."

We finished the short conversation with small talk and signed off. Immediately my phone rang again. It wasn't Carla.

"Gumshoe?"

"Well, hello, Bett . . .er, Liz."

"Hello. Been thinking about your offer. Three months--if I don't like, three months' severance. Still on the table?"

"Absolutely. When you starting?"

"Monday morning, 8 a.m. Too soon?"

"Heck, no! Pick up a desktop, a printer, a laptop for yourself if you need a new one,*Negra,* two bottles of *Martell Cordon Bleu* and one of those french press coffee pots, a small office refrigerator, coffee, office supplies, a case of *Anderson Valley Bourbon Barrel Stout* if you can find it . . . otherwise, *Modelo* whatever you drink."

"Depends on the company I'm with," she answered. "At work it will be tea . . . at least for the first day," she giggled. "You want me to bring all that Monday morning? It will cost you another day. I agreed to *start* Monday morning, not before. But as it's a new job and all, I guess I can overlook your unreasonable demands. Just don't expect me to acquiesce again."

"Liz, I'll make unreasonable demands every day . . . and often," I shot back. "If that's unacceptable, we may as well forget the job offer."

"I've already accepted, Gumshoe, so either tell me where I'm coming Monday morning, or send me my three months' severance pay."

I gave her the address, thanked her for coming on board, and for her *voluntary* service.

I spent the rest of the afternoon and early evening walking along the water watching the scores of plovers scurry to the edge of the outgoing tideline, then rush back to escape the inflow. Seagulls were further up the sand, searching for ocean shoreline critters or scraps and bits left behind undoubtedly by sunbathers or other slothful visitors.

Last, I walked the length of the pier, picked up a taco plate, sat and ate as the sun disappeared. Started back up the hill to my place when my cell phone rang.

"Garrett?"

"Yeah, this is Garrett. Inspector?"

"Yeah. You busy tomorrow?"

"Morning's free. Busy after 4 p.m. I'll be at my new digs at 9:30 a.m. You want to meet me there?"

"Give me the address."

TWENTY-EIGHT

Enjoyed a cup of coffee with Pop Saturday morning.

"How's the case coming along?"

"Slow and cumbersome, but we'll get there."

"Who's we?"

"Oh, you know, the ladies and me. I'll be leaving in a few minutes. I have an appointment with Inspector Morris. Can I use the car this afternoon?"

"Sure. Did you buy that Caddy?"

"Done deal. Being picked up late today. Your buddy Walt is going to go through it and make all the repairs."

"Mind if I tag along on the inspector chit-chat? Three heads might be better than two."

"Uhh, Pop, I have no problems. I don't even know what he wants to talk about, but, sure. Bring a deck of cards and a couple of books in case you end up reading or playing solitaire."

Pop shrugged, went to a games drawer for cards, then proceeded to grab a couple of books.

He hadn't seen my new digs since we made the deal with Old Man Grinnell. He was impressed.

"This office is stunning, Son. You've made it very presentable."

"Thanks. My money works hard at times."

* * *

Inspector Morris arrived right on time, carrying two paper cups of coffee. And a file folder under his arm. When he saw Pop he apologized. "Sorry, Mr. Garrett. I figured Alan wouldn't have a coffee pot in here yet, so I brought coffee for two."

"No problem," Pop laughed. "I'm just a fly on the wall. We flies don't drink coffee."

"Alright, I want to go over the questions you had for me." Morris took a swig of coffee. "I have found a few things; maybe they'll help a bit.

I like what you've done with this old complex; you're going to brighten the outside as well, right?" Morris handed the folder to me. He had neatly typed it out in *point* fashion.

"Absolutely. I have some plans to make it look vintage all the way," I assured him.

"I'm on my way to see that Gina Rowling lady," Morris continued, obviously not listening. "She's the one you called and . . . "

"Yeah, I know, I know. She hung up on me. That doesn't mean she's hiding anything."

"No, but . . . "

"Inspector, you're the cop. I'm just a nerdy, forty year old wannabe; she'll open up to you."

"I'll share what I learn," Morris promised.

"Put it in bullet points like these. They're

good. Do you have any leads that point in a certain direction?" I asked him.

"Not yet," he shook his head and winked, "but we're looking for someone with a big freezer. I have copies, these are yours."

"Good luck," I mumbled as he smiled and walked out the door.

* * *

Way to go Morris! I'll have to study these bios to see if they help me put this puzzle together.

I looked at Pop, "Efficient, isn't he?" I commented

I started to plow through Morris' pointed notes. He had them in alphabetical order, so that's the way I listed them, starting with:

Rachel Block:
- 1981 born Margaret Block, father: James, mother: Joan Hayes
- 1999 graduated high school
- 2002 El Camino College-Administration of Justice degree
- 2002 married Chris Evans, policeman-Hermosa Beach
- 2005 back to school Cal State Long Beach-psychology
- 2009 husband Chris killed -shot-no witnesses -cold case
- 2009 changed her name to Rachel, took back maiden name Block
- 2011 Psychology degree CalState LB with honors
- 2011 became mental health counsellor at VA Long Beach
- 2016 left for private practice - works part-time- one-on-one

Hmmm, she told me her uncle was a cop. Would that be Charles White? Nah!

Next was

Sharon Etts:
- 1982 born Sharon Carne, father: Fred, mother: Betty Etts
- 1994 parents divorced, took on mother's name Etts

•1999 graduated high school
•2002 AA degree from El Camino College
•2002 employed by Mattel
•2005 hospitalized with HIV- 4 months under control
•2008 mother died; took over family home, never married
•2014 sold family home, moved to Fallbrook
•2019 missing persons report filed May 17, by Gina Rowling

Next was
<u>Regina Leone:</u>
•1961 born Regina Olds, father: George, mother: Pat Dodd
•1981 married Jonah Evans, a policeman
•1982 twins, Chris and Virginia born
•1983 children went to live with grandparents, the Olds.
•1984 the Olds moved to Arizona-children returned to
          parents
•1984 divorced, twin children split--son, Chris went back to   live
with Olds, Virginia to her father, Jonah
•1985 remarried to Frank Leone-son, Teddy, born the   same
year
•1995 Frank died- Purchased marina same year

Next was
<u>Ruby Salinas:</u>
•1981 born Ruby Salinas, father: Tomas, mother: Rachel   Ames
•1999 graduated high school
•2000 killed in single car crash, power pole, possible suicide
          autopsy revealed HIV positive, pregnant

Next was
<u>Trudy Wells:</u>
•1982 born Trudy Wells, father: Martin, mother: Dorothy
          Adams
•1999 graduated high school
•2001 AA degree from El Camino College
•2004 BA degree Pepperdine University
•2008 MLS(Master of Legal Studies)Pepperdine University
•2009 Rape and Sexual Abuse Counsellor - Orange County

•2014 wrote Book: <u>Aftermath -- The Mind-Numbing Side Of Sexual</u>
        <u>Abuse</u>
•2016 taught at Pepperdine: *Can Adult Consensual Sex be a*
        Crime?
•2018 on sabbatical Sept. 19 to travel - disappeared, no   trace

And last was

<u>Charles White:</u>

•1944 born -- father: Henry, mother: Ruby Sears
•1963 married Catherine Evans, single mother of one year   old
   son, Jonah
•1968 graduated police academy, joined Beach Cities Police
•2005 retired, distinguished record.

"Well, take the rest of the weekend off, Son; there's always tomorrow--that is, Monday," Pop was convincing. "Let's go get a quick burger."

"Okay. Let's have lunch. I'm meeting Walt at Rachel Block's house at 5:30 tonight; he's going to haul the Caddy to his garage, then I'm taking Rachel to dinner, but I can have something light."

TWENTY-NINE

"So, did you bring your swim trunks?" Rachel smiled as she opened the door. She was dressed only in a bra and pink-laced panties. It was 5:15 p.m.

"Ahhh, no! Sorry," I answered, waving a check, staring at her curvaceous body. "Just a twenty thousand dollar check, an appetite, and a reservation for 6:00."

"Oh, good. I'll take the check now, thanks!" She grabbed the check from my hand and slammed the door in my face. No amount of pounding on my part opened that door. Instead, Rachel called out, "Go away. My boyfriend will be here at 5:30. I'm getting ready."

Walt pulled up right at 5:24 p.m. The garage door opened, revealing the beautiful Cadillac. The tarp was gone, and it had been wiped or washed so that it was spotless and sparkling. No one was in the garage. I tried the garage door into the house. It was locked.

Walt took great care to set the Caddy on his flatbed. I shook his hand; he disappeared around the curved driveway with my new car. I stepped out of the garage as the door dropped down, and retraced my steps to the front door.

At precisely 5:30 p.m. the door opened . . . Rachel appeared stunningly dressed in a cobalt blue sheath. "Where are you taking me, Alan?"

"Do you like fish? I've made reservations at Baleen Kitchen."

"In Redondo? Splendid! It will be a new experience; I've never been there."

"By the way, Rachel," I said, looking at her appreciatively as I opened the Subaru door for her, "you look lovely."

"Why, thank you, Alan," she smiled. "Just for you. And, by the way, you should have seen the look on your face when I first opened the door tonight."

"It was a bit of a shock, Miss. And boyfriend? Where did that come from?"

"I try to make everything exciting, enjoyable and fun. But I'm also very careful."

"Oh, so you don't open up the door naked to just anyone?"

"Oh, heavens no! You have to pay for that pleasure. Look at you. It cost you twenty grand for the privilege, boyfriend."

We pulled into the valet parking area at the Redondo Beach Pier on Portofino Way; handed the valet my key. Then I walked around and opened Rachel's door. She took my arm. It felt good.

We were directed to a window seating I'd booked that looked out over the marina beyond.

"Lovely spot, Alan. Nice choice."

"Let's make a final decision after the meal," I suggested.

Rachel laughed. "Good idea."

We started with cocktails--Rachel enjoyed a <u>Still Dreamin'--</u> *consisting of Havana Club Rum, orange curacao, coconut, pineapple and orgeat.*

For myself a <u>Cali Love--</u>*Grey Goose Pear Vodka, agave, apricot liqueur with a squeeze of lime.*

The meal was delicious. Rachel chose baked black sea bass, I decided on grilled salmon.

During dinner Rachel brought up the 'demands' I had made on her recollections, but I shushed her.

"Let's enjoy each other and the dinner," I suggested. "We can discuss business some other day."

"Deal," she laughed. "I like that *enjoy each other* idea."

Alan, that was, perhaps, a poor choice of words, I told myself.

For dessert we enjoyed one piece of keylime pie with two forks, and washed it down with something they called a Peppermint Patty--hot chocolate, Bailey's Irish Cream, and Peppermint Schnapps.

We left Redondo Beach satisfied. Rachel scooted tight against me as though we were seventeen again . . . and I didn't mind. I didn't mind one bit.

* * *

Twenty minutes later we pulled into Rachel's drive. She pulled my head to her and kissed me.

"As I asked a bit ago, Alan, did you bring your swim trunks?"

"Answer is still no," I said, laughingly, as I walked her to the door, "so, thank you for the lovely evening."

"Oh, no you don't, Alan Garrett! I have swim trunks as we discussed before, the night is young, you work for yourself, tomorrow is Sunday. I'm not on a schedule, you have nothing pressing; just lock your car and come in. Now!"

She unlocked the door, opened it, smiled and closed the sale with, "I have Martell Cordon Bleu. And, by the way," she changed the subject soberly, pointing to a manila envelope on a table by the door, "there is my report for you to take home with you. You will find it complete, I'm sure."

"I'm sure," I agreed.

"You'll find a pair of trunks under the envelope. I'll be right back."

We swam a little, drank a little, embraced a little, talked a little, sat in the hot tub a little (*I think that's where we lost our swim suits*), swam a little more, drank a little more, embraced a little more, and a little more than that.

Some time after, I dressed and started for *Pop's*, envelope tucked under my elbow. It was Sunday morning, 4:15 a.m.

THIRTY

Climbing out of bed at 7:30 a.m., I put the coffee on. Then I opened the folder Rachel had provided last night. Pop came down, enjoyed a coffee with me and asked about the Cadillac.

"Walt picked it up right on time," I confirmed.

"Oh, I know," Pop acknowledged. "Walt called me once he checked a few things over in his garage. He says it's a sweet-looking vehicle. He'll have an estimate for you by late afternoon tomorrow."

Then Pop tried to be casual. "Where did you have dinner last night, Alan?"

"Baleen Kitchen in Redondo. Why?"

"Just asking. I thought maybe Bakersfield or San Diego."

"Very funny, Pop. She has a hot tub and a pool; not that it's your business, but, we enjoyed some of each. She a very vivacious lady; fun to be with."

"Uh-huh! Right! Good coffee, Alan. I'll leave you to your investigating. Oh! I'll need the car this afternoon."

"Sure." I tossed him the keys. "I'm probably just going to take it easy today, anyway. Make sure you're back before the 10 p.m. curfew, Pop."

We both had a good laugh. Pop lumbered up the stairs, calling back, "You be careful out there, Son. Thanks for the coffee."

* * *

I poured myself a fresh cup, opened the file folder Rachel had given me and began reading. She had, as she said, double-spaced the two page manuscript.

To: Mr Alan Garrett, Private Investigator.

Re: four suspicious deaths July 31, 2019,

High School Reunion Eye witness account of

Rachel Block:

Arrived-- 4:22 p.m. As I walked up the ramp, there were at least two dozen graduates ahead of me, and many more on the ramp behind me. A few were pulling rollered luggage; one case ahead of me was especially large--checkered black and tan, being pulled by a brunette. [You {A.G.} have my sketch of the lady.]

I picked up my name tag at the "welcome desk" then went back to my car because I'd forgotten my yearbook. (I wanted to have it to compare today with yesteryear.) Going back down the ramp I came face to face with a gentleman having an identical suitcase. The press of people coming up the ramp made me scurry on my way. It just seemed strange that such large luggage would come to the reunion. I described the gentleman to a sketch artist for A.G. as well. He was a large man, muscular, like possibly a football player in high school.

Coming back up the gangplank (about 5:00 p.m.) I was one of a group of single ladies. Our group decided to sit together. I knew one or two of them, but not all. One was Patti Brown, one Gina Brand and one Roberta Cordero. Tom Wellings tried to sit with us, but was shooed off by Patti . . . they were divorced. He sat with Gerry Kitchens and a few others at the next table, where he kept trying to talk with Patti. She finally got up and moved to another table. Later I meandered through the crowd of people, dancing with some, drinking with some, going from table to table. I may have seen the lady later in the cafeteria, but I'm not certain. I don't think I saw the man again.

I opened my yearbook only twice: to identify the group of ladies I was with at that first table. I remembered Patti Brown from school, but kept looking from the real Roberta to her picture-- would have never recognized her. And you, Mr. Garrett--I would never have guessed that it was

your picture in the yearbook when you stood to
address the crowd.

I stood and was headed for the door to leave
when Tom Wellings stood and asked where Patti
was. I didn't learn of her death until days later.

Love and Kisses

Rachel Block

I didn't learn a damn thing. Well, okay, two things:
1)she says the man with the luggage was a football
player type. 2)she left just before Patti was found dead.

The fact that she went back to her car for the
yearbook, then met up with the other gals as they were
boarding clears up that seeming confliction in my mind.
It was back to the drawing board.

Some days ago I had put Morris' attendance list in
alphabetical order. I yanked my yearbook to the
desktop and put the Inspector's attendance list in front
of me.

Turning to the athletics section in the book, I
compared the twenty-two member varsity football team
to the reunion list. Came up with four members who
attended that could probably fit the description of a
large, muscular kid, now a man.

There were three more heavy-set seventeen year
old fellows I chose from the yearbook as well. I emailed
most of the names to Inspector Morris along with the
following note:

*Alan Garrett here. Please interview these six
attendees of the reunion. I have one more I will*

*check on personally--a Mr. Krup. He lives near
the marina where Roxy DeVry died. -- A.G.*

A pair of scissors was handy. I cut out pictures of the seven young men, and tacked them on the   cork-board, squeezing the others closer together to make room for the new additions, apologizing as I did so with, *Sorry all, but you have more company.*

Then to the coffee pot for my third or fourth mug, after which I went to the window, mug in hand. This is the worst part of investigative work--the menial, no action, head in hands--thinking part.

I'd much rather be in a car chase, or breaking down a door to put cuffs on a dirty Air Force smuggler, or perhaps boarding a tramp steamer off the Florida coast to put the brakes on a trafficking ring involving Navy or Air Force personnel.

No, of course military is 99% clean . . . but it's the 1% that just blows the tin lid off my brain. The difficulty, as I see it, is time--the hours and hours spent preparing to get to that tramp steamer.

I looked at the pier through my antique Griffith telescope. A couple of old-timers were leaning over the far rail fishing. As I watched, one of them seemed to be having some luck . . . his rod was bouncing up and down . . . *probably a jack mackerel.* I could never handle the taste, but I'm told it's oily flesh is filled with Omega 3 fats.

My attention shifted to the rest of the pier. Typical Sunday pedestrian traffic--elbow to elbow. Things have certainly changed in twenty years. Used to be able to walk the pier even on a Sunday without bumping into anyone. "I miss the good old days," I mumbled aloud.

Pop was just coming down the stairs on his way out. "So do I, Son. So do I."

I waved at him. "Remember the curfew, Pop."

* * *

1:15 p.m.

I needed a nap.

My cell phone woke me with the jingle I had chosen. The number was one I didn't recognize, telling me I could get a reduced price on solar panels. Their workmen were in the area.

"Good. Where are you right now?"

"I'm sorry. What?" the young lady asked.

"Where are your workmen at this moment?"

"Uhh, let me check." The line went dead.

It was 5:30 p.m. anyway. I had a good nap.

The cell phone jingle repeated its little ditty. *I think I'll change it. It's beginning to jar on me.* I figured it was the girl calling me back, so I was prepared to ignore it, when a familiar female voice said, "Alan, are you there?"

Carla!

"Hi. Carla?"

"Hi, Alan. I have some sign sketches for you to look at. I can e-mail them or swing by tomorrow and go over them with you, and we can make a decision if you like any of them."

"Swinging by sounds better to me," I said, "how many do you have?"

"Five. Each a bit different. Would 10:30 a.m. be a good time?"

"Perfect. At my new office, Carla. Thanks. See you." We signed off.

The cork-board, with its seven new faces, stared back at me as I compared them to Rachel's sketch of the reunion *suitcase man*. I shook my head.

"Ladies, do you see any similarity?" I asked the four dead gals. "Can you pick him out? Look closely. Sometimes I can see a similarity and sometimes absolutely nothing, depending on how intently I look at that sketch.

When I first looked at it days ago it could easily have been Inspector Morris, for crying out loud.

Hey!" I smiled, "maybe a drink would help. Any of you care for a snifter of booze? No? Your loss. I'm going to have a drink right in front of you!"

The glossy faces--with pushpins through their foreheads--looked back at me, most smiling, but all stone-cold sober. Teetotalers, all.

* * *

Pop made his curfew . . . with five hours to spare.

THIRTY-ONE

Monday 7:00 a.m.

I said goodbye to Pop and the crowded, motley bunch on the cork-board, I started down the hill toward my new office, full coffee mug in hand, feeling like I should have packed a lunch in a brown paper bag.

7:45 a.m. An old, green sedan parked against the front curb. Betty-Anne McConnell emerged, dressed elegantly in a chic, steel gray business suit, as if she belonged in an uptown attorney's firm. Maybe a little overdressed; but for now, I was simply pleased to see her show up early. I smiled as I opened the door.

"Good morning, Liz," I greeted her.

"Gumshoe," she nodded. "I'm going to need some help unloading my car."

She opened her trunk; I brought in the small refrigerator, printer and desktop with monitor she had managed to squeeze in there. Meanwhile, she brought in a new laptop, coffee pot, coffee and four large mugs.

"I figured you'd like some new coffee mugs; I picked up a few for you. I'll be right back."

She returned to her car for a bag of office

supplies and a case of the stout beer on my list. Again, she left for her car. She came back with two bottles of Martell. Then she dug through the office supplies to find two straws.

"For the end of the day, Gumshoe?" she asked, handing me one.

"I like the way you think, Liz."

"So, where do I sit, Bossman?"

"Here in the main foyer. My desk will be in there so we can eyeball each other when my door is open."

"Alright. I'm sitting. What do I do all day?" adding, "besides looking lovelier than a forty-three year old fox ought to look."

"Ha! I'm having a sign painter come over later this morning to show some designs for the outside sign, but perhaps, I should consider the name, _Gumshoe and Fox_. Has a nice ring."

"I like it," Liz agreed. "Of course, you'll have to change it after three months."

"Why afte... Oh! Yeah. A defeatist, huh?"

I opened my checkbook. Wrote out a check made out to Miss McConnell, dated it November 1, and using my new stapler, stapled it to the side of the desk where she was sitting. Upon examining it she whistled and turned to me.

"_Gumshoe and Fox!_ When is your painter coming?"

* * *

We put everything in order, then I sat in my office making a "to do" list for Liz, when it struck me--show Rachel's sketches to Liz.

"Sure, I think I know who they're supposed to be," she said. "The man could be officer White, the woman, his wife. I'm going back a few years of course, but they could be."

"Why, you're right!" I exclaimed. "I can see it now that you say it. But how do you know the Whites, especially Mrs. White?

"I was interviewed, of course, by Detective White regarding the cabin cruiser, and Mrs. White was . . ."

The front door opened, interrupting our conversation.

"Are you open for business?" a gray-haired gentleman asked as he pushed his companion through the door.

"Yes, we are," Liz smiled graciously. "Please sit," she said motioning to the chairs in front of her desk."

"How did you hear of us?" Liz asked. "Our signage isn't even up yet."

"Inspector Morris suggested we drop by. Our daughter, Maureen, was one of the two CSI investigators at your reunion. No one should die like our Maureen and those other women did. The police said you are spending most of your time searching for motives and clues. We're prepared to pay you to find our daughter's killer, and we spoke with the other CSI's family. They, too, are willing to pay."

"Not necessary, Sir," I assured them. "Leave your contact information with Liz. Whatever we find we'll share."

"But, we nee . . ."

"Don't worry about it," Liz shushed them, "the man works for free." She handed them one of my cards. They left.

Liz took a sidelong glance in my direction. "I need some cards, Gumshoe--at least three months' worth--before you go broke. By the way, who's doing our monthly books?"

"Funny lady, Liz. That would be you. We're going to get along just fine."

* * *

I scribbled a few more items on our want list:
- Business cards for Liz
- A two-sided flip board: cork one side whiteboard on the other
- whiteboard pens and push pins
- Good Surveillance Camera
- Listening devices
- Cassette tape recorder and tapes

I handed the list to Liz. "We'll discuss later what we were talking about earlier. If you think of anything else we need, run it by me before ordering. Use this credit card and order on-line. Get free shipping wherever you can. Oh, by the way, park in our parking lot. Here's a set of keys to the padlock, and the back door. Chain link fence on left."

"Can I order a new outfit?" she asked soberly.

"As I said, run it by me," I shot back. "We'll talk." "And I'm doing the monthly books? Aww, are you sure you can trust me, Gumshoe?"

This could be an interesting three months.

* * *

A black sedan pulled up. "We have company, Boss. Oh, oh. Looks like cops."

"I see it," I replied. "Inspector Morris . . . alone. Maybe just to give us an official welcome to the world of crime-solving, but make some coffee, please."

THIRTY-TWO

"Ahh, fresh coffee! Great! I can use a cup. Thanks, Miss--?" Morris asked as he took the mug.

"Fox!" Liz said, winking at me.

"Inspector. Nice surprise. Pull up a chair. Let me introduce you to my new office manager, Liz McConnell. She's considering the Fox thing but hasn't yet made the official move."

Morris smiled, "Congratulations on your engagement, Miss McConnell."

"Not hardly, Sir. Gumshoe, here, doesn't play the game right." As Liz handed me a coffee, her nose wrinkled, her upper lip formed a masterful sneer.

"Ahh, my dear, no time for games." Morris turned to me. "Do you have some time to go over some notes of mine?"

I looked at my watch. 10:05 a.m. "I have an appointment here in a half hour. What's up?"

"I met your two ladies, Gerri Kitchens Alvarado and Gina Brand Rowling. I spent an hour with each. The bottom line of the whole thing is that their best friend, Patti Wellings is dead, and they think you are the murderer. You had the time, opportunity and motive."

"Motive? What possibly could that be?"

"Some longstanding hatred over an incident in high school. Patti made a fool of you, and the ladies figure her death was payback. They fear for their lives as well."

"Almost laughable, Sir. They shared the same exact story with you? Were they together?"

"No. I interviewed Gerri mid-morning. Got hold of Miss Rowling that evening. Same story."

"Ah, collusion. Were they at all believable?"

"Bizarre, more like it," Morris laughed. "But an interesting take on the evening."

"You did some homework before you made your visits, right? Do you have a pointed report for me as you did with the others?"

"Oh yes, I did my duty!" he smiled as he handed me the reports.

I glanced at the neat lists. "I'll review them later, thanks."

"What kinds of leads does your forensics team and your own investigations point you toward, Inspector?" Liz asked. "Your CSI parents were here early this morning; they told us you sent them here. We spoke for a few minutes."

"We can't accept a reward, and they want to reward someone . . . may as well be you. You're working on the case."

"We appreciate it," she nodded, then turned to me, "don't we, Gumshoe?" batting an eye at me.

"Sure we do. Thanks, Morris. By the way, I gave Bradley Swazer photos of the skipper of that doomed craft from twenty years ago. Have you had the chance to put them through photo recognition?"

"Hmm! Good question. I'll look into it. Leave it with me. Just wanted to give you what I have, Gumshoe," the inspector smiled as he got up to leave. Turning to Liz, he added, "Fox."

We turned to the Inspector's reports on Gina and Gerri. Again, he was concise and logical.

First was

<u>Gerri Kitchens Alvarado:</u>

•1982 born Gerri Kitchens, father: Karl, mother: Ann Cook
•1999 graduated high school
•2004 married Roberto Alvarado -works for Cal Trans
•2006 teaching credential UCLA
•2008 Masters of Education UCLA
•2009 son, Richie born
•2010 began teaching elementary LA Unified School Dist.
        currently teaching

•2019 August -- interview conducted by Inspector Morris:
    •last contact with Patti Wellings before reunion? -- *three weeks before reunion - she called to let me know Alan Garrett was back in town - she said she wanted his address to invite him, to bury the hatchet.*
    •who murdered Patti? *Alan Garrett*
    •why? *he hated her. She embarrassed him in school*
    •who is the other dead woman? *likely, Sharon Etts*
    •why? *she promised Matt Wallis to be at reunion*
    •do you have a large freezer? - *no*

Next was

<u>Gina Rowling:</u>

•1981(?) born--vague recollection of birth family -- placed in
        orphanage
•1984   adopted by Jeffery and Judy Brand, Las Vegas
•1995   moved to Manhattan Beach
•1999   graduated high school

•2000   El Camino College
•2001   son, Peter born
•2002   Cal-State Long Beach–nursing program
•2003   married Kevin Rowling–pharmacist
•2004   daughter, Tina born
•2005   enrolled in Blackstone 5 year paralegal course to be
        certified as legal counsellor for wills, trusts, and
        estates
•2008   husband and children killed in freeway auto accident
•2008   undergraduate legal internship for Gunn and
        Gunn law firm
•2011   set up private practice as estate planning paralegal
        her current occupation

•2019 August -- interview conducted by Inspector Morris:
   •how well did you know Patti Wellings? *Best of friends --
        she lived with me for a few months after my husband
        and children were killed*
   •who do you think killed Patti at the reunion?
        Alan Garrett–she was afraid of him.
   •why? *She made fun of him in school. He swore to get
        even. I heard him tell her he was going to kill her.*
   •but high school kids say things like that all the time.
        You've seen him. His threat was real.
   •but she was the one who invited him -
        *She was toying with danger. Even giggled
        about it nervously.*
   •who is the other dead woman? *Trudy Wells*
   •did Alan kill her as well? *Yes*
   •why? *She rejected him in high school*
   •do you have a large freezer? *– Absolutely not!*

   "Interesting, Gumshoe. Gina was an orphan!"
   "Correction, Liz. Almost an orphan. She has vague
recollections of family. One thing we know for certain:
we cannot trust anything that comes out of Gina's
mouth!"
   "Do you think she's lying about that as well?"

"No, *Foxy*," I said, emphasizing her newfound persona, "her telling Morris that I threatened someone with murder."

"So, you weren't a switchblade-carrying bad-ass dude as a seventeen year old, huh?"

"Not even funny, Liz. You seem to be having fun, Liz," I smiled. "It won't ever wear off, will it? I rather like the sense of humor. But, I'll give you some real work before you start your shopping."

* * *

"Okay, coffee break over; now back to business." Liz stood, one leg on the floor, one leg against the wall, with a pen and pad in hand.

"What's next? Send your shirts to the dry cleaners? Mop the floor? Oh that reminds me, we need cleaning supplies."

"Top right drawer of your desk--open it," I instructed. "You'll find two files; they are affectionately known as skips. I'd like you to . . ."

"Skips?" Liz let out a cry of delight. "I love skips! I was a skip tracer for over a year when I was going to college. One of my favorite jobs! And I'm good at it, too." Then she added, "Your 10:30 appointment is late, by the way. It's almost 10:40."

No sooner had she finished her last thought than a knock came on the back door. I opened it to Carla.

"You said parking spots in back. You didn't say you were going to lock me out," she said, breezing in.

"That's my fault," Liz said. "I just automatically locked it after I came in. Sorry."

"Liz, Carla; Carla, Liz," I said. They shook hands.

"Let's see what you have for me, Carla."

"For us, Gumshoe!" Liz interjected.

"Us?" Carla turned to her in surprise.

"Three month deal," Liz declared. Possible name modification."

"Oh, nice try, Foxy, but I don't think so." I looked at Carla and laughed out loud. "Let's see your sketches, Carla."

She spread them out all over the desk. One caught my eye and was particularly appealing. It incorporated a vintage wrought iron railroad clock as I had envisioned:

Private Investigations
555-9876
Alan Garrett

"What do you think?" Carla asked.

"I like it. Can you do the entire project, including the clock?" I asked.

"Of course, I have a modern-day blacksmith who . . . "

"I don't like it," Liz countered. It's not, uhh, *vintage* enough. She grabbed a marker and drew the following:

Gumshoe & Fox
555-9876
Private Investigations

"Oh, I like that!" Carla said, "and it is certainly vintage. I understand Gumshoe and I assume Fox would be you, Liz, but isn't it a bit premature?"

"Certainly not!" Liz answered. "When have you ever seen a successful firm with only one name? Anyone can be Fox. I'm Fox for the next three months, maybe more," she winked at me.

"You should also have the word, GUMSHOE, in big, bold gold leaf, gilded in an arched vintage style," *Now Liz was getting carried away*, I thought . . . "with *Alan Garrett* in smaller letters underneath, on--like a," she continued, "a milk glass, half-door panel on the door to your office, Bossman. That way, no one will mistake the *Fox* for the *Gumshoe*.

"Carla," I asked, shaking my head. "Can you do that--the gold leaf thing?" I was actually beginning to like the idea.

"Oh, absolutely!" Carla said enthusiastically. "Not sure I can still get the milk glass, but a fine sand-blasted glass or maybe even a glue-chip would do the job beautifully. All we need is a door with a half-glass panel."

"I'll get on that right away," Liz assured us. "Now, if we're finished here, I have much more to order for our office." Liz turned and walked away.

I laughed. I couldn't help myself.

THIRTY-THREE

Carla and I finished our sketch designs, I initialed my approvals, Liz wrote her a deposit check from our company check book--the first one. A peck on the cheek, a goodbye wave to Liz, and Carla departed through the rear door.

"Let's lock up and go to lunch, Liz." I wanted to finish our earlier conversation. It was just getting interesting before we had a client walk in.

"Never before had a boss take me to lunch on the first day, Gumshoe. Shouldn't we wait a week or so, so I know you're sincere?" She winked.

"You're impossible, Liz. I should just cut you loose right now. Never know what's going to come out of your mouth!

But, no. I'd like to hear the end of your boat story. There's a pub right around the corner. Let's go grab a burger or taco, and have a chat." I grabbed my fedora.

We found a comfortable corner at the Shellback Tavern--good view of the pier, a bit before the lunch crowd. Fairly quiet.

"Back to the Whites," I smiled at Liz as we ordered, "how could they be the subjects of those sketches?"

"Obviously, they may not be, Gumshoe," she answered as she unfolded her napkin, "but they sure look like them."

"I know you were interviewed by White, but how would you know his wife?" I asked.

"Oh, didn't you know? The Whites are Regina Leone's former in-laws. When Regina lost her husband and bought the marina, the White's were always there . . . well, the Mrs. anyway. And, might I add, it was always, or almost always an unhappy visit. Arguments from one end of the dock to the other. I was around quite a bit; I knew them both quite well."

"What were they fighting about?"

"Money. I don't know the details, but I heard the word *investments* a couple of times."

"A little detail they forgot to tell me. What about Regina's first husband . . . that would be Mrs. White's son?" I asked.

"Yes. Disappeared, no trace. He had custody of the kids-- took them. Some said he was still in the area, some said to Texas."

I shook my head, "So the Whites were in their forties when Regina married the son." I reached in my pocket, pulled out my notes. "Let's see, that would be . . . "

"Jonah." Liz nodded.

"Hmm, Jonah. More interesting all the time, but also more confusing."

"Yeah, small world, Gumshoe. Good burger."

"Umm," I agreed, nodding, mouth full. "So, Now, Fox, best guess . . . was Rachel on that boat?"

"To tell you the truth, Gumshoe, I don't know.

I'm told a small boat came up and dropped off two girls and picked up a couple. I was counting heads, not memorizing faces."

"Two girls off; two girls on? You sure, Fox?"

"No, but that's what some of the girls said. I heard the speed boat approach the cruiser a couple of times, like they were shuttling people on and off."

We ordered a second draft beer. Liz raised an eyebrow, but clinked my glass with hers.

"I was told it happened only once," I said. "two guys sped up in a speed boat, picked up two girls and dropped off one young fellow."

"I don't think so, Gumshoe. Six young girls plus, of course, Roxanne DeVry were on that boat at the end."

"Did White interview everyone? actually talk to everyone that came off the boat?"

"He talked to me, mostly," Liz confirmed what I was thinking. "I think most of the guys and gals split as soon as they got off."

"Did he actually board the cabin cruiser?"

"Oh, yes! He was aboard by himself for twenty minutes. Came off gagging and shaking with rage!"

"I suppose we should head back," I said. "Otherwise, we'll be in trouble with the boss."

"I think I may be in trouble already," she laughed. "Don't let him smell my breath."

"Don't worry," I assured her, "he won't get that close."

"Ohh! Touché!"

THIRTY-FOUR

Liz placed orders for the items on my list, while I used 4 x 6 cards to jot down each of the various facts, notes or questions--one item per card. It was a technique I'd used as an Air Force investigator.

"You have scotch tape, right?" I called to her.

"Sure do, a four pack. I'll bring you one."

I taped cards on the wall in front of me and grouped them as I thought they related to each other. Liz watched for a few minutes.

"Easier to move around than a white board," I explained. "White boards are good for scheduling, lists and such, but not notes."

"Nice idea, Gumshoe. I'll buy more 4 x 6 cards. I have a white board on order. And there's a guy coming in tomorrow a.m. to take your door away as a template for the new one with glass."

My cell rang. "Garrett here."

"Hi, this is Walt. Got an estimate for you on that Caddy."

"Great, Walt. What's the damage?"

"You sitting down, Alan?"

"Yes. Hit me with it."

"Changed out all fluids--oil, brake, tranny, new rad, water pump, gas tank, all the hoses and lines, belts, new fuel injector, and new tires all around."

"Walt, it sounds like you've already started the work. What are we looking at?"

"Parts, labor and the tow, it comes to $3,166.00. Too much, right?" Walt smiled.

"Walt, I love you," I almost shouted.

"Hey!" from the other room, "thought I was your one and only."

Walt continued, "I was afraid you'd say it was well within your budget. I'm outside--sitting in it, halfway down the block."

"I'll be there in a minute with a check," I said. Then to Liz I said, "Liz, lock the doors and follow me."

I walked out, looked both ways, saw the Caddy and hastened my steps. Walt was standing outside the vehicle, waiting. He had put current plates on it, but they couldn't belong to the Cadillac. I had sent the DMV the change of ownership paperwork already, but had yet to receive new plates.

"She's a beaut, Alan. Here's my detailed repair report." I looked at his bill, pulled my wallet out and wrote a check for $3,400.00.

Liz caught up with us. "So this is the car I've been hearing about. Nice!"

"Thanks for the bonus, Alan. I need a ride up to your dad's place for a late lunch. He and I haven't talked in months, and haven't seen each other for a couple of years. I missed the get-together the fellas had recently, so we'll have a good visit."

"Fine. Jump in. You, too, Liz. We'll give Walt a ride," I said, opening the rear door for her.

Liz beamed, "Yessir, Bossman. Don't I get shotgun?"

"Absolutely! But on the way back!" I smiled.

Liz frowned, playfully stuck her tongue out at me, but dutifully slipped within.

Pop was waiting for us outside as we drove up the drive. Walt stepped out from the front passenger side and shook his hand warmly.

"Alan," he cried, as Liz and I emerged, "she is a beauty!"

"Oh, Thank you, Sir!" Liz piped up. "I try."

Everyone laughed, of course; but when I introduced Liz to Pop as my new office manager she changed from silliness to total respectability.

"Mr. Garrett," she started, "it is a privilege to meet you. Your son is a fine boss. Intelligent, witty, quick, willing to compromise. We work together well," she turned to me, "don't we?" Then, not waiting for me to respond, she said matter-of-factly, "Yes, we do."

Pop raised his eyebrows."All that in just one day, young lady?"

"Well, Sir, I'll have a complete report by week's end, but . . . Oh, I forgot! He's a good-looking dude, as well," she said. Then looking directly up at me, she added, "Figured I'd just throw that one in there as well."

"We're going to run, Pop. Nose to the grindstone and all that. I'll get your plates back soon, Walt."

"Again, Alan," Pop said, throwing a wide smile at Liz, "the car's a beauty."

"I call shotgun," Liz exclaimed. She scooted next to me, causing just a bit of consternation.

* * *

We drove the two or three blocks back to the office. As we pulled in front to park, a silver Mercedes came to a stop just behind. In the rear view mirror it was easy to see Rachel Block behind the wheel. I had seen the car following, as far back as the corner near my house, but I wasn't absolutely sure until now. *Hmm? Coincidence? Interesting, indeed, Alan.*

Rachel emerged from her car and walked briskly to the passenger side of the Cadillac. I did the same . . . just as Liz was opening her door.

"You conniving vixen!" Rachel screamed, yanking Liz by the hair, "Get Out Of My Car!"

"Whoa, whoa! Rachel! Stop!" I yelled. "What are you doing? You get back in that Mercedes and you go home! Cool off!"

"Screw you, Asshole! and," she turned to Liz, "you, too, Bitch!" She hadn't let go of Liz' blond hair; twisting it more, she gave Liz another yank before I could stop her.

I grabbed her wrist and forced her hand to loosen its grip on that large hank of hair. Then I pressed her hands to her sides to keep her from lashing out and hurting someone or getting hurt.

"Are you calm, Rachel?" I asked after almost a minute. "I'll let you loose. Come in the office. We'll talk." Meanwhile, Liz opened the office door.

Rachel's eyes grew narrow with anger. "She has a key? Who is she, Alan? Why was she in the Cadillac? And why are you running around with her? Alan, she was practically sitting in your lap!"

"Step into my office, Rachel." I motioned with a sweeping arm for her to enter my private office, and after asking Liz if she was okay, I shut the door behind us.

"First of all, Walt, the repairman just brought the Caddy here today about 2 p.m. Here's his repair bill, $3,166.00."

She only glanced at it. I continued:

"I gave you $20,000.00; I figured to spend around $28,000.00 total. On that basis I have a check made out to you for $5, 000.00."

I pushed the check across to her.

"I don't want the money, Alan. I just want to know about the woman in the other room." She pushed the check back at me.

"Her name is Liz. I hired her as my office manager. Today is her first day. She's very qualified. And since I was shuttling Walt up to visit my Pop, I invited Liz to join us."

"And before that," Rachel spat out, "you invited her to lunch at the Shellback Pub. I can't trust you at all, you womanizing, cheating prick!"

"You don't own me, Rachel, and I'm not committed to anybody. We enjoyed the other evening, and perhaps will again, but . . .?"

"Never! You hear? NEVER!" She picked up the check, slammed my office door damn near off it's hinges, gave Liz the finger and hissed, "Die, you whore!" as she stormed out.

The Mercedes squealed away from the curb.
I ran to the foyer. "Are you okay, Liz? She had murder on her mind."

"Methinks she was jealous, Gumshoe. And yes, I'm fine--thanks for asking. I Don't know why or what triggered her mindless action. Certainly can't be jealous of me."

"Nor of me, Liz. We spent a casual night together recently, but those things do happen in the real world; I have feelings for her, sure, but that was beyond the pale."

"Ahh, but it was you, then!" Liz laughed. "Silly men. None of you understand the effect you have on women."

"I suppose I'm familiar with only one side," I agreed. "Let's knock off for the day. We have a full day tomorrow, Liz."

She frowned, "That's Fox to you, Gumshoe. A full day tomorrow? What should we call today, then? Foreplay?"

THIRTY-FIVE

Tuesday morning, 7:49 a.m.

I parked in the lot and tried the back door. Surprise . . . it was unlocked. Obviously I was late.

Inspector Morris was sitting with Liz, enjoying a mug of something hot. "Alan, we began to worry about you," Morris stood to shake my hand.

Liz poured a mug and handed it to me. "Thanks, Liz. Is our coffee better than yours Morris?" I asked.

"Had a couple of things to go over with you, and decided to swing by again. I'll try not to be too big a nuisance in your house."

"You may swing by our house any time," Liz assured him. "Friendly faces are welcome."

"Got a DMV ping on your boat pilot from twenty years ago. Drew Penn, age forty-six, lives in Fullerton, works at *Medieval Times* in Buena Park. Clean, couple of traffic tickets, married, three kids. Something for your cold case.

I still shake my head that your detective White was so dismissive at the burning of that craft." Morris went on, "almost like he was anxious to sink her." He handed me the Penn contact information. "Not my business, not my case."

"Tell me, Morris," I asked, "Have you identified the dead girl yet? You must have her DNA by now."

"We have her DNA, just nothing to match it to."

"What about that Matt Wallis fellow's note?" I asked. "He seemed awful worried about a lady no-show at the reunion."

"I don't remember the note, and we're not up to W yet, tracking the attendees down."

"Step into my office, Morris. It's on the board. I like you Morris, but you have old-fashioned ways."

"Well, damn! I completely overlooked this one," the Inspector exclaimed as he read and re-read Wallis' note:

'I expected to see my high school sweetheart, Sharon Etts here tonight but she never showed up. We just talked on the phone last month; she assured me she was coming. In fact, she was to be here with a couple of friends.'

"Have you followed up on Wallis?" the inspector asked.

"No. I figured I'd do the heavy lifting and give you the easy pick-up stuff, Sir. But I do have Matt's contact numbers, and we can call him right now."

"Let me call the office first," Morris laughed, "Let them know I'm in my other office."

"Oh! That reminds me," Liz turned to me while she dialed the number, "I think the office or my office is too ordinary a name, don't you think? We should call it some unique, catchy name like *the lair,* or *the study,* or *the den.* Foxes have dens."

The Wallis call went to voice mail. Liz left a message for him to return the call regarding the information he had given to the police at the reunion.

Two minutes later Matt called. "It was her, wasn't it?" he burst out, "I know it was."

"We don't know that at all," Liz answered him. "We'd like her address, phone number, and anything else you may know--perhaps about the friends she was to go with. Let me put you on to the inspector." She handed the Inspector the phone.

Morris started writing. When he hung up he had Sharon's phone number and address and her expected traveling companions.

"You want me to go with you?" I asked him.

"No. I have urgent business at home; gotta be off. She lives in Fallbrook. I'm not going, Alan. You can. If you decide to go, I'll call the Fallbrook police to insure you won't be shot as an intruder. Thanks for the coffee." He was gone.

"I've got *The Lair* covered, Gumshoe, if you want to go to Fallbrook. I have a couple of skips to track down, and that door guy is supposed to be here soon. I can stay busy, promise . . . plus, I'll have a great name for this place by the end of the day. The Lair's not bad, though, eh?"

"I'm thinking, I should go to find Drew Penn first," I said. "Ring him up for me, Fox Let's see what he has to say."

A few minutes later she had him on the line. Turns out he was available until 1:30 p.m. He had to be at *Medieval Times* by 2:30 p.m.

"Decision made, Liz, I'm going to see your friend Drew. Do me a favor," I continued, "call the Fallbrook

P.D. Let them know we have a dead girl that might be Sharon Etts. Ask them to please knock on Sharon's door.

See if they can enter and get a DNA sample from something--hairbrush, toothbrush, anything--to compare to the dead gal Morris is holding in the morgue. Have them bag it and send it to Morris. Then, while you're at it, see if you can track down those two girls Wallis gave the inspector." I looked at the note for the first time. "Oh, just one of them, Fox--a Gina Rowling. The other is Patti Wellings."

"And she's dead, right?"

"Yup."

"Got it, Gumshoe. You run along. *The Lair* will still be here when you return."

I can play. I smiled, "Lock the back door to *The Cavern* when I leave, Fox. Not safe to have two open doors when you're here by yourself."

"Cavern's good, too. When do I get a gun, Bossman?" she asked, sweetly.

I smiled, "Lock the door, Fox."

THIRTY-SIX

First solo run in my Caddy. What a ride! She handles smoothly, purrs quietly, and responds beautifully. *Nice car, Alan,* I told myself.

I parked in front of the address in my notes, and hopped up the steps of the small, neat-looking cottage. The young man who answered the door, I assumed, was Drew Penn.

"Twenty years? You're joking, right?" Drew asked, taking my offered card.

"No jokes, Drew. There's a connection between that day and another, more recent murder. You skippered the cabin cruiser. I heard you were tied up until the end of the voyage. Is that correct?"

Drew's frame seemed to sag; he closed his eyes, hung his head, reliving that tragic day. "Why did you come, Sir? Just to torment and bring it all back after twenty years."

"Drew, I'm here to put some pieces together. Until now, I'm looking at the backside of a thousand piece jigsaw puzzle, with maybe eight hundred pieces on the table, and all I have is the bottom and the right side edge pieces--nothing else. I need more pieces.

I hope you can help, Drew. I'm not talking about the regrettable cabin cruiser atrocity. I'm speaking of a recent high school reunion murder involving many of the same players."

"You mean the same kids that were in the cruiser were involved in a murder at their twenty year reunion?"

"Could be. Not sure, but it looks that way." I repeated my question, "Were you tied up until the end of the voyage?"

"Miss McConnell, I think that was her name--she and I were tied up, but with all the crying and screaming coming from the number 3 berth, something had to be done. I struggled, got loose, and ran to where the commotion was."

Drew's face turned ashen, eyes began to tear up at the recollection of the horrible scene. "Sorry, Mr. Garrett, but it was awful. I screamed for everybody to get out, but two girls had become insane with rage. Most of the other kids ran, jumped overboard, or up on the main deck, where they cut Miss McConnell free.

The two girls had cut up a red-haired girl from her neck to her belly. I don't know where they got their knives or razors, but they had them. Then they came after me! They were crazy!"

"Please continue," I encouraged him. "Take all the time you need."

"I yelled at Miss McConnell to bring me two or three giant trash bags we always kept on board. She brought me two. In the meantime, I was trying to avoid being cut up by the two with the razors. I finally hit one really hard. She fell to the floor. When that happened the other one jumped off the boat and I threw the first one off."

"Did you recognize them from earlier?"

"Honestly, I don't think they were among those on the roster. I think they boarded later."

"Could you recognize either of them?"

"Oh, I don't think so, Sir. It's been so long."

"So, you're the one responsible for bagging the body and throwing it overboard. Am I right?"

"Yes and no, Sir, it was me. I flipped the girl over, wrapped her entrails into a sheet, flipped her back over on the mattress, then put the mess in a garbage bag, dragged it all out on the railing. Then I took the other body--it was in pieces all over the floor, and shoved those pieces into the other garbage bag and dragged it out as well. But I didn't throw either one of them overboard."

"Whoa, whoa, Drew! What other body? Miss McConnell said nothing about another body, neither did the cop on the scene."

"I wouldn't let Miss McConnell come into the berth, Sir. She never saw the real mess. I couldn't stand any more of it either. I was puking while I filled the bags. Once I dragged the second bag to the rail, I dove overboard, and never looked back.

But one thing I do know Mr. Garrett. The second body was male, not female. I'd not seen him on the boat initially; he must have swum out from shore. . . or perhaps was brought out by that speed boat. He was younger than the seniors, fourteen or so. A freshman maybe. He had been beheaded, eviscerated, his genitals chopped up, and limbs savaged as well."

THIRTY-SEVEN

A young boy was chopped to pieces on that boat? How can that be? I asked myself on the trip to *Pop's*. My mind was a-whirl with more questions--no answers. Who threw the garbage bags over the rail if not Penn? White said *it* surfaced a few days later.

Was there really a second body? A male? Why was there not a missing persons notice? (*There might have been, Alan . . . it was twenty years ago.*)

Why was Liz not more observant? She was supposed to keep a watchful eye on the whole cruise . . . *Oh yeah, Alan, she was tied up, remember?*

I drove into my parking spot, unlocked the office back door and, entering, was greeted my assistant. She gave me a big smile.

"Afternoon, Gumshoe. Learn anything from Mr. Penn?"

"A good bit actually," I said as I gave the hat rack a try with my fedora . . . *missed again . . .*

"Remember, you told me White was on the cruiser by himself for about a half hour and came off puking his guts out?"

"Yes, that's true. Why?" Liz asked as she scooped up my hat.

"How long after he exited was the boat dragged out a mile and set on fire?"

"Oh, Gumshoe, sounds like you learned more than you should have. To answer your question, I don't know for sure. I heard it was that same day, but I don't know.

That was just a job to me, Gumshoe. When I drove away that afternoon I didn't go back to work for Regina. I call her every so often, but I've never gone back to work for her. What did Mr. Penn say?"

"Mr. Penn told me there were two dead in berth #3. One was a younger teen . . . and not a girl. He said you gave him two bags, he filled two bags with human parts, dragged them to the railing and dove overboard; never went back."

Liz sat dumbstruck! "Gumshoe! You think White had the *Gone Fishin'* burned to destroy evidence of a young dead boy?"

"Sure sounds that way. I guess I make a trip back to see him. Any coffee?"

"I'll make some. We going to lunch or is that a 'one day only' habit?"

"So, what happened while I was gone?" I asked, ignoring her question.

"Door guy came, picked up your door. He thinks they can cut a panel out of the existing door and put a glass pane in.

Then I called Fallbrook," Liz handed me the steaming mug and continued, "they promised to have a squad car roll to the address we gave them, check it out, and hopefully, have Sharon Etts' DNA sample sent to Morris."

"Any calls?"

"Just getting to that. A call came in from a Captain Albert of AFOSI. Phone number is on your desk."

"Thanks, Fox. I'll take it in there. Anything else exciting happen?"

"No, Sir, well, I mean, I finished placing orders for everything on our list. We should start receiving shipments starting tomorrow--white board, listening devices, etc."

"Okay, good. Any progress on the skips?"

"On my desk for this afternoon, as soon as we return from lunch."

"I have a better idea. Call a local cafe for home delivery . . . we'll have a picnic."

"Really?"

"Sure, why not? You can do as you wish, but I'm going to brown bag it four days a week, order out maybe one day a week . . . call it a picnic; then once a month go out for lunch in lieu of the picnic . . . unless we're out of the office."

"Like, on assignment?" Now the lady was just baiting me; I refused to bite.

"Exactly," I said. "Just make the call. I'm going to get hold of the Captain."

"Sounds like a plan. You feel like a burger, taco or pizza, Gumshoe?"

"Whatever, Liz, make a decision."

The decision was made . . . it was Taco Tuesday. "Lunch in twenty minutes, Gumshoe! It's Taco Tuesday!" Liz yelled from the foyer.

I smiled and shook my head . . . *fine, Fox, just fine. Taco Tuesday sounds fine!* I told myself. I dialed Captain Albert. After the niceties . . .

"Alan, I have a job for you if you have some time for it."

"Working on a major, Sir," I answered, "you have a time frame?"

"Not really a time frame," the Captain said. "Disappearance of Brigadier General Maggorie's son. Remember Paul?"

"Sure do; basketball player. Would be about seventeen by now."

"He's the one. From all accounts he ran away. We can't put it on the Air Force tab; can't use our team, you understand."

"How long has he been missing?"

"About the same time you left us."

"Three months? Damn, Albert! He could be in Madagascar by now."

"Madagascar?"

"Just an expression, Captain. I mean he could be anywhere. I'm on a case. Not sure how much longer; maybe a week, maybe a month. If you want to send me file info, I'll let you know when I'm free to look, and if he's still missing, I'll spend some time on it. He have a budget?"

"He figures you'll be fair with him; he knows the kind of time that goes into an investigation. He said he'll put you on a daily at four hundred-fifty per. He said to tell you a seventy-five thousand dollar bonus if you end up finding the boy and bringing him home."

* * *

"A seventy-five thousand bonus? And all you can say is 'you'll think about it'?" Liz exclaimed in total shock. "Think about it? Are you made of money, Gumshoe?"

"When will our door be delivered?" I asked her.

"Oh . . . is that a hint? A little snippish, Bossman, don't you think? As your office manager I recommend you take on as much work as the business can handle, and you have me to do much of the preliminary searching...after all, I am a skip expert. Kid sounds like a skip, his dad is worried sick. Let me take a look when Mr. Albert sends the file over."

I had to laugh. "Sure, Fox. We'll take it on if you collect from all the skips, including the one in Arizona that blew me off the other day."

"Done! And don't worry, Gumshoe. Nobody blows the Fox off!"

Again I laughed as I saw the nose wrinkle, and upper lip create that silly sneer. "You are one rough, tough lady, Fox." I gave her a wink. "I'm ready for a beer. When are our tacos coming?"

THIRTY-EIGHT

3:39 p.m. Tuesday afternoon I received the promised *pdf* file from the captain. It was time for a drink anyway. I printed a hard copy of the file, stapled it together, put my feet up on my desk; then I leaned back and read it through while sipping cognac.

Typical story of a kid--became involved in a physical altercation with a strict military father, said *screw you* and left home. That was May 10--almost three months ago to the day.

"Bring a glass, Fox, and come on in," I invited my office manager.

I poured two fingers in her glass, pushed the *pdf* file across the desk to her.

"What's this, Gumshoe? Termination papers already?"Liz asked.

"Oh, no, Fox. I think everyone deserves a two-week window to dangle before cutting them loose. You'll know probably by next Wednesday or Thursday. Hey, stay positive and focused. You might make it beyond two weeks."

"Whew! I'm so relieved. I've already made it through two days."

"Not quite . . . still an hour and a half, Fox," I corrected her. "This is the file we expected from Maggorie regarding his son, Paul. Take it home and read it through--we'll talk about it tomorrow morning. You can take the rest of today off if you wish."

"I think I'd like another two fingers, Gumshoe," Liz smiled.

As Liz pulled out of the alley onto the street I took a closer look at her green sedan. *That gal could use a new set of wheels,* I thought. *I'll have to see what can be done for her.* I called Walt.

Before heading to *Pop's* I tossed my fedora at the hat rack, determined not to close up until I accomplished the feat. Twenty minutes later I locked up.

* * *

Pop wasn't at *Pop's* when I got there. Note was on the refrigerator: *Gone to see a movie. Back by curfew. Have a date!*

Right, Pop. A date! With whom I wondered. Aw, what the hell. Pop should be able to take care of himself without my interfering . . . or laughing.

I sat facing the troupe on the cork-board for a few minutes. Then I spoke aloud.

"Ladies and gents, here's the deal. Someone among you is holding out on me . . . perhaps more.

Patti, I think you were on that boat weren't you? I think that's what you were going to tell me in that elevator, wasn't it? Who else was on that boat with you . . . you know, the one that pulled up last? The one where you brought razor knives and butchered Roxanne DeVry and the young lad.

Oh, yeah, Roxanne, did you know a teen boy was cut up and killed as well? He was. I think White knows . . . he may even know who it was. Hell, Regina may even know who it was.

But who else was with you, Patti? Why didn't you open up to me on that elevator? Someone filled with venom, for sure. Toward Roxanne? Perhaps furious toward a boyfriend or even a girlfriend for that matter?"

After pouring another Martell, I leaned back and stared at the cork-board.

"I guess I need to go one more time to see the Whites . . . and probably Sandpoint Marina. I'll spend an hour or so in the morning with Fox, then make the trip."

A gourmet chef I am not. I made myself a beef bologna sandwich and Caesar salad for dinner, then sat and watched *Beau Geste*, an old Gary Cooper movie. Pop wasn't back by his curfew time; guess I'll have to have a talk with him.

After a warm shower I retired for the night.

* * *

6:30 a.m. Wednesday morning Pop was up first, with coffee and donuts waiting for me.

"Where'd you go on your date, Pop?"

"It was a retired fireman's do. All the units get together maybe twice a year at an area steakhouse. This time it was in Orange County. Got back here around eleven."

"Oh! I was just sure you and our neighbor, Mrs. Mason, were out on the town. She's a widow, right, Pop?"

"She is a widow, and a right fine looking woman, Alan. As a matter of fact, she and I have gone to a movie or to lunch together a time or two. We haven't since you've been back at *Pop's*, but we're good friends. You don't think I just sit upstairs watching TV do you?"

"No, as a matter of fact, I've often wondered why you haven't remarried, Pop. You're still a young man. There are many a pretty lady out there who would think a handsome devil like you, fireman and all, would be a damn good catch."

"Hard to imagine anyone but your mother, Alan. When you find the right one you'll know . . . and when she's no longer there, it's a mighty big hole to fill. I'm not saying it's impossible, just saying that when you look, you always compare."

"Well, Pop, you have my blessings. Thanks for the breakfast. I'm gonna run. If I see the widow Mason, I'll send her up here," I laughed.

* * *

I was a few minutes late. Fox had the coffee ready . . . and, would you believe, donuts?

"Busy day, Fox," I told her. "Going south to see our friendly policeman, White."

"Before you go, here's news. We received a phone call this morning at 8:oo, straight up. Inspector Morris says Fallbrook cops replied to him. Roommate says Sharon is missing, but the DNA samples picked up there aren't a match to our body. What do you think of that, Gumshoe?"

"What can I say? Just another dead-end road. I'm thinking, what if we approach it from another angle . . . the reunion I mean. What if we used a tip line. We'll send an email with a hotline phone number for all incoming communications.”

“Great idea,” Liz agreed. “I can set that up today while you’re gone.”

“You’ve done it before?”

“No, but how hard can it be, Gumshoe? Get a dedicated phone number, email everyone on Morris’ list with the number and the specific request for information.”

I nodded, “And make sure you stress that tips will be anonymous.”

“Exactly. I have it handled, Bossman. Get out the door and head wherever it is you’re going.”

“Keep the rear door locked, Fox.”

THIRTY-NINE

I had driven only a few blocks south on Highway 1 when my cell sounded. I pulled over.

"Garrett here, can I help you?"

"Garrett, Morris. Disturbing news here in the Southland. Your Ms Fox said you're heading south to interview the Whites once more. Thought you should be prepared."

"Prepared?" I almost didn't get the word out.

"Looks like a murder-suicide," the Inspector continued. "It's all over the news, Alan. Police are swarming the place, but I made contact with a Sergeant Jerry Hopkins. Told him you were making inquiries and assisting on a current case up here that may have ties to a twenty year-old case. Friendly enough fellow. I gave him a two minute AFOSI military background on you. He said he'll keep an eye out for you, then share or let you snoop when they're finished with their investigation."

"Murder-suicide? Where? Who?"

"Oh, sorry," Morris said. "The Whites."

"Oh! No!" It was hard to believe. "Why on

earth?" I blurted out, shaking my head.

"Let me know if you find anything linking to our case. Meanwhile, I'm busy here, locally. Take care."

"Got it Morris. Thanks." I flipped on the radio. Sure enough, the AM channels were blasting out the sad news of a retired cop and his wife dying apparently at the hands of one of them and then the gun being turned on the shooter. Both dead on scene.

Less than a half hour later I was ducking under yellow tape, shaking hands with Sergeant Jerry Hopkins, handing him my business card.

"His old police service revolver, a Colt M1911, was used; it was in Mr. White's hand," Hopkins said. "Neighbors heard the shots and called it in. Just how do you figure into the Whites' affairs?"

"Boat fiasco and tragedy twenty years ago, He was officer in charge on scene. You were probably still a kid at the time."

"I heard about that. I think I was in what they called Intermediate School--Middle School they call it now. But when I graduated from police academy I heard stories of White's escapades. Great cop, great stories. Your Morris is also a legend."

"Mind if I stick my nose inside?"

"Not at all. My guys are finished anyway. Fill your boots."

He turned to his crew. "Fellas, let's wrap it up. Any computers or suspected evidence, bag it. We have a visitor who wishes to stroll through the house for any things that may be pertinent to a different investigation."

Turning back to me he asked, "Is it okay if I

tag along with you? I understand you have been an investigator for some time--military and all."

"Oh, no problem. This makes no sense to me, Hopkins. I've visited the Whites twice before. They seemed a loving couple. I, in fact, was on my way down here this morning to clear up one disturbing story I heard recently."

"And what was that, if I may ask?" Hopkins asked.

"Let's walk through the house. Your boys have taken the electronic evidence out of here, right? I'm not interested in any of that anyway.

Tell you what, after we walk through the house, let's have a cup of coffee. I'll go through the reason I'm here and we can discuss it. Hard to believe they're no more, Hopkins. I liked them both."

"Fair enough," Hopkins replied.
We entered. The front room carpet was blood-soaked; the bodies were already gone. Then on to Charles White's study. The computers, copiers, and other devices had disappeared, of course, and all of his notes from the last ten years were missing, but the steno pads prior to 2005 were still there. I asked if I could box up and sign out White's 1998 to 2002 steno pads.

He scratched his head. "I guess so."

Next we went into the dining room. I rummaged through cabinets and book shelves, found family albums that looked like the younger Whites, possibly in their early marriage days to age fifty or so, and asked Hopkins the same. Again, he nodded agreement.

"You think something happened years ago that led to this calamity, don't you?"

"I'm looking at everything, Sergeant. I don't

know what I'm looking for, but when I find it I'll know . . . at least I think I will."

Main bedroom was down the hall to the right. I popped my head in, looked through the dresser drawers, glanced in the closet--satisfied nothing there was of interest to me.

Next, I walked across the hall to the bath, and simply poked my head in there. Again, nothing of interest. Smaller bedroom, same thing.

"The only thing left is the shed out back," Hopkins said. "If you want to take a peek, be my guest. We had to break the padlock to get inside."

"Yes, I may as well since I'm here. What about the garage, Jerry?"

"Oh, yeah, I forgot about the garage. Strange garage for a senior couple. No shelves or cabinets at all. Just a car, a shovel, a hoe, a rake and a garden hose."

We were almost at the door of the shed. "I believe you, but if you don't mind, I'll take a look in the garage as well, but let's take a look in here first."

Hopkins opened the door by the hasp and stood aside. Inside was an absolute jumble. As different from the garage as could be, from Hopkins' description. There were sporting goods, toys and games, old wooden furniture piled high and totally awry. I took some pictures.

"Mind if I pull a few things out and set them aside for a moment? I think I see something under the window in the right corner," I said motioning to a stack of chairs and books, while donning a pair of latex gloves. I took more pictures.

"No problem," from Hopkins. "Pull it out, I'll set it aside."

I thought I had seen something partially hidden by a blue tarp; I was right--a long, enameled deep-freeze. The compressor motor was still running, but as we opened the lid, we discovered it empty, sides covered with heavy frost. I took some pictures of the freezer, inside and out. It looked new.

"Have your forensics inspect the freezer, Hopkins. Might prove interesting. If you discover anything unusual, forward a copy please.

"What are you looking for?" Hopkins asked.

"DNA, fingerprints, blood-- usual crime scene garbage," I answered, with a smile on my face.

"Let's take a quick look in the garage, Jerry, then I'll buy you a coffee."

We walked back to the house, entered the kitchen and side door into the garage. Hopkins was correct, the two-car garage was almost empty with the exception of a 2016 Lexus sedan and the few tools the sergeant had mentioned.

"I'm sure you checked the car from one end to the other."

"Oh, sure. There's some luggage and a few other things in the trunk; and definitely blood spatter on the driver's side door panel. Probably the old man had a bloody nose."

"You said luggage in the trunk? Did you dust for prints in the car and trunk?"

"Why would we do that? I see no reason. The old couple offed each other in the living room," Hopkins frowned.

"Humor me. Call your forensics back right

now to collect DNA, dust doors, car and trunk. Pretend this crime was committed by an *'unsub'*. In the meantime, let's go have a coffee. I'll fill you in.

But before we go, I'd like to take a look at the luggage in the trunk. Can we pop the lid?"

I reached in the car's open driver's window and pulled the trunk latch. Hopkins opened the trunk all the way. There they were: Two large black and tan checkered suitcases, neatly stacked, one atop the other. A bamboo cane, a bag of various articles of clothing and a cardboard box filled with empty paint cans as well. I shook my head as Hopkins watched.

"Not what you expected?" he asked.

"Afraid of what I would see. Sorry to say, I was right. Make sure they examine the luggage."

Hopkins made the call, then we jumped in my Caddy and took a short ride to a coffee shop. Over a quick lunch I explained the entire reunion evening to him, including the luggage, dog's blood, and how it may relate to that long ago tragedy.

Then I drove him back to the White's home. The CSIs were already there, wondering why.

"Make sure you examine those suitcases thoroughly. DNA samples inside and out," I yelled to the sergeant as I drove off.

FORTY

Before I left the White's driveway I called Morris. "Can you meet me at my office this afternoon, Sir?"

"4 p.m. okay?"

"Yes, 4:00 is just fine," I said. "I may have some information for us from the crime lab down south. The Whites are definitely dead."

I opened the Caddy up and sped to the office. Fox was all smiles when she saw me as I unlocked and entered through the rear door.

'Gumshoe, am I glad to see you. A workman was here today to install the pole for the sign and clock; I didn't know exactly where. I asked him to return at 2:00 p.m. It's almost that now. I would have made the decision had you not returned."

"And it would have been perfect, Fox," I assured her. "Let's go outside."

We walked out front, I marked a spot on the sidewalk.

"Vertical mark. Pole with bracket goes up there, plumb with my mark. When your guy comes, take care of it. Did you have lunch?"

"Yeah, I brought a brown bag, remember? This is where I would have put the pole as well, Bossman. Are you okay? You sound agitated, Gumshoe."

"I am a bit. The White's are dead."

"No!" Liz exclaimed. "That can't be! That's what Morris called about?"

"Yes. Looks to be a murder-suicide, but something is wrong with that speculation. Much more to investigate."

* * *

For the first time I looked around the office. Some deliveries had arrived, including a white board/cork board which Liz had assembled and placed in my office. Then she had transferred all of my 4x6 cards from the wall to the board, just as I had them. *Excellent, Fox.*

Carla's workman came a bit later; Liz took him outside to show him the correct location--he lagged the bracket into the wall and was gone within twenty minutes.

"So, Fox, tell me about your reading last night."

"No! First, you tell me what happened with the Whites."

"No. You first. You'll be sitting in when Morris gets here around 4:00 p.m. So tell me, Fox, what's your first step in skip-tracing this runaway kid?"

Fox went through a litany of steps as well as could be expected of anyone.

"And how is your real job coming along? Any progress?" I asked her.

"Absolutely, Sir. The only one I haven't any information on is the guy in Arizona. I have a name and phone number; I've called him, actually talked to him, but he says in effect, 'go, pound sand'. Everything he does seems to be done in cash. No credit cards, onshore bank accounts, nothing."

"Okay. We'll get to him later. For the other two, all we need is paperwork to collect money due. Tomorrow morning go to Judge Hamlin for signatures. Get authorization to freeze their accounts--credit and checking. Take all the demand letters from Grinnell to support your claims."

"You sure you want me to go get the authorization, Gumshoe?"

"You're the skip tracer aren't you? That's what you told me." I said to her, winking. I suspected she did the leg work back in the day, then turned the information over to a company attorney or V.P. and of course, that was the case.

"I am the skip tracer, Gumshoe!" she said defiantly. "When I finish with these two tomorrow, I'll be boarding a plane to Phoenix to take on that s.o.b. down there."

"Whoa, Ms Fox, I don't think there's enough money in it for us to bill Old Man Grinnell for a percentage plus air fare. What does he owe?"

"The Grinnell file has it at $1350.00 per month from February 1, so as of September 1 the arrears rent will be $9,450.00. Then there's a clean-up and property damage invoice in his file amounting to $2761.41. The total is $12, 211.41."

"Oh, I remember, now. I checked into that file a few days ago. Twelve grand is a bit of coin, isn't it? You'd think Old Man Grinnell is made of money the way he let all these cases slide."

"He was just waiting for me, Bossman."

"Absolutely," I agreed.

We were both laughing when Morris walked through the door.

"Is this the private investigations office?" he asked. "Every time I come in here you seem to be fooling around. Do you ever get any work done?"

"We try," Liz told him, "but when you're working with Gumshoe here, you need to keep everything light and breezy."

"Did you receive anything from the White case down south?" I asked Morris. "A sergeant Hopkins handled the case. Specifically looking for some DNA sample results. I asked that he send them to you and/or me, and I haven't received anything."

"Unlike you two, I've been on the job most of the day," the inspector grinned. "Let me check with the office." He pulled his phone from his pocket and punched in a number.

"Any messages?" he asked. "Hmm, fax them over to, uh, just a minute . . . what's your fax, Alan?"

Liz rattled off the numbers. Morris repeated them to his secretary. Two minutes later we had DNA results from the two large suit cases, the side door panel, and the freezer.

<u>Luggage</u>: recent DNA evidence of human skin tissue, hair, and blood.

<u>Door panel</u>: canine blood - recent

<u>Freezer</u>: finger prints - exterior only. No DNA inside unit.

There was also a scrawled note attached.

Inspector Morris,

Freezer is in new condition. Forensics has confirmed it has never had anything inside. A neighbor confirmed it was delivered by two men in a small U-Haul van only two months ago. They unloaded it directly into the shed, padlocked the shed behind them and left.

If you need further assistance in your investigations, my office would have to approve the time spent. From our standpoint there is no crime in a freezer delivery. The luggage is queer, as is the the dog's blood, but I think our case is a murder- suicide only. Any more is probably better left in your hands, or with the P.I. you sent down here.

If I can be of further assistance let me know.
Until then,
Sgt. Jerry Hopkins, 21ˢᵗ Precinct

"Well, I'll be!" Morris breathed, looking up from the note, rubbing his chin, "what do you make of that, Alan? Have a new freezer brought in, lock it up in a shed, and there it sits, unused, for two months. That's a head-scratcher."

"Or," Liz chimed in, "how about this? Two U-Haul guys drive up, don't even knock on the front door, and dolly a freezer to a shed behind the house, set the freezer up, plug it in, cover it with a tarp, put a padlock on the door, and then drive off; no paperwork to sign, no signature, nothing."

"Or," (I had already passed empty glasses around) now I reached for the Martell, "or, we have some clues staring us in the face. We have a U-Haul truck, and delivery boys' finger prints. There must be a paper trail for the truck, and we should find a match for those prints. Somebody paid for that truck and that freezer within the last two to three months. And we also have a nosy neighbor."

I turned to Liz, "Get hold of Hopkins before you go home tonight. Find out which neighbor. I'm going to send you down there tomorrow to interview him or her. Just get information on who has visited the Whites in the last six months, besides me. Descriptions, car, anything." I took a sip of my cognac, and continued, "Take my Caddy."

"Really, Gumshoe? What about going to that Judge Hamlin on the skip matters?"

"Yes, really. The skips can wait. I'm going to chase down the U-Haul and the freezer purchase. Get the freezer model and serial number off that freezer."

Morris sat sipping his cognac all this time, smiling at the *Gumshoe* moniker and the positive vibes inside our office.

"Sounds like you have this handled. I'll check the DNA in the luggage against the body to see if it's a match. It will be, I'm sure."

"Oh, and that's disturbing as well!" I interrupted Morris. "Why would the Whites leave two pieces of incriminating luggage in their trunk?"

"Perhaps they were preparing to take a load to a thrift shop," Liz commented as she dialed the police precinct where Hopkins worked. "You said there were other things in the trunk as well, right?" She held her hand up to indicate she made a connection.

"Is Hopkins there? . . . oh, it is? . . . Hi, Sergeant. Alan Garrett's partner, Fox here. Listen, I'm coming down tomorrow. Just want to make sure I can access the Whites' shed. I'd like to get model and serial number off the freezer . . . okay, good . . . one other thing, can you tell me which neighbor remembered the delivery? . . . Thanks very much. I'll see you tomorrow."

"Mysterious empty freezer, empty paint cans, bag of old clothes in the car's trunk?" Morris laughed sarcastically. "I'm going now." Then he smiled and added, "Fine team: *Gumshoe and Fox*. I'm sure you'll get it all sorted out. Let me know when it gets close to the end, because I need to take the credit." With that, he walked out the door, laughing.

"You forgot the cane!" Liz called after him.

"Busy day, Liz." I raised my cognac, "I don't suppose you had the chance to set up the tip line, but there's alw . . ."

"Of course, I did, Bossman. I set up a dedicated phone line and private email this morning; then sent out emails to the list Morris gave us. All done," she clinked her glass against mine, "before I opened my bag lunch."

"Liz."

"Yes, Gumshoe?"

"You are not my partner, Liz," I said forcefully, but with a smile. "You can say you're my assistant, my aide, pointman, part of my staff . . . but you're not my partner. Got it?"

"Absolutely, Gumshoe," Liz was quick to apologize. "Sorry. Won't happen again."

I watched Liz pull out of our parking alley in her rusted green sedan, which tweaked my brain. I called Walt.

"Hey, old man," I greeted him when he picked up, "Alan Garrett here. Did you come up with a good used vehicle for me?"

"I did, Sonny Boy," Walt retorted. "I was going to call you at home this evening, but this is fine. I have two that should work for you. Six grand for either, your choice."

"I'll swing by with a check within the hour if that works for you," I suggested.

"Sure. I'm here all evening, Garrett. You'll like them. I've checked 'em out. Everything works well on both. One is a black 2010 BMW sedan with a moon roof, only 73K on the odometer, 'as new' tires; the other is a 2016 silver Kia hatchback with 31K, clean throughout. Again, tires are like new. Both have cold air, smart key, pretty much everything you would want."

"See you in a bit then." I signed off, and reached for my laptop. There were six U-Haul truck rental outlets in the beach cities. I jotted down phone and addresses of each, then finished my last swallow of Martell. I locked the front door, let myself out the back and locked the door. As I pushed the remote entry button for my Caddy gunfire exploded from a point nearby. Three shots, accompanied with shouts of *Bastard!* and *You're dead!*

Immediately a car squealed away from the curb and sped down the street. I couldn't tell who it was; I was too busy ducking.

Drawing my weapon, I raced to the street in time to see an older sedan hang a right up Ocean Avenue. Couldn't tell if it was green or brown in the afternoon shadows. I holstered my weapon, walked back through the back door to see if there was any damage.

No damage at all in the foyer. I stepped into my doorless office; three bullets had created a triangular pattern in the plate glass window. Had I been sitting there I would be bleeding by now.

The bullets had slammed into the back wood-paneled wall; I pried them out one by one. Large caliber, like a police service revolver. I stuck them in a bag to give to Morris.

Back outside I cranked the Caddy engine over and headed for Walt's place.

FORTY-ONE

I chose the Kia and wrote the check. Walt and I then delivered it to my house, visited with Pop for an hour after which I drove Walt home. Our conversation centered around the cars with no mention of the gunfire. At this point I didn't want to upset anyone, especially Pop.

* * *

Thursday morning, quick coffee with Pop, I pointed my Caddy toward the shop. It was 7:15 a.m. Morris wasn't in yet; I left a message on his voice mail for a return call. Water was boiling in the microwave. I threw some grounds in the French press and had coffee ready. After trying unsuccessfully with the fedora/hat rack thing I poured a mugful of the steaming brew when Liz stepped through the rear door.

"You're early, Gumshoe," she remarked as she opened the refrigerator door and deposited a brown bag inside. "So you still want me to take your Caddy to the White's place?"

"Yes, of course, Liz. Just leave your keys in case I need wheels while you're gone. Does it drive okay?"

"It gets me from A to B," she shrugged. I've

been threatening to trade it in but it still runs."   She popped a mug of water in the microwave, then tossed a bag of green tea in the hot water and dunked it up and down a couple of times.

"Follow me into my office for a couple of minutes," I beckoned her, waggling a couple of fingers as I led the way.

Dutifully she obeyed. "What's up Gumshoe?"

"See anything strange?" I asked her.

"No, except your back wall has some scratches. How did that happen, Bossman?"

"Bullets."

"Bull . . . " Liz wheeled to face the window. "Wow! When did that happen, Gumshoe?"

"Last night as I was closing up. I'm only telling you because it could have been worse. I think it was a warning, but I'm going to put an electric latch on the front door. No one comes in here unless invited. And again, keep that back door locked at all times."

"I'll call that door company before I leave this morning and have them install that latch," Liz said. "You think it was a warning? Are we getting close to breaking this case, Gumshoe?" she continued. "I don't see it, do you?"

"No, Fox, I don't. I think we'll end up stumbling over the big break, then look back and say, OH! Look at that!"

Liz called the door company. The workman could swing by tomorrow for the installation. She finished the last of her tea, then held her hand out for the keys to my convertible.

"Careful driving out there. Get back to me as

soon as you have the information off that freezer. If you can, get as close to the delivery date from the neighbor. Make sure you . . . "

"Gumshoe! Relax! This is Fox you're talking to. Just watch the office. Don't turn down any business while I'm gone!" She winked.

She exited through the rear door; I heard the key turn in the lock.

Replacement glass was next on my list. The local glass shop sent an estimator. He arrived within the hour.

"Those are bullet holes, mister, did you know that?"

"Yes, I know. Someone was target practicing last evening."

The phone rang. "Garrett here." It was Carla.

"Alan, are you busy?"

"Hi, Carla. No, not really." I smiled at the glass man; he proceeded to take measurements. I continued with Carla.

"I'm expecting Morris to call, maybe swing by. What's up?"

"I have your clock and sign. Is it okay to do the installation this morning?"

"Absolutely."

"I'll be there in a few minutes. Convince the Inspector to swing by. I'll pick up a dozen donuts."

She hung up, but before I could finish with the estimator the phone rang again. Morris.

"You nearby?" I asked. "Five minutes? Care for a cup of coffee?"

He hung up.

After a bit of haggling, I agreed to the

glazing estimator's second firm quote. I paid him in full. He called his shop then shook my hand, promising to complete the job this afternoon. He walked out as Morris walked in.

"Who shot your place up?" Morris asked as soon as he walked through the door. "I saw the business logo on that car." He poked his nose in my office. "Were you sitting in here at the time?"

"No. I had just walked outside to my car. Heard three shots; someone--a female I'm sure--yelled obscenities then drove off. I have the slugs in a bag. Can you test them for me? Like to know the type, and if the gun is in the system."

"Sure. Is it possible to get that cup of coffee you promised?"

Front door opened as I was making more coffee. Carla followed by Bruce, her workman, walked in.

"What the hell, Alan?" Morris asked, smiling, "a party going on?"

"I brought the donuts," Carla laughed.

* * *

The sign and clock were marvelous. They suited the atmosphere I had meant to achieve. We all four with coffee and donuts in hand, stood on the corner looking up. The clock above the sign stood out from the wall, looking dramatically antique.

"You really did it, eh, Alan?" Morris laughed. "*Gumshoe & Fox. . . .* very classy.

Oh!, by the way, we had a slow afternoon yesterday. Remember that list you gave me back a way? I put Bradley Swazer on it. He was able to get some information on that Trudy *whats-her-name*--Wells, was it? Anyway the one that worked at Pepperdine and wrote some books. Her passport records show she returned to the states in late February at Long Beach.

Brad called her parents out in Hemet. They didn't know she had returned from her world travels. Here's their information." He handed me a piece of paper.

Bruce and the Inspector left together. Time to lock up the shop and head to *Pop's* to pick up the Kia.

"You want to walk up the hill with me, Carla? I have some business to attend to; I'll cut you a final check and drive you back."

"Sure. I could use some exercise."

We walked the short distance up the hill to *Pop's Place,* chatting about my first week in the new office, the sign and clock, and my new office manager.

"Oh, by the way, Carla, do you mind making whatever arrangements with the door company for the glass you need for my office?"

I gave her the address and phone number, then we stepped inside. I introduced Carla to Pop, then went to my desk and wrote out a final payment while the two of them were busy chatting. Pop accompanied us outside.

"Can you give me a hand?" I asked Carla. "I want to empty the contents from the old car into the Kia."

"What's this, Alan?" she asked. "You bought the young lady a new car?"

"Let's put it this way, I bought the Kia as a company car to be used by whomever works for me. Right now Liz works for me," I answered.

Pop transferred a few things to the trunk; then he walked around the silver Kia. "Nice looking vehicle," he commented. "Walt found it for you, did he?"

"Yes, it seems that firemen in these parts know a lot of widows who no longer drive," I winked at Pop, "and it's time to empty their garages."

"Umhuh, I thought so. This looks like Charlie Hanks' car. He bought it new the same month I retired, and less than two years later he was dead. How many miles did he put on it before he cashed in?" Pop asked.

"Just over thirteen thousand.

We gotta go, Pop. See you tonight." We drove down to my office and parked in the spot belonging to Liz.

Carla said goodbye and was on her way. I went back inside the office after another look of appreciation at my sign.

Liz had left me a message: the freezer was a Kenmore, serial Number 2213897A2018; and the neighbor said the delivery was either the third or the fourth of June. Then she said she loved the Cadillac and *might* be back soon. I had to laugh.

I started making calls to U-Haul outlets in the beach cities for a freezer delivery in the first few days of June. Four U-Hauls laughed and said something like, *Mister, once a truck pays their money and leaves here, who cares what they're hauling?* But the fifth one said, *funny you should ask that. I was on duty, and a young man came in and specifically said he needed to take a freezer to an old geezer's place and stick it in a shed. Shouldn't be gone for more than four hours.*

"Do you have a name?"

"Well, yes and no," he said. "When he returned, took his credit card receipt back, and paid cash. I have no record at all. Maybe a George somebody."

"What about the contract?" I asked him. "It has his driver's license, address and everything on it, right?"

"He, uhhh, I uhhh . . ."

"You gave it all back to him didn't you? Like It never happened, right? That's illegal, you know. How much did he give you?"

"An extra hundred bucks."

"Bad move, Son."

Then I called Sears in Hermosa, asked if they had sold a deep freezer in June. *Buddy we sell lots of freezers. Are you missing a freezer?* He laughed, turned to an associate, *Hey Marta, Did you sell a deep freeze in early June?* Turns out Marta remembered selling one to a lady on June 1, even laughed about it with the lady. *Having it picked up by my own delivery guys.*

I asked Marta if they could trace the purchase records. *That's the strange thing. She pulled out a wad of twenties, paid in cash. She had a Sears credit card in her wallet, but paid in cash. No name, no insurance, just cash.*

I called Liz. "You on your way back, Liz?"

"I am indeed, and I think I have some interesting news as well," she said excitedly.

"Well, spit it out!"

"No. I'll wait until I get back home," she retorted. "Not the same over a phone. You'll probably shoot it down anyway, but I think it's a key bit of info."

"Okay, pick up a burger for me. Get one for yourself."

"Already ate, Gumshoe. Bringing you the bill for reimbursement. You can have my brown bag lunch in the refrigerator."

"Well, I have so . . . Liz?"

She hung up.

I opened the refrigerator. *So, what have we here? Ahh, a roast beef sandwich!* I washed it down with a bottle of *Modelo Negra* . . . good lunch.

FORTY-TWO

I called the number Morris had given me . . . Trudy Wells' folks out in Hemet. They lived in a mobile home in a park on Lyon Street. Mr. Wells was receptive to a visit. I told him that either an associate or I would come by Monday for a chat.

"Is something wrong?" he asked. "You're the second person asking about Trudy."

I decided to be upfront with him. "The police discovered four bodies, all female, at a high school class reunion, under rather unusual circumstances. I'm working the same case from another angle, giving them a hand.

We have identified the two older ones as police officers and one of the younger as a member of the class of 1999 at the high school your daughter attended. According to records, your daughter was also a member of that class."

"I see. Unrecognizable, eh?"

"Afraid so, Sir."

"Need some DNA, right?"

"Yes, Sir."

"I'll have some samples--toothbrush, hair, that sort of thing for you. Don't tell the wife, so far as she's concerned, Trudy is still in Rome."

"Just a visit, then, Sir. Not sure how I'll mask it, but I'll think of something."

"The last letter we received was from Athens," Mr. Wells said. "Trudy was going to Rome and then on her way home."

"When was that?"

"Sometime after mid-January."

"Do you know if Trudy knew a Patti Wellin . . . .never mind, we'll talk when I get there. I'll call first."

* * *

The glazing company sent glass and two glaziers; they were finished in forty-five minutes. They even washed my new window in and out. Liz was back before they finished.

"Sorry, Gumshoe. Friday afternoon traffic was miserable."

"Right, Fox! Especially when you're driving a convertible."

"Aww, how did you find out, Bossman?"

"Call it a hunch . . . although, it's been an hour and a half since you called, and it's a forty minute trip at the worst of times. But never mind, what's your exciting news, Fox?"

"The neighbor says there was a freezer pick-up as well as a delivery, Gumshoe, a-*n-n-n-d,* the one they took out was heavy. The crew laughed about it, they tried to open it, but it was locked."

"You learned all that from the neighbor?"

"See? You need me, Bossman. I'm not only a good secretary and skip tracer, I'm also a good sleuth, right?"

"Been all of one week, Fox. But I must say, I am pleased thus far. A second deep freeze, huh? And no doubt, full--or at least, not empty. I wonder where it ended up?"

I pulled the Martell off the shelf and grabbed a glass . . . then took a sidelong look at Liz . . . grabbed a second glass. She made no move or acknowledgement.

"Do I need to inspect the car for dents or scratches? No? Okay, you can come in Monday. Have you ever been to Hemet?"

"No, but I know about where it is. Down by Riverside, right?"

"Right. Do you want some cognac or no?"

"Oh! Yes, please."

"Oh! Before I forget. I need my keys back." I said. "And here are yours." I handed her the keys for the Kia.

"These aren't mine. I don't have one of those new-fangled keys. The others are mine but not this one," she held up the black computerized key.

"There's no other car in the lot," I answered casually. "Gotta be yours."

Liz walked outside and walked around the Kia; then took another tour around it, laughing and clapping her hands. Pressing the buttons on the remote entry, she jumped inside and started the engine.

"Is this mine?" she squealed, climbing out.

"Company car, but you won't need another one so long as you work for me. Your sedan is at *Pop's* any time you want to trade back."

"I won't!" She threw her arms around my neck. "Thank you, thank you, Bossman!"

We walked back inside.

"Could I have another cognac?" she asked.

"Sure, but just a short one."

Liz sat sipping her drink. She suddenly turned to me, "Have we had any response to our tip line?"

"You haven't shared where you have it embedded," I accused her, "neither have you shared the email site or password for the written tips."

"Didn't I? Sorry. I meant to." She wrote down the access codes for each. "Let's see if we've had any activity."

We were not prepared for the responses:

Sorry you weren't at your desk; maybe next time! That was the first of several voice mails on the phone. The voice had been distorted and gravelly; difficult to tell if it was male or female. It sent a chill up my spine. I assumed it was a female because of the woman's voice outside my alley on Wednesday.

The next voice was completely different . . . a falsetto, 90% sure it was male: *Reunion matter. To the P.I. Gina is the key. Look deeper. The dead girl is Sharon Etts.*

"That's gotta be Matt Wallis," I said to Liz. "She was his missing date at the reunion."

There were a few other messages, one was also distorted, but interesting: *You're cold!* and others, most of which were remorseful words of condolences to the families, but there was one other worth noting in the form of an email:

Check the residences of Patti and Tom Wellings. You'll find your answers there.

"Well, that was interesting," I said. "Oh, well, tomorrow is another day. We'll take these up next week.

I'm going fishing tomorrow morning with Pop and Inspector Morris. I have a few questions for our inspector. Maybe I can get some answers. And you? What are your plans?"

"I'll be at the beach. Right down on the water below your house. I was going to invite you, but . . . You know what they say, Gumshoe. All work and no play. How did your fishing trip come about, anyway?" she asked casually.

"Pop set it up. He and the inspector hit it off a couple of weeks ago. One thing they discussed was fishing. I want to ask Regina a few more questions anyway."

"You're going to *Sandpoint*?" Liz seemed surprised.

"So," I continued, "Pop made 6:00 a.m. reservations for a small fishing boat at Sandpoint Marina; and yes, to answer your question, I'm going to Sandpoint."

FORTY-THREE

Morris knocked on my door at 5:15 a.m. Saturday morning. Coffee was already brewing. Pop came downstairs, a baseball cap on his head, and a windbreaker draped over an arm.

"Just in case the wind kicks up out on the water," he explained. "You put our tackle box and gear in the car, right, Alan?"

"Everything is packed and ready to go, Pop. Yours, Inspector?"

Morris had on khaki long sleeve shirt, baggy jeans and a pork-pie hat. "It's all leaning against your Caddy. Shall we go?"

* * *

In the darkness of the morning with subtle hints and the promise of a beautiful day on the water, we didn't notice the pair of eyes that followed us as we headed down the hill, nor did we notice the figure creeping with the gallon of gasoline that was to destroy the tranquility of my neighborhood on that Saturday morning . . . indeed, we were five or six miles from home before flames climbing the garage walls of Pop's Place were noticed by a neighbor.

The call came in from Walt just as we were unloading our equipment into the rental boat.

"Where are you, Alan? Is your Pop with you?"

I started to explain when he interrupted with news of the fire. I motioned for Morris and Pop to gather round. I put the phone on speaker; we listened to Walt.

"Two cars sitting outside were destroyed," Walt started. "Some garage contents damaged beyond salvaging as well, including your Pop's Subaru.   The good news is the fire didn't penetrate the wall into the house. Our boys were there within minutes once it was called in . . . clearly arson, Alan. Whose cars are these, by the way?"

I told him. He laughed bitterly

"So a police inspector's personal car, eh? Is someone out to get him or you?"

"Oh, no question, Walt," I said. "Something I've done has disturbed a hornet's nest."

"Well, your Allstate agent is here if you want to speak with him. I assumed you still have Jerry Williams, so I called him. He came right away."

Morris piped up, "Let me speak with him if I may."

Walt handed the phone to the agent.

"Yes?"

"Mr. Williams. My name is Carl Morris. I own the CRV that evidently was destroyed. May I give you my agent's name? He's with State Farm . . . "

As the two men exchanged phone numbers, Pop and I discussed our plans for the day. Should we abort our fishing or should we carry on as planned? We voted to stay, if Morris, of course, was in agreement.

Overhearing, he pointed a thumb up, and handed the phone back to me.

"Walt," I asked, "can you have someone stick around the place until we get back this afternoon? We've decided to go fishing."

"Good choice, Alan. Nothing you can do anyway except go shopping for a new washer and dryer. Don't worry about your place, I'll stick around. We broke a window to get in to see if there was any damage. There is none.

I'll just sit on your patio, read a book and have a beer or two. Already checked, Alan--you have plenty. Catch lots of fish."

The three of us shrugged our shoulders after the phone call.

"Sounds like minimal damage but for the cars," Pop was first to speak. "We dodged a bullet."

"We were targeted," I shook my head, "and I suspect the culprit knew our movements."

"Well," Morris said, "I for one will not let a little fire spoil my first fishing trip in ten years. Let's go get some frozen anchovies."

We followed his lead to the bait shop. The young man I had met previously stood behind the counter.

"You're not here for Miss Leone?"

"No. Today we're here to get some sardines," I said to him.

"Anchovies," Morris corrected.

"Anchovies, sardines; sardines, anchovies, Pop laughed. "What seems to be working, Son, and what do you have in those freezers?"

"I'm Bill. We have both. Right now, the best

bait seems to be anchovies. Squid works pretty well, too." He pointed to two large freezers. "Help yourself. Prices are on the lid. By the way, Miss Leone isn't here today. Two week vacation. Been gone a week. Be back a week from Monday."

Morris lifted the lid to the first freezer. It was about a third full, with bags of ice, plus different bins for shrimp, anchovies, squid and sardines. In the meantime, I lifted the lid of the other one. It, too, was only little less than half full with the same four types of bait plus the ice.

I laughed. "You have squid, sardines, anchovies and shrimp in here as well, Bill. Why two deep freezers for the same kind of bait?"

"Funny story," Bill said. "Gearing up for the new season Regina supposedly ordered a new freezer for ice cream bars, popsicles and such, but when the delivery came it was the used, dented one that you see here. I was out cleaning up a rental boat at the time; when I got back inside, it was all set up and running, but it was padlocked.

Regina kept calling the delivery people. They promised to return and correct the mistake. Never did. One Monday morning I came to work. The padlock was gone, Regina had it filled up with what you see. I don't know why we have two half full deep freezers in the shop. Ask Regina."

"Are we going fishing, or are we just going to stand around gabbing?" Pop asked.

I grabbed two packs of anchovies, one of Sardines and one of squid, showed them to Bill, then tossed a ten spot on the counter. "Thanks, Bill. Fellas, let's go fishing."

FORTY-FOUR

"So how are you going to handle that, Inspector?" I asked, opening up the throttle on the 16' outboard. "That's our missing deep freeze for sure."

"It appears to be, alright," he answered, threading a hook through an anchovy. "But didn't you tell me the Whites were meticulous? That deep freeze looks pretty old and beat up."

"But there must be a connection," Pop joined in. "Too coincidental. Regina is mixed up in these murders somehow."

"That's not a leap," Morris said, "but it doesn't flow as easy as maple syrup."

Pop cast his line out, hook baited with a squid. Almost immediately he had a strike, surprising all three of us. I cut the engine as Pop pulled in a 20" jack mackerel. He immediately released it, rebaited the hook and tossed it out once more.

"Let's leave it here for a bit," Morris said, tossing his line out, "where there's one, there are more."

Dutifully, I let the boat drift, while I set my line up using an artificial lure designed for 'jigging'. With this jig, called a buzz bomb, the line goes through a two or three inch heavy piece of metal, with a treble hook at the end. The idea was to slowly lower the lure to the bottom, then lift the rod maybe four or five feet, then snap it down as fast as you can. The lure flashes downward like a roiling, wounded minnow, enticing a game fish to strike.

"I'll send a CSI team down here Monday morning to swab that deep freeze. Maybe we'll get lucky. I doubt Bill is involved, so then if there's been a crime here, we sit and wait a week for, uh, what's her name, again?"

"Regina Leone," I said.

"Regina Leone," he repeated, suddenly jerking his rod upward. "Damn! Missed!"

After twenty minutes the score was Pop- five fish, Morris- five fish, me- one fish. I switched to an anchovy.

We moved the boat about a quarter of a mile further out and again tried our luck. Morris snagged something heavy. I pulled my line in to avoid entangling. Pop did the same. Not a fighting fish by any means, but once in a while the rod would twitch, so whatever it was, it was alive.

After ten minutes we saw it below the surface . . . a halibut. A few more turns of the reel and the real fight began.

"I'm keeping this one, boys!" Morris shouted. "Get the net!"

It seemed the halibut became alive once it realized it was being dragged against its will. It took several more minutes of fighting and the large landing net to bring it aboard. Thirty-seven pounds, ten ounces of halibut!

We continued fishing for another almost three hours, I landed eight fish, kept three: a nice eight pound striped bass and two red snappers. Morris caught twelve total, kept, in addition to the halibut, two snappers. Pop landed a total of fifteen fish, so he took home the prize for most fish caught, including five keepers. Morris, however, won the fish of the day. We steered the boat back in, agreeing to do it again in a couple of months.

We prepared the fish at the marina's cleaning station, salted and packed it in ice, and put it all in a tub I had put in the Cadillac's trunk. A good day on the water.

FORTY-FIVE

Walt met us, beer in hand, when we drove into the circular drive of Pop's Place.

"The two cars outside the garage had been especially targeted. That was the assessment of the incident inspector for the Fire Department, the garage being a secondary objective of the arsonist. I agree. What do you think, Pop?"

Pop nodded, "Definitely. Sorry about your car, Inspector."

"Your boy's not the only one with enemies, Roland. I could have been targeted this morning-- followed and torched."

"Doubtful, Inspector," I added my two cents. "I suspect I've made a couple of enemies since returning home."

"Here's your Allstate guy's card and damage report," Walt said. "He said get an estimate of the property damage. Just a formality. He'll approve it right away.

He called your State Farm fella, Inspector Morris. Gave him a rundown of the situation. Just send your guy the claim. He says there's a deductible, but of course, you know that."

As I was inspecting the damage to the garage interior, Mrs. Mason came walking up the street.

"So sorry, Roland, Alan," she said. "I saw the fire trucks coming up the hill. I couldn't imagine it was your place until . . ."

"Until it became obvious," I finished her thought. "We were very fortunate. I thought perhaps it was you that made the 911 call."

"No, and there was no one else up here when the trucks got here either. I followed them up. It was early . . . before 6 a.m."

"And you saw no one else?" Morris asked her. "No car, bicycle, pedestrian?"

"Oh, sorry, Mrs. Mason, I interjected. This is Inspector Carl Morris; Morris this is Rita Mason."

"No one at all, Inspector."

"A car most likely," I added. "Carrying a gallon of gasoline as a bicyclist or walking would be difficult up this hill. Now, do you need a ride home, Sir?" I asked.

"No. I called the wife. She'll be here within a half hour. If you don't mind, I'll just look around a bit more. A beer would be nice."

Pop disappeared, returning minutes later with five bottles and a glass. He passed beers all around, then offered a beer to Mrs. Mason. When she accepted he poured it into the glass.

A building contractor I didn't know drove up.

"Need an estimate?" the fella asked, handing me a card. "Jose," he said holding out a hand.

"Not much damage," I answered. "Broken window next to the car. Looks like the culprit tried to pour accelerant on the car, then toss a match in. Most of the liquid ran down on the cement under the car, but enough to get the undercarriage oils going. Other than the car, it's mostly smoke, and repaint two inside walls. I need to order a new washer/dryer. I haven't looked at the electrical. I may need wiring behind the washer."

"Let me take a quick look," he offered.

"Fine."

I didn't see him write anything on his pad. He came back smiling.

"You must have friends at the firehouse." He shook his head. "Usually a garage fire with this much vehicle damage includes an explosion. A gallon of Zinsser odor control paint and a gallon of topcoat should cover the damage . . . Oh, and there's a bit of bubbling on the drywall next to the car, but I think a bit of finishing mud will cover that."

He turned to me, "Half a day, $480.00 total, window glass and all, tax in."

"Done! By the way," I said, introducing him to Pop and Walt, "Pop just retired two years ago as Manhattan Beach Fire Chief - Station 11, and Walt here, just one year to go at Station 9. This house is still the meeting place for poker nights and get-togethers - active and retired firefighters."

"So you *do* have friends at the firehouse," Jose laughed. "Next Thursday morning okay?"

* * *

Morris chopped the halibut into several slabs in our kitchen, and shared the steaks among us-- even included Walt in the spoils. Pop and I did the same. There was plenty of fish to go around; I decided to package a couple of fillets of striped bass to share with Liz on Monday.

Monday morning, 7:15. I pulled into the parking lot to start the day. The phone was already jangling.

"Alan." It was Morris. "Listen, I'm sending my Forensics team down to the marina. Any questions I need to ask Bill or whomever is in the bait shop?"

"A description of the freezer delivery man might help," I suggested. "By the way, I received a tip to check Patti Wellings place. Have you or Bradley been there?"

"Interesting you should ask. She listed Tom Wellings' place as her address on her driver's license. But she had moved out of there some time back, right? She said she lived with one of those two girls I interviewed . . . that Gina if I remember correctly."

"Yes, I guess I should knock on their doors as well. Maybe they won't shoot me," I laughed. "So, have you gone to see Tom?"

"Not yet, sorry. My caseload is stacking up. Bradley is going on vacation in a couple of weeks, so I have him working overtime as it is."

"Well, there will be no one in my office today. I'm heading to Hemet to visit with Trudy Wells' parents, then on to see Sharon Etts' roommate down in Fallbrook. I'm sending Liz to see Mr. Wellings today if he's home. If he's not there, I'll adjust my plan and send her down to Fallbrook."

"Oh! You're not going to see Tom Wellings yourself?" the Inspector asked. The way he said it raised an eyebrow.

"You concerned about Wellings, Inspector? You think I should be the one to see him?"

"Alan, I've known many men like Wellings," the Inspector came back. "I'm not saying he has anything to do with the current situation. But I am saying one wrong question and things could go sideways."

"That's how I sized him up, as well," I smiled. "That's why I'm sending Liz. Ahh, here she is now," I continued to Morris, while waving at Liz as she walked through the rear door. "You have a good day Inspector. I'll think about what you said. Did you buy yourself a new Aston Martin?"

"Who's buying an Aston Martin?" Liz asked.

"That was Inspector Morris. We had a little fire at Pop's while we were fishing. Lost three cars: Pop's Subaru, your sedan, and the Inspector's personal car."

"You're kidding!" she exclaimed. "Arson? Is the house okay? Who did it? Do you know? Did they catch the guy?"

"Yes, yes, we don't know, we don't know, and no . . . all in that order. We were fishing," I said.

"My old car totaled?"

"Yes. Sorry. It got hauled away Saturday afternoon. My Allstate guy said the book on it is five hundred."

"Oh, I know the car wasn't worth much, but it was mine, Bossman. So, the Inspector's car was totaled, too?"

"All twenty-nine grand worth," I said. "A 2017 Lexus RX-350."

"Thirty grand!" Liz whistled.

"Oh, yeah, but not to worry. Fully insured."

"And who are you sending Liz to see? I overheard you talking to Mr. Policeman."

"Morris says you can't handle Tom Wellings if I send you to interview him."

"Let me have a gun, Gumshoe. I'll interview anybody."

"We'll see after the three month probation. Then I'll take you to the range and teach you to shoot, then we'll talk."

"Really, Gumshoe? You serious?"

"So, back to the subject, are you up to a visit with Tom Wellings?"

"Absolutely, Gumshoe. The Fox is ready!" Then Liz turned and frowned. "But I thought I was going to Hemet?"

"Change of plans. Let's see if the gentleman will be in this morning. If so, you go there. If not, you travel to Fallbrook. Deal?"

"Sure, Gumshoe--if our call to Fallbrook is picked up by a real, live person."

"Here's Wellings' number. Give it a try. It's after 8:oo." I gave Liz a slip of paper; she dialed the number.

"Hello?"

"Mr. Wellings? Liz McConnell from Alan Garrett's office. I'd like to swing by to do some follow-up if it's convenient."

"It's never convenient, Ms McConnell, but if you must, come ahead. Come at noon. You can buy my lunch. I'm sure your boss, Alan has a slush fund for such occasions."

"11:3o a.m. sound okay?"

Liz turned to me after her phone call ended.

"You'll be gone most of the day? Then I'm going to follow up on those skips; I'll go see Judge Hamlin. Get a court order for collection."

* * *

I was about to bid Liz adieu when the phone rang. It was Carla. "I have your door ready, Alan. I'll bring it by this morning if it's convenient."

"Not for me, Carla, but Liz will be here. How does it look?"

"Fabulous, if I do say so myself! I glue-chipped and sandblasted one surface, and on the other surface I painted gold leaf in a half-moon shape with a slender black outline. You will like it, I promise."

"Liz will cut you a check. Thanks, Carla."

"Liz? I know Fox," Carla sounded quizzically sincere. "Who's Liz?"

"Funny lady. Okay, sure. Fox. I'm on my way to Hemet. Thanks again, Carla."

I turned to Liz. "Carla will be here this morning, *FOX*." (I stressed the byname). "Cut her a check. Give her a 25% tip.

Have a good interview with Wellings. Rattle him a bit. Why did he have a change of clothes after only an hour or so? Did he use his rented berth other than to change? Make him sweat a little, feel uncomfortable."

"All without a gun, Gumshoe?"

"Find out who he sat with," I continued, ignoring her wit. "Get names if you can, why he tried to sit at his ex's table. Most of all, find out what he had to do with our reunion disruptions. See you later. Oh! Bring back a lunch receipt."

FORTY-SIX

Hemet is an interesting town with a long history. It was at one time one of the larger towns in Riverside County, thanks in major part to damming the San Jacinto River to form Lake Hemet at the turn of the 19th Century. With a water source, the town grew.

Retirees discovered mobile home living in the Inland Empire wasn't all that bad--fully landscaped plots, swimming pools, clubhouses, planned community activities. In the late 1950's and 60's Hemet became known as a mobile home community for seniors. It remains, to some extent, that way to this day. I had never been there before; I was headed there for the first time to check it out for myself.

The Wells' home lived up to the town's reputation. They lived in a well-kept mobile park. Their home was a double wide, from the outside it could have been a nice 'stick home' on a normal foundation.

Mrs. Wells stuck her hand out. "Good morning, Mr. Garrett. I'm Dorothy."

She was a little bit of a thing, dressed in slacks, striped long-sleeve shirt and covered in a full apron. She ushered me in, saying, "Martin will be here in a few minutes. He's at the clubhouse for his morning workout."

"That sounds energetic. Is that a ritual with him?"

"Every morning like clockwork. Ever since we've been out here. Coming up on seven years."

"Do you like mobile home living?"

"Love it. Wouldn't ever go back to a regular house."

Martin Wells walked in as I was about to say, "Interesting."

"You the P.I.?" he asked.

"I am. Alan Garrett," I held out my hand. He took it in his. A huge man, probably 6'5, 280 lbs. His hand enveloped mine with a strong grip. I tried to determine his age, but he had the look and movements of a man as young as sixty. *And they've been here for seven years?* I asked myself.

"Care for a lemonade, Garrett?" he asked. Ignoring any response, he opened the patio door and walked out under an awning in the back garden. A couple of orange trees, along with a grapefruit and lemon tree graced the small, but efficient grounds.

"I usually have a lemonade after my workout." He turned to his wife, "Dot, a lemonade for Alan if you would as well. We'll be on the patio."

"Alright, Sweetie," came a call from inside.

"Best woman in the world, Garrett. You have a wife?"

"Not yet. Runs through my mind from time to time but never matured into a real project."

"Don't wait, Mr Garrett. How old are you, anyway?"

"Pushing forty. How old are you, Mr. Wells?"

"Hmm, same as my Trudy. That's why you're here isn't it, Mr. Garrett."

"Alan, please."

"And I'm Martin, and I'm seventy-eight."

"Never! What did you do before you retired, Sir?"

"I started out in the merchant marines, six years. Then met and married Dot. We decided to travel while still young, so we tramped though Europe for three years in the early sixties."

"Quite a honeymoon," I observed.

"Came home to the beach cities, went into construction, became a licensed contractor, built two large construction companies, both successful.

But, became tired of it all: the red tape, permits, exorbitant fees, subcontractors cutting corners, all the bullshit.

Decided, if I can't beat them, join them. I became a private building inspector, working for some of the largest, most respected builders in the southland. Became a whistleblower of sorts, but I separated the quality builders from the riff-raff.   Dot quit her job and came to work with me. We made a good team for eleven years. Then we pulled the plug--came out here. A good move. Bottom line Alan, get yourself a good lady. You'll not regret it.

Now, what about my Trudy?"

"Did Trudy live here with you?"

Dorothy stepped out on the patio with the lemonade and a tray of oatmeal-cranberry scones, hot out of the oven, complete with butter and some Kadota figs.

"I see what you mean, Martin." We both laughed. I complimented the baker. She smiled, curtsied and retraced her steps back into her kitchen.

"Did Trudy live here with you?" I repeated my question.

"No. She taught at Pepperdine. While teaching, she lived with a friend, actually, a relative by marriage."

"How so?"

"It's complicated. Originally, our family name was Wellingsly. A few generations ago, three or four, a family feud broke out, and one of my grandfathers changed his name to Wells, and the brother to Wellings. So it's been Wells and Wellings ever since."

"So Trudy and Tom Wellings are cousins going back. Was Trudy staying with Tom?"

"No!" Martin was quick to deny that thought. "She stayed with Tom's ex, a lady named Patti. Then when the school term ended, September of 2018, she came home until she took her sabbatical."

"Was she seeing anyone that you know of?"

"No. Strange, too. In high school she was a popular girl. Boys knocking at her door all the time. But as a young woman she changed . . . became a total workaholic. Very few friends. Became sort of an introvert."

"Did Trudy and Tom know they were cousins when going to high school?"

"I never told them."

"Don't mean to be rude, Sir, but that wasn't my question. Did they know?"

"Yes. Trudy told me she was in school with a fellow who said he was a cousin, that his grandfather and hers were first cousins, that their dads had changed last names over some kind of family scandal."

"Okay, so Trudy stayed with Patti Wellings. For how long?"

"Over a year and a half. They were good friends. They even visited out here together a couple of times."

Did she bring any other girlfriends out here?"

"Yes. Just before Thanksgiving she brought a Gina somebody--Dot knows the name--out for two days. Nice lady. A little pushy, but nice. They left together. That was the last time we saw our girl. Gina was driving her to LAX on November twenty-seventh.

Now I have some questions for you, Alan. This reunion thing, How does it all fit?"

"I'll answer your questions in a minute, but first, what do you mean, pushy?"

"Oh, the old used car salesman routine. Figured I should have all my personal and real property in an estate, and offered to draw up a document for me. When she learned that our home is under DMV and not real property, she backed off. Now, is my daughter dead? You said four dead -- two cops and two others. Talk to me, dammit!"

"To start with, the class reunion was July 27. I, too, am a member of the class of 1999."

I proceeded to go through the entire story in detail, from the gruesome dismembering of Roxanne DeVry on a senior outing in 1999 to discovering a dismembered female body at our 2019 reunion, and the subsequent three murders--one of whom was Patti Wellings, Trudy's friend and roommate.

As I spoke, I could see Martin's jaw quivering in rage and shock.

"Sick bastard! Find him, Garrett. Put him away."

He handed me a small bag he had tucked in his shirt.

"You'll find enough there for identification I think. You call me immediately one way or the other, you hear?"

I was just putting the bag in my attaché when Dorothy emerged with a jug to refill our glasses.

"Will you join us for lunch, Mr. Garrett? Tuna salad sandwich and canned pears. Not much, but it's nourishing."

"Thank you, no. I'm on my way to Fallbrook. Perhaps another time, if I'm invited," I smiled.

"You'll be invited, Mr. Garrett," she assured me. "May I say, too, I'm glad you're the investigator on our daughter's case."

Martin twisted his large frame around to stare in disbelief at his wife. "You heard?" he asked.

"I knew there was a problem when we didn't hear from Trudy in February. I was keeping a stiff upper lip," Dot said--showing a wistful smile, wiping a finger across her left cheekbone. "Then police calls, and finally, here comes Mr. Garrett. As my husband says, Alan, our daughter deserves justice."

"Not sure if we have the right victim yet, Ma'am. There are still a few other people whose whereabouts are not yet accounted for, thus my trip to Fallbrook. Might I have a recent photo of Trudy?"

FORTY-SEVEN

Sharon Etts had disappeared from her Fallbrook home less than a month before our reunion. Matt Wallis had expected her, in fact they had made arrangements to link up after twenty years. But that didn't happen. Another mystery to solve.

Connected to the bigger case? Yes, in fact, it may be the nucleus of my case, but not straight forward--like: solved--done! . . . Why did I pull the short straw?

Fallbrook was about forty miles south of Hemet; it took a bit over an hour, zigzagging through orchards: persimmons, pistachios, and of course, avocados and oranges. I had called ahead to make sure someone was home. I pulled in beside a white Chevy Volt.

Amy Wynne met me in the driveway. "You must be Alan Garrett. Nice car."

Over a coffee Amy and I went over Sharon's movements up to the time of her disappearance. I asked what progress the Fallbrook police had made since the filing of the missing persons' report.

"They called here a couple of times in July, then nothing."

"Who owns this house if I may ask?"

"Sharon. I rent from her," Amy said. "She bought it free and clear from the sale of her mom's home."

"So what do you know about Sharon?" I asked.

"We're like sisters. I helped her move down here when she bought this place. I've known her since university."

"How is it that a Miss Gina Rowling filed the missing persons' report? She lives up near Inglewood."

"Gina was down here quite often. They were good high school pals. Neither of the women was ever married, and they both worked from home, so their time was their own.

Gina would visit a friend down in Oceanside or Vista, then pop by to see Sharon on her way, coming or going. In fact she stopped by to see Sharon on her last trip and discovered Sharon missing. She filed the report immediately, worried sick, and stayed with me for two days, hoping for good news before heading home."

I wasn't going to correct Amy's story, even though I knew Gina had been married—lost her husband and daughter in an auto accident some years ago. Just chalked it up to another of Gina's lies.

"What does Sharon do for work?"

"She's a freelance book editor; has worked into quite a clientele."

"And, do you know what Miss Rowling does?"

"I believe she's like a lawyer. Helps people set up their estates."

"Interesting," I mused aloud. "Did she assist Sharon?"

"Yes, I believe so. They sat up one night about six months ago, until two or three in the morning working on something."

"Were you aware of what they discussed and decided?" I asked.

"Just that a couple of weeks later Sharon told me she thought she had made a mistake and would have to fix it."

"Did she?"

"Fix it, you mean? I don't know."

"And you? What do you do, if I may ask?"

"I'm a freelance writer/photographer. I submit candid shots to magazines, regional papers and so on, with a short byline . . . sometimes I'm lucky enough to get published."

"An old-fashioned way to make an honest buck! Don't you use the internet?"

"I'm not into the commercial, plastic lifestyle," Amy answered. "I may get sucked in one day, but not today."

"Do you have a current photo of Sharon I may borrow? I can mail it back."

"Certainly." She pulled a framed photo off a shelf and handed it to me.

"Did a Trudy Wells ever visit here?" I asked.

"Sorry," Amy said, "I don't remember any Trudy Wells."

* * *

I headed north on I-15. It was 1:30 p.m. In Corona just before hanging a left on State 91, I stopped for a whopper from Burger King and a call to Liz.

"Just checking in. I should be back in the shop in an hour or so. How did your talk with Wellings go? Learn anything interesting?"

"Yes. You'll be proud, Gumshoe. I'm back, still alive and safe. You drive safely coming home, you hear?"

"I hear, Mother. Do me a favor. Find a physical address for Patti Wellings for me. Morris must have it. I know she stayed with others, but she must have had some personal notes, perhaps a journal, worth going through."

"You got it, Bossman. Just get your butt home."

Getting home was a breeze; traffic was headed the opposite direction for the most part. I kept the Caddy within bounds; I'd never live down a speeding ticket--not with my smart-mouthed office manager.

The electric latch buzzed to allow me entrance. Liz smiled as I walked in. (As an aside, Liz and I had decided to keep the latch secure only from 6 p.m. to 8 a.m., or when only she is in the office.)

"Glad you have that thing on, Fox," I said. "At least I have the assurance that you're safer today than you were last week."

"When do we go to the gun range, Gumshoe?"

FORTY-EIGHT

"First of all, Gumshoe," Liz said, handing me a slip of paper, "here's the address Morris gave me. It's in Inglewood--a condo Patti Wellings bought quite recently.

Now, here's my morning report." She handed me a few sheets of paper labeled

Interview with Tom Wellings:

•1981 born Thomas Eugene Wellings, father: Albert, mother: Ruth Kramer
•1999 graduated high school
•2002 El Camino College-Associate of Arts degree
•2004 married Patricia Brown--Office manager/bookkeeper for car dealership in Whittier, where Tom worked as a salesman
•2007 became a transfer student to Whittier College--Business Administration major
•2007 divorced Patti--she was cheating
•2010 graduated from Whittier with BA in accounting
•2010 secured a position with an accounting firm
•2011passed examination--became a CPA

And then the questions turned to the reunion night-
•why did you rent a suite on reunion night?
I was hoping to get lucky
•did you have a suitcase?
No. I took a small briefcase

•did you get lucky?
>   *No*
•why not?
>   *All hell broke loose with the discovery*
>   *of the body*
•why did you change your tie after less than an hour?
>   *I changed tie and shirt because I was bumped-*
>   *spilled red wine*
•who did you sit with at the reunion?
>   *At first I sat with Gerri and a few others. But I*
>   *visited with several people so I sat at several tables,*
>   *mixing and visiting with people from yesteryear, but I*
>   *especially liked seeing Patti and my old pals, Barry*
>   *Franks and Matt Wallis*
•did you know the others at Patti's table?
>   *I knew Gina, and Roberta. There was another gal, too.*
>   *Gerri said she thought it was Margaret, but I used to*
>   *date Margaret; no way was it she, even after*
>   *twenty years I'd have known*
•did you remember Alan Garrett from high school?
>   *No I do not. We didn't run in the same circles.*
>   *Three weeks before the reunion I heard Patti had*
>   *especially invited him. Why she would is*
>   *beyond me*
•did you know Barry Franks was dying of aids?
>   *yes, he told me*
•did he tell you how he contracted it.
>   *everyone knew the risks of having sex with Roxy-*
>   *we did it anyway. We were stupid kids*
•twenty years ago you shuttled several people to that cabin
cruiser with a speed boat. How many trips and how many
people?
>   *I made two trips. I delivered a kid out there who said*
>   *he worked for the Marina, and I dropped off Patti and*
>   *Roxanne-(they heard there was a party going on out*
>   *there) I picked up Gina Brand and Gerri Kitchens and*
>   *brought them to shore -- Then later I took Gina and*
>   *Gerri back out there and picked up Trudy Wells, Ruby*
>   *Salinas and Sharon Etts*
•who killed Roxanne twenty years ago?

> *I wasn't on the craft. We all supposed it was a frenzied act of juvenile sexual stupidity. Barry didn't know -- he dove off and swam ashore.*

•did you know a young boy -- probably the one you shuttled out there that afternoon -- was also murdered out on the water?

> *Oh, no!*

•who killed Patti?

> *I have no idea. Some of the ladies think it was Alan Garrett, your boss. I don't. In school I knew Alan by reputation only as keen and studious, but not a murderer.*

•Who do you think the dead lady is, and who killed her--that lady Alan discovered at the reunion?

> *I don't know. Possibly Sherri Foote, Sharon Etts or Trudy Wells. They were all supposed to be there that night. Who knows? Whoever killed her was someone who hated Alan intensely; the only one I can think of, possibly is, oh, I won't say, but the reason? payback? jealousy? Fear?*

•who brought the cabin cruiser back to shore?

> *We were told the skipper dove overboard and never went back. I never boarded the boat. probably that older gal that was aboard, the one that got tied up. She was the first one off the boat. She called the police and met them at the dock.*

•did you meet that gal? Would you recognize her after twenty years?

> *Oh, yeah, we all met her. I'd know her for sure*

•do you think she cut Roxanne up?

> *Uhhh, no. Well, I guess she could have*

•do you have a large deep freezer?

> *That's a terrible question to ask, Miss. Absolutely not!*

•I noticed a large cabin cruiser parked in your drive. Do you take it out much?

> *As often as I can. It's my fishing boat. I also have a motor sailer I keep tied up at Seal Beach Yacht Club. Do you sail?*

· Never have.

Exhilarating! You should go out with me some time.

"What do you think Bossman?" Liz asked as I looked up at her after reading and rereading the interview notes.

"I think we need to buy you more note pads. Was he comfortable?"

"It went smooth as glass all the way through, Smart Ass. You said be thorough. I was thorough."

"What'd you have for lunch?"

"Pastrami. Both of us. Receipt on your desk."

"So, do you remember Tom Wellings from twenty years ago?"

"Oh, yes. He was on the boat. I could hear him bossing the others around. Seeing him brought back some memories. I'd forgotten a few things, but now I remember him shouting something like, *I'm going back for another load.* But I don't think he was there at the end. He took the speedboat back with some girls."

"You're sure, Fox? You were all tied up, remember?" I queried her with a smile.

"Yes, Mr. Gumshoe. I thought about it all during lunch and on the way home. I'm sure."

This is the second or third time I've heard the name Sherri Foote bandied about, I thought to myself. *She was not at that reunion . . . at least alive. We need Sherri's current information.*

I turned to Liz. "Call Tom Wellings back, since you have a history with him. He may know if Sherri married, has a different last name, her address or workplace if he knows. Then, if that's not successful, call Morris. Get DMV records on our Sherri Foote."

"On it."

Tom was helpful. He hadn't seen Sherri in years, but the last he knew--about 2012--she was married (no children) but kept her maiden name; she was an attorney with Gunn and Gunn, a Glendale firm on Broadway.

Fox found the firm and placed a call. Sherri--out of the office since July 20. She and her husband had a six week African adventure planned for several years, target date was their tenth anniversary--Tuesday, July 22nd--left a general itinerary, *no phone calls unless plane can't land at LAX due to earthquake,* is the way the receptionist described Sherri's instructions.

"Call the inspector anyway, Fox. Let's get an address."

"It's after 4:30 p.m., Gumshoe. He won't be there. He's enjoying a . . . Oh! forget I said anything," Liz said with a giggle. "We obviously have better booze. He's pulling up outside as we speak."

"Good. We have a few things to talk about."

"Two things before I forget, Gumshoe, I'll be late tomorrow. I'm going to collect some skip money or put a brick on a couple of accounts."

"You can leave now, Fox, if you wish."

"Who's leaving?" Morris asked as he walked through the door.

"No one's leaving just yet!" retorted Liz. "Gumshoe, he's just trying to hog all the booze." Without objection, she grabbed the Martell and three glasses off the shelf.

"Well, I have news," Morris said. "You have any?"

"A bit," I said, and took a sip.

"Good!" the inspector said, saluting with his snifter. "I'll start."

FORTY-NINE

"Slugs you dug out of your wall are a match to some found in a cold case murder victim."

"You're joking, Morris!" I blurted out. "Who?"

"Cop by the name of Chris Evans. Ring any bells?"

"Rings a *gong*!" I shook my head. "Oh, Inspector. Your people sure it was that gun?"

"Couple of my guys are picking up your friend, Rachel right now. I'll be going back to ask her a few questions tonight. I doubt we'll hold her overnight, but we'll squeeze pretty hard before we take her home."

"You can do that?" Liz was surprised, "match slugs from a few days ago with slugs from ten years ago, and say conclusively that they came from the same gun?"

"Yes," said Morris simply. "Slugs are probably from a high-powered revolver. So what's your news, Alan?"

"Would you do me a favor? Run down Sherri Foote's DMV records and get an address for me? Seems she is another question mark. Just want to eliminate her as our dead body.

Next thing, I brought back a couple of photos from my trip south. I want to have Carla compare them to the corpse we have in the morgue. It's still there, right?"

"Sure is. Do you have a time?"

"I don't even have a day, yet, but I'm hoping tomorrow. I'll let you know."

"Well, that's easy," Liz frowned and dialed a number. "I'm calling her. That's what you do to arrange things."

In the meantime, I handed Morris Trudy Wells' hairbrush and toothbrush for DNA samples. "Picked these up today," I explained.

"Hi, Carla. It's Fox. Can you meet with Gumshoe tomorrow?"

I grabbed the phone and took over. "Good evening, Carla. Our dead corpse is still a Jane Doe. I have photos of two possibles. Can you reconstruct or envision what the face might normally look like to make a professional evaluation?"

"I'd be happy to try," she said. "I'm free tomorrow after 1:30 p.m. if that works for you."

"Great! See you at my office at 2:00."

Morris had finished his cognac. "Keep this lady on, Alan. She makes sure you get in your full eight hours a day."

He bid us adieu and headed back to police headquarters.

Liz poured another short cognac, reminding me she wouldn't have coffee waiting for me in the morning.

"What was the other thing you wanted to tell me before leaving this evening?" I asked her.

"Take a look at Gina's 4x6 card. Notice anything

in common with what we just learned about Sherri?"
She set her glass down, "See you sometime tomorrow,
Gumshoe."

I sat at my desk for ten minutes, staring at the
three holes in the wall. There must have been
some mistake. I poured myself another cognac, but I
didn't take a sip. Instead, I pored over my notes,
especially of Gina and Sherri, and found what Fox had
noted: both Gina and Sherri had at one time worked at
Gunn and Gunn.

I spent a few minutes looking for imaginary clues
for Rachel's vindication. I found none. Then I spent a
few minutes listening to the tip line. Nothing new. A
few days ago, *Gina is the key,* this time, *Gina is the
answer.* Maybe I need to have a sit down 'one on one'
with Gina.

Frustrated, I tossed my fedora at the rack a few
times--70% success. Time to go home. I started out the
door when my cell phone rang.

"Hello, Garrett here."

"Alan? Can you pick me up at the police station
and take me home?"

FIFTY

Rachel was standing inside the lobby frantically looking for my Caddy as I pulled up. She came running out, hugged me, whispered a quick *thank you*, and ran to the passenger side and hustled aboard.

"They think I killed Chris, Adam! They think I killed Chris!" she sobbed uncontrollably.

I put my arm around her and drew her close as we motored toward her home.

"Take a deep breath, Rachel, then slow down and tell me exactly what happened and what was said. Did you speak with Inspector Morris?"

She could only nod. I had some Kleenex in a box on the floor; I offered, she took a couple and blew her nose.

"Oh Alan, it was awful. Two cops came to my door and asked me to come with them. They didn't say a word the whole trip. I asked them several times what it was about. The driver just looked in the mirror at me and said, *Inspector Morris has a few questions. You'll see.*

When I get there this Inspector Morris asks if I own my own gun--I say yes. Then he asks if I have Chris' police revolver. I say yes. He asks how many hand guns are in the house, and are they all legally permitted. I tell him I have four, and yes they are. He says, bring them to the police station tomorrow at 9:30 a.m. Alan, what is going on?"

"You didn't use one to try to scare me the other night in my office did you?"

"What? Of course not, Alan Garrett!"

"Then you have nothing to fear." We were just pulling up Rachel's drive to her door. "Just take the guns to Morris tomorrow."

I walked around, opened the car door and took her hand. "Everything will be fine, Rachel. Comply with Morris. Whatever he asks. It'll be okay." I gave her a peck on the cheek. "I'll talk to you tomorrow."

"Would you stay with me awhile, Alan? I'm so sorry I blew up the other afternoon. It's just that I was so shocked to see that woman in *my car* . . ."

"No, no. We both have things to do, Rachel. Call me tomorrow after you see Morris. We can do lunch if you'd like."

"I would," she said.

I watched as she unlocked her door and disappeared inside, then headed to Pop's Place..

* * *

Pop met me at the door. "You're late, Alan. I fired up the bar-b-que half an hour ago. Fortunately for you, I didn't throw the steaks on yet. You're supposed to make the salad, so get in the kitchen and get with it!"

"Sorry, Pop . . . a bit of overtime, I'm afraid. Salad in ten. Dinner in fifteen?"

"Perfect. Wash your hands before you grab a knife!"

Dinner was washed down with a Bourbon Barrel Stout. Pop and I discussed a replacement car for his Subaru.

"I'm having Walt send out some feelers," Pop said. "My check from the insurance company came in today, so I can plunk down a few bucks. Your check is on your desk as well."

"I'm going to take a walk down on the pier. Feel like joining me, Pop?"

"Not tonight, Alan. Been thinking about what you were saying, my being a young man and all. I invited, and the widow Mason is coming up for a game of scrabble. By the way, her name is Rita."

"I won't be long, Pop; early start tomorrow. You're not going to keep me awake all night with giggling are you?"

"All depends on the widow, Son," he answered, shaking his head, sagely. "All depends on the widow."

* * *

The early morning was dark and wet with fog-- moist and thick--typical of our coastal area. I was forced to turn on lights and windshield wipers; the mist obscured my view, after only the short drive to my office.

The landline phone was blinking as I flipped on the lights. I ignored it. Instead, I tossed my hat at the hat-rack (bullseye!), made a pot of coffee, then poured myself a cup, then finally sat at Liz's desk and clicked the phone voice mail. It was Morris.

I understand you picked up Rachel Block from our facility and took her home this evening, he said on the message. *Do not accompany her tomorrow morning. Things don't look good for her. I'll call you after.*

I didn't want to plow up that ground right now. I had a definite purpose for coming in early this morning. I grabbed the White's notebooks, photo albums and a few blank sheets of paper. I began:

The Whites--
  •Were their deaths a murder-suicide?
    Were they ashamed of a past act?
    Did they hate each other?
  •Was Mr. White's service revolver used?
  •Family Ties
    Was Mrs. White really Regina's mother-in-law?
    If so, was that relationship good?
     Why did their son, Jonah, gave up custody of the
    grandchildren--namely, twins, Chris and Virginia -- to
Regina's parents
    Did they keep in touch with Jonah and Chris?
    Did they know the adoptive parents of grandchild,
    Virginia, and did they know her whereabouts?

Too late to ask these questions of the Whites, I thought to myself aloud, *but perhaps of Regina, perhaps even of Rachel. Surely, Rachel talked with her husband before he was killed. They were married for seven years.*

I opened the photo album. It had belonged to the Mrs. I was sure . . . pictures of her as a young woman, then of her all smiles with an infant . . . then photos of the wedding to Charles--with evidently, young Jonah by their side. The lad looked perhaps just a year old. That would be 1963.

From there the album showed scenery, photos of Charles graduating from the police academy, Jonah graduating from high school, the White's anniversary photos, vacations; two or three of the twin children, Chris and Virginia as very young children--but, strange--Regina's face had been cut out of each of those photos.

I struggled with that fact. Not one photo of Regina! And a complete lack of Jonah and Regina's wedding day, which should have been a day of joyous celebration. No love lost there!

Now I had a few more questions. I'm certain Rachel's murdered husband and Regina's son Chris are one and the same. But--
> •Was there no communication between Rachel and Chris and the rest of the family (Mother-Regina, Grandparents-the Whites)
> •Where is Jonah Evans?
> •Where is Chris Evans twin sister, Virginia?
> •Where is Regina's son, Teddy Leone?

I poured another cup of coffee--my third--and set everything down on paper. . . then sat and stared at all the pieces. Here it is, going into the fifth week of investigation, and I still haven't put any of the puzzle together. I figuratively threw my hands up. Another thought pounded its way in my head: *Maybe I should consider Morris' offer . . . Maybe I should be driving around in a patrol car.* Phone rang--startling my brain back to reality. I glanced at my computer--just a bit before
8:oo a.m. Morris again.

"Got that address you requested, Alan; that Sherri Foote."

"Oh! Thanks, Morris. I'd completely forgotten I'd asked you for it." I jotted down the address--on Wawona in the hills of Eagle Rock.

"One more thing, Alan."

"Sir?"

"My forensic team found human DNA in that marina freezer . . . the one delivered in June, compared it against the reunion corpse. It's a match."

"As we suspected, Morris. And, as I remember," I added, "Regina is supposed to be back this week , Right?"

"Yeah, that's right," Morris replied. "I'm calling her about nine, and if she's there I'll be heading to the marina after I have my interview with your friend, Ms Block. Want to take a ride?"   "No, I can't," I replied. "I have my own interview to conduct, unless you intend to keep her in chains."

"Rachel?" Morris asked incredulously.

"Yes," I replied, "Rachel. We're having lunch, after which I have several questions for her. You might do me a favor, though, Inspector--if Regina is there today, ask her if she owns a handgun."

We hung up. I turned to my laptop, plugged into google maps for directions to Wawona Street in Eagle Rock. I didn't have time to go there now . . . perhaps after lunch. I closed my eyes . . . *No!* My eyelids flew open in the realization I had a commitment. *Carla at 2:30.* I settled back in my chair again. Closed my eyes a second time. *I have a date with Carla . . . at the morgue.*

The phone startled me from my momentary funk.

"Alan Garrett?" Male voice. "Good, you're there. See you in half an hour." The line went dead.

FIFTY-ONE

The latch clicked on the strike plate as the door opened. The guy looked somewhat familiar as I stood and waved him toward one of the two chairs before Liz' desk.

He reached out a right hand, "George Nichols," then slumped in the chair. "I think I did a bad thing, Mr. Garrett. I understand you've been out at the White's place, and then at the marina in Ocean Vista."

"Deep freeze connection, George?"

"Yes, Sir. I knew there was something wrong with the whole thing, but the money was so good I couldn't turn it down."

"Tell me what you know, George. Who gave you the money?"

"That's just it, Mr. Garrett . . ."

"Alan."

"That's just it, Alan, we never met. Everything was communicated through email and texting."

"You're not just here for the deep freeze are you, George? I thought I recognized you from somewhere. I think I have your picture tacked to my white board. Just a minute."

I walked into my office and came back with the two sketches Rachel had provided.

"Is this you, George?" I handed him Carla's sketch of the male figure.

"A very good likeness. Yes, Alan, that could be me."

"So who's this?" I handed him the sketch of the female figure.

"If I knew I'd tell you, but I don't know her--honest."

"Same person deal with you?" I asked him, pouring him a cup of coffee.

"I think so," he responded. "Thanks. Good coffee."

"What did you do with the suitcases, George?"

"I took my case to a suite . . . uh, Suite 14A. There was a case in there already. I simply dropped mine off as instructed and picked up an envelope on the dresser with my name on it, checked the cash inside, and split."

"Were you aware of the contents of the deep freeze you delivered to the marina?"

"I have not been told; I do not know; I have no interest; I only know you have been snooping around the White's place and the marina. I only suspect it has a connection to delivering the luggage to the cruise ship on July 27. I want it on the record that whatever involvement I had was purely cash received for a job done as instructed."

"I appreciate you coming in, George. If you'd be so kind," I handed him a note pad, "would you jot down your contact information for me? You may be contacted by Inspector Morris of the local police. You did hear that the Whites are dead, right?"

"You're kidding!" George looked at me in genuine shock. "No, I did not know that, Alan! We didn't even knock on their door. We were instructed to go directly to their shed, drop off the new freezer, pick up the old one and deliver it to the marina, the only paperwork being a receipt saying something like--*drop off at Marina bait shop. See Bill, the guy that runs it.*

Oh, I'm so sorry, Alan. I hope I didn't have anything to do with their deaths."

"Not at all, George. You were used as an unwitting pawn by your mysterious caller. Inspector Morris will probably ask you to come in to answer some questions. Just be honest with him, consider anything more that might be important between now and then . . . for instance, why were you chosen, who knew your movements, your free time, those kinds of things."

George stood to go. I watched his body language carefully as he set the coffee cup on the desk. I decided he was genuine. I handed him my card, and told him to expect a call from Morris.

That was interesting, I told myself. A piece of the puzzle came into focus--not as I had suspected, but welcome, none the less. It appears the luggage with the body wasn't brought to the reunion by graduates, but by two paid lackeys of a diabolic schemer or perhaps schemers.

The clock on Liz's computer told me it was 10:13 a.m. I should be getting a call from Rachel any time. The phone, as if on cue, rang. I picked it up, expecting to hear Rachel on the other end.

"Alan?"

It was Pop.

"Got a car. Walt got me a 2017 Subaru Impreza. You doing anything for lunch?"

"Yes, I'm waiting for a call from Rachel Block. I'm picking her up from the police station as soon as Morris is finished interviewing her."

"Well, I need to take this little beauty for a spin. I'm picking up the widow Mason . . . uh, that is, Rita, and coming to your office in a few minutes. Thought she and I would take you down the coast, maybe somewhere like Seal Beach for lunch, but if you're busy we'll make it another time."

"Sorry, Pop. I'm sure there's time for a short visit, but a raincheck on the lunch. See you in a bit."

I had to smile as I sat at Liz's desk. Pop getting involved with the widow Mason. *Way to go, Pop!*

The phone rang. It was Rachel.

"Hi, Alan. The Inspector and I will be finished in about a half hour. Are we still on for lunch?"

"Make it 11:30. I'll be there."

"I'm leaving my car in the parking lot. I can pick it up later."

A small candy apple red sedan pulled up . . . undoubtedly Pop's Subaru. Nice looking ride. I walked outside for a chat.

FIFTY-TWO

Rachel was on the police steps waiting for me as I drove up. She looked unhappy. I pulled to the curb.

"Ah, Mademoiselle," I smiled as broadly as I could muster, "may I offer you a lift to your destination? Perhaps a little French bistro or possibly an open air boardwalk cafe, or a picnic on the beach?"

"Take me away from here, Alan." *No sense of humor.* "It makes no difference where I go," she continued, "so long as it's away from here."

I pointed the Caddy toward Highway 1, preparing to drive as far as Rachel wished. She surprised me.

"Just take me to the pier in Manhattan, Alan. I want to sit at the far end. I want to rent a fishing pole and catch a mackerel. I want to run away. I want to take a long, hot shower."

I made a U-turn and retraced the route to the police station.

"Leave it to me, lady." I decided to go big! "We'll pick up your car, drop it off at Pop's Place, then walk to the beach. We'll go to the far end of the pier. I'll rent some fishing gear and set you up. Then I'll order a couple of beef franks from Barb's. She's a buddy of mine--been going there for years for one of her dogs."

Rachel's jaw dropped. "You're serious aren't you?" Then she rubbed her hands together, "Sounds wonderful, Alan! Makes me smile! Thank you!"

We did just that. As expected, Pop and the widow were not home. Both cars parked and locked in the drive--we walked to the pier.

We sat on a bench at the end of the pier, lines out. After the first hot dog, Rachel leaned into me and laughed.

"This is really fun, Alan. First time fishing. Ever!"

I broached the subject. "So what happened today with Morris?"

"He wanted my four guns; I gave him my four guns. He tested them all. He returned them all. He has asked that I be available for any further questioning; I assured him I'm going nowhere."

"So he's satisfied--good!. On another front, Rachel, we found your male sketch subject. Not a 1999 graduate, simply a goon used by someone to shuttle the luggage upstairs."

"So, where are we on our case, then?" Rachel squeezed my arm. "I mean your case, Alan."

"Well, for one thing, we know in which suite the luggage was delivered, so Morris should know who rented it. We have the phone number George used; should be able to get a call history off that phone. And we . . ."

"Oh! I caught one!" Rachel shrieked! "Alan, help! What do I do? I caught a fish!"

Her rod was jumping up and down crazily. The Penn reel drag screaming as line went out.

"Help me, Alan!" she repeated. "What do I do?"

Someone in the growing crowd yelled, "You reel it in, Lady!"

I heard another say, "It's probably just a leopard shark. Already two this week."

And sure enough, after more than fifteen minutes, Rachel had a leopard shark ready to be pulled up. One of the bystanders, an old-time fisherman, grabbed the common rope with net attached, dropped it to the water, guided it under the fish, then pulled it up hand over hand to the top of the pier.

Rachel was elated. She stood with rod in hand, the fisherman beside her with the shark held out in front of them. I took the picture. Then she watched with sheer joy as the shark was unhooked and released over the edge and back into the water.

"Oh, thank you, Alan! That was amazing. I needed that! "

"Good. Now you know what to do the next time you get stressed. Pick up a fishing pole and head for the nearest pond. Works every time."

We walked up the hill to Pop's. Rachel slid into her Mercedes.

"You want to come shower with me, Alan?"

"Ha! No, Miss. That was on your list, just not mine. But, before you go, and it's kind of a touchy subject right now in light of what Morris pulled you in for, but what did you know about Chris' family? His mom and dad, brothers, sisters, that kind of thing?"

"Strange . . . the Inspector asked me the same question. Chris never talked about it. Said only that his folks were dead. He ended up in an orphanage.

He was working as a short order chef at Norms, going to school. So, when we married, I had no in-laws. We joined my folks for Thanksgivings and at Christmastime--before they moved to Florida a few years ago."

"Rachel," I said, looking at my cell phone, "I'm glad Morris is satisfied with everything from this morning. Go home for a nice long, warm shower. It's been fun, but I must go. I'm heading down to the office to prepare for a meeting."

I gave her cheek a quick peck and started for my car.

"Hop in, I'll give you a ride, Alan."

"Nope, you skedaddle--I'll take my Caddy, thanks."

"You never call me, Alan. Did I do something wrong?"

"Not at all, Rachel. We had a great morning, right? Now I have a busy afternoon, and, no--I'm not seeing anyone on a regular basis, if that's what you're worried about."

She drove off, squealing tires. I shook my head and climbed into my Caddy.

Liz was at her desk as I walked to the door. She buzzed me in.

"Gumshoe! Glad to see you." She held out two folders. "I have news."

"Good or bad?"

"Look in the folders."

The folders contained checks made out to Grinnell, one for the complete amount he owed, the other with checks at 30, 60 and 90 days, complete with prorated interest.

"You did good, Fox. Any messages while I've been out?"

"That's all I get, Boss? *I did good*? . . . Boss, I did fantastic!"

"Okay, Fox, you're right--you did fantastic! Any messages?"

Liz mumbled something under her breath. I leaned over her desk.

"Fox, it's a great job you did for us today. I minimized it so you wouldn't get a big head, but really and truly, you did great!"

"Aw, shucks, Bossman," Liz smiled, "weren't nuthin." She bent one nostril with a forefinger while snufflling noisily. "By the way, there was a message from Carla. She can't make it today. Call her tomorrow."

"Oh! Okay. Change of plans. Get your purse; we'll swing by Grinnell's office with the checks, then you and I are heading to Eagle Rock."

"What's in Eagle Rock, Gumshoe?"

"Sherri Foote's home on Wawona."

Grinnell wasn't in his office. We stuck the four checks into an envelope along with a business card and note from Liz, slipped it through his office mail slot-- making sure it landed well within his office-- then pointed my Caddy up I-110 N.

FIFTY-THREE

Wawona snakes its way along the crest of a gorge in the San Rafael Hills. Nestled in the highs and lows of the area lies Eagle Rock.

Many of the residential streets are two-way, but traffic is able only to proceed in one direction, while any oncoming cars duck in wherever the curb allows-- very congenial neighborhood. Most of the dwellings are crammed along the street--small, on two levels; the payback is the lovely view, and the fact that no one can drive in excess of 10 mph.

The walkway going down to Sherri Foote's front door was protected by a wrought iron gate and an ivy-covered fence line. There were two vehicles in the driveway. I let Liz out, then squeezed in as close as I could, blocking the cars in.

Liz beat me to the gate, and discovering it was unlocked, proceeded to the door and rang the buzzer. No answer. She tried again. I walked to a window and peered inside. No signs of life. Wasted trip if I couldn't get a DNA sample. I walked around the house to try to find a way in. I was about to break a window when a car horn beeped.

Liz called out to me, "Bossman! Need you out here!"

Back to the front . . . an older teenage boy was standing outside the gate, talking with Liz.

"Why are you snooping around here, mister?"

"I'm a private eye, son," I said, handing him my card, "working on a case that involves the lady that lives here."

The lad stared at the card for a moment. "No lady lives here, Mr. Garrett, my dad just sold this place. Signed the papers day before yesterday. I'm staying here, kinda camping out, while he's out of town. He'll be back Friday. In two weeks the new owners will be moving in."

Liz and I traded equally shocked expressions at the news.

Liz piped up, "May we take a look at the inside of the house. We only want some DNA samples of the previous owners. They're linked to a criminal investigation we're conducting."

"Uh, I guess so. The place is really clean. I don't think you'll find much, but if you do, can I take pictures?"

"Absolutely!" Liz assured him. "If you see anything like a toothbrush, a towel, even hair, don't touch it, but show us. Take all the pictures you want, but don't touch, okay?"

"Sure. Name is Ron, by the way."

"Your last name, Ron?"

"Graham."

"And your dad's name?"

Ron laughed, "Graham, Sir. Oh, sorry. Alex."

We all laughed.

"Do you have a mom, Ron?" Liz asked.

"She died in childbirth when she had me. Dad tried remarrying . . . didn't work."

We went through the bath, kitchen and living room. The kid was right. Not even dust on a window sill.

"Did the previous owner leave any furniture in this place . . . anything at all?"

"No, Sir. Nothing. Two or three plants in the sunroom and some outdoor furniture. Nothing upstairs, either. Two bedrooms and another bath . . . oh, and an attic space."

"Liz, take a quick look outside," I suggested. "I'll go upstairs with Ron."

"No," Ron said, "I'd rather that we all go together. I want to take pictures if you find anything."

"Okay, then, upstairs we go."

The bedrooms were squeaky clean. Ron's sleeping bag was the only item in one of them.

But the attic was another story. It took a flashlight to find them, but there was a small cardboard box with three small photo albums in it, along with other trinkets. After Ron took his pictures of the box I pulled it out of its hidden corner.

"May we take this box? We'll return it if you'd like."

"I'll ask Dad, but I don't think he'll want it. Do you still want to look at the outside furniture?"

I shrugged, "May as well, while we're here."

We walked out on the patio. Liz rummaged through the potted plants, then opened the potting shed and glanced in.

"I see nothing here, Bossman."

"What about tools or garden gloves?" I asked.

"Yeah, rake, shovel and a pair of muddy gloves is all," she answered as she turned to secure the hasp on the door . . . "oh! I see, Bossman--the gloves!"

"Absolutely! The gloves!" Turning to Ron, I asked if we might borrow the gloves as well.

"I don't think Dad wants the gloves back," Ron laughed. Liz placed them in a fresh plastic bag as she had done with the photos.

"Please have your dad call me when he gets back from his trip," I told Ron, as Liz and I returned to the Cadillac. "Thanks for your help today. What does your dad do for a living, by the way?"

"He's a real estate specialist. Buying and selling properties that have legal complications. That's all I know."

"Hmm. Interesting."

"Do you want me to send you the pictures I took?"

"Please do," Liz was quick to answer. "You have our cards, right?"

"Neat name: *Gumshoe & Fox.* You must be Fox, right?" he asked Liz.

"Sure am, Ron," she assured him. "And the old man, here, is Gumshoe."

Liz kept her eyes closed as we guided the Caddy back through the San Rafael Hills, opening them only when she felt we were going more or less straight, heading for Manhattan Beach.

"What do you make of all that, Gumshoe?"

she asked. "Sherri Foote was supposed to be paddling up the Amazon, knowing that her home would be safe and sound when she returned home."

"With her husband," I chimed in with a smile, "but you have the wrong continent/wrong river. They didn't go to South America, Fox, they went to Africa, maybe the Nile or the Congo."

"Whatever," came a sardonic reply. "Ah, I know!" she continued without taking a breath, they sold the house on the way to the airport or even before; they had the deal in the works for months, and now, maybe they're enjoying . . ."

"Maybe she's on a slab in the morgue, Fox. Maybe the husband was buried in the back garden with that muddy shovel in the potting shed."

"Oh, I hope not, Gumshoe. I like my scenario better."

"Yeah, so do I," I agreed. "Besides, that whole hillside is probably solid rock."

Neither of us spoke for three or four minutes. I concentrated on driving, making sure I took the correct off-ramps in this unfamiliar section of the Los Angeles sprawl, all the time juggling the possibly new wrinkle in my already confusing case.
Liz broke the silence.

"How did you know, Gumshoe?" she asked, turning to me. "I mean, you suspected something awry, didn't you?" Without waiting for me to respond, she added, "I'm proud to be working for you, Bossman. You have good instincts . . . in fact, you're a great detective. Are you thinking what I'm
thinking?"

"I think I am, Liz."

"What's our next move?"

"Tomorrow I want you to call Gunn and Gunn. Arrange a meeting with a principal. Tell them it's a police matter. We need everything they can remember regarding time spent together between Sherri Foote and Gina Rowling back in 2008, anything abnormal, any memories, cat fights, collaborations, anything; then ask about Sherri's plans regarding her current African trip, and anything on her husband."

"Got it, Bossman. I'll take the recorder so I won't miss a thing. I assume you'll be heading to see Morris with the gloves and box of photos."

"Of course. But then I'll be checking the county records for that transfer of title for Sherri's house. And, by the way, thank you. We're going to get this son-of-a-bitch, Liz, and soon."

It was too late to call Morris. Instead, I dropped Liz off at the office and continued to the police headquarters, dropped off the gloves and box with photos, marked it DNA testing please, and finally, left Morris a message to call me in the morning.

Without bothering to return to the office, I called it a day. A day of angst and trepidation at what the police lab might find tomorrow.

FIFTY-FOUR

My fedora was still swinging from the hat rack when Morris called me. It was Wednesday morning, 7:40 a.m.

"Got your package, Alan. It's at forensics. Should have some answers for you this afternoon. You going to be around?"

"Probably. I'm hoping Carla can meet me at the morgue today. Maybe I can schedule that for sometime this afternoon and see you both.

Oh, in case I forget, can you pull paperwork for license and concealed carry requirements for me? Liz is looking to become a P.I. She has good instincts, I've tentatively agreed, just haven't moved forward on it yet."

"She can do everything online, Alan. Just have her Google it."

"Right." (I heard the back door open, Liz had come in...) "Okay," I continued with Morris, "I'll call you after I make arrangements with Carla. Oh! One other thing--have a pen handy? I had a visit from a George Nichols. He was both our freezer and corpse delivery man at the reunion." I gave Morris the information. "He's expecting your call."

"Wait, Ala . . ." I hung up on him. *That'll irritate the hell out of him,* I thought with a smile.

"It's just me, Gumshoe!" Liz sang out. "You beat me here. You have coffee already or shall I make some?"

"Please make some. Morris called before I could turn around." I stepped into the foyer and smiled at her. She was dressed to kill.

"You expecting to see the attorneys at Gunn & Gunn today? Usually, you need to set up an appointment, then wait anxiously for a few days before they'll see you. It isn't like we're hiring them for representation on a new case, simply buying some time for an *in-house* interview."

"Someone will see me today, Gumshoe. I'm sure of it," she smiled confidently.

"And you know this because?"

"Because I called late yesterday before I left the office. The only one there was the president, Peter Gunn, and he thought his wife was calling. When he answered with, *Sweetheart, I was just leaving,* I explained I wasn't his sweetheart, but I needed to speak with a company principle that knew Sherri Foote; that it was a matter of urgency. He said he would meet with me personally at 10:30 this morning."

"Wow, Fox! Interviewing Peter Gunn! Now that's a feather in your cap."

"A little too late for that Peter Gunn. You're not that old, either, Bossman. Nice music, though. Anyway, I'll be seeing him this morning. I have a list of questions. Take a look, and see if I need to ask others or go a different direction."

I could add nothing to her list. I handed it back to her. Then I stopped.

"Oh! Yes! Ask Mr. Gunn who or what firm he would recommend for an education in fraudulent title transfer of real property. Ask that question first if you will, then call me. I want to spend some time studying the problem this morning. It may be nothing, but it may be very much related to our case.

Something else I want you to do, Fox. Start your paperwork for a gun permit and license."

Liz sat with a slight smile as I spoke. I continued, "You can get what you need off Google to start the process. Then . . . why are you looking at me like that?"

"I have a gun, Bossman," she laughed. "It's licensed. I've had my Beretta for probably ten years and I shoot pretty well. What I don't have is a concealed carry permit."

"You are a sly one aren't you, Fox? Alright, when I see Morris today, we'll move forward on the *concealed carry* part."

"So can we plan on a visit to the gun range tomorrow? I want you to teach me how to shoot."

"Smart ass . . . No! Tomorrow's Thursday. I want you to spend this afternoon in preparation for a trip to Arizona tomorrow. Let the guy know this afternoon that you're coming. Call Judge Hamlin. See if he has a friendly counterpart in Phoenix. Hamlin has already signed off on it here in California, right?"

"Uhh, right, Sir, but I don't have an airline ticket."

"That's because you're going to drive that

new car of yours to Arizona. If you stop in Vegas and don't get there until Monday, make sure you take your own credit card with you. I expect you back here warming your seat on Wednesday morning or before with a big, fat check in your hand. You need to start on Brigadier General Maggorie's missing son."

"We're taking that case on, Bossman?"

"We already have, Fox. I made the call to Captain Albert before I came in this morning. Son is still missing. Maggorie will be sending a retainer to us. In fact, it should be in our account as we speak."

Liz tapped a few keys on her computer.

"Nope . . . nothing yet."

"Gotta be there," I said with conviction. "Captain Albert said he'd make sure it went out immediately. Try my credit card account or yours, maybe I gave him the wrong account number."

"Who would deposit a retainer in a credit card account, Gumshoe? That's ridiculous."

"Humor me, Fox. Check!"

"Sure." More keyboard strokes, followed by a "Nope," then more taps and a shriek!

"Alan Gumshoe Garrett! I now have a $20,000 credit balance in my credit card account. Vegas, look out!"

"Back in your seat by a week from today, young lady, with a check for Grinnell. Then we go to the police gun range for that first step in your concealed carry."

FIFTY-FIVE

Liz left at 9:45 a.m. for Gunn and Gunn; I called Carla--arranged a meeting at the morgue.

"2:30 this afternoon okay?" she asked.

"Absolutely. See you then."

I called Morris to confirm the time.

"2:30 p.m.?" Morris hesitated, "just a minute, Alan." I could hear his chair squeak as he shifted. Then muffled voices, then he came back to the phone, "2:30 should work just fine. Lab should have DNA results. We have other business to discuss as well."

"Business to discuss?" I repeated. "Tell me!"

"It can wait. Be here at 2:30 this afternoon. We'll talk."

I sat for a moment shaking my head, then went to my *current* business at hand . . . business on the computer. Using Google, I opened up a few sites warning homeowners of scammers bent on taking possession of their homes. Evidently there is a surge in this type of activity, falling into two major categories:

1. the simple, easily-detected, easily-rectified--and usually poorly-planned schemes perpetrated by tricksters or swindlers. This type, from what I could read, is typically the renter who tries to sell the dwelling using false documents to convince the unsuspecting *buyer* that he needed to sell the house quickly to pay overwhelming hospital costs, or some such fable.

2. the professional, well-educated, well-read, white collar con artist who has honed his craft to a polished edge, perhaps involving setting up dummy revocable trust accounts to show potential *buyers* that the properties are secure, mortgage payment slips into the trust accounts are up to date, that ownership papers show signatures of duly-signed trustees, notary's stamps and such, of course, to show authenticity.

The phone pulled me away from the computer. It was Liz.

"Gumshoe, I'm here with Mr. Gunn. He says one of the best experts in, as he calls it, *adverse possession* actually works at Gunn and Gunn. The gentleman, Mr. Eric Betters, is available to speak with me any time this morning right up to 12:30 p.m. Or, we could include you in a conference call around noon if you would like."

"I'll be here until 1:00 p.m.," I said. "A conference call sounds good. Call me when you're finished with Mr. Gunn. We'll set up a conference call at that point. I'll be here. Thanks, Liz."

* * *

I made a quick call to Captain Albert, assuring him we were finishing with a case and would be spending full time on the Maggorie boy by a week from today, with a progress report by that Friday and every Friday until the boy was found.

I sat in the foyer at Liz's desk and flipped on the tip-line tape. There were no new messages. I rewound the tape to the beginning, and pushed play. Various voices: *Gina is the key; dig deeper. You're cold! The dead woman is Sharon Etts. Sorry you weren't at your desk.*

I unplugged the recorder. Perhaps by taking it to the police lab they could modulate the voices to remove the distortion. Who knows? Might be of no help, but if we could identify a voice or two, especially the *Sorry you weren't at your desk . . .* I was just tucking the recorder into a satchel when Liz called.

"Bossman, we're ready for the conference call. I'll give you the number. Call back in exactly three minutes from now."

She hung up. I waited the appropriate time and dialed the number for the conference call. Mr. Betters answered.

"Is this, uhh, Gumshoe?" he laughed. "I couldn't help it, Mr. Garrett. A fun name, and sounds like a fun place to work. Your assistant is a charming lady. Now how may I assist you?"

"Good morning, Mr. Betters. Yes, Alan Garrett. Liz has probably filled you in on our findings yesterday at the home of Sherri Foote."

"Yes . . . without keeping you in suspense, to our knowledge Sherri has neither sold, nor has she ever contemplated selling her home. We tried calling her this morning, but were not successful--which is not surprising, considering the nature of their planned adventure.

Now, regarding the problem of adverse possession, it is becoming a more and more sophisticated, shall we say, industry for the greedy, ruthless con artist and a growing serious problem for unsuspecting home owners, especially the elderly."

Betters continued, obviously in his element, as an expert on the subject of fraud.

"In today's economy, with so many avenues and niches to put surplus funds, the trusting homeowner or mortgagor oft-times gets confused with terms like annuities, living trusts, revocable trusts, and so relies upon experts in the field to protect his assets--perhaps opening up an offshore bank account, perhaps shuffling his money in ways he's never heard of, and perhaps, unfortunately, dropping all of his assets into a phony trust. Ninety-nine percent of the time the expert is one of us; but one percent of the time he or she is a fraud. So, now as to the fraud--

This *expert* guides him, adds recommended, *safe* trustees, perhaps even making an associate or himself the beneficiary--second or third place--to the trust. The client feels protected; the *expert* scores a win and waits for his reward.

We have even found some of these scum eliminate the beneficiary above them, and if they format the agreement skillfully, it's tough to fight it in the courts."

"Tell him who your undergraduate intern was while working for Gunn and Gunn," Liz piped up.

"Well, yes, a Gina Rowling was under my wing for a few months; a keen student as I recall. It's been ten plus years."

I interjected a few well-chosen words, like: *damn* and *son-of-a-bitch,* but Betters explained it sufficiently without any questions.

"Look," he continued, "I have written a paper on fraudulent estate planning. It covers much more than I covered on this call. I've given it to your young lady. I trust it will assist you in your investigations, Mr. Garrett."

Liz said something about being a young lady just as I was saying, "Thank you, Sir," . . . so I added, "please send the old gal back."

We laughed.

"I'm usually here mornings," Eric Betters continued. "Let me know if I can help further. Tata."

While waiting for Liz, I went over the latest communication from Captain Albert regarding the missing son. Maggorie worked out of Quantico, so the young man, Paul, was last known to be in the DC area.

Albert had forwarded the kid's main identification numbers: his Virginia driver's license, cell phone, credit cards, social security; however, Paul had taken his passport.

I heard the Kia pull into the drive; got up and met Liz at the back door.

"Don't bother coming in," I said, "we're going to lunch around the corner."

"Sorry, Bossman. Gotta come in. Gotta pee."

"Of course, you do," I shook my head. "Hurry up and pee. You're buying."

"No sweat, Gumshoe. I got twenty grand in my purse." Then as she scurried by, she called back at me, "I'll even buy you a drink."

FIFTY-SIX

The Shellback Tavern had become my *go to* place for a quick lunch. It was time for Liz and me to have our weekly outing anyway, and a taco and beer sounded good. We sat in the same booth we had before and ordered the same fare. Liz even ordered four beers, two for each of us.

"Mr. Gunn was kind enough to allow the use of a recorder," Liz began, "but I'll give you the highlights.

Sherri Foote and her husband, Jerry, were chauffeured to the airport by a company limo on July 21. They were to be gone until September 10, which is what, next Tuesday, right?

Sherri is a valuable asset to the company. As their attorney who covers estate planning and trusts, Gunn said, she is one of their busiest, especially with the retired population. Over the years she has saved their clients well over a hundred million dollars in scam attempts, some very sophisticated--which of course has earned big fees for the company and to Sherri personally as well."

Our tacos arrived. I took a sip of beer and watched as Liz stuck a taco corner to her mouth and crunched down on it like a ravenous wolf.

"Hungry!" she apologized. "Sorry, Bossman. Too nervous to eat breakfast earlier. Afraid I'd say something stupid to that attorney and be an embarrassment to you."

"No, Fox! You were great! Don't sell yourself short. I can't have my wing woman second guessing her actions. Make a decision and stick with it. I'll back you up. Today's interview with Mr. Gunn gave us good information. You did that, Fox! Now, eat your taco."

It was close to 2:00 p.m. We finished lunch and walked back to the office.

"I should be back before closing time, Liz. You'll find a dossier on the Maggorie kid on your desk with everything Albert sent me. Maybe while on your visit to Phoenix you can spend some down time doing research.

I've asked Albert again if we can use some federal resources under the radar, but looks like we're on our own. The kid has no car; you can start with his credit cards, social security number and driver's license."

"That's all fine, Gumshoe, but we have some murders to solve, and I have a skip to take care of first. Some breathing room, please."

"You're right. Finish up your beer. Let's get out of here. I have an appointment at the morgue . . . would hate to be late."

FIFTY-SEVEN

Carla was waiting with Morris and the police Medical Examiner when I drove into the lot. After a quick greeting, I handed Carla the two photos I'd taken from Hemet and Fallbrook, of Trudy Wells and Sharon Etts, respectively.

"I can save you the trouble," Morris informed us-- the DNA doesn't match the samples you gave me last visit."

"My job is done, then," Carla smiled. "Perhaps I can still reconstruct the dead lady's face using what I know. She was a redhead, yes?"

"Yes, of course," the M.E. said . . . "but does her hair color make a difference?"

"No, not at all. Just to get a picture in my mind."

The drawer was opened, the body uncovered. Carla walked around the nudity, careful to examine bone structure and build of the frozen corpse in front of her. Then she produced a sketch book and a tool kit, complete with a two part molding compound.

"You can leave, Alan. I think you and Inspector

Morris have business to conduct. I'll be about a half hour, and I work better with no one standing over my shoulder. Trust me--we'll have a recognizable lady to look at when I'm done. It won't be today. I'll be taking the mold back to my workshop and finish up tonight."

"Bring it in tomorrow around 11:00 a.m.?" I asked. "Maybe we can do lunch?"

"It's a date," she smiled.

I followed Morris up the stairs to his office. On the way he stopped to ask his assistant for a couple of files, then we continued to his office.

"Oh, by the way, Inspector," I said, showing him the cassette I had brought, "do you have a contraption to take the voices off this tape and modulate them to sound more human? They're distorted on purpose."

"Leave the tape with me. We'll get it done for you. Now," he paused, "about the ladies in the photos . . . we know neither of them is our corpse in the morgue, Alan. Have either of them been located?"

"No, Sir. I would have heard."

"I'm surprised I don't yet have the results of the package you dropped off, either. Just a minute." Morris buzzed his assistant. "Has forensics returned information on the evidence I gave them this morning?"

"A few minutes later . . . "Just bringing them upstairs now, Sir."

The phone on the inspector's desk buzzed.

"That'll be her now." He picked it up, "Bring it in . . . Uh, sorry. Who's this? Sergeant Hopkins? Oh, yes. How are you, Hopkins? . . . You're pulling my leg! . . . My, my! . . . Is that right?"

There was a long period where Morris simply listened. Then, "But you corrected your mistake,

Sergeant. Now, out of curiosity, could you send that report to me? . . . Yes, my guy, as you call him, is here with me now . . . He may want to . . . I'll have him call you. We have your phone number. Thanks, Sergeant. You keep me posted, you hear?"

Morris turned to me. "This is getting a lot more interesting, Mr. Gumshoe. A couple more shootings, this time at the marina. Regina Leone and Bill, her bait shop fellow."

"You're kidding! Are they both dead?"

"Afraid so, Alan. And the strangest thing. Ballistics show a match with the gun that shot the Whites. Hopkins is sending the report to us."

"But I thought they had the damn gun that killed the Whites," I said--raising my arms in the air, disbelief in my voice, "it was in Mr. White's hands . . . a Colt M1911."

"They made a seriously wrong assumption," the Inspector answered. "I'm sure heads will roll. But for right now, the whereabouts of that revolver isn't known, nor is the reason for those new murders."

I started to respond when a tap came at the door. A female police officer entered.

"Here's the forensics report you were looking for Inspector." She handed Morris a folder and walked out before he could thank her.

"Here's our report, Alan. Let's see if we can identify our corpse."

Morris scanned the report as I closed my eyes and said a quick prayer. I didn't want that cold figure on the slab downstairs to be my old friend, Sherri Foote.

"Well, Alan," Morris started, "we do have a match,

but not to our unidentified corpse." He handed me the paper.

"Now what?" I asked sarcastically as I reached for it. "This is getting to be a bit much."

I quickly found the important clause and whistled. The DNA match was inside the gloves-- identifying Patti Wellings.

DNA evidence was also found on the photo journal as well--in fact, three separate samples-- but no one to match it to. We could only assume it was from family members--possibly a husband and others, but none from the corpse.

I asked the Inspector if I could borrow the photo album for a day.

"Sure. I'll call downstairs for it. You know I can't ignore the implication, Alan." Morris said. "I have to call the police chief of Eagle Rock and recommend a court order to conduct a search warrant for that entire property, both interior and exterior."

"Agreed, Sir. I'm heading back down to see Carla."

But she was already gone. The morgue's only occupants were dead. I drove the nine miles back to the office deep in thought. Regina Leone dead! *She must have been a liability to the murderer,* I thought. *Maybe she suspected something and telegraphed it? Maybe a phone call or email?*

Then what about Bait-shop Bill? Maybe simply collateral damage? Maybe. I made a mental note to speak with Sergeant Hopkins soon.

I pulled into my parking spot with a couple more questions for myself:

What the hell was Patti Wellings doing at Sherri Foote's place?

Did she mean to reveal a diabolic plot as we stepped into the elevator that reunion evening? . . . She did seem anxious to talk with me the following Monday.

Was her murder inevitable, not simply a consequence of walking into the ladies room and surprising the murderer?

Enough, Alan! Go inside and pour yourself a Martell Cordon Bleu, put your feet up and call it a day. I unlocked the back door, tossed my fedora at the hat rack, then reached for a snifter.

A note from Liz was pinned to the cork board: *I'll be back by Wednesday with a check.*

I found the new tapes for the tip line, inserted one in the recorder, plugged it in, and turned it to record.

Then I pulled the photo album from the bag forensics had given me and opened to the first page. A happy family looked back at me--husband, wife, three children--all under ten. I flipped through the rest of the photo album. I poured myself two ounces of cognac, then added another. Not one picture of Sherri Foote! Ooops!

There's always tomorrow. Go home, Gumshoe!
No! On second thought, Gumshoe, you still have some time today. Get yourself over to that condo in Inglewood. See if Patti left clues.

With fedora firmly atop my head, I pointed the Caddy toward Inglewood.

Three hours later I was back at Pop's, chewing on a piece of Kentucky fried chicken, washed down with Bourbon Barrel Stout, satisfied with my afternoon.

I had another puzzle piece tacked to my corkboard.

FIFTY-EIGHT

Thursday, September 19. Until yesterday it could have been July 28, so far as my case was going. Pop was downstairs sipping a cup of steaming coffee when I emerged from the bath. He pointed to the cork board.

"I see new visitors on your board, Alan," he began. "Are we celebrating? Pull up a chair and bring me up to date."

"Sure, Pop. First off, I sent Liz to Arizona to get a court order for collection of a debt; I'm meeting Carla this morning at the office with a casting of my mystery corpse; I have a photo album we found in Sherri Foote's home which doesn't appear to be hers; Sherri didn't sell her house, but it lies empty, and some fellow says he bought it to flip and was going to show it this weekend to potential buyers; Sherri is one of three missing ladies; two new murders happened within this last week. Shall I continue?"

"There's more?"

"I'm just getting started, Pop," I said, shaking

my head. "One of those killed in the latest murder was Bill from the marina."

"Oh, no! Bill? What did he do?"

"Wrong place, wrong time is my guess. And not only him, but the owner as well. And get this, Pop, same gun was used to kill the Whites and that policeman over ten years ago."

"That husband of Rachel what's-her-name?" Pop interjected. "Same gun that left three slugs in your wall, too, Son, don't forget that! More coffee?"

"Please," I handed him my mug, and nodded.

"Now, the three new photos on the board are some I found just yesterday. Looks like Patti hired a private eye to snoop. The foursome all lovey-dovey in the group photo are--left to right--Gina, Tom Wellings, Sherri and some guy I don't recognize. The other two are puzzling. Sherri is definitely arguing with her husband in this one," I said, pointing . . . "and this one is Tom and Gina embracing.

Also, I found a notepad by the phone in Patti's den. Only one word, but she repeated it over and over: *Bastard! Bastard! Bastard!* She must have written it nine or ten times."

"She obviously meant Tom," Pop said, running his hand through his hair; "no clue who the guy is, huh? Not Sherri's husband, I can see that from the photos."

"Just more for me to ponder, Pop. I'm heading to the office. I brought back a stack of reading material from Patti's condo. Going through it today."

* * *

As I unlocked the office back door the phone was ringing. It was 7:30 a.m.

"I'm in Phoenix, Gumshoe. I've been on the phone with a Judge Spalton. He's the judge our Judge Hamlin hooked me up with. Going to see him just before lunch with my paperwork. Easy trip. Love my, uh, our car. Anything new there?"

"Not yet. Every time I try to stir things up they just settle to the bottom."

"You need me, Bossman. I'll be back soon." "Just bring back a check."

"Never fear, Bossman. The Fox is on the job."

I had to smile. "Right. Go get 'em, Fox." We hung up.

The tape Liz brought back from Gunn and Gunn was on my list of things to attend to, so I flipped it on and listened to the conversation. Liz had hit the highlights quite well, but one thing Mr. Gunn had emphasized was that while Gina was with the firm for only about a year, she had a great teacher in Sherri Foote.

Gina was well on her way to becoming a star for our firm is the way Mr. Gunn had expressed it.
Became very adept in explaining and guiding clients through the task of asset planning and revocable trusts. Sorry she left us.

A thought struck me. Using my smart phone I took ten shots of the photos in the photo album we retrieved from the Foote household and the group shot I had liberated from Patti's place. Then I called Gunn and Gunn and asked to speak with Mr. Betters.

"Mr. Garrett. What can I do for you this morning?"

I asked him if I could forward the photos, to see if he or any staff could identify any of the subjects.

"Certainly. If I can't, I'll pass it around to some others. Incidentally, we have made several attempts to reach Sherri with no success. You say some realtor claims he intends to sell her home? I'll have staff run a title search on the property and let you know."

"Thanks. That will be a big help."

We ended the call. I sent the photos. Twenty minutes later I received a call from Peter Gunn.

"Garrett. Photos are of a past client, a Mr. and Mrs. Caldwell. The photos go back probably twelve-thirteen years or so. Clients of Sherri Foote. They died in a house fire, the whole family--five of them--in September, 2009."

"So sorry to hear that, Sir. Next of kin?"

"Ahh, spoken like a true detective, Mr. Garrett. I'll have someone pull the file. At this point, no laws broken in sending it to you."

"Thanks. I'm tied up this morning. I'll pick it up this afternoon."

"Don't bother," he laughed, "I'll have it couriered to you today after three. I may need to hire a good P.I. one day; your assistant says you're a good one."

* * *

The sheaf of papers I had taken from Patti's condo proved interesting--mostly back and forth notes with a private eye. In one note, he identified the unknown fellow in the group photo as Alex Graham.

"Huh! So, you're Alex Graham!" I said aloud, as though I were being introduced to a stranger. "How do you figure into this vicious alliance? Your son said you are a realtor. Somehow, I think it's more."

Carla walked in . . . right on time.

"Do you want to take a look at the bust of our lady now, or should we enjoy lunch before we get down to business?"

"Let's do lunch first, Carla. I need a clear brain; I don't want to think about what I'm going to have for lunch while I'm discussing business. What do you feel like?"

"Burger and fries. Your little pub around the corner looks great."

So it was back to the Shellback Tavern. The waitress, Karen, came over with a laugh. "Four beers?"

"Why not?" Then I turned to Carla, "Or would you prefer a wine?"

"No. A beer sounds good. In a glass, though."

We ordered, ate, then walked back to the office. I tossed my fedora at the rack. It swung back and forth as if to say *look at me*.

Carla looked impressed but refrained from mouthing a compliment. Instead, she had me close my eyes and sit in one of the two chairs in front of Liz's desk. Then she opened the bag and stood the bust on the desk facing me. That done, she sat next to me.

"Okay," she said. "Open your eyes, Alan, and tell me who you see."

FIFTY-NINE

There was no question in my mind. The lady staring at me was indeed, one of my missing ladies. Carla saw the look of recognition, the frown and emotion spill across my face.

"It looks like I hit a nerve, Alan. You know this lady, right?"

"Oh, yes. Look at this photo." I retrieved the framed photo I had picked up while in Fallbrook. "The DNA I have from her house doesn't match, but your creation can only be one person: Sharon Etts! You've done an incredible job, Carla. How did you manage the recreation?"

"Portraiture. Comparing bone structure of the known subject to photos of faces with similar characteristics. It's been used for over a hundred years. Plus a lot of guesswork, of course."

"But," we both blurted out, then laughed . . . I continued, "Carla, how could a package of mystery DNA samples be confused with Sharon's?"

"I have no idea, Alan Garrett, but I have a Private Investigator friend, who I'm sure, will be able to make some sense of it."

My mind was working overtime. One puzzle piece falls into place, but more fall off the table.

"What do I owe you?"

She gave me her regular price, then chopped it in half. I waggled my finger and added thirty percent to her original amount.

"This has been a breakthrough, Carla. Much obliged."

"Alan, I . . ."

"Yeah?" I said, while examining the bust of the dead Etts woman.

"Alan, uhhh, thanks for the lunch."

"You're welcome. Is something wrong?"

"No. Well, maybe. One of my clients asked me out. I've been toying with it for two weeks. I wanted to speak with you about it. I like you, Alan. I know you're a busy man, just as I am a busy woman, but I feel secure in myself, and am ready for a permanent relationship.

The fellow that asked me out is probably not the one, but there have been others, Alan, just as there will be again."

"Ah, Carla. You have me at a disadvantage, but I must say, I appreciate your directness. You're secure in yourself because you've proven yourself; I've just begun . . . haven't even solved my first case."

"Oh, Alan, I . . ."

"No, Carla, listen. I'm not ready to settle down. If this is your time to have a serious relationship, you must look elsewhere. I am hoping though, that we can be the best of friends."

"Oh, Alan, you are a special friend."

We embraced, I kissed her cheek and she mine.

"Whatever help I can give you on cases, make sure you call me."

She walked briskly to the front door, then on to her car.

I followed her to the sidewalk and waved. Then it was back in the office. I called Morris.

"Did you convince Eagle Rock to get a search warrant for Sherri's property?"

"You must have telepathy, Alan. I'm on my way to join them right now. They invited me. Have a cadaver dog with them. I'll let you know what we, uh, dig up."

"Not even the slightest bit funny, Morris." We laughed anyway.

"Before you go, Morris, did you have the chance to decipher the tape I gave you?"

"It's somewhere at H.Q. but I don't know what's been done with it so far. You know if you have an Apple computer, just go on their Garage Band program you can probably do that kind of thing yourself. Talk with you later."

Sharon Etts. Why cut her up and leave her in front of me? Why me? Was I just a convenience? Was there a message there somewhere?

I called Matt Wallis. No answer. Without giving him a reason for my call I asked him to get in touch.

My second call was to Barry Franks. He answered after four rings.

"Barry, Alan here. How are you feeling?"

"I'm still here."

"Up for a chat tomorrow?"

"Make it between 8:oo a..m. and 10:oo a.m. I'm

good for maybe a half hour; not much good after that. What's it about, Alan?"

"I'll explain tomorrow." I needed to change the subject. "Oh! How is Turk doing?"

"He's still hanging on. It won't be long, now."

"Would you feel up to a visit to him?"

"You would do that?"

"If you're up to it. I don't remember him at all from high school, but perhaps if I saw him . . ."

"He was a smart ass in school; you probably won't remember him."

"I'll see you just after 8:oo a.m. tomorrow."

A cherry red Audi pulled up in front just as I was polishing my best snifters. I made sure a fresh bottle of *Martell Cordon Bleu* was where I left it in a cabinet, and welcomed a gentleman from *Gunn and Gunn* into the office.

"Alan Garrett? Peter Gunn," he said, extending an arm.

"Ah, so good to meet you . . . I didn't expect the CEO to hand-deliver that file, but thank you, Sir."

"I needed fresh air. Haven't been down here in three or four years. Besides, I wanted to meet you; as Betters said to you this morning, there are times our firm finds it necessary to hire an outside investigator.

We decided I should come and make an assessment for the firm. We were impressed with your assistant. I see she is out at the moment."

"She is indeed. I've sent her to Arizona to collect on a court order."

"Arizona?! My goodness! I gather you aren't afraid to take your business wherever it leads."

"Can't be any different, Sir; if I take on a case

I see it through. Please have a seat, Mr. Gunn; would you care for a cognac?"

"Well, uh, why not? Please. And my name is Peter."

"Mine is Alan." I poured a respectable amount of *Cordon Bleu* into our snifters.

"Now, about the file I brought, I've included the work that both Sherri Foote and Gina Rowling supplied; they both did good work. Looks like no next of kin," Gunn continued, "but all the assets the Caldwells had were in trust. The beneficiary account to that trust is pretty much standard with a twist.

In first place of course were the children or any remaining children. In the event--as in this case--there were no living children, the assets were to go into a separate revocable trust controlled by Sherri herself, which is a bit strange . . ."

"You mentioned Gina Rowling was involved. In what way?"

"Sherri drafted the original document. Gina made changes at the Caldwell's direction; they insisted that should no family members remain, Sherri would be included as final beneficiary.

Sherri said she would only consider it if it were to go into a separate trust designed for worthy causes--but that she couldn't ethically draft such a document, so turned it over to Gina. And from there on, Alan, whatever assets were in the account aren't under our purview."

Mr. Gunn took another sip of his cognac while I mulled these facts over in my head. I toyed with my snifter, shaking my head, then took a sip.

"All legal?"

"Your money, your house, whatever--you can give it to whomever you wish."

"Oh, I know that, Peter, but to be the author and beneficiary of such a contract . . ."

"Obviously why Gina got involved. I see nothing completely out of context, here. Strange things do happen in walking the line of legalities. Very nice cognac, by the way."

"May I top it off for you?"

"Oh, no. I must be going."

"A question before you go, if I may," I said.

"Ask away."

"Were you able to do a title search on the Eagle Rock property to see if Sherri sold it recently?"

"Ahh, I have Betters and his staff working on that. We may have an answer already; let me check right now."

Mr. Gunn used my office to make the call. I only heard his side of the conversation, but it was filled with expletives and disbelief. When he hung up he walked back out into the main foyer and sat down, his face drained of blood. I again offered a "topper" of cognac; this time he didn't refuse.

"We have a dilemma, Alan. County records show the property was never owned by Foote or Ashcroft. In fact, legal title up to late 2007 was the file I just brought you: the Caldwells. Then title changed to The DeVry Memorial Trust."

I sat bolt upright. "Really?"

"Really, Alan." He shook his head. "Sadly, we had no idea. We thought Sherri and Jerry owned the home.

By 2007 the Caldwell account had been turned over to Gina. Sherri was her oversight . . . no one thought to check further.

You've uncovered a major breech; Gunn and Gunn owes you a huge debt. We'll be doing a review and taking corrective steps."

"I'm equally shocked Peter. I knew Sherri from high school; always thought she was a straight shooter. I guess we can all be fooled."

"I suppose," he said as he stood to go. We shook hands and I held the door for him.

* * *

I poured another couple of fingers of cognac, put the bottle away, and leaned back in my chair, eyes closed. Then opened the Caldwell jacket to begin reading.

Clients of Gunn and Gunn since 1995, the Caldwells became clients of Sherri Foote starting in 2003. Then in 2007 Gina Rowling took over as Gunn and Gunn representative, instituted a subsidiary trust in the event no family members remained: *The Roxanne DeVry Memorial Trust*--Sherri Foote as beneficiary . . . all signed and legal.

Another terribly repulsive thought flashed through my mind . . . all five members of the Caldwell family were destroyed in a fire in 2009. A tragic accident or a planned, horrible murder? I felt sick to my stomach.

SIXTY

The Roxanne DeVry Memorial Trust! I closed my eyes and tried to reconcile this . . . what did Peter Gunn call it? A twist? Yes, more than a twist . . . did Gina Rowling author it at the behest of Mr. Caldwell, or was he constrained against his better judgment? In either event, he made Sherri Foote the beneficiary . . . well within his rights.

But the name made no sense to me. Whose choice? Hopefully, I'll have the opportunity to ask Sherri.

I was startled awake by a hand gripping my shoulder.

"One of the first signs of old age, my friend."

I recognized the voice, but I was still half asleep, and the comment didn't fit my dream. I was somewhere in a cabin in the Northwest Territories sweeping sled dogs out the door. One of them turned on me and bit my shoulder. I looked up.

"Oh, it's you, Morris. I was dreaming. What time is it?"

"Time for a stiff drink, Mr. Gumshoe," Morris sighed. "Where's your brandy?"

"Bad News, Inspector?"

"The worst, I'm afraid, Alan, you were right. The back garden is a graveyard. A damn killing field. They've found three bodies so far--one male, two females. Eagle Rock coroner will do the work and share their findings with me. They suspect there are more."

"Damn!" I reached for the cognac, poured Morris a double, and a small one for myself. I shrugged, "I had company earlier.

What about the fellow who thought he had the place sold. Kid said the buyer was moving in next weekend?"

"He'll have to contend with about four officers, a backhoe and a lot of yellow tape. No one showed up while I was there. Maybe the kid was joking."

"But he had a key," I said. "No, he wasn't kidding."

"Let Eagle Rock worry about it, Alan. You don't have enough cognac."

SIXTY-ONE

Another day! What would this one bring? Pop wasn't up yet; I made the coffee. Pop was going to complain; he says my coffee is too strong. I steeled myself as I heard him coming down the stairs . . . oh, well!

"Good morning, Alan! Beautiful day isn't it?" He held his mug out for me to fill.

"Wow! That's robust coffee!" is all he said as he took a sip. "Rita and I had a lovely evening last night, Son. You were right, I still have some good years ahead of me."

"You were out last night, Pop? I thought you were upstairs watching TV or reading. I went to bed early; showered about nine and guess I was already dreaming when you got home."

"I guess you were," Pop agreed, smiling. "Even stepped over the squeaky step so I wouldn't wake you." Pop took another sip. "Good brew!"

"We went to see *The Treasure of the Sierra Madre* at the Old Town Music Hall in El Segundo," Pop continued, "delightful vintage venue stuff! Got home at 11:45 p.m. We'll be going again."

"Good for you, Pop. I'd like to know more, but I have an appointment this morning early. There are cookies on the counter. Keep smiling!"

I pointed my Caddy toward the Barry Franks bungalow in Torrance. I got there at 7:51 a.m. Barry was sitting as he had before, on the front porch. He waved as I pulled in the drive.

"Garrett!" Barry seemed genuinely pleased to see me. "Garrett, you're right on time. I just walked out here, wondering when you would show up."

"I do try to be timely," I grinned. "Drilled into me from an early age. Appreciate your seeing me." As he stood, I hopped up the steps, shook his hand, then gave him a hug. He was nothing but bones.

"How's your strength, Barry?"

"I have good days and bad. Today's starting out as a good day."

"You quit your security job, right?" I asked.

"Oh, yeah. The boss let me go a week ago today so I could be on unemployment. Then I had vacation coming, until my disability kicks in, so I'll be good until the end, Alan."

"Anything come up, you need some cash, let me know, Barry. I mean that, okay?"

"I appreciate that, Garrett, but I suspect you came here with purpose in mind . . . what's up?"

"Come right to the point, eh, Barry? No small talk." I laughed. "That's okay; I do have a serious bit of news and a request.

"Then spit it out." Barry's turn to laugh. "I can't wait around all year."

"We've identified the murdered lady at the reunion. She's Sharon Etts."

"Sharon?" Barry burst out. "Oh, no!" His shoulders sagged even more than before. "What did Matt say?"

"I suppose the police have contacted him, or soon will. We found out just yesterday. That's really not why I'm here, Barry. May I have a look at your final financial papers? Your trust and all."

"My trust? What do you want that for? Isn't it straight forward?"

"If it's handy, I'd like to go over it with you."

"Oh, sure. Wait here. It's in my file cabinet in my bedroom."

He disappeared and returned in a couple of minutes with a thin file folder. He handed it to me.

"Fill your boots, Garrett. God knows I've got nothing to hide."

I scanned the trust and found what I thought I would find.

"Just a minute, Barry, I want to check something." I handed him his trust, jumped down the steps to the Caddy, grabbed my attaché and pulled out a folder. As I retraced my steps to the porch I peeked at the last page of the Caldwell Trust.

"Here, my friend. Take a look."

Except for the name of the original trust which was *The Barry Franks Trust,* with its meager assets, everything else was identical to the Caldwell Trust, right down to the exact same trustees . . . and, as Barry had no next of kin, Sherri Foote was named as beneficiary.

The writer of the Barry Franks Trust, had in turn, set up a second revocable trust with Sherri Foote as *grantor.* And as in the Caldwell Trust this new trust was the Roxanne DeVry Memorial Trust!

"Yeah, Gina explained that to me when she drew it up," Barry said. "She said she and Sherri would be good stewards of my assets--house, car and all. They called it after Roxanne DeVry as a commitment to do good for young girls in trouble."

"Sounds good, Barry, but I have a gut feeling the Roxanne Trust is pure deception, preying on the unsuspecting and innocent."

"You're just being negative, Garrett. This is a good thing. What do you mean, *unsuspecting and innocent?*"

"I have more investigating to do, Barry. For the time being let's just say we're putting together a case. Shall we go see Terrance?"

"Let me call the hospital, Garrett. I spoke with him yesterday. He was pleased you and I would be coming. I told him I'd call when we're on our way."

Barry dialed a number. "Room 434 please . . . Terrance Perle . . .Is that right? . . . No, that's it, I guess, thanks."

Barry turned to me, "He died just after midnight, Garrett. He's gone. My best friend. Just to let you know-- you'll find out anyway--he had his trust made the same time as I did. We all sat around a breakfast table and drew them up."

"Who is we?" I asked. "And when?"

Barry looked at his trust. "This was August 3, 2008. I remember a group of us, the first meeting of the planning committee for the ten year reunion. We were at a cheesecake factory. There was Sherri, Gina, Tom and Patti . . . they were still together, Turk(Terrance),

Gerri and Roberto Alvarado, and me. I don't think there was anyone else there.

We decided to set up our own trusts. Of course, Sherri and Gina were experts among us, so we decided to use their expertise in drawing up the trusts. Those with next of kin put beneficiaries in place; Patti and Tom listed each other of course, as did Gerri and Roberto.

Turk was going to list me, and I him, but Sherri suggested we create a beneficiary trust for a worthy cause to put our assets in, in the event no one of us had family to leave assets to. Gina suggested naming it the Roxanne DeVry Memorial Trust, which suited everyone around the table.

So, Garrett, we all had a hand in creating the Roxanne DeVry Memorial Trust."

"I get the picture, Barry. All written showing Sherri Foote as being the *grantor*. Did you determine the worthy cause?"

"We left that as a *to be determined at a later date* thing."

"You hungry, Barry? Feel like breakfast?"

"No. I haven't been hungry in weeks. I eat only because I know I should. Let's go back to your *unsuspecting and innocent* remark. What are you thinking, Garrett?"

"Let me just say this. Sherri and her husband are in Africa. Supposed to have just arrived home this week. In the meantime their home has been emptied, completely vacant, even sold out from under them while they're gone. There were clues. We became suspicious of foul play, a search warrant was conducted, and bodies were found, buried in the garden."

"Bodies? No!" Barry blurted out. "At Sherri's? Who?"

"We don't know yet. I heard just yesterday, late. Police are still looking. Three so far. They think there may be several more. I'll know more later today. I'll keep you in the loop."

"Yeah, Okay. I'm wearing out, Garrett. Call before 6 p.m. if it's today."

We said our goodbyes. I drove to the nearest McDonald's for a coffee. McDonald's has good coffee. I'll skip breakfast. I sat in a window booth and dialed a number.

SIXTY-TWO

"Amy?"

"Yes?"

"Amy, Alan Garrett here. I have terrible news for you. The body of your roommate and landlord, Sharon, has been discovered. I'm sorry to say, but she's dead."

"Oh, no! How? When?"

"The worst, I'm afraid, Amy. She was our reunion lady."

"That can't be. You took Sharon's toothbrush and hairbrush for samples."

"That's what we thought, too, but there was a mistake somewhere. We actually had some expert face recreation done and identified her from the photo you gave me."

"But . . ."

"I know. We'll figure it out later. I just wanted you to know. One more thing, Amy, I need you to find Sharon's revocable trust . . . I'd like a copy of it."

"I know where it is, but I don't have proper authorization to get it. Oh, Alan, what will happen now?"

"If it's accessible, don't worry about what's

permissible, Amy, just fax me a copy of it if you can. The legal aspects of it will be sorted out later."

I hung up and made a second call. Second time to call Matt Wallis. Still no answer. I refilled my coffee and went over a couple of notes. I really should call Morris, I thought.

I made the call.

"Yeah, Gumshoe. What's up?"

I had to laugh. "What happened to all the niceties of telephone etiquette, Morris?"

"Got an answer on your taped voices if that's why you called," he continued, "they are all made by one person--a female."

"That's impossible, Inspector. There were different men and women on that tape,"

"Sorry, Alan. All female and all one person."

"Very puzzling, Morris. Very puzzling indeed. What's the latest on the Eagle Rock property?"

"I haven't spoken with them yet, but the day is still young. So what did you call about?"

"Just checking in to see if any of the dead in that back yard have been identified. I have another visit or two to make, then I'll be in my office."

"Where are you now?"

"Torrance. Visit with a reunion attendee, Barry Franks. He's terminal. I give him six months, tops. Gotta run, Morris. Swing by for a drink later if you want. Bring that tape with the voices if you would."

Next I called Gunn and Gunn. The receptionist connected me to Mr. Gunn's secretary. I asked her for a favor--for a photo and background details on Sherri's husband. I hung up, drained the coffee, and stood to leave when my cell phone sang out. Gunn and Gunn returning my call.

"Mr. Garrett, Eric Betters here from Gunn and Gunn. We must have a couple of photos around here. I'll send a photo as soon as we find one, and I'll have someone put together and send whatever file we have on the husband. You should have that in PDF format within an hour."

"Appreciate it. Still no sign of Sherri Foote's whereabouts?"

"Nothing at all. Hopefully, no foul play, Mr. Garrett."

"I agree, Sir. If I see or hear anything I'll let you know. Take care."

Time to head to the office. I was there in fifteen minutes, just in time to hear the tip line phone ring. I hustled to unlock the back door. Caught just the tail-end of the call . . . unfamiliar female voice, no distortion that I could tell.

. . . in danger. So is mine. Be careful. -- click!

I tossed my fedora toward the rack, and picked up the phone as my hat swung on the peg.   Too late. I punched *reverse* on the recorder and hit 'play'. *Alan! I'm calling to warn you. Your life is in danger. So is mine. Be careful.*

What the? I stared at the recorder for a moment as if to say, *Tell me more!* But it sat there like the lifeless machine that it was, and wouldn't reveal another syllable. Instinctively, I reached for my weapon, checked the cartridges to insure I had a full load, then thrust it back in it's holster. *You're a little bit jumpy, aren't you, Gumshoe!* I scolded myself, *Maybe you need some breakfast.* I wondered what Pop was doing. I called him.

"Hi, Pop. You busy?"

"Not really. What's up?"

"Wondering if you've had breakfast. I've had about five cups of coffee but no food. I'm just a bit hungry. You want to join me?"

"Yes, but join me and Rita instead, Alan. She and I spoke earlier, and are having brunch together at 11:00 a.m. Come on up. I'll rustle up enough for the three of us."

"You sure I'll not be in the way?"

"For heaven's sakes, no. Come on up, Alan."

"On my way."

The meal was simple but tasty. Roasted chicken with sautéed vegetables. The company was delightful. Rita was bright and cheery--just what Pop needed. It wouldn't bother me if he took their relationship to the next level . . . whatever that was to be.

"Something on your mind, Son?" Pop asked as we sat and enjoyed a glass of iced tomato juice. He had obviously seen me deep in thought. I decided to share one or two of them.

"Yeah, Pop. I have a few twists and turns in my case, one of which is that we identified the dead reunion lady, and she's not as I expected. Five people are dead, shot with the same weapon, and somehow I know they are linked, but haven't yet pieced together the connection."

"Same gun that shot up your office, right?" Pop interjected.

"Same gun, Pop."

"What about the arsonist?" Rita asked. "Is that fire connected?"

"I think so," I nodded. "why else would I be targeted?"

"So, what's your next move, Alan?" Pop asked.

"I'm working on another angle, but I'm not ready to share it yet."

"What do you mean, you're not willing to share it yet?" Pop seemed mildly irritated. "We're family."

"Now, Roland," Rita spoke up, frowning. "Alan knows what he's doing."

"Thanks, Rita," I laughed. "Pop and I often have differences of opinion, but we almost always end the day with a glass together . . . unless you steal him off to the theater." I winked at her; Pop mumbled something incoherent.

I stood. "Thanks for lunch, Pop. It's back to work."

* * *

My email had a large PDF attachment from Gunn and Gunn. I opened it and printed it off. Then I leaned back in Liz's chair and read it--a brief on Sherri Foote's husband, one Jerry Ashcroft. Along with the brief was a nice close-up portrait of Sherri and Jerry together at some Gunn and Gunn celebration. Jerry I didn't know, Sherri I would never have recognized. Didn't look like a happy, loving couple. Just my opinion.

Jerry was a self-employed computer tech. Among his many clients was Gunn and Gunn. I copied the photo and stuck it on the cork-board.

SIXTY-THREE

While waiting for Morris I called Sergeant Hopkins at the 21st Precinct.

"Sergeant. This is Alan Garrett. Don't know if you remember me, but I'm investigating the deaths relating to the gun used against the Whites and the marina people."

"Of course, I remember you, Garrett. Been expecting a call from you or Inspector Morris. How can I help you?"

"My office is delving into the estate planning of those involved. We've discovered a string connecting a few of the deceased in this area, and wondering if the string continues to the Whites and possibly the marina owner."

"Not sure what you're theory is, but we haven't opened any of the files at the marina, so whatever they had is still in the marina's office, locked up.

Now, so far as the White's paperwork is concerned, we allowed a rep from their attorney's office to remove it. He was there a week ago or so."

"Oh?"

"Yes. Just looking for any wills or financials, bank

accounts and such. My guys were there and monitored him. Took out two or three boxes of stuff. Obviously, no valuables or personal items were taken."

"Understood. I'd like to come down and pick up the files from the marina, and the files from Regina's home."

"What for, Garrett?"

"We're looking for inconsistencies, odd or peculiar retirement documents. I'll be doing this as part of my investigation. I have no problem in making your precinct the lead, Sergeant--you'll be thoroughly involved."

"Oh! Okay, when do you want to come down?"

"Tomorrow morning will be fine if you're available."

"Tomorrow's Saturday. Make it 9:00 a.m. I'm off, but I'll take a couple of hours to help. Meet me at the marina."

Morris called to tell me he'd be at least an hour. He'd been tied up on a call involving a shooting. I told him we could make it another time, but he seemed anxious to meet. I think it was the cognac.

I stood to take another look at the photo of Sherri and her husband when the fax lit up and began spitting out pages--five total--The Sharon Etts Trust. Amy had come through. *Thanks Amy!* I said under my breath.

The first page--the cover sheet from Amy caught my eye. *"To Alan Garrett, Here is the Trust. I've locked up Sharon's house. I can't continue to live there, knowing she's dead. I'll be in a motel tonight, but not sure where I'll be staying starting tomorrow. Haven't made any plans, but I can't stay at Sharon's. I am very frightened. My cell phone is 555-607-1122.*

I stapled the trust together, then skimmed over the instruction and assets, all of which looked nicely and professionally prepared. It was dated May 10, 2019.

My eye then fell upon the distribution portion. The three trustees' names were exactly the same as the Barry Franks Trust. Illegal? No, but interesting. The beneficiary was disturbing, but as I suspected: The Roxanne DeVry Trust, with Sherri Foote as grantor and beneficiary to be determined.

There was a scribbled note in black ink at the bottom, crossing out the instructions for the second trust but leaving the last few words 'to be determined'. I could only presume Sharon had written the note. It read as follows:

This trust is flawed. I feel as though I was rushed, even coerced into making it. After much consideration, I am revoking it as of this date. I will draft my own trust with the help of my lawyer, John Cantrell. In the meantime, if anything should happen to me, all of my assets are to go to Amy Wynne as beneficiary or for dispersal as she sees fit.

Signature: <u>Sharon Etts,</u> date: <u>May 22, 2019.</u>

Witness: ________________ date: ____________

  c.c. Gina Rowling ✓
    Sherri Foote
    John Cantrell ✓

I understand now why Amy was spending the night in a motel and determined to lay low. She must have read the trust for the first time today. My brain screamed, *you need to call her, Gumshoe! Now!*

I dialed her number.

"Amy! Alan Garrett here. I just got your fax--thank you."

"Mr. Garrett! Did you read Sharon's note at the end? I am terrified. I can't stay at that house, knowing that Sharon met with such a horrible death."

"I know it's early," I continued, "but what are your immediate plans, if any?"

"I have none, Alan. I just packed up the back of my car and split."

"Her attorney, John Cantrell. How did she choose him? Is he her family attorney?"

"Oh, yes. She used him to settle her mother's estate years ago. I've met him; funny, wizened old man. Very proper, but with a sense of humor."

"Listen," I said. "I have an appointment tomorrow morning at Sandpoint Marina in the Hermosa Beach area, I'm meeting with the Police Department there at 9:00 a.m. Would you care to join me? I may have an idea or two for you to consider."

"Oh, I'd be in the way, Alan. No, I'll do my own thing."

"Okay. If you change your mind, call me."

"I will. 9:00 a.m. The Sandpoint, Right?"

We said our goodbyes. I reread Sharon's note at the end of her retracted trust. I felt better.

The check marks after Gina Rowling and this attorney, John Cantrell told me she had emailed those two notifications off immediately, and that she hadn't yet sent it to Sherri. Did that result in her being butchered? I think so. Did Amy also come to that same conclusion? I think so.

My electric strike buzzed. Morris was at the front door. I let him in.

"Inspector," I said, and walked to shake his hand as I welcomed him in. "Busy day."

"Yeah, right. Some guy barricaded himself and four hostages in a credit union on Pacific Coast Highway for three hours. We were the back-up crew, assisting SWAT. Frustrating as hell. I would have done everything differently. Damn!"

"Are you asking for a drink, Morris. Quite a story." I laughed. "Must have taken you ten minutes to perfect it on your way over here."

"Story, hell, Alan! Gospel truth! SWAT will get all the credit. The real hero of the day is Brad. He talked the guy down."

"You talking about Bradley Swazer, your young assistant, just out of high school?"

"Yeah, Gumshoe, who knew? So, anything exciting happen in your day?"

"Actually, yes, Morris, but let's start with Eagle Rock. Did you hear anything from them?" I reached for the cognac.

"Five bodies, Alan. So sad! Positive I.d.'s on three--recent buries--but the other two are, as yet, unknown . . . been in the ground a long time--at least three years, maybe more."

"And?" I handed Morris a full snifter as I asked the question.

"And, of the three more recent casualties, one was identified as Trudy Wells. I believe she was a fellow graduate, Alan?"

Without waiting for an answer, he continued, "A man and woman were identified from fingerprints on file as Jack and Wilma Brighton, husband and wife, of Santa Monica. Disappeared about six months ago. All three dead about the same time. The other two will take a day or two more to identify. Ran through AFIS. Not a thing. One man, one woman."

"Perhaps I can help find their names, Morris. Here, read this while I send an email," I said, handing Morris the emailed trust Amy had sent me. "Give me a moment."

The email went to Peter Gunn, asking if any clients other than the Brightons had disappeared in the last five years.

Morris was rereading the trust, sipping his cognac.

"So, what do you think, Inspector?"

"Concerning, for sure. Do you think she'll be alright?"

I nodded. "She seems quite capable. I was afraid we'd find Trudy in that ground, Inspector. Has anyone contacted her parents?" I asked.

"Yes, they will be on their way up tomorrow to identify the remains. Swazer will assist them."

"What do we know about the Brightons? Any family?"

"Don't know. I expect we'll find out soon enough," Morris said, shaking his head. "I must go, Gumshoe. It's Friday, and I try to hit the road early on Fridays whenever I can. Oh, Yeah, here's the thumb drive with the voices no longer distorted."

He drained the last of his cognac, and stood. I opened the door; as we stood in the doorway shaking hands, we heard a car engine, followed by three shots. Morris fell. An angry hornet ripped into my left arm just above the elbow.

I watched a gray sedan roar down the street and round the corner up Ocean as I dragged the Inspector inside and leaned him against a wall. I grabbed the desk phone -- called 911 for an ambulance, then looked at my own wound. The bullet had taken the hair and carved out a groove of flesh. I wrapped it with a bit of gauze and taped it. No big deal.

The floor around Morris was turning red with his blood, but I jerked my head up when I heard his raspy voice.

"I'm okay, Alan, really, I'm okay, Dammit! I just need to call my wife, to tell her I'll be late."

"Quiet, Old Man! You have a hole in your right shoulder and there's a quart of blood on my floor. What's your home phone number?"

I dialed. "Hi, Mrs. Morris. Alan Garrett here."

"Oh, yes, Alan. Carl isn't home yet. I'm expecting him any moment."

"That's why I'm calling. He's with me. He's going to be okay, but a bit late. He's on his way to the hospital with a slight gunshot wound."

"Let me talk to her!" I could hear Morris in his weakened state trying to yell at me. "Give me that phone, Alan!"

I handed Morris my cell phone, and listened in on the conversation.

"No!" Morris was rasping on the phone. "Listen to me. You don't need to come into Manhattan Beach, Lucy! I'll be home before you . . ." He turned to me, "She hung up, Gumshoe. Why did you tell her all that?" Then he dropped the cellphone as he passed out.

An ambulance screeched to a stop in front. In two minutes he was whisked off to the hospital. I mopped up all the blood, thinking, *there were two people in that car. I'm sure of it.*

SIXTY-FOUR

I followed Morris to the Kaiser Hospital on Sepulveda. I found him in emergency. I called his wife and directed her to the correct facility, then held her hand as he went into the operating room.

The surgery went well; the bullet missed the shoulder socket, went through soft tissue and came out the back just above the fleshy armpit area.

The surgeon pushed through the double doors of the operating room to meet with us.

"Very fortunate you got him here when you did," he started. "He had lost almost three units of blood. But, he's going to pull through."

"What happens now?" Mrs. Morris asked the surgeon.

"He'll stay here for two days, after which he'll be on bed-rest at home if you can tie him down. Then he'll undergo a four-week regimen of physical therapy, with limited physical work."

"I've never been able to keep that man from his work," Mrs. Morris bemoaned. "What happens if he ignores the order?"

"He could lose the complete use of the arm."

"Please put that in writing," she insisted.

She turned to me. "What happened Alan? He spent the better part of the day in a hostage situation, walked away unscathed, and then gets shot while enjoying a visit on his way home. I don't understand it. First Carl's car gets burned up at your place, now this. Are you a curse, Alan?"

"I hope not, Mrs. Morris. This case we're working on keeps getting more and more complex. I'm so sorry, Ma'am."

"Well, Alan, thank you for your quick thinking. I'm going to stay here for awhile. You may as well be on your way."

"Tell him I have an appointment tomorrow morning, but I'll get in here as soon as I can--probably by noon."

"I'll tell him," she assured me.

I headed straight for Pop's.

* * *

Saturday morning, 9:00 a.m. Hopkins was right on time.

"I heard the Inspector was shot yesterday, Garrett."

"You heard right, Sergeant. Happened in my doorway. Means we're getting closer to solving this case."

Hopkins raised an eyebrow. "Related to what case?"

"All of it. The Whites, Regina, the reunion lady, five bodies buried in a backyard in Eagle Rock."

"Five bodies? Have they been identified?"

"Working on it. Not all, not yet."

"Okay, Garrett, let's go inside. Grab the files and whatever papers you want to borrow and get going. I have plans for the day." He unlocked the marina office door.

I thumbed through the first file cabinet. All were of boat owners with long-term moorings, and photos of Marina doings. The second had Regina's business tax papers going back to 2009. The third cabinet was the treasure I was looking for: housing her financial documents, employee agreements, and retirement documents. This was worth gathering up, but her will or other final papers were missing.

I put the papers in a box I had brought, and nodded to Hopkins that I was finished.

"Let's head to her home. She may have her final documents there."

We locked up and walked to our cars, just in time to see another vehicle pull into the drive.

"Who's this?" Hopkins asked, putting his hand on his weapon.

"Ahhh, it's Amy. I told her I'd be here. I may ask her to accompany us if that's okay with you."

"Sure, sure, but let's hustle up," Hopkins said. "The wife made plans I wasn't aware of when I said I had a couple of hours this morning."

Amy agreed. We followed the sergeant in our own cars just a matter of few miles to Regina's home. She lived in a gated community. Hopkins had made arrangements for us to enter, and gave us a map to the address. We entered.

Regina's office walls were lined with photos and books. Hopkins looked bored and restless.

"You've not been in here since her death?" I

asked him. In my mind I wondered at the Sergeant's methodology. I shook my head.

"A forensics team should go through this place completely. There may be a useful clue or two."

"Not enough time, Garrett. I'm short-staffed as it is. Fill your boots. I'll leave the key. Bring it back when you bring the files. I'm leaving. Lock up, and . . ." he smiled, "don't destroy anything."

"Before you go, Sergeant," I asked, "do you remember the name of the fellow who picked up all the papers from The White's home?"

"Not offhand--tall, thirties or forties--but I think I have his business card in my car, if you want to follow me outside."

"I'll get it," said Amy as she followed Hopkins out.

She returned, card in hand. "What are we doing here, Alan?"

"We're looking for any retirement plans, trusts, wills or any such files of the owner, Regina Leone."

"She's dead?"

"She's dead, and I have the feeling her death is connected to Sharon's in some macabre way." I glanced at the card. I didn't recognize the name, John Drake, Esq. but the company was Gunn and Gunn.

I turned to Amy.

"So you decided to come up here to join me," I said, "what are your thoughts?"

"I'm in limbo, Alan. You said you may have an idea or two, so I stared at the motel room ceiling all last night, didn't sleep a minute, and . . .
here I am."

"I see. Fair enough. I work in Manhattan

Beach and live there with my Pop. We have lots of room there. How about following me. We'll stop at Pop's for lunch. Then I need to visit a friend in the hospital--while I'm doing that, you can relax. We'll sort a few things out when I return. Sound reasonable?"

"Sure, I guess," came her reply.

I spent a half hour going through files, pulling out several to add to a box, while Amy searched through photographs for any faces that might have visited Sharon in Fallbrook. I wished Liz was my partner for that chore, but Amy might surprise me.

We locked up, waved to the gatekeeper, and in separate cars, headed for Pop's.

SIXTY-FIVE

"Pop, meet Amy Wynne. Amy is staying with us awhile until she gets herself sorted out."

"Oh! My! Well, my dear, welcome to our humble abode," Pop winked. "Alan called me and asked if the two of you could barge in on me for lunch, so, what was I to do?

Take your jackets off and go wash up. Alan will show you to the bathroom. Lunch will be ready in three minutes."

Cold cuts, slices of tomatoes, pickles, cheese, condiments, and of course, bread and butter--with mugs of steaming tomato bisque soup. Choice of beer, juice or soft drink for Amy . . . she selected a beer; Pop and I did the same.

That's when both Pop and Amy noticed the wrapped blood-stained gauze on my arm.

"What happened to you, Alan?" Pop asked.

"Shot," I said simply. "Yesterday."

"Let me see that!" Amy demanded.

"It's just a scratch," I contended.

"Let me look at your 'scratch'." she countered. "You could have blood poisoning and not even know it."

I took a swig of *Bourban Barrel Stout* as she peeled the gauze away from my arm.

"Hmm, you seem to have cleaned it well. The gauze doesn't stick. Took quite a groove out of your arm, though. Do you have more gauze?"

"Yes, doctor," I said, smiling. "Now just eat. When I get back, we'll set up your bedroom. I'll sleep on the couch so . . ."

Pop picked up on the conversation. "What about Rita?" he interrupted. "She has two extra bedrooms. She would love to have a lodger, even if just for a few days or weeks."

"Sure. Ask her," I said. "It's a consideration."

"Just a minute!" Amy demanded. "Go ahead and ask all you want, but I have the final say in what I do for the next few days or weeks!"

"You're right, of course," I said. I was beginning to see a stronger lady than first presented. I liked her.

We enjoyed the lunch, thanked Pop, I prepared to head to the hospital. As I pulled my windbreaker on, Amy said, "I'm going with you."

"Why?"

"I've met your dad. I feel quite comfortable. Now I'd like to meet your policeman friend. It will   help me decide how and where I wish to spend the next few days. Oh! Then I'd like to see your office. I'm going with you."

Sure, why not? Strange lady . . . hmm, don't know. Haven't decided yet.

I held the Caddy door for Amy, hopped behind the wheel, then off to inspect the Inspector.

SIXTY-SIX

Morris was sitting up, his left hand wrapped around a steaming mug, drinking a vegetable-based drink when we arrived.

"Hi, Alan. A word of thanks is in order, so, thanks." Then looking up at Amy, he said, "Miss, hello. I'm Carl Morris. They have me tied to this bed, so you'll forgive me for not shaking hands."

He lifted the mug. "Hot V-8 juice, or some kind of vegie juice. Tastes better than it sounds."

"Very good for you, I'm sure. I'm Amy. Amy Wynne. I'm visiting Alan and his dad for a few days. Good to meet you."

"Just to let you know, Inspector, Amy was the roommate of our reunion victim, Sharon Etts."

"Of course, now I understand. You're the young lady who sent the Sharon Etts Trust to Alan. Good to meet you, Amy. You'll be safe with Alan; that is," and Morris tried to laugh, "unless you stand in his office doorway."

We made small talk for a few minutes. I could see Morris' strength was waning.

A nurse walked in and pointed to her watch. Morris shrugged.

"Well," Morris said, "that means visiting is over, children. Lucy was here all morning. She left ten minutes before you arrived, and I'm worn out. Amy, sorry I'm not much company. I'd like to continue our chat. Perhaps in a few days if you're still in the area."

"She'll be around," I assured him. Amy only frowned.

Once outside the hospital, Amy reminded me we were on our way to my office. I just smiled.

Pulling into my parking spot, I unlocked the back entrance, and pushed the door open for Amy to enter. Next I took the boxes of files inside. And set them on the two chairs facing Liz' desk. I looked around for Amy, then realized she had ducked into the bathroom upon entering.

I inspected the front entry; I had done a pretty good job cleaning the floor of blood the day before, but decided it could use a bit more. Then I remembered *Oh, Oh, the shower stall is full of bloody towels. Amy will flip out if she opens that shower door.*

I sat at Liz' desk and grabbed a folder from the box I'd marked <u>R. Leone.</u> Amy was just rounding the corner, coming into the main foyer.

"I found some plastic bags," she smiled, "would you like me to bag the bloody towels to take to your place for washing?"

"Yes!" I was indeed surprised. "Yes, please, and thank you. I didn't have time yesterday."

"I understand that. Saving a man's life is a bit more important."

"There should be latex gloves in an upper

drawer. Put a pair on."

"Have them," she sang out.

I noticed the tip line light blinking as I skimmed through several papers in one file, laid it aside and grabbed another folder. *The tip line can wait*, I thought.

After a few attempts I came across what I was looking for: a folder marked Estate Planning. Stapled to the inside of the folder was Regina's trust. Stapled to the front of the folder was a business card identical to the one Hopkins had given us. I sat bolt-upright as I read.

Amy returned just in time to hear me whistle and say, "Strange."

"What's strange, Alan . . . or should I call you Gumshoe?"

"Either is fine," I laughed. "Take a look at this trust, Amy. It's dated November 2006. Notice the format is the same as Sharon's, and the trustees are exactly the same as well.

The beneficiary schedule is a bit different. In first place is Chris Evans. There is no other immediate family member to inherit, and Chris died in 2009, so the trust assets, including the marina, her house, car--in short, everything was to go to his widow.

But just this summer, July 20, in fact . . . one week before the reunion, Regina, with expert help, changed the trust beneficiary from the widow to the Roxanne DeVry Trust to be directed by Sherri Foote, beneficiary to be determined at a later date. The expert help she used for this change was the person on the business card, a John Drake, Esq. whoever he was, and was witnessed by Norman Nestling, another name unfamiliar to me.

What do you make of this, Amy?"

"Are you kidding me, Alan?" she exclaimed, sitting down in the just emptied chair. "How many of these DeVry trusts are there? Alan, they can't all be legal, can they?"

"I suspect none of them are legal, Amy. What's the phone number on that card?"

Amy called out the numbers as I dialed. It picked up on the first ring. *Leave a message. We'll return the call.*

"Perhaps they're closed Saturdays, Alan." Amy suggested. "Attorneys make plenty in five days per week anyway."

"You may be right, but an odd way for a professional firm to answer the phone, don't you think? Plus, I don't recognize that phone number."

"By the way, Alan," Amy said sweetly, "and I don't mean to tell you what seems obvious, but your phone has been blinking since we walked in here, detective."

"Yes," I answered with a droll look. "I told myself I had a message over fifteen minutes ago, Miss. Then I told myself I would look at it later. It's now later."

I picked up the tip line and pressed *play.*

Alan, did you get my message? I'm sorry I blamed you for the reunion murder. Now I know you didn't do it. I know who did. Here's my phone number. Please call me. Soon!

She left a phone number.

Wait a minute, I asked myself, w*asn't it Amy that sent that last desperate tip line call?*
I turned to Amy.

"Didn't you call my tip line yesterday?"

"Not me. I faxed you, silly man. I didn't even know you had a tip line. Find out who it is. Call the number."

I called.

Third ring; a man's voice--deep. "It's done."

"Who's this?" I asked.

"Who's this?" came the voice on the other end--surprised.

"This is Alan Garrett, private investigator. I . . ."

Click!

Oh, Oh! Someone didn't want to talk to me.

More than one way to find out who called. I trotted to my office, pulled a folder off my desk, thumbed through my notes and found the names of the reunion attendees. Found it.

"Amy, let me take you back to Pop's. I have a little run to make. I'll be back later."

"No! I have a better idea. Let's go back to your dad's place and pick up my camera. I'm a photographer, remember? Maybe some interesting pictures wherever it is we're going."

SIXTY-SEVEN

We could see the smoke and the emergency vehicles as soon as we rounded the corner and pulled onto Russell Way. The Alvarado home at the end of the cul-de-sac was totally engulfed in flames, as were the homes on either side.

Amy jumped from the Cadillac, camera in hand, and trotted as near as she was allowed. I looked for the chief on scene. There were no media people on the street. Only one squad car.

"Anyone inside?" I asked the chief.

"Are you the owner?" he asked.

"No. Private Eye. The owners of the end house are part of my investigation. I was contacted by someone living there within the last few hours. I called back just a bit ago, someone inside hung up on me. I knew we had a problem, but I didn't expect a fire."

"Stay out of the way, Sir. We'll let you know."

The media and another squad car arrived at the same time, the cul-de-sac was beginning to cram with emergency vehicles. I backed the Caddy out and parked half-way down the main street, then walked back, searching for Amy. I found her, camera in hand, in an animated conversation with a lawman.

"Alan! Come here!" she shouted. "Officer Mallory has a question for you!"

I joined them just as the last of the visible flames were being beaten down, allowing the fire crew to enter. The cop held out his hand, I shook it.

"You're the fellow who took Inspector Morris to the hospital, eh? Quick thinking. Amy here says you visited him already today. You must be buddies."

"We've have spent quite a bit of time working jointly on a murder case."

"That must be the one on the cruise ship, right?"

"Right."

"I'll let you know what we find inside," he said. Then, turning to Amy, "Follow me."

What the hell? Why is Amy going with him? I asked myself. *Did she just get a job as a police photographer?*

Ten minutes later she returned to my side, smelling of smoke.

"Three bodies, Alan," she whispered, just barely audibly, shaking her head. "Sitting in what's left of chairs. One was a youngster, the other two were adults, burned beyond recognition! Fire chief says they were tied up. Hard to look at, Alan, but I got a lot of pictures for Mallory."

"Are you okay?" I asked. The adrenalin and excitement of the moment seemed to have been replaced by nausea . . . she was visibly shaken by her experience.

"Yes, I'll be okay." She handed me her camera before putting her hands on her knees. After thirty seconds with eyes closed she stood upright and gave me a smile.

"There. All better now." She emptied her lungs with a long breath of air. "Let's go home. I need to email Mallory these pictures."

I'm thinking, *Home?*

*   *   *

The photos were graphic. Inside, the horror of the three dead; outside, fire crews standing on the roof, or almost in the midst of flames . . . I stood over Amy's shoulder as she scrolled through them before emailing them off to Mallory. Ten minutes later he emailed her back. *Thanks, Miss Wynne. Sending them off to Chief James at Fire Station #3. If you have time Monday, swing by the station. Garrett has directions. Lt. Mallory.*

Pop came downstairs. "Rita's coming up at 5:00 p.m. That's only ten minutes. She and I are cooking tonight. We'll need your kitchen, Alan, so you two, kindly retire to the den. Then, if you're into it, we'll play a game of cards or perhaps, scrabble after dinner. I must warn you, Rita plays for blood."

"She sounds like fun," Amy said.

Pop opened the door for Rita. She was carrying a roasting pan in front of her, and a shopping bag under her arm. I took the pan from her and set it on the stovetop, then Amy and I retired to the den and flipped on the 6 o'clock news.

The fire was mentioned only briefly, with pictures of the firemen manning hoses, but no details of the three dead inside.

"You scooped everyone, Amy. Every other news photographer got the periphery; you got the heart of the story, inside and out."

"Dinner!" Pop yelled from the kitchen.

We enjoyed the evening, complete with shortbread cookies and vanilla ice cream for dessert, followed by a rousing game of partnered pinochle. Pop and Rita won, but the game was close. During the evening the ladies made arrangements for Amy to spend the night with Rita.

Pop retired upstairs leaving me to the solitude of the evening at my desk, sipping cognac, staring at the cork-board with all its sets of eyes staring back at me.

The Sharon Etts mop of red hair--my first photo that reunion evening--now identified and flipped back over, took her _rightful?_ place among the other three from that evening. Next I searched the yearbook pictures pinned below those four,   and found Trudy Wells and Gerri Kitchens; I added their smiling faces to the top row.

Then I thought about that first phone call from the obviously, now unsmiling Gerri. I cursed as I poured another half inch into my snifter.

Why didn't you identify yourself in that phone call, Gerri? I might have saved you, I thought. Now you, your husband, Roberto, and your ten year old son, Ritchie are dead--lives snuffed out along with your home.

Murder? Oh, most definitely! They were obviously tied to chairs while the culprit poured accelerant throughout the house.

Who was he? I must have called just as the arsonist was finishing. It's done, he had said. Who did he think was on the other end of the phone?

Lifting my snifter for the last sip of cognac, I promised myself that Monday would bring a turning point to this tragic case . . . but tomorrow I must visit my friend, Inspector Morris.

SIXTY-EIGHT

It seems crime never sleeps. My cell phone woke me. Squinting at the illuminated alarm clock confirmed it was a bit early for a friendly call . . . only 3 o'clock a.m.

"Garrett here," I tried to sound awake.

"Mr. Garrett. Mallory here. Better get your butt down to your office. Bring your girl." He hung up.

Dutifully, I rang Amy's cell. "Put your clothes on, grab your camera and walk outside. I'll pick you up in three minutes."

"What?"

"Your pal, Mallory just called. Said to pick you up. I know nothing else." I explained.

She was waiting at the curb as I drove down. Approaching my office I saw a considerable police presence--at least four vehicles' worth--one ambulance, one coroner's wagon and two squad cars. Mallory stopped us before we entered my driveway.

"Need you to take a look at a body, Garrett." Poking his nose further into the Caddy driver's side window, he continued, " Bring your camera."

"Do you recognize this fellow, Garrett?" Mallory asked me. "He didn't have any I.D. on him.

No driver's license, nothing. Just a set of car keys."

The man, quite dead, lay in a pool of blood next to my chain gate. Two plastic pails full of what smelled of gasoline were on the ground beside him, bolt cutters and a revolver lay on the sidewalk two feet away from him

"No, can't say that I do . . . Oh! Wait a minute! I think I do. Let's go inside. What happened, by the way?"

Two other cops walked up. One was in uniform, the other plain clothes: Bradley Swazer. Mallory answered, "We've been watching your place since Friday when you and the Inspector were shot, figuring--since someone has it in for you, perhaps they would return. First they tried to torch your house and shoot out these windows. Bradley, here, thought . . ."

"We have eyes on your house as well," Bradley interrupted. "I thought it was a good chance they'd try to do more damage."

"Looks like you thought right," I said, shaking my head. "So, what happened?" I asked again as I unlocked the front door. Amy had been busily snapping pictures; now she joined us as we entered. They followed into my office and looked at the photo I had taken weeks ago of George Nichols--our freezer and corpse delivery man at the reunion-- on the cork-board. Everyone agreed, we were looking at the dead man outside.

The uniformed officer said, "He had a pair of bolt cutters about to cut the lock on the gate. I yelled, he pulled a gun and put two bullets in the squad car windshield. I dropped him right there."

We walked back outside. Body, ambulance and Coroner were gone. Parked halfway down the block was a an older green-gray sedan .

"Hand me that set of keys, Bradley. I think they fit that sedan," I said, pointing.

"We'll do that, Garrett," Mallory insisted. "Bradley, check the keys out; if they fit, get forensics down here to go though that sedan."

"Okay, Garrett, who is George Nichols?" Mallory asked in a demanding tone.

I frowned. *You're the one that woke me from a perfectly sound sleep, Buster! And the lady as well!* I decreed I didn't like him . . . that whole <u>first four seconds</u> thing . . . I decided to share as little as possible. I'd give a bit more to Morris when I visited him later today.

"He was one ballsy fellow!" I exclaimed. "He's a puzzle piece in a missing person's case I'm working on, Sir. Morris' case as well. He has whatever information we have on him."

"Thanks for your help, Alan." Swazer said.

"Thanks for inviting us. We're done here. Amy and I are heading back to Pop's."

"Still hope to see you Monday morning?" Mallory asked Amy. It was 4:17 a.m.

"Sure." was her reply.

"Mallory certainly has moxie," she offered as we hopped into the Caddy.

"The guy has gall," I replied. "Is he offering you a job?"

"I'm not sure. It's been exciting, so far, but nothing has been offered."

I laughed as I stopped at Rita Mason's home to drop her off. "Until tomorrow then, Amy."

Sunday 6:27 a.m. I'd looked at the clock for the tenth time at least. Couldn't get back to sleep. Got up, made a pot of coffee.

I shook my head. *Unbelievable!* I told myself. *He comes into my office a couple of weeks ago all innocent-like, telling me he had delivered luggage to the reunion not knowing what was in it, and then the same with the freezer--like, Oh! I didn't know. I was simply doing a job. And I bought it! Damn!*

Pop must have the nostrils of a grizzly bear; he was downstairs with his coffee mug extended before I could say *Where's your shirt?* I said it anyway, but I poured his coffee.

"Where's your shirt, Pop?"

"I was sure you were on your way out, and I wanted to catch you before you left. What happened last night?" He sipped gingerly. "I heard the door close very early; came downstairs; you were gone."

"Attempted arson--my shop. Caught red-handed and shot. I identified the body for the police. I was back in under an hour, Pop."

"Who died trying to burn you down?"

"Haven't worked it all out yet, but it's my newest case."

"You have another case?" Pop was surprised.

"Nope." I knew that was an old, hackneyed sucker move, but it felt good for a moment.

Pop smiled a sick, smirky smile. "Another reunion player, eh? Male or female?"

"A delivery boy." I filled Pop in on my George Nichols story. "A sly one for sure."

"Until now," Pop reasoned.

"Right. Until now." I took a long swig of coffee. "Gotta go, Pop. Visiting Morris this morning."

"Alan, Are you running out early to avoid that young lady?"

"Ahh, who's the gumshoe now?" I winked.

My Caddy rolled past the widow's place a bit before 7 o'clock a.m. I looked to see if any lights were on . . . no signs of life . . . good. They can sleep in, it's Sunday morning anyway. No one should be forced out of bed early on a Sunday morning.

I parked the Caddy in my spot at the office, locked the gate, and walked to the beach. Ocean was calm. Except for a half dozen optimistic surfers, the early risers that would soon be dotting the sand here and there, bringing their picnic chests, blankets and umbrellas hadn't yet arrived. The shore birds and I had the beach to ourselves.

I took my shoes and socks off, rolled up my trousers and walked a quarter of a mile through the calf-deep sudsy surf, with no one but my Creator. It was a good feeling. It was rejuvenating. Necessary. I walked back up the hill.

"Well, now I know why you didn't answer your door." Amy sounded frustrated. "I've been standing here ten minutes, pounding. Your car is parked behind the gate, so I knew you were inside. I was about to call Mallory."

"Guess what?" I said.

"What?"

"No need. Come on in." I said as I unlocked the front door. "Did you bring your camera and the pictures you took? I'm hoping to have copies of the fire victims and of the shooting outside my office."

"Yes. May I accompany you to see the inspector? I'll take my own car. Then, when we leave the hospital, give me directions. I'll plug into my GPS and be out of your hair."

"Sounds like a plan." I agreed to her request, with one caveat. "We'll ride together in my car. I have a few questions for Officer Swazer while you're chatting with Mallory, after which I'll bring you back here; if it's close to lunchtime we'll enjoy a lunch together; then you can be on your way and out of my hair."

"Wow! I am impressed! And, do you know what? I'll agree. By the way," Amy continued, "what were you doing earlier? Having breakfast somewhere?"

"No. I was being one with nature . . . along the water," I pointed to the beach.

"Nice!"

I locked up. We headed for the hospital. My early morning walk had recharged my batteries. I was going to have a good day.

* * *

Morris was just finishing his breakfast when we knocked on his open door.

"Thank the lord . . . someone to talk to," he said. "Even if it's you, Gumshoe."

"What have you heard from Mallory, Sir?" I asked him.

"Fire destroyed a house with a family in it, is all. The young lady, here took some good photos, and we should consider using her talents if she stays in the area."

"That's it?"

"I haven't seen him yet this morning. Why? Something else?"

"Uhh, yes, Amy will show you the shots she took. But first, a question. Do we have any more information regarding the Eagle Rock bodies?"

"Don't know. Talk to Swazer. He's carrying my load while I'm in here." Looking at Amy, he said, "Young lady, what do you have to show me?"

While Amy opened her computer and showed Morris the fire and arsonist photos, filling him in with the back stories, I called to make sure Swazer was in his office. He was. I listened to the exchange between Amy and Morris. He looked over at me.

"You telling me that George whatsisname is the dead arsonist? We were both snookered weren't we?"

"We were, Inspector."

"Damn!" Morris exclaimed. "Sorry I caught this case."

"We're heading over to your office right now Inspector Morris," Amy said. "Any messages?"

"Just tell Swazer to keep me informed so I don't get the pertinent information from a casual visitor."

"I'll tell them that for sure," she laughed, "emphasis on the *casual*."

We said our goodbyes and headed for police headquarters.

Desk sergeant met us. "Good morning, Mr. Garrett, Miss. You're here to see Officer Swazer?"

"I am. The lady here would like to talk to Officer Mallory."

"You're the photographer? Mallory said he's expecting you."

"Mr. Garrett, you know where Morris' office is. Bradley is hiding out in there. I'll let him know you're on your way. Miss," she continued, "I'll get the detective. Wait here."

With minimal recognition, Mallory and I passed each other in the hallway. Swazer was waiting in the doorway to Morris' office as I rounded the next corner. He ushered me in and shut the door

"You saw Morris?"

"Just came from there. He could probably use more communication."

"I'll see him after lunch," Bradley said in a manner I thought rather officious. "And to answer your first question, the gun used last night is not the murder weapon you're looking for. Next question?"

Now I was sure of it. I suppose sitting in the old man's chair gave him a touch of arrogance.

"Come on, Bradley, this is me. Don't let Mallory's insolence rub off on you. You have a classy boss. Take notes and follow him."

I continued, "Forensics went through that sedan last night. Did they find anything of value?"

Bradley sat upright. "A couple of things, Sir. We got two sets of fingerprints from the vehicle--one, the dead guy and one other, identified from an FBI database as Gerri Alvarado.

I shook my head. I'm familiar with the NGI program. I had access in the Air Force. It expands the FBI's criminal and civil fingerprint database to include other identifiers--iris scans, palm prints, face-recognition photos, and voice data, and makes that data available to other agencies, state and federal. But Gerri Alvarado? Must be old prints.

"And the other thing?" I asked, still wondering about that second set of prints.

"Our dead guy had two wallets, two sets of I.Ds . . . business cards and driver's licenses." Swazer handed me a printed copy of the forensic report.

"Well, this is interesting," I said. "One of his wallets has a driver's license showing a John Drake, Esq. Of Gunn and Gunn, Attorneys at Law, and the second one belongs to a Mr. Norman Nestling, Market Street Real Estate Brokers in San Francisco, CA, right down to family portraits. Who knows who they are; probably paid for posing."

"Looks like you recognize the two names. Do you?" Swazer asked.

His phone interrupted our conversation. It was Mallory. He had a message for me. Amy would be a while. Mallory would bring her back. I could leave.

"Good," I said. "That makes it easy," I continued. "To your question, yes. As Nestling he was witness to the signing of a few trusts, and as Drake he picked up the White's paperwork. Can all of this be shielded from the media for a while?"

"Oh, I think so. They weren't even there last night. Only your lady friend."

"One more question, if I may," I asked. "Do you have a name of that officer in Eagle Rock? The one that Morris was communicating with?"

Swazer flipped through the Inspector's notes, came up with a name and a phone number. I jotted it down in my notes.

"Thanks, Swazer. I'll be off."

"Garrett!"

"Yeah?"

"Thank you for your advice."

* * *

Pop and I had homemade tacos for dinner, washed down with Bourbon Barrel Stout. That was at 6 o'clock. Now I was spending a quiet evening watching a Dodger game. It was 7:42 p.m. by the digital readout at the bottom of the TV screen. Pop was at Rita's playing gin.

The Dodgers were ahead by three in the bottom of the sixth. Amy was AWOL.

My snifter was empty. More, my bottle was empty. I went to the kitchen, pulled another bottle of *Martell Cordon Bleu* from the cupboard.

I poured two fingers of the smooth stuff, considered taking the bottle with me into the den, but the better part of wisdom prevailed--instead I added to the snifter, put the bottle into the cupboard and worried my way back to the den.

The Pirates had tied the game in my absence. It was still the bottom of the sixth. Amy was still AWOL.

SIXTY-NINE

Monday morning, 6:45. I had coffee and donuts waiting for Pop as he descended the stairs.

"Umm! Good coffee, Alan!"

"Thanks." Pop always said, *good coffee*, and I almost always said *thank you*. It was a ritual.

"How was your evening, Pop?"

"It was terrible, Alan! Rita won every game. I was determined to win at least one just to gain some self respect; but it was not to be. Every game, Alan! At least one would have felt good!"

"Yeah, I know how you feel, Pop. I've been there! But cheer up! Next time may be your turn. Things like that go in cycles."

"They'd better! Anything new in your case? I understand you saw the detectives yesterday."

"Oh, so the prodigal daughter returns!"

"Huh?"

"Thinking out loud, Pop." I smiled. "Just curious how Amy fared yesterday. I was hoping to speak with her last night but she didn't show up."

"She got home--that is, to Rita's--at 8:45 p.m., watched a couple of hands of gin, didn't say anything to us except goodnight. I didn't see her after that."

"If you see her later, have her call me. I'll be on the road. See you, pop."

I was driving before I realized I hadn't answered Pop's question. I called and told him about the two aliases that died with George Nichols.

"Where are you off to?" Pop asked.

"A minute at my office to make a couple of calls, then either Gunn and Gunn or Eagle Rock P.D., or both."

"If Amy comes up what do I tell her?"

"Tell her to sit and have a cup of coffee. She's a big girl, Pop. Has her own car and everything."

I hung up and pulled in front of the office. It was only 7:25 a.m. My first call was to the phony Gunn and Gunn number on the business card of John Drake, aka George Nichols, now very dead.

Picked up on the first ring. Same abrupt message as before. I should have given that phone number to Bradley to track down. I'll do that today.

I hopped out of the Caddy. Unlocking the front door, I stepped inside, but before I had the chance to grab the coffee maker the door opened behind me.

She spoke before I could turn to see who was entering at 7:30 a.m. I recognized the voice.

"Cup of coffee, Rachel?"

"Good morning, Alan. I think you've been avoiding me. I had to pop by to see how you're doing. Yes, please. One suga . . ."

"I remember. One sugar and heavy on the cream. It'll be a minute."

My eye spotted the thumb drive Morris had brought me Saturday. I'd forgotten about it in the excitement of the shooting. I plugged it into my computer. Rachel was speaking. I turned to her.

"Did you find out yet who was murdered at the reunion?"

"Yes, Sharon Etts. DNA results conclusive. Came in last week."

"Oh, I'm so sorry," Rachel said with a shocked look on her face. "Poor Matt. I wonder how he took it?"

"I haven't heard. I suppose I should have tried his number one more time."

"Oh, do it now! Doesn't he know?"

"I'm sure he does. The police were going to question him after they identified her."

"Who did this terrible thing, Alan?"

"Getting closer," I assured her as I dialed Matt's number, "but needs fine tuning before we know for sure." Still no answer at Matt's.

"Do you have a revocable or living trust, Rachel?"

"That's an interesting question, Alan. Yes. Why do you ask?"

"One of the key facets to the murders, and there are many, seems to be the drawing up of certain trusts and the beneficiaries of same."

"I shouldn't have a problem, Alan, I had Sherri draw mine up shortly after Chris was shot."

As Rachel sipped her coffee I pulled three files from a drawer--those of Sharon, the Caldwells, and Regina Leone--and laid them on the desk in front of her.

"All dead, Rachel."

I pointed to the author, the trustees and the beneficiary clauses of each: Sherri Foote drafted each one, then Gina took over with the secondary beneficiary--namely, the Roxanne DeVry Memorial Trust, naming Sherri as beneficiary.

Rachel studied each one carefully, stacked them carefully, then folded her hands.

"Okay, so now I'm totally alarmed, Alan. I have this exact format. I don't remember the trustees--it's been ten years, but I remember the Roxanne Trust as a dumping grounds for my assets if I didn't make any life changes."

"Did you notice, Regina originally named Chris as beneficiary until it was changed back in July?

I want you to be careful, Rachel. I'd even recommend you put one of your four guns at the front door and keep one under your pillow. You're strong, Rachel, but please use caution. Don't trust anyone!"

"Sounds like good advice, Alan," she smiled, "but I have a better idea. Why don't you come home with me and protect me?"

"Ha!" I couldn't help but laugh. "And who will protect me?" I said, winking as I refilled both our cups.

Rachel took another sip of coffee, and pondered my question. Then she smiled, "I'll be gentle with you, Alan. Promise."

An idea floated through my mind . . . share the thumb drive with Rachel. She may recognize the female voice.

"I received some messages, Rachel. Whose voice is this?"

Without hesitation, "Gina. That's Gina."

"Can't be," I argued. On one of them the speaker says, *Gina knows. Ask Gina.*"

"You asked me , Alan. I told you. Gina is on the recording."

Changing subjects, Rachel asked, "What time does your office manager show up? I owe her an apology. I want to do it face to face."

"She's on an assignment out of town. Probably back Wednesday."

"An assignment? Who for? You?"

"Yes. She's in Arizona." I said nonchalantly. "On a case. Haven't heard from her yet, but she should be wrapping it up today or tomorrow. She's supposed to be back in the office Wednesday for a new case."

"Then I'll swing by Wednesday morning to speak with her. What's on your schedule for today? Do you have time to swing by for a drink later?"

"Let me call you, Rachel. My day includes a trip to Eagle Rock, a stop at Gunn and Gunn Law offices, and sometime today I need to spend time with Inspector Morris. I think he's still in the hospital."

"Do you want some company?"

"No. I'll be gone most of the day. I'll call you."

"You'd better. I have Cordon Bleu."

She was gone. I picked up my phone; my first call: Gunn and Gunn. By now, the receptionist recognized my voice.

"Good morning Mr. Garrett. Let me see if Mr. Gunn is in and can take your call."

"Alan!" Peter Gunn greeted me. "I've had company records pulled for both Sherri Foote and Gina Rowling trust preparations since they were employed here.

Sherri prepared over one hundred forty trusts in the twelve plus years she was with us. All disbursements seem in order with fourteen exceptions, the Caldwells being one, and just Friday the terrible news of the Brightons.

Gina had only six on her own. I'm having the lists printed out for you. You may pick them up anytime after noon today."

"Thank you, Sir. One other thing," I flipped through my notes, "does the name Alex Graham mean anything to you?"

"A client, perchance?"

"Don't know. If the name shows up in your files, I'd appreciate a call."

"Alan, we appreciate what you're doing. Whatever we can do to assist in this tragic ordeal."

* * *

Bradley Swazer had given me the Eagle Rock Police contact, a Joe Watts. I decided to call Watts before heading out this morning. He was in. I introduced myself to the detective. Three new bodies had been found. They are now sure there are no more.

Three husband-wife couples, identified as the Sinclairs, the Brightons, and most recently, the Bells. All were buried two plus years ago. Then one male and one female--the latter identified as Trudy Wells, confirmed by the parents from clothing and jewelry.

The other body, as yet unidentified, was estimated by forensics to be male between fifty-five and sixty-five years of age and to have been in the ground for years.

"Can you have a DNA sample from the remains pulled and sent to me?" I asked.

"Perhaps, but what's your interest in my case?"

Watts asked. "I know you went looking for someone at the Wawona address and grew suspicious, but that's all I know. What else?"

I filled him in on the murders beginning with those at the reunion; by the time I finished, Watts whistled and promised to keep me in the loop.

* * *

My day of travelling turned into phone calls. The only trip I would make would be to the hospital to see Morris. Even that turned into a quickie. I reached the front door to the hospital just as his wife was wheeling him out to their waiting car.

"I'll be resting up a few days at home, Alan. You're welcome to swing by any time for a visit."

"But not today," Mrs. Morris interjected. "And you call me first before you visit."

"Lucy, I can't watch soaps all day long," Morris groaned. "You play cribbage, Alan?"

"Ha! I'll call you tomorrow, Carl. Latest news from Eagle Rock . . . total of eight bodies in that yard."

"That's enough!" Lucy Morris announced. "Get in the car, Carl."

"Yes. Get in the car, Carl," I repeated, laughing. "I'll call you tomorrow."

Mrs. Morris slanted a look of hostility at me. "He wouldn't be in this condition except for you, Alan."

I heard Morris say, "Oh, Lucy," as they drove away. I started toward the office. Then I pulled the Caddy to the curb and looked at the time. I may as well go to Gunn and Gunn to pick up the list of worrying Trusts in Sherri's caseload.

I shook my head, and found myself arguing with

myself. *Can't be! Gina is on that tape? She made all those calls?* I listened to it repeatedly as I drove--finally had to conclude they were definitely the same voice.

* * *

4:15 p.m. I had two lists in front of me--the first was of clients known to have died or disappeared under less than usual circumstances, and those known to have used Sherri Foote for creating trusts under the auspices of Gunn and Gunn. I checked off familiar cases--the Brightons, Bells, Caldwells, Gerri Alvarado and her family.

The second list was of people I knew of whose final benefactor was the Roxanne DeVry Trust. They included Barry Franks, Rachel Block, Sharon Etts, Regina Leone, Tom and Patti Wellings--Patti was dead, Tom still alive, Terrance Perle, Gina Rowling, and of course, Sherri Foote.

Then there was Trudy Wells, buried in Eagle Rock, an older unidentified male buried there, and the Whites. How do they fit?

I picked up the phone. "Your invite still on?"

"Of course, Silly. I wouldn't have invited you if I didn't hope you'd come."

Before I closed the office I replayed that latest hotline message--*"Alan! I'm calling to warn you. Your life is in danger. So is mine. Be careful."*
Comparing that voice with those from the one I shared with Rachel, I concluded the voice was the same!

An eerie sensation struck me. Did Gina know Gerri was in imminent danger? Is that why she left Gerri's phone number on the tape? How would she know?

I grabbed my fedora, locked the office and headed for Rachel's.

* * *

"Busy day, Alan?" Rachel greeted me at the door, dressed in about two dollars worth--off a bolt of hot red satin fabric, fashioned into a sheer sarong--barely enough to cover her stomach, hips and not much more . . . and was split up both sides. Perfect attire for the boudoir; however . . .

However, I was here for a friendly drink. My eyes shifted to the full brandy snifter she held out for me. "So glad you decided to join me."

I took the cognac and followed my hostess to the back garden. She had chosen two of the lounge chairs by a poolside table. The Martell bottle and her drink were already there.

"How are you certain that voice belongs to Gina, Rachel?"

"It is. Trust me, Alan. Gina and I were at one time very close." She shifted a bit in her chair, revealing more of her lovely anatomy. "Please, no more questions, Mr. Gumshoe. Let's just enjoy our evening."

"Can't think of any more right now, anyway, Ma'am," I said, smiling. "Oh, there is one. What do you mean, *'Gina and I were at one time very close'*?"

"Gina, Chris and I were very close. When she and Kevin married we went to concerts, movies and dinner dates together. Then, when Chris was killed, there was a noticeable change in our relationship.

Now, Alan," Rachel continued, "I received a sizeable insurance payout from the city as well as a private life policy Chris insisted on, which paid for everything you see," she spread her arms out. "Eight months later Kevin and their children died in that freeway accident, and that ended our friendship. I did nothing except profit under the most horrific of conditions. It wasn't my fault that Gina wasn't thus protected."

I was struck by this new wrinkle. Gina was jealous? Felt cheated? I mulled it over in my mind as my eye followed the slit in Rachel's skirt to the top and back down the other side. I suppose my silence, by the time I had traced and retraced that same cul-de-sac five or six times, caused Rachel to speak.

"Cat got your tongue, Gumshoe, or are you simply in awe at what you see?" she laughed.

"Oh! Sorry, Rachel. Forgive me, but I wasn't looking at . . . uh, anything. I was . . . uh, deep in thought."

"I'm sure you were. How about a salmon sandwich?"

"Sounds lovely, Rachel."

"Back in a minute."

She obviously knew I'd agree to the salmon. She returned almost immediately with sandwiches cut into quarters, spicy pickles, swiss cheese and green and black grapes. In her other hand I recognized the same pair of swim trunks I had used on a previous visit.

"I'll stay for the meal," I smiled at Rachel.

"If that's the only thing that looks delicious, Alan Garrett, I just might show you the door right now."

I stayed for dessert . . . it was past two a.m. as I pulled into my garage.

SEVENTY

6:30 a.m. comes way too soon when you hit the sheets only four hours earlier, but Tuesday September 24, 2019 comes but once in my lifetime, so I decided it should demand the same respect as all other workdays.

As the aroma of coffee wafted upwards, Pop came downstairs with his usual smiling face.

"Missed you last night; take a wrong turn?" he asked as he held out his coffee mug.

"No, not really. Oh, well, it did get a bit interesting after hours, but I made it home early enough to get up by 6:30. In fact, I have another clue to my puzz . . ."

The door bell rang. Pop and I looked at each other, both frowning. I opened the door to Amy Wynne.

"Are you avoiding me, Mr. Garrett?"

I managed to finish filling Pop's coffee mug, but before I could get a word in edgewise she continued,

"I stopped by your shop twice yesterday for a visit. I wanted to share the news."

"Let's hear it, then," I laughed, handing her a steaming mug. "Cream and sugar on the counter."

"Umm, good coffee," Amy said, approvingly. Pop and I shared a smile, as Amy resumed, "Is your coffee shop open all day or just from 6:30-7:00 a.m.?"

"If the lights are on in the kitchen the coffee is on, Pop answered. So, what's your news?" Pop was as anxious as I.

"My photography was a hit with a lot of different people," Amy sounded excited. "I've been offered a retainer with the Police as a crime scene photographer."

"A retainer?" I asked.

"I'll keep my independence, work for them in an on-call capacity."

"Sounds good," Pop said. "How much?"

"They'll give me $1,200.00 per month. I use my own transportation, my own equipment, have to be available 24/7, but . . ."

"That's less than minimum wage!" Pop almost shouted.

"But I tally my own hours," Amy laughed, "and, from the time I'm called in until I get home all hours over thirty a month I will bill as overtime at $40.00 per hour."

"Wow!" Pop declared, "where was I when the dishy jobs were handed out?"

"So your plans are?" I asked her.

Amy smiled, "It gets better. Rita and I sat up last night and talked. She's renting a room out to me, I'm sharing in household duties, and a few other things."

"You did pretty well, Amy," I joined the conversation. "I may be able to use your talents as well as time goes on."

"I was hoping you'd say that, Alan," she said.

"Okay, kids," I said, after finishing my coffee and pulling my fedora from the rack, "I'm out of here. See you Pop, Amy."

I left them to their coffee, settled my hat firmly on my head, and headed for my office. Today I had only one major thing on my agenda--visit Gina Rowling.

She shouldn't deny me today. *Perhaps a breakfast meeting?* I thought. *She doesn't punch a clock. I'll wait until 8:30 before I call.*

Decision made, I unlocked the gate into the parking spaces and drove in. I found, to my surprise, I wasn't first to arrive for work. A silver Kia sat in Liz's spot. I turned the key to the back door and entered my domain.

"Bossman!" Liz reached up and kissed my cheek. "Mission accomplished, Sir," she beamed, pointing to the envelope on her desk.

"Good to see you back in one piece! When did you get back, Liz?"

"I pulled in at 2:00 a.m., showered, caught a few hours of sleep. But I couldn't wait to see your smiley face, Gumshoe, so here I am. We go to the police gun-range today, right? I've cleared all the skips," she added, handing me a mug of coffee.

A promise is a promise. Still . . . "When did I promise that, Liz?" Before she could answer I said, "Morris and I got shot Saturday evening. He was in the hospital until yesterday morning."

"Liar!" she looked at me and laughed. "You did not!"

"Oh, it happened," I assured her. "He won't be able to work on your carry permit for a week or so, but . . ."

"Gumshoe! Okay, Smart-ass, let's see your wound!"

I rolled my left sleeve above the elbow. I had long since rid the arm of any bandages; the two inch groove left by the bullet had scabbed over until now it was simply a long, ugly, half-inch-wide, brown gash encircled by a rosy circle. God was busily at work using His healing powers.

"OH! Bossman!" Liz squeaked. "You did get shot! Sorry I doubted you. Okay, the carry permit is on hold for a while. So," she continued, "what's on tap for today? I know I start on that Air Force brat tomorrow, but let me check my calendar . . . yup! Today is free."

"I'm going to call Gina Rowling at 8:oo a.m. and ask her to breakfast. If she's home, I think she will accept. You should join us."

"Absolutely."

"In the meantime, let's see your success in Phoenix, Liz."

She pointed at the envelope on her desk. "Open it," she beamed.

I opened the flap and slid the contents onto the surface. Four pages stapled together with two signatures on the bottom of each--Liz's and the debtor. The fifth sheet was signed by Liz, the debtor and a witness. In addition, a packet of six $2,000.00 checks fell out, dated the first of each month, beginning September 1, 2019, and ending February 1, 2020.

"You did well, Liz."

"Fox," she corrected.

I briefed Liz on the happenings during her absence while she summed up her trip. It took the better part of an hour. At 8 o'clock I called Gina.

"Good morning, Miss Rowling. Alan Garrett here."

"It's Gina, Alan. I've been expecting your call. You figured out that I was sending you messages?"

"Yes. You said my life and yours are in danger. Did you mean yours or Gerri's?"

"All of our lives are in danger, Alan. I'm very frightened, especially after what happened to Gerri."

"Do you feel safe leaving your home?"

"I guess as safe as anywhere," she said.

"Then let's get together for breakfast this morning if you're available. I have tons of questions that need answers, Gina."

"I can juggle things around and meet you about 9:15 a.m., so long as it's close. Just a suggestion," she added, "there's a Norms right down Hawthorne Boulevard."

"Norms it is. See you. By the way, I'll be bringing my office manager, Liz."

I turned to Liz after we hung up. "Ask whatever questions come to mind, but don't box her in. She is the consummate liar. If we press her, I'm afraid she'll clam up, and we'll create an enemy."

* * *

We arrived at Norms at 9:10 a.m., were seated two minutes later, then waited for our guest.

At 9:30 we ordered. 9:39 our food came--an unbelievable amount for the money--and by 10:10 a.m. we had finished breakfast; Liz made a trip to the ladies' room and back. Still no Gina.

"What now, Bossman?" Liz asked.

"The only sensible thing. Head for Gina's."

* * *

As we drove, Liz called Gina's number. It went directly to voice mail. The house was just off Rosecrans; took but ten minutes. The front door was locked. I walked around to the back and tried the back door; also locked.

Fox was on the front porch. She stood peering through a large picture window as I came around the corner of the house.

"Gumshoe, come back up here, take a look."

SEVENTY-ONE

"I don't think anyone lives here, Gumshoe, do you?" Liz asked.

Other than an unplugged floor lamp in one corner, a kitchen step stool adjacent to a hallway leading into the rest of the house, we were peeping through the window at a fully carpeted, bare room.

I turned to Liz, raised an eyebrow, "Shall we?" Liz nodded with a crafty smile.

"Grab some gloves from my car console, please, while I pick this lock."

My lock-picking was adequate; the door was open by the time Liz returned. We entered.

The carpet was imprinted with evidence of recently moved furniture. We frowned and carried on, through the hallway to an open kitchen-dining area . . . again, void of furniture except the built-ins. All seven rooms were the same--empty. No signs of violence.

"Let's hit the garage; probably nothing there, but what the hell," I added, "we're here."

The garage was like most--walk-in door on the side--easy to pick the lock.

"Well looky here, Gumshoe," Liz acted almost

like she was in a toy store.

One whole wall was covered with stacks of file storage boxes, the cardboard, economy kind. There was a desk with desk-top computer and land-line phone. Phone had a dial tone. An idea hit my brain. I flipped through my note pad, came up with a number and dialed it from my cell phone. The phone on the desk rang. I signed off.

"Am I missing something, Bossman?"

"Thinking, Fox, thinking," I said, rubbing my chin. "Let's see if there's anything of value in those storage boxes."

There were twelve stacks, three boxes high, on one wall, all numbered, one through thirty-six.

Liz opened the very first one, marked plainly #1. "Look at this, Gumshoe!" Liz said, "Two files: Bell and Caldwell. Wasn't Bell one of those the fellas found up on Wawona?"

I nodded as she opened the top box on the third column, marked #4. "Files on Franks, Perle and Sinclair."

I opened the top box of the eighth stack, marked #22. Two more file folders--Farley and Torkon--names not familiar to me, and not on the Gunn and Gunn list.

"There's a key somewhere, Fox, to these boxes. Let's see if there's a notebook in that desk, then let's get out of here. Leave everything. We'll have Morris' people get a judge to sign off on a search warrant."

Liz opened the desk drawers--all empty.

"Changed my mind, Fox. Help me load this last group of boxes into the Caddy."

I picked up boxes #34 and #35 and put them in my trunk; Liz followed with box #36. I pulled the garage door shut and made sure it was locked. We pulled the Caddy out into the street and headed for Manhattan Beach.

"Where to next, Bossman?"

"Let's call on Grinnell. Then I'm going to visit Morris at home. Join me if you wish, or I'll drop you off."

"No, I'm going with you."

* * *

Grinnell was delighted! "You did it, Garrett. I didn't think you'd be able to bring that creep to justice. Why, I'da been happy with half."

"It was this young lady. I sent her to Arizona to settle with the skip. She did it all."

"Well, you keep her!" he exclaimed. "What's your name, Miss?"

"Call me Fox, Sir."

"Well, Fox, you got almost all of it. Take this," he added, pulling some bills out of his wallet, "as a cash bonus." Then turning to me, "And you make sure you invoice me, Garrett for the full amount we agreed on, you hear? I'll be letting my friends know who to go to for the best investigator in L.A."

We thanked him, and headed for the Morris household. Liz called ahead.

"He's not here," Mrs. Morris bemoaned.

I took the phone, "What do you mean he's not there? He was ordered to stay home for a week."

"Well, he woke up this morning, dressed, kissed me goodbye and left for the office. I can't tell you any more, but if you see him, kick his sixty-three year old butt and tell him to get it home. I can't control his bull-headed hide."

"We'll head there now, Lucy. I'll make sure he comes home soon."

We turned the Caddy around and headed for the police station.

* * *

"I know, I know, Garrett," Morris moaned. "She's called twice already. I promised I'd be home by noon, so make it fast or I'll be in even more trouble. I had to come down here to see how much trouble Bradley had caused. Turns out, I'm quite pleased."

"How fast can you have a judge sign off on a search warrant, Inspector?" I asked.

"Who? Why?" he raised an eyebrow.

I filled him in on Gina's no-show for breakfast, the empty house, the garage with the phony Gunn and Gunn message phone, the storage boxes filled with fraudulent trusts of people now very dead.

"You need to send a van to pick up those thirty-three boxes, and check for fingerprints and blood in both house and garage."

Liz gave me a sidelong glance as I mentioned the boxes. If Morris saw it, he ignored it.

"I may be able to get the warrant this morning," he said looking at the wall clock. "Anything else?"

"Not for now; one other warrant, but it can wait," I said. Morris was already on the phone.

"Yes, Judge Hamlin. Good cause," Morris was explaining. "Homicide suspect's home. We've seen files inside house and or garage that may provide major evidence of a fraudulent trust scheme. We'd like those files. Yes, Sir. Thank you, Sir. I'll have Bradley Swazer pick it up right away. Thank you."

"Are we going back to Gina's when the police get there?" Liz asked.

"No. That's a police matter for now. A forensics team will cover the place like a blanket. No, we're heading back to the office. I'm curious to see who is in those boxes."

Within fifteen minutes we were unloading the boxes into the office. My phone rang . . . Morris.

"You make it home alright?" I laughed.

"Yeah. Lucy still loves me. Not why I called."

"What's up?"

"It's Gina's place, Gumshoe. The house was torched, garage is completely in ashes. Swazer says looks like several gallons of gasoline used. Worse, he says a body was at the desk, or rather more correctly, draped over it.

Desk is embers, body is charcoal. Forensics is at this moment going through the ashes." He hung up. I could hear Lucy yelling in the background.

"Damn!" I closed my eyes and tried to make some sense of it all.

"Someone was watching us load your trunk, Gumshoe," Liz said. "We need to be on the alert. Whoever this is, they're serious."

Phone rang again. This time it was Amy.

"Alan, I just shot a homicide scene. The guys say it's Gina's place. Did you know about it?"

"Yes, the Inspector just called," I answered.

"It's awful. I don't think the body is Gina's. It's too long. A man, I think, but I I'm not sure."

"How did you get there so fast, Amy?" Fox asked, sounding very surprised.

"I was out shopping when Mallory called. I drove right over."

I butted in, "Amy, are you still at the scene?"

"Yes, two dozen or more police and firemen, and of course, a crowd of onlookers."

"Be discreet, Amy. But take lots of pictures of everyone there, if you would, then bring them by the office, please."

"I will."

* * *

"Okay, Fox," I said, picking up box #34. "Let's see what we have in these boxes."

Three names in the box. Two of them, Jordan and McGee, were on Gunn and Gunn's list. The third, Smith, was a name new to us. The last page of that trust confirmed, there were no family member beneficiaries.

I reasoned aloud. Liz listened.

"Sherry Foote was named in first place as the beneficiary of record on this trust. The trust itself is called the Roxanne DeVry Memorial Trust--authored in 2009 by Gina Rowling. There's a handwritten note clipped to the first sheet--says -- *deceased 4-16-12 -- S.F.-p.12*

I assume the S.F is a set of initials belonging to Sherri Foote. The p. 12 has to be page twelve of the notebook we're missing. We need to find that notebook or spreadsheet, Fox. It's key to the Roxanne DeVry Trusts . . . plural. How many? I have no idea."

"There were handwritten notes on a couple of the files I saw in that garage as well," Liz noted.

"Yes--me too," I admitted. "I simply thought we would have time to pick them apart in detail, so
I didn't pay too much attention."

I glanced through the other two files. They were basically the same, but for dates and page numbers. The deaths were before 2011.

We opened box #35. It contained four files, all names were on the Gunn and Gunn list, all with handwritten notes showing completion--all dates before 2011.

Box #36 could have been a carbon copy of Box #35. These were again four names on the Gunn and Gunn list.

"Looks like these are the first ones they've profited from, Bossman, and all closed. Ten of them were when they worked for Gunn and Gunn. The other one, the Smiths, Gina did on her own in private practice."

"Sure looks like it, Fox. Wonder where the assets are being funneled. There's an end game somewhere. We'll find it."

* * *

The front door opened. A middle-aged well-dressed gentleman entered. He came equipped with an attaché and a two thousand dollar suit. I recognized him immediately from a photo I had tacked on my corkboard, but tried hard not to show it.

"Good day. Is Alan Garrett here perchance?"

"Who's asking?" I asked.

"Name is John Cantrell," he said with a deep, strong voice. He offered me a business card. "I am the attorney for Sharon Etts, and it appears now, for Amy Wynne."

"Ah, yes. I'm Alan Garrett," I said. "Have a cup of coffee. We are expecting Amy to swing by within the hour."

"Is it true that Sharon Etts has been murdered?" he asked.

"Afraid so," I said. "Sometime after February. Her body wasn't discovered until the end of July."

"And not identified until around the first week of September," Fox supplied, handing him a fresh coffee.

"How did you get involved?" Cantrell asked.

"Long story. We were high school classmates. But her homicide is just one of many, and a small fraction of a much larger case involving revocable trusts."

"Really? What's this world coming to, eh, Garrett?" Our visitor took one of the chairs in front of Liz, and turned it to face me. I caught sight of a shoulder holster under his jacket.

"What's with the name, Gumshoe and Fox?" he asked, smiling.

"Oh, just something I thought would give the place some vintage charm."

I *felt* as much as saw Liz sit up straighter and pay closer attention to our visitor. Her Beretta was in her top drawer; hopefully she wouldn't be forced to use it, but I wanted her to be prepared for anything.

A small, white hatchback pulled to the curb.

"Ahhh," I said, "here comes Amy now."

SEVENTY-TWO

Our guest turned and walked to the door to allow Amy in. I took the opportunity to pull my weapon and drop it in my jacket pocket. I watched Liz open a drawer as well.

"Thank you Sir," Amy smiled as she entered. "Hi, Alan. I brought some interesting pictures for you to look at." She was now well within the foyer.

"Ahh, hello, Amy. Allow me introduce you to my assistant, Liz--better known as Fox." The ladies nodded to each other; "And," I continued, "the gentleman you already know, attorney John Cantrell."

Amy looked up at the face for the first time and gasped.

The newcomer reached frantically to put his left arm around her, but I had my gun trained on him before he had the chance.

"Don't even try it, Ashcroft!" I yelled. "Amy, get behind the desk, please."

Ashcroft tried anyway. I put a bullet through his right elbow as he reached his gun. With his arm rendered useless, the gun fell harmlessly to the floor.

"Fox, call Bradley Swazer. Tell him to bring

an ambulance--suspect shot. Amy, you're the camera lady. Do your thing."

"Now, Mr. Ashcroft, I have lots of questions for you. Sit!"

"You shot me! You bastard! You shot me! I'll sue you, you hear me?"

I picked the handgun off the floor by the barrel--a Glock-19, magazine holds fifteen rounds, nice weapon.

Liz pulled a fresh towel from the bathroom closet and tossed it to Ashcroft.

"Wrap this around your arm," she instructed. Tight! I don't want you to die before you stand trial for nine or ten murders!"

Amy set about snapping pictures of the wounded man and the scenes within the office.

"First question, where is Sherri?" I asked. "And then, where are you depositing the assets of all these fraudulent trusts?"

Ashcroft looked at Amy, then me with a pained, but hollow expression on his face. From experience, I realized he was going into shock. We could hear an ambulance in the distance.

"Fox, check his pockets for keys. We may get lucky."

"You wanna get lucky, Bossman, *you* check his pockets for keys."

"Fox!"

"Okay, okay." Dutifully, she found a ring with three keys in a front pants pocket, and dangled them for me to see.

The desk phone rang. Amy answered. It was Morris.

"Did Alan shoot someone, Fox? Bradley says he did. Or was it you?"

"It's not Fox, Sir. It's Amy. A little hectic here. Take a deep breath, Inspector. Here's what happened--Jerry Ashcroft, that husband of Sherri Foote walked in a few minutes ago, tried to pull a gun on the three of us--Fox, Gumshoe and me. Gumshoe was faster, and shot his arm almost completely off at the elbow. An ambulance is on the way . . . in fact it's parking in front just now."

"Have your boss call me when the dust settles," Morris instructed.

Swazer pulled in just as the ambulance crew was taking Ashcroft out.

"Put a cuff on him Bradley, he's a killer," Fox yelled from the doorway. Swazer looked at her with a blank stare.

"Who is he?" he asked.

"Part of the reunion murder crew," she answered.

Swazer held up the ambulance until he could instruct the crew of two ladies to make sure their passenger was in restraints. He watched for a full minute, then entered our office. Amy filled him in on the happenings; he recorded it all in a notebook, assured us it was a good shoot, my account being corroborated by the two ladies.

I wrapped the Glock and handed it to him for ballistics; he asked me to swing by the station when I could, then left us to follow the ambulance.

"Who's hungry?" I asked. "Fox, here has a $500.00 bonus that's burning a hole in her pocket; says she'll spring for lunch."

SEVENTY-THREE

Karen, the waitress at the Shellback Tavern smiled and waved us to what had become *our spot*. We settled in, the two ladies on one side, I on the other.

"Good to see you back, Fox," she said. "And who is this young lady?"

"This is Amy Wynne, a police photographer," Fox introduced them.

"The usual, Gumshoe?" Karen asked.

"Absolutely! and give Fox the bill; she's loaded."

Karen brought a large pitcher of beer. "Cheaper than six mugs," she explained.

Meanwhile, Amy opened her laptop to show the photos she had taken at Gina's home--the devastating fire, what was left of the human remains draped over the desk, and all the curious onlookers milling around outside.

"Arson investigators were still on-scene when I left, but there wasn't much left." Amy reiterated. "My photos don't begin to show the devastation. It was horrible."

Of the twenty or so onlookers, I didn't recognize anyone in the photos. Liz frowned.

"Isn't this the man I interviewed, Gumshoe?" she asked, pointing at a figure standing behind others in the crowd--we could only see his face. "That Tom Wellings fellow? Sure looks like him."

I picked the computer up for a closer look. "It could be," I agreed. "We have a magnifier in the office. Let's check it out there."

Tacos came. They were delicious.

* * *

Ashcroft's car hadn't moved. I unlocked it. Both ladies and I, with latex gloves, searched it top to bottom.

The trunk held a prize: three boxes taken from the White's home--reading materials for later. Inside the cab we found a box of shells, a black address book, and insurance and car registration for a Maude Torkin.

"Torkin. That was a name in one of the boxes in the garage, Fox."

"It sure was, Gumshoe. Car is probably an asset in her trust."

"The address book will be an interesting read. See what you can find in it, ladies. I'm going to call Morris, then going to see Swazer."

Morris was asleep according to Lucy. I gave her all the details of the encounter with Jerry Ashcroft, our findings in the car he was driving, especially the address book. I told her to tell him to hurry up and heal; we missed him.

Lucy only grunted, "Sure."

* * *

I met Swazer just after 2 o'clock to file my

report. They checked my weapon against ballistics. It was clean, but for today's shooting. Ashcroft's weapon had been fired recently, but was otherwise clean. I expected it to be; it looked new.

"He'll be okay, Garrett, all but his arm. I'm afraid it's permanently done. I couldn't get anything out of him except he was screaming for an attorney. He's going to sue your ass off, is how he put it."

"He'll be in federal prison for murder, forgery and graft for at least two hundred years; he can sue me after that."

I started out the door, then I remembered.

"Oh, and Bradley, please schedule Liz at the police range for her marksmanship-gun handling assessment. She needs her concealed carry permit to continue working with me."

"Sure, tomorrow morning 9:30 okay?"

"Done. Thanks."

"One last thing that might interest you, Garrett. We have his credit card and cell phone records. You interested?"

"You're kidding. Of course, I am," I said.

"Here are visa transactions for August and up to yesterday and phone for last 30 days."

"You fellas really move fast!"

Swazer continued, smiling, "Especially these two numbers--one local, one international he's called many times. Here are copies; tell no one where you got them."

I zipped my lip, tucked the copy in my shirt.

* * *

Amy was still at the office when I returned.

The ladies were examining the black address book; unfortunately, it was all in code. When I brought the phone call sheet into the mix, we spent the next half hour going through all of the lists in our possession, from the reunion attendee list Morris had first given me, to the Gunn and Gunn list of trusts, comparing them to the cell phone printout.

The most often called local number was the one in Gina's garage, but the international one was another message phone in Belize. The message was the same--man's voice: *leave a message.*

The three of us looked at each other. Belize?

"Belize!" Amy sounded shocked. "What's in Belize?"

"It's a tax haven, my dear," I answered. "I ran into it several time as an AFOSI officer; a place to shuttle funds in any amount in and out of the country with privacy and anonymity."

"Wow! Are you thinking what I'm thinking, Bossman?" Fox looked at me with a raised eyebrow.

"I am. Money must be shuttled out of the U.S. secretly, but from there it can move freely. Let's check the phone number."

We found the number was for an exchange in San Ignacio, population under twenty thousand, but on theoutskirts of the populous Cayo District with over one hundred thousand. A major banking facility, the Atlantic International Bank, had a branch there.

"Amy, another subject," I said. "How much do I owe you for your help today?"

"Oh, Alan, nothing! You saved my life this morning. You owe me nothing!"

"And don't forget, Bossman, I bought her lunch!" Liz piped up.

"No. I want it made clear, when I ask someone to do something, I owe them."

"Okay. Starting tomorrow, Alan," She said. "Starting tomorrow. Forty bucks an hour. Cash only!"

"Good. Now, Fox, I may be going to Belize for a few days, but before I do, you have an appointment with Swazer tomorrow morning at 9:30 at their gun range."

"Whoopee! For my concealed permit? Oh, Bossman! I love you!" She hugged my neck. She turned, almost deliriously, to Amy.

"I'm going to be a private detective!"

"When you get back from the police range tomorrow you start on the Maggorie job."

"Yes, but I'll be a private investigator. I'll need new business cards, Gumshoe."

"Not until you're licensed, Genius. It takes thirty days and five hundred dollars. And, by the way . . ."

"Just a formality, Bossman. I'll ha . . ."

"As I started to say, Your three months isn't up yet. Who's to say you'll be around after October thirty-one?"

"Is that what the check is all about?" Amy broke in, laughing. "Sorry, I was snooping. I saw a check tacked to the side of your desk, Liz."

"Yeah, I'm guaranteed three months employment; then I may be kicked to the curb. Can you imagine? Me, who does everything to keep the doors open, the place clean and the guy in cognac."

* * *

Using a magnifying glass, Liz was still unsure about the fellow in the crowd at Gina's. I took a close look as well. There just weren't enough markers to verify if we were looking at Tom Wellings or a close look-alike.

We were getting close; I could smell it. We simply needed a couple more pieces to fall into place. It would be nice to think we could wrap this case up by the end of the month . . . one more week. Loose ends, false leads, so many questions . . . and tomorrow is another day.

* * *

7:30 Wednesday morning. Liz and I enjoyed a cup of coffee and discussed her 9:30 appointment.

"We'll call Captain Albert first. I'll introduce you to him as my associate, and explain that you will be taking lead on the disappearance of the Brigadier General's son."

Fox looked at me with a gleam of admiration. "Thanks, Gumshoe, I'll make you proud."

We made the call.

SEVENTY-FOUR

Fox left for her appointment at the police range. I thumbed through the boxes we had retrieved from the trunk of Ashcroft's car--the files belonging to the Whites.

There was the usual DeVry Trust, the all too common denominator . . . it's usual beneficiary and trustees.

This time I examined each page thoroughly, returning it into a new box, writing notes I felt possibly needing follow-ups.

I finished one box and had started another when I came across a photo tucked between the folds of a triple-folded letter. Completely out of place. On the back, in handwriting I recognized from a photo album in my possession--was that of Mrs. White. The subjects-- her son, Jonah with twins Chris and Virginia. Each of the three had an X through their faces. I estimated the children were probably about 18 months old in the photo.

I read the letter. It was typed, except for the signature. It was not dated. It started out by saying,

Catherine,

I'm returning your photo.
How dare you accuse me of being a horrible mother?
Your son was a cruel son of a bitch; his own mother's
son. I was happy to rid myself of him. I'm only sorry
the courts believed your fiction and took my
children from me after my mom and dad left for
Arizona.

If I ever hear from Virginia, I will let her
know who her grandparents are. As you know she
was diagnosed with the same affliction as your son.
Had I only known! It would have saved a ton of
heartaches, and I would never have had to deal with
you or Charles!

Regina

Now, what do I make of that? Too bad I didn't
have this letter in my hands a month ago. I could have
asked one or the other of the parties involved. I shook
my head and continued my search.

I had just finished the second box when my cell
phone rang. I suspected it to be Liz but it proved to be
Sergeant Joe Watts from Eagle Rock.

"Garrett, Watts here. I promised to keep you
informed should we find anything of interest.
Remember the unidentified male body we found on
that property? DNA conclusive. A close relative of a a
known shooting victim, one Chris Evans. We picked it
up off police files; he was a police officer, correct?"

"Yes, he was. Shot and killed about ten years ago.
The dead guy you unearthed. You said he was an older
gentleman. Perhaps what . . . father?"

"That's my thought, Garrett. Looks like it."

"Huh! . . . well, Sergeant, thanks for the info.

Very interesting." I hung up.

Immediately, the phone rang again. "Alan Garrett here."

"Okay, Gumshoe, now I need new business cards!"

"You qualified?" I asked as though in total shock.

"With flying colors!" Fox burst out, excitedly. "Gun knowledge, gun safety, range marksmanship--I impressed Officer Swazer, Gumshoe, isn't that great?"

"When will you be back?"

"Come on, Gumshoe. At least *sound* excited. My carry permit will be mailed to me within ten days."

"I'm excited. This is just step one. You still have a PSI test to take; then I'll be really excited," I laughed.

"I know. I just wanted to share the moment. I'll be taking the state PSI test Saturday in Los Angeles. I've been studying the investigative side online for almost a month. Now, to answer your question, I'll be back in twenty minutes."

She was back in fourteen. I gave her a hug as she walked through the door.

"Well done, Fox. Now, here's the Maggorie file."

"Up yours, Gumshoe!" Liz feigned anger, but returned my hug with gusto, and took the file from me enthusiastically.

I started to pick up the last box taken from the Whites when Fox turned to me.

"I almost forgot, Bossman. That crispy body at Gina's place was identified. DNA tests came back while I was there. The fellow worked at the L.A. county recorder's office. Swazer says the name was Alex Graham.

"Well, well. His son said he bought and sold

complex real properties. In his position he had access to, and could have falsified title searches, altered deeds of trust and other documents. Perhaps our investigations are having an impact on our little gang of murdering thieves.

I'm guessing three down and perhaps two or three remain, Fox."

"Call the Eagle Rock Police. They need to track down that son of his--Ron--and place him in a foster home or somewhere safe."

"On it, Bossman."

SEVENTY-FIVE

My cork board was filling up with corpses. The top row stayed the same. There was the now- identified Sharon Etts, the two forensic ladies, and Patti Wellings.

But, I changed the rest of the board. I removed all the reunion attendee photos that were now cluttering it, and began replacing them with photos and/or 4 x 6 card notes more pertinent to my case.

Those I considered other victims of crime-- starting with Gerri Alvarado and her husband and son-- complete with Gerri's high school photo, a photo of the Whites with a note on their demise, same with Regina Leone and Bill, her marina hand.

Next came the Caldwell family of five, with photos from the album in my possession . . . I figured they were one of the first if not the first casualties of the gang, followed by the eight in the Eagle Rock garden: the oldest, a male whose DNA matched Rachel Block's husband, Chris Evans, the Sinclairs, the Bells, Brightons, and of course, the most recent, Trudy Wells--photo included.

"Good Grief!" I heard myself saying aloud.

From the front office I heard Liz, "Is everything

okay in there?"

"Oh, yeah, Fox. Just hard to imagine . . . two dozen people dead, and I haven't even begun with the bad guys yet."

"Sounds like a serial killer on the loose, Gumshoe," she sang out.

"Ya think?"

Finally, I set down on the cork-board those I considered bad guys . . . those who had a hand in the slaughter.

First, George Nichols--delivery boy/arsonist who was shot and killed by a cop while trying to torch my office--justifiable homicide.

Then Jerry Ashcroft--Sherri Foote's husband. Tried to pawn himself off as Attorney John Crofton in an attempt to do harm to Amy. I put him in hospital with a gunshot wound to the elbow.

Finally, Alex Graham--L.A. County Recorder's Office--an "inside man" who could falsify, alter or stamp as legitimate, phony title searches or deeds of trust. Alex was now a corpse--burnt up in Gina's garage.

The last grouping was our prime suspect list. I flipped the board over and wrote three names--Sherri Foote, Tom Wellings and Gina Rowling--the only three on my list thus far.

Sherri must have been complicit with her husband. Was she still alive? If so, she wasn't at the reunion, so that left the other two.

Tom and Gina certainly were there, and they had ample time to mix, dance, go to the bar, go to the bathroom, slip out and drop off a corpse or slice a jugular vein. That took strength and a frenzied hatred-- or perhaps simply a heavy dose of adrenalin.

I put the three names on the board, then sat back with a Bourbon Barrel Stout and studied the board. Should I have added other names? No one else came to mind. People did leave before the night ended, but still, I didn't think anyone else was involved.

But what did the killer have to gain in bringing a corpse to the reunion, and calling it Roxanne DeVry? Unless to strike fear in certain of the attendees? The CSIs--simply collateral damage? Probably. But Patti? To shut her up? The more I thought about it, the more it made sense. She certainly wanted to talk.

Then last but not least, phone calls to Belize. *What's that all about?* I asked myself.

"Hey, Fox! You have a minute?"

She appeared at the door almost instantly. "What's up?"

"Am I missing something in my outline?" I asked.

She read and re-read the cork side of the board. "You weren't kidding were you, Bossman? Twenty-four dead . . ."

"That we know of," I interrupted. "Who knows how many more. Flip the board over."

After reading the white board side, she spoke. "Isn't this what you thought all along, Gumshoe? Tom, Sherri and Gina, along with a couple of different players, but now you sound unsure. Why?"

Pulling at the hairs of my imaginary beard, I said, "Just a nasty feeling."

"They're probably out enjoying the sun on Tom's yacht, away from the maddening crowd."

"It's *Far From The Madding Crowd*, Liz," I corrected her. "And if they're on his yacht, who knows when they'll be back."

"Or if!" she laughed

"How far have you delved into your that kid's whereabouts?"

"Paul? Two hour's worth, Bossman. I need another half hour."

"Did you get hold of Homeland for his travel information?" I asked.

"Huh?"

"Passport, commercial travel--trains, buses that sort of thing."

"No. Do you have an inroad?"

"Yes. Could be. I think Morris is back at work. Let's call and see."

I made the call. The Inspector was there.

"Morris. Good to have you back."

"Believe me, Garrett, good to be back. What news do you have for me?"

"We have four people we need to locate, Morris. Hoping you may have some contacts in FBI, Homeland or Border Patrol that can put out a BOLO or run some passport info for us."

"Do you have pictures? And just why are they so important? I can't be asking for frivolous favors."

"We're looking at more than twenty-four suspicious deaths--among them at least twenty murders, Carl. You could have been number twenty-five, but you were lucky."

"You know the FBI will take over this case once they find out the numbers involved."

"Swing by after work; we'll talk."

"Fine. Just don't tell Lucy."

An hour later, cognac in hand, Morris sat, studying the cork-board, then the whiteboard once m o r e . He shook his head and offered a couple of expletives between swallows.

"So we tell'em we're chasing some culprits fleeing the scene of a crime who may be headed out of the country; cell phone records show calls to Belize. We have photos and fingerprints to help in the search. Then," Morris continued, "who is this one, Gumshoe? The kid."

"A new job, Morris. Fox will take the lead on it. A missing person, not a crook. We have his last known address. It shouldn't be a matter of national security, but we need to find him. Fox will send you everything we have on him. I may be flying to San Ignacio, Belize tonight."

"Good for you, Alan," Morris said, ignoring me. "I have a couple of friends who may be able to help without asking too many questions. I'll see what I can find. Now I gotta be off. I'll call you in the morning."

"Say hi to Lucy for me."

"No! Lucy is never to know I talked to you today, Alan!" He sounded serious as he walked out.

"Going to Belize tonight, Bossman? Really?"

"No. I have a couple of things to do here tomorrow, but perhaps in a couple of days."

"Are you being paid anything for this job, Bossman? Almost two full months, and I haven't seen a dime in your coffers from this reunion gig."

"Don't you worry your head about our finances, Fox. It's called advertising. Gumshoe and Fox will be around for a long time. I want the Beach cities to understand we are the private investigators that get the job done."

SEVENTY-SIX

Cup of strong coffee and I was out the door. Pop was still asleep. He and Rita had gone once again to the Old Town Music Hall in El Segundo. I pulled into my parking spot, locked the gate and again I walked the block down to the beach. My early morning walks along the surf were always exhilarating--today was no exception. I had jogged a quarter of a mile toward Hermosa when I heard a voice behind me. Female.

"Garrett! Slow down! Wait up!"

I turned to see who knew and was following me. Then I smiled at Amy, put my hands on my knees and waited for her.

"You're a tough man to keep up with, Alan!" she complained, panting as she spoke.

"Why did you follow me here?" I laughed. "Don't you believe in sleeping nights?"

"It's almost 6:oo a.m. Alan. I saw your car pass by, so I thought I'd join you. I didn't realize you were a racehorse."

"Can you keep pace? I normally jog to a marker down the beach and back, but it's quite a distance--about 2.5K each way."

"Are you kidding? That's three miles, Alan."

"That's correct. There's a bench about a half mile down the beach. Pace me to there, then wait for me. I'll pick you up on the way back." I offered.

"Deal! Then I'll buy breakfast at the *Ocean View.*"

This is awkward, I thought. I have too much to do this morning to spend it socializing. But I suppose . . .

I picked up the pace just enough to make it a bit of a strain on legs and lungs. If Amy noticed she didn't complain. The bench came into sight. I dropped her off as agreed, then slogged on in the surf.

At my marker I stopped just long enough to take in about five or six strong, long gulps, then reversed direction and jogged back to meet Amy.

"Gotta swing by the office to throw some different clothes on, and run a comb through my hair. Be just a minute."

I escorted Amy into my office and followed behind. She sat at Liz's desk while I freshened up in the bath. As I was emerging into the foyer, the tip line rang. I'd forgotten it was there.

"You have a phone call. Aren't you going to answer it?"

I weighed the pros and cons of sharing the message with Amy. I opted for the latter. Without answering, I wrote a note for Liz:

Be back by 7:30 a.m. Please answer the tip line. It rang at 6:30.

"You're preoccupied, Alan. We should do breakfast some other day."

"No, no, Amy. Really, I have time. Especially at this hour. We can walk. It's only five blocks."

The place was already filling with laborers and the retired old men who had to have a go at cursing or defending current political leadership while enjoying hash browns, a couple of eggs and coffee.

Amy and I found a table in the middle of the floor. We sat and listened to the humorous exchange . . . at least humorous to me. Very serious stuff for the old-timers.

The waitress came; we ordered. Amy's phone rang. She excused herself and went outside the front door to answer. She was back in a few moments.

"Sorry. I told him I'd call back. No big deal."

"Amy. Relax! It's a free country," I laughed, "but who's calling just after seven in the morning? I thought that was only for fellows like Morris and me."

"Mallory looking for me. Says to hurry up with breakfast. He's got another situation for me to photograph. I may have to cut our breakfast short. "

"Depends upon how hungry you are, Amy. I'm ravenous, myself."

We ate like starving wolves. It was almost funny. I kissed her on the cheek . She thanked me as she slid behind the wheel of her Chevy Volt, and I watched as she drove off.

I shook my head. Why could she not have answered her cell phone in my presence? Perhaps for the same reason I didn't answer the tip line in her presence. *Stop it, Gumshoe! Ahhh, we private investigators are a much-too-suspicious lot*, I told myself.

I walked up the hill to my office. It was 7:22 a.m. Fox wasn't there yet. I made coffee, then flipped the tip line tape to play. A male voice.

Mr. Garrett, You're very annoying. My team has been compromised almost beyond repair. I must even the score, then rebuild. Believe me, I will even the score! Oh, and Mr. Garrett. I guess I don't have to tell you, watch your back! Tata.

Liz had just unlocked the rear door as I sat with a look of obvious alarm reflected across my face. Hell, I even jumped when she walked through the door.

"Are you okay, Bossman? What happened?"

I replayed the message for her.

"Bossman! This is serious stuff! Who else knows about it?"

"I've told no one yet. Do you recognize the voice, Liz? It sounds familiar. A bit distorted, perhaps. Does it sound distorted to you?"

"No and no. Exaggerated enunciation. Crisp voice, like taunting you . . . or us."

We listened to the tape again. Then I called Morris. He should have some information for me anyway. I put the phone on speaker.

"Hello, Alan. Yes, I have some information for you. You have the coffee on?"

"I always have coffee on for you, Inspector. We need you to listen to another tape."

"I'll be right there."

* * *

Morris listened and re-listened to the tape as he sipped his coffee.

"I can't put a 'round the clock' watch on your place, Alan, but I can include your home and office a couple of times per shift until we catch this guy."

I nodded appreciatively. "Thanks, Inspector."

"Well-educated," Morris continued. "Precise, determined and a sense of humor, wouldn't you say?"

"My goodness, Inspector. You're a profiler now," Fox laughed.

"This is no laughing matter, young lady. This so-called team of sons-a-bitches is ruthless. You have a board in the other room with two dozen names on it to prove it.

Now," Morris continued, "as I said, I have some news--starting with your missing young man. I have nothing yet, but a Homeland contact is working on it when she has some free time. She says give her a day or two.

In other news, the FBI was able to plot the movements of one Sherri Foote earlier this year--July 21, as a matter of fact. She missed a flight to Johannesburg, South Africa. Her traveling companion, however, a Jeremiah Ashcroft, who paid for both tickets with a credit card, showed up for the flight, checked in, then decided to abort. He actually got off the plane at the last minute. Three hours later he purchased a round trip ticket for one to Belize, and flew there alone.

And, get this: three days later, July 24, a Mrs. Sherilee Ashcroft boarded a plane to Mexico City, stayed there until the twenty-seventh, then caught a one way flight to *Philip Goldson International*, in Belize."

Fox and I stared at each other at the news. I was intrigued. I watched as the Inspector flipped a page on his spiral bound notepad and continued.

"Further, on August 5, our Mr. Ashcroft returned to LAX. Now if I'm not mistaken, we have Jerry Ashcroft in a hospital bed with a gunshot wound to his elbow. Then Mrs. Ashcroft returned on August 23, almost a month later. My FBI contact has no other international activity per passport documentation."

"Wow, Inspector," Fox exclaimed. "You were able to gather that information that fast? Your FBI guys are good!"

"The world has become a neighborhood, children," Morris chuckled.

"Speaking of a neighborhood," I said in a more serious tone, "I'm going to talk to the fellow I put in a neighborhood hospital. You want to accompany me, Morris?"

"No, I'm swamped since returning to work. Take a recorder; I'd like to hear what he has to say . . . if he'll talk to you."

"I'll let you know."

"He has a security detail. I'll call ahead to let them know you're on your way."

* * *

A cop sat outside Room 23B as I approached. It was 9:41 a.m.

"You're Alan Garrett?"

"Yes."

"He's in there with his attorney right now. The guy has been in there for almost a half hour. I told Ashcroft you were on your way here for a visit. He just about exploded; shouted *absolutely not*, but the attorney popped his head out the door a few minutes ago and asked that I let him know when you arrive."

Hmmm, his attorney, I thought. Change of tactics.

"I'll be right back. Don't announce me yet."

I ran back to my Caddy, dropped the recorder on the passenger seat, pulled two UHF micro-bugs and a video pen from my attaché. I stuck the pen in my shirt pocket and retraced my steps to Room 23B.

"Okay, officer. Let them know I've arrived."

SEVENTY-SEVEN

"Alan Garrett! Good morning!" he stuck his hand out. "We spoke on the phone some time back. Eric Betters."

"Of course!"--brain working overtime--I should have known Ashcroft would call an attorney with whom he felt comfortable. Who better than a Gunn and Gunn attorney?

"Ashcroft worked with you folks, didn't he?" I took his hand in a firm grip.

"I recommend you distance Gunn and Gunn from your client's activities. He is a murderer and a scoundrel."

"Thank you for that, Mr. Garrett," Betters smiled. "I have agreed to provide counsel for Mr. Ashcroft, and as such, whatever he and I talked about is confidential. But I would appreciate whatever information you have to share."

"May I speak with him?" I asked.

"Certainly--but not without my presence."

"Fair enough."

I dropped one of the two bugs in his coat pocket as we turned to enter the room. They have a three hundred yard range. I hoped it would be of value. It was attached by voice activation to a recorder in the Caddy.

A barrage of expletives met me as we entered.

"My arm! You see my arm, Garrett? It's in a sling. I may lose it! But your ass will be in a sling when I'm through with you, Garrett! You hear me? Your ass will be in a sling!"

I decided to play innocent. "Where is Sherri Foote, Jerry? Did you kill her as you did Sharon Etts, Trudy Wells and Lord knows how many more. Police unearthed seven bodies at your old home in Eagle Rock."

"I don't know what you're talking about. I never owned a place in Eagle Rock," Ashcroft spat.

"That's enough, Mr. Garrett," Eric Betters said in even, clipped tones. "My client will answer no more questions."

"I'm just getting started," I complained. "This man has more than twenty counts of murder hanging over his head. I strongly recommend you not take him on as a client."

There was no sense in sticking around. I decided to walk out and talk to a nurse or the attending doctor, to ask when Ashcroft would be well enough to go to the county jail.

"Thank you for your concern, Mr. Garrett. I suppose I'll be seeing you in court."

"At Jerry's arraignment," I agreed.

"No. When he sues you," he smiled. "Tata."

I nodded to the deputy outside, then strolled down the corridor to ask at the nurses' station how long Ashcroft would stay in the hospital. The answer-- probably two more days. He wouldn't lose the arm, but would lose much of its function.

I sat in my Caddy and listened to the ongoing conversation. Betters was cautioning Ashcroft to say nothing to the police or to me. I heard the two exchange goodbyes and watched as Betters walked into the sunlight.

As I drove back to the office I thought to myself, *should have shot Ashcroft in the head, Gumshoe. Save the world the expense of locking him up for fifty years.*

I punched in Morris' number--told him Ashcroft would be in the hospital for a couple more days before being transferred to the jail; also told him that I couldn't ask questions because Ashcroft's attorney cut me off. But I did make a video of our meeting, whatever it might be worth. Afraid my visit didn't accomplish much.

* * *

Morris suggested I lock the office and work from a motel while this madman's *team* was on the loose. I had other ideas.

"Go home and pack, Fox. Just as soon as Morris brings us any news of Maggorie's son, you will head there, wherever there is. I suspect it will be on the eastern seaboard. You up for that?"

"I am, Bossman."

"Put your car in a secure garage, take an Uber to LAX."

"You're going to Belize, aren't you, Gumshoe?"

"Just as soon as I know you're safely on your way. I'm going up to Pop's to fill him in on the situation. You can ride along if you wish."

"No, I'll stick around here; maybe check out flights to Belize for you. Besides, Morris may call with information on Paul."

"Paul?"

"Paul Maggorie, Gumshoe. You know--my case. Forget already?"

"Okay. Here," I said, handing her the pen and the cassette I had recorded with the bug. "Watch this video, and listen to the recording of their conversation. I'll be back within an hour."

I sped up the hill in my Caddy and pulled up in front. Pop was surprised to see me.

"What are you doing here so early? Did you forget something, Alan?"

"No, Pop. I came to pack a bag and give you a 'heads up'. We received a threatening phone call early this morning. Some fella says I'm a bother to his business, and that he'll have to deal with me."

"So, you're packing a bag?" A slow smile crossed Pop's face. "I see the irony of it, Alan. That's alright. I'll deal with him. Do you have a name or a picture so I'll recognize him?"

I laughed with him. "No, Pop. But, I think I've spoken with him recently. Morris is going to have this place patrolled a few times while I'm away. But, you might do well to keep a weapon under your pillow and your firehouse buddies on speed dial."

"Where you going?"

"Belize. I mentioned the possibility a day or two ago. Now it looks like a sure thing."

I prepared my carry-on bag for the trip, grabbed my Beretta, along with ammunition, packed them in a locked case to go into the luggage compartment. Then I made copies of my carry permits and credentials. I was ready to head for Belize.

I Gave Pop a hug.

"You make sure you keep a sharp watch for any unusual movement coming up our road. Don't hesitate to call Morris or 911."

I drove down the lane to the office. Passing by, I noticed Amy's car was still out. For a fleeting moment I flashed on a thought, *Mallory may have had more than a photo shoot on his mind this morning.* Then another thought, *So what, Gumshoe? She's a big girl.* Then, as I opened the gate to park, I had yet another thought, *You kinda like that moniker, "Gumshoe" don't you, Alan?*

My phone was ringing even before I got back in my Caddy. It was Fox. Excited.

"Bossman! Where are you? Please get yo . . ."

"Whoa, Fox! I'm right outside. Coming in the back door now."

I left the convertible in the drive and ran to the rear door. Fox was waiting with the door open.

SEVENTY-EIGHT

"It's Amy, Gumshoe! And Mallory! Ambushed according to Bradley Swazer! Amy's in hospital, just barely hanging on; Mallory's dead."

"Oh, no! Where and when, Fox?"

"I made notes," she said, handing me a pad.

• *7:09 a.m. Anonymous tip--shooting at vacant residence on 160th Street in Lawndale*

• *Officer Mallory responded. Per patrol car camera, he arrived on scene with police photographer, Amy Wynne at 7:33 a.m.*

• *Discovered open door. Entered. Shot immediately per audio on camera. No trace of shooter*

• *Victims discovered by real estate agent 10:22 a.m. Officer Swazer, ambulance responded 10:38 a.m.--*

• *No other victims on scene*

• *Amy transported to Memorial Hospital, Gardena*

I felt anger boiling up inside. The caller on my tip line earlier was making good his promise. I needed to stop him before we lost any more to this madman. I was pretty sure I knew who it was.

I called Morris. The desk sergeant informed me he was at Memorial. I called his cell to tell him I'd join him there. Liz elected to stay at the office. As she said, her desk was secure from outside view.

"Gumshoe! Before you go, what do you think of your hospital visit this morning?"

"You mean what do I think of Eric Betters, don't you, Fox?"

"Listen to this, Bossman." Liz pushed the button on the tip line.

Mr. Garrett, You're very annoying. My team has been compromised almost beyond repair. I must even the score, then rebuild . . . Liz stopped the recording.

"That's the same voice, or at least, very similar to the pen video from the hospital, Bossman."

"I know. I came to that same conclusion during my hospital visit. Keep your weapon handy. I may have to postpone my Belize trip."

I tucked the pen in my shirt pocket and exited through the rear door, locked the gate and headed for Memorial Hospital on Redondo Beach Boulevard in Gardena.

Morris met me at the nurses' station.

"She's still in intensive, Alan. Shot through the stomach, missed her spine; Doc says she will recover . . . maybe a week's stay."

"Were you able to speak with her, Morris?"

"No. She was all drugged up and in emergency surgery by the time I arrived. Going back under the knife once she's stronger. Probably tomorrow morning."

"Damn shame about Mallory," I expressed my sympathy. "Has his family been notified?"

"Swazer called it in. I sent him to the Mallory's home as soon as the paramedics arrived on-scene."

"I think I know the person responsible, Inspector. I'd like you to swing by the office to listen to that same tape we listened to this morning and compare it with a recording I took later this morning."

"Well," Morris said with a shrug, "no sense in sticking around here. Let's head back to your office."

* * *

"It's definitely him," Morris confirmed. The tone, the expressions--especially that taunting *'tata'* he seems so fond of. Did he have time to gun down Mallory and Miss Wynne before visiting Jerry Ashcroft this morning?"

"Absolutely, Sir," I said. "Strange, isn't it? Amy and I were having breakfast this morning just before 7 o'clock. She cut it short to meet with Mallory."

"Gunn and Gunn is in Glendale, right?"

I nodded.

"We'll pick him up today. Do you have their address and phone number?"

Fox gave him a Gunn and Gunn card.

"Drive safe, Inspector," she said.

Morris started out the door, then turned.

"I haven't forgotten your young man. I received an email just an hour ago. My Homeland contact says she'll be faxing some pertinent information shortly. When it arrives my sergeant will shoot it over to you.

"Watch yourself young lady," he said to Fox. He gave me a rueful smile as I opened and held the front door for him, "At least no one shot me as I walked in today."

I looked up and down the street. No cars were approaching from either direction. We shook hands, he stepped off the curb and into his car. I watched as he hung a right at the corner.

"Eric Betters!" Fox exploded. "Can you imagine? He was so friendly, so knowledgeable and so helpful, Gumshoe. He's been there for decades! Why, I . . ." Liz suddenly came to an awful conclusion . . .

"Gumshoe! Do you realize he may have been killing people for decades to inherit their assets?"

"I came to that same conclus . . ." I hadn't finished my sentence when music sounded from the front desk.

"What's that?" Fox asked. "did you buy a stereo, Bossman?"

"No! That's my bug in Eric Betters' pocket, I'm sure of it!" I exclaimed. "The stereo in his car. That recorder is sound-activated only within 300 yards, so he's close by!"

"He's on the hunt, Gumshoe!" Fox whispered.

"And I think I know his quarry. Grab your Beretta, Fox, and head for the hallway."

We listened as the recorder volume increased, became clearer, then suddenly, only silence. A car door opened and shut, followed by the sound of footsteps.

Our visitor peered through the window but he couldn't see me. He pushed the outside bell. I yelled, "Just a minute!" made sure Fox had a wall between her and the front door, and pushed the electric strike.

"Oh, there you are, Mr. Garrett," Betters smiled and put out his hand. "I didn't see you at your desk."

I ignored his hand. "Betters, turn around; hands behind your back. I'm arresting you for murder."

"You what?" He acted incredulous.

I grabbed his arm before it could move, twisting it behind his back.

"I said turn around, you sick slime!"

I slapped a cuff on the right hand and jerked him around. Eric's left hand came free from a jacket pocket, complete with a handgun. He tried to bring it up but I chopped his arm with the heel of my hand, wrenched the gun from his hand and joined both hands behind his back in cuffs.

"Fox! Come out here, please. Call Morris. Tell him turn around and get back here."

"On it, Gumshoe."

"You're making a big mistake, Mr. Garrett. That gun is for my protection and it's legal. I came here to discuss my client."

"No, you came here to--how did he describe it, Fox?"

"To uh, 'even the score' is the way he put it, Gumshoe."

Morris pulled up outside.

"Well, who do we have here?" he asked, looking from Betters to Fox to me.

"This is the s.o.b. that shot Mallory and Amy this morning, Sir. The attorney, Eric Betters."

"I shot no one!" protested Betters. "I've never even fired a gun!"

"So this is the brains behind all your trust cases!" Morris said, looking Betters up and down. "Murdering son-of-a-bitch!"

The Inspector turned to me, "I'll take it from here, Alan. Thanks," he said. He ushered Betters into the back of his squad car and headed for police headquarters.

"One more down, Gumshoe, and nobody died," Fox looked at me and smiled.

"Nobody died," I agreed. "And with Betters in custody we can breathe a bit easier. Nothing yet from Homeland, eh? Go home and pack, Fox. I'll watch the store until you get back."

Coffee sounded good. I made a short pot, sat back at my desk and enjoyed a mug, while checking the internet for hotel accommodations and flight information to Belize. I had just about drained my mug when the fax began spitting out paper. I walked back to Fox's desk--three sheets came through from a Homeland agent.

The gist of it was that the movements of young Maggorie had been traced to a visa card used at a motel in Morehead City, North Carolina, close to the Marine Corps Base Camp Lejeune.

That was July 19. Nothing further, with a caveat: the visa statement had been paid monthly right down to the penny by a money order through the mail. Someone was keeping the young man's finances current. The payments were being made from Panama City, Florida. Not much to go on, but it's a start.

SEVENTY-NINE

Friday, September 27. Carry-on and two pieces of luggage, one of which was a carry case for her Beretta, Fox was ready for her trip to North Carolina. She didn't have a concealed carry permit yet, but she shouldn't need one. She was simply going to pick up the trail of young Paul Maggorie and track him down. She would start at his last known location. Our Homeland contact would keep in touch.

Fox had called the motel; they were as helpful as one could expect. They should have had his license plate number, but they forgot to ask for it, but they were sure he had a vehicle.

I took Fox to LAX. Uber was too cold. I wanted to see her off.

I now had two days before I would head for Belize . . . my scheduled flight was early Monday. Pop and I arranged for him to pick Amy up from the hospital when she was released. Ashcroft had been transferred to the jail. Neither Morris, Liz, nor I have had success in locating either of my three missing persons: Tom Wellings, Sherri Foote or Gina Rowling. Even Morris' FBI friend had no success.

I sat in my office with hands wrapped around a mug of fresh coffee. Morris sat across from me with two pieces of news--

First, that Eric Betters was dead. Evidently committed suicide in a holding cell last night.

Second, that his FBI contact reported that the Ashcrofts, both husband and wife, flew to Mexico City Wednesday, and were on a flight this morning to Belize . . arrived there at 9:17 a.m.

"That's a barrel-full of very surprising news, Inspector. It's 12:34 p.m. I think a Martell is in order. Join me?"

"I will."

"So Mr. Betters took the coward's way out," I said pouring each of us a snifter of cognac. "I suppose he figured death was cheaper than spending twenty-five consecutive life sentences.

And now, we have someone posing as Jerry Ashcroft . . . he is still in the hospital isn't he?"

"No, he's in jail," Morris assured me.

"So, while we're speculating on who flew to Belize, do you have time to take a ride with me?"

"Sure. Where are we going?"

"A surprise."

* * *

The Bahia Marina at Seal Beach was a sprawl of piers with slips along the waterway between Long Beach and Huntington Beach. We stopped at the gate and I asked the gatekeeper for directions to the slip belonging to Tom Wellings. He called the manager. The answer came back immediately.

"Tom Wellings owns a yacht?" Morris sounded dumbfounded.

"Comes here quite often so it seems," I answered.

The gatekeeper circled the location on a map, drew with a red marker the easiest route and handed me the map.

He wrote down my license plate and mumbled something about parking only in designated spots and visitors must leave within two hours unless they have a parking permit. The Inspector waved a badge at him.

"Official police business," Morris barked as we moved forward.

The sailboat was gorgeous. A 46 foot Hunter. Must have set someone back about two, two hundred fifty thousand bucks. The fellow patrolling the piers on this end of the marina watched as we strolled up to the boat.

"Can I help you?" he yelled from the next pier over.

"Looking for the owner," Morris chirped. "Has he been around here recently?"

"Took her out with a couple of ladies about two-three weekends ago. Gone for a few days. When I came in to work Monday following she was still out; but Tuesday morning, there she sat.

"Mind if we take a peek inside?" I asked.

"Go see the director. If she says it's okay then I say it's okay. But she's probably going to tell you to get a warrant."

"Probably," I agreed, "but we're investigating a homicide case. Several people missing, probably tossed overboard into the Pacific."

"See the director," he repeated, with a pained look on his face.

"Where did you come up with that tall tale?" Morris asked as we approached the main office.

"I've been thinking about it for a couple of weeks. Simple, clean and final once you're out beyond currents, maybe ten to fifteen miles."

"A search warrant would have been nice, Alan."

* * *

Mary, the director was charming. "Tom Wellings' boat? That's slip J-33 out on the end isn't it? He normally pays once every three months, but in August he paid for twelve months. In cash, no less."

"Did he give any reason for such a change in routine?" I asked.

"No. He just said that way we wouldn't be bothering each other for a year. Now why are you fellows interested?"

"Homicide investigation. We have reason to believe Tom may be a victim. He's missing. We'd like to be allowed to inspect his yacht."

"By all means, so long as his locking mechanism isn't compromised."

"Thank you. We won't disturb a thing. What we will do is bring our forensic team on board to take finger print samples and such."

We walked out before she could change her mind. We called police forensics to drop everything and get out here. Then, while waiting, we enjoyed lunch at a local eatery.

We returned a few minutes before they appeared at the gate; we went in past the guard together. My locksmithing skills went to work, opening the hatchway door with ease.

Morris and I inspected every nook and cranny while the forensics team swabbed and dusted for prints and organic matter. The galley had dirty dishes and wine goblets in and around the sink for easy DNA samples. Garbage cans had been emptied in an outside dumpster at the end of the 'J' pier, but a used condom was under a bed in the forward berth.

The two forensics went topside. Next to the davit they discovered evidence of a considerable amount of blood.

The four of us spent more than an hour there, after which we wrapped yellow tape across the face of the slip, notified the director that boarding the yacht was prohibited for the time being, then headed back with items that held promise.

By the end of the day we had a notebook full of information, some very surprising.

•Fingerprints of nine different people were in the dusted samples--those of Tom Wellings, Jerry Ashcroft, Sherri Foote, Gina Rowling, Eric Betters, Trudy Wells, Alex Graham and two ladies police have identified as high-priced escorts.

•The wine glasses on the galley counter suggest that only three people were on board during the last trip, which corresponds with the pier security fellow. DNA and prints showed those imbibing were Tom, Sherri and Gina.

•The used condom showed DNA of Tom as we expected. The vaginal fluid residue belonged to Gina.

•The blood sample on the aft of the yacht would take more time; the area was mixed or at least smeared with fish guts and blood. The sample was not pure. The team may have to return to Seal Beach for a better sample.

•The most surprising fact that came from our visit is that the DNA samples pulled match DNA on file. One of the two ladies is a familial match to an unsolved cold case.

EIGHTY

Early Saturday I jogged my usual beach run, then continued my trot to the end of the pier, where I sat on a bench and watched three inveterate fishermen. I had come here often--I knew several of these fellows by name. Today, however, my mind was elsewhere; I hardly spoke to them at all.

"Hey, Mr. Private Eye," one of them growled. "You ain't exactly sociable this morning."

"Oh, sorry," I replied. "Just thinking about a case I'm working on. Came here to sit and clear my head, not ignore you."

Our conversation was cut short when one at the rail shouted "Fish on." and I watched until I saw his catch--a small yellowtail, then waved at them and jogged toward my office, stopping to pick up a glazed buttermilk bar on my way.

The pastry was gone, my second mug of coffee was about to disappear when Fox called from North Carolina.

"I'm heading for Florida, Gumshoe. The latest from my Homeland contact, Shirley, is that Paul's credit card was used in Panama City Beach. $137.33 for a dinner at the *Saltwater Grill*. Just a week ago. Awful lot of money for a meal. Think he has a traveling companion?"

"Or he drinks expensive booze," I suggested.

"I'll find him in a week," Fox declared. "This is too easy. I forgot to ask, what happens when I find him? Should I shoot him, handcuff him, what?"

"Your job is to find him. When you do, then you get hold of Captain Albert and ask for any further instructions. If I know the Captain, he will probably catch the first flight to Florida. At that point he takes over, you come home, we figure total expenses, send Maggorie a final bill, return the excess from the retainer, and live happily ever after."

"But there will be no excess, Gumshoe!" Fox protested. "My expenses are mounting. I may need to call you for . . ."

"Funny lady!" I laughed. "Just find Paul so you can get home."

I filled her in on the progress here and we hung up.

Pop was up when I walked into the house.

"Have you had breakfast, Alan? I made extra . . . kept expecting you to join me. Still some of my famous hash browns in the refrigerator."

So I enjoyed a real breakfast, after which Pop and I visited Amy. She was awake. "Doc says I'll be discharged by Tuesday at the latest," she smiled. "Is my camera equipment safe?"

"Yes," I assured her. "Morris put it in the Police impound along with your car. We'll make arrangements to have the car delivered to Pop's."

"Then I'll pick you up and bring you home when you're released," Pop added.

* * *

Philip Goldson International Airport in Belize City serves the nation quite well. I arrived at 11:20 a.m. Monday morning. From there I rented a late model sedan and drove about two hours to San Ignacio, the logical place--in light of all those phone calls--to start my search for Sherri--and, or, Gina.

San Ignacio is what we in California would call a suburb--in this case a suburb within the Cayo District, with it's more than one hundred thousand. A major banking facility, the Atlantic International Bank, had a branch there. The bank was my first hope in finding my quarry.

My reservations at a downtown hotel did not disappoint. It was lovely. I unloaded my suitcase, took a quick shower and put on a suit and tie . . . my formal wear. Then, armed with a fluency in the Spanish language, pictures of Tom Wellings, Gina Rowling and Sherri Foote, and of course, my personal magnetism, I headed for the Atlantic International Bank.

The teller, as I walked through the front door directed me to an assistant manager, Natalia Duran. We shook hands, I identified myself as a U.S. investigator working with the FBI, which wasn't entirely untrue. I explained to her that a group was suspected of laundering money through some vessel in the San Ignacio area, and that it might possibly be through her bank.

"We just had a complete audit for mischief at the end of last year, Mr. Garrett. Our assets were frozen for weeks. We were cleared of any wrongdoing, but the examination of our records was stringent. I believe you must be mistaken; however, I'll help you any way I can."

"We're looking for U.S. citizens who make large deposits from time to time in some kind of depository-- savings account, trust account, that kind of thing, going perhaps as far back as 2008 or 2010."

"There is so much American money here," she smiled. "Is the money wired here or do they bring it in personally?"

"Not sure, but most likely they fly in, spend a few days, do their banking, then fly back to California."

"Okay. Let's start with a name or names."

"Sure. Ashcroft, Foote, Rowling and Wellings to name four."

"Let me check my client listings. You say you're working with the FBI?"

"Yes. The case started as a suspicious death, but as incident linked to incident it became clear it wasn't so simple."

Ms Duran found nothing under those names.

"Sorry, Mr. Garrett; nothing."

"I almost forgot. I have photos." I spread photos of the four, then added a photo of Eric Betters to the group.

The assistant manager studied the photos closely.

"I'm sorry, Mr. Garrett. This one," she said, pointing to the picture of Jerry Ashcroft, "may have been in here a few times over the last few years, but I can't be sure."

"Okay, I have one more for you. Do you have a trust in-house named the *Roxanne DeVry Trust*?"

"Roxanne DeVry! Oh my, yes! One of our largest client depositories. Monies flow into this account usually every month. Almost always hand-delivered, but occasionally wired from Mexico. In fact, I believe a deposit was made just this morning."

Ms Duran scrolled through her client list once more. Then with a few more strokes on her keyboard, she looked up and smiled.

"Ahh, yes. $138,331.68 USD was deposited at 10:22 a.m. by Sophia Cortez, lovely old lady. She lives in Mexico, comes the odd weekend, makes either a deposit or a withdrawal for some worthy cause per the terms of the trust.

I understand she owns a condo at the Villages in Florida as well. Her husband died when she was fifty. She's devoted to philanthropy--has done some good things for the youth here in San Ignacio."

"Do you have any photos of Ms Cortez?" I asked.

"No. For the first three or four years we checked her passport photo, but as she's grown older, she now has a hearing aid, hair is turning white and she uses a cane; she's like family. We all know and love her."

"I see," I replied. "Does she have a local address when she's in town?"

"No. Only in Mexico City. But we must have a contact phone number on file. I don't think we've ever called it."

"I probably have that number," I said. I thumbed through my notes and read off the one which had led me to this town in the first place.

"That's it," she affirmed, raising an approving eyebrow.

"My superiors will be asking me a series of questions. Is it possible to have a print-out of the account activity? We can block or cut off the account name and number so the pages will simply be a series of numbers."

"From it's inception? I can't do that without a court order, even for the FBI, Mr. Garrett. You know that!" she smiled. "I can say that the assets as of this morning are just shy of $200,000,000 USD."

I decided to push further: "And the charitable outlay as per the trust's charter . . . to worthwhile causes?"

Ms Duran scrunched up her face in a sardonic frown, as she looked over 2018 and 2019 figures. "You're being impossible, Mr. Garrett," she laughed. "I'll say this. In the last twelve months, outlays are in excess of $4,000.000 USD."

I thanked her for her time, exchanged cards with her, told her where I would be staying for a few days, and walked out, hoping she would call that suspicious contact number.

I went back to my hotel room, hoping to lay a trap for our *"lovely old lady, Sophia Cortez"*.

* * *

The outdoor table seating at the bistro across from my lodging gave me a good vantage point to observe traffic flow through the ornate double doors of the hotel. But I had another challenge . . . just how much coffee could I drink?

I called Morris.

"Forensics confirms DNA of the human blood on the deck of the yacht belongs to all three of the people aboard: Sherri Foote, Tom Wellings and Gina Rowling, Alan. Looks like they all drew a bit of it, mixed it with fish blood and poured it on the deck and over the side. Weird friends you have, Mr. Gumshoe."

"I think it's more than that, Inspector," I said.
"I think they intend to disappear, leave everything behind. It's their last hurrah. They have well in excess of $180 Million USD in a bank here in Belize under the *Roxanne DeVry Memorial Trust*. Someone needs to put a brick on that account immediately, Morris. I expect they'll know I'm here nosing around very soon. They may already know."

"I'll call my FBI contact right now. Maybe he can tap that contact line, too. He may want to call you back. You stay safe, Alan, you hear?"

EIGHTY-ONE

After two hours, five cups of coffee and a couple trips to the "*gents*", I decided the little cane-wielding lady wouldn't show. Perhaps my banker lady didn't call that contact line after all. I strolled across the cobblestone esplanade toward the hotel entrance.

The cobblestone suddenly exploded around me; chips of clay and lead ricocheted toward the hotel walls and a small panel delivery truck parked at the curb, spattering them with a mixture of surface gouges and deadly destruction.

I was being targeted--by, fortunately a very poor sniper. I raced, zigzagging across the street. My assailant had a suppressor on his or her rifle; I couldn't tell where the shots were coming from, except probably from one of the bungalows on the knoll behind my right shoulder.

As glass from a hotel window crashed to the sidewalk, I ducked behind the truck. Bullets strafed the truck's side, shattering glass and tearing holes in the metal. A cadre of police came running--the sniper fire ended.

"Who was shooting at you?" an officer asked me. "Where did the shots come from?"

"I can't be sure, but I'm here in conjunction with an FBI investigation into the movements of a team of U.S. criminals."

"And just what does this team do to attract the FBI enough to send an agent to Belize," the officer continued.

"Setting up illegal trusts and murder," I answered. "But, I'm not an FBI agent--I'm a private investigator, and I followed them here." I handed him my card.

"I assume you are carrying a weapon and have the proper paperwork." He didn't wait for an answer. Instead, in rapid fire he asked, "Where are you staying? What is *Gumshoe*? Is *Fox* with you?" all the while staring at my business card.

I answered his questions, noting that he spoke perfect English. He raised an eyebrow and smiled.

"Stay safe, Gumshoe. If you need any help from us, please ask for me, Jose Gallo."

The policemen entered the hotel lobby; I hustled in on their heels and up to my room. I grabbed my viewing binoculars and stood at my window scanning the row of seven or eight bungalows on the hillside behind the bistro. No curtains moved, no cars drove off, not even a stray dog was roaming the neighborhood; all was quiet.

I decided to go on the offensive. I changed clothes into something more *"touristy"*, checked my handgun for a full clip, and descended stairs to an exit onto a side street. From there I climbed into my rental car and sped up the hill.

Why not? I told myself. Start with the home at the end of the row. I knocked. The small, older lady answering the door knew everyone and everything that happened on her block. The fourth house--the green one--was usually vacant . . . occupied only occasionally by a middle-aged couple; sometimes just one of them shows up.

She thought they were together in the village right now, but of course, she wasn't sure. They kept to themselves, not very sociable. They kept an expensive black car in the garage.

"Strange, though," she confided in me. "When the man comes alone, he brings an older woman--a cook or housekeeper I presume. She's not always there, but I see her once in a while. Wears glasses, walks with a cane."

"Thank you. Very helpful," I told her as I walked back to my car. I opened the trunk, pulled my camera bag out, put it on my shoulder, and made my way as a tourist down the street, taking shots of the village below.

As I neared the green bungalow my cell phone rang. I sat on the steps of the house next door as I spoke to an FBI agent.

"Mr. Garrett. The *Roxanne DeVry Memorial Trust* account has been frozen. It happened ten minutes ago.

The FBI will have agents on the ground within two hours and in San Ignacio shortly thereafter. What are your plans?"

"Five minutes ago I was being shot at in front of my hotel; right now I'm sitting next to the house from which those shots were fired, planning on retaliation . . . and I'm a much better shot."

"Can I ask you to stand down?"

"It depends upon the occupants of the house next door, Sir. I can only say, get your boys here soon."

I pulled my listening device from the camera case, and pointed it toward the green bungalow. The bits of conversation I heard were innocuous until the phone in the house rang. *"Leave a message. We'll return the call."*

"Hello. Is this Sophia Cortez? This is Atlantic International Bank. I must inform you that the Roxanne DeVry Memorial Trust account has been frozen. We received the order just fifteen minutes ago. It seems your government has concerns, the cause of which we haven't been notified." The call ended.

Screams of rage came from the green bungalow.

"Kill that bastard!" a female raged.

"Oh, I intend to!" a male roared, just as fierce and even louder.

A door slammed. I pulled my weapon, expecting to see someone come flying around the corner of the house. Instead, I was surprised to see the garage door open and a black sedan screech forward, out and into the street. The driver, a man, didn't so much as turn to look back at the house, but instead, headed down the hill. I didn't get a good look at the fellow behind the wheel, but I assumed Tom Wellings.

Sitting on those steps I wondered how I would handle the coming confrontation with this murdering couple, but on an impulse I slipped into
the garage before the door re-closed.

Brilliant move, Alan, I said to myself. *Now what? Not sure,* I answered, bu*t here I am.*

As silently as possible, I tried the garage hinged door going into the house. It wasn't locked. I slipped inside. Kitchen.

Epithets, screams of, "I should have killed you weeks ago, Alan Garrett!" and a woman's crying came from beyond the kitchen hallway accompanied by noises like dresser drawers opening and slamming shut.

Decision made. I walked into the front room and chose a chair situated so that anyone coming into the room wouldn't see the occupant until exposing themselves totally. I made myself comfortable on the reclining chair and waited.

It took ten minutes. I didn't recognize the woman that carried the two pieces of luggage past me to the front door. An old woman with glasses. She dropped them there, turned and spied me.

"AHHGGGH!" she screamed. Her eyes were as big as dollar coins; her hands went involuntarily to her temples and pushed up through her gray hair, which lifted to reveal the blond tresses beneath. "What are you doing here?"

"Waiting for you." I tried to sound nonchalant. "Sophia Cortez is it? Or how about Gina Rowling? Or maybe your real name. Virginia, isn't it? Virginia Evans?" I kept my gun trained on her.

Her shoulders slumped. "You *know.* How long have you known, Alan?"

"Started as a hunch from the very beginning--you know, Virginia--Gina--an easy transition. Then I dismissed it just that fast; but the thought kept niggling away and I couldn't shake it. That combined with all the violence against your family members, and to top it off, your own error, which we only recently learned. The gun used in family member shootings is the same gun, even including your father's killing. It was his service revolver wasn't it?"

"Ahh, yes. My dear family. I have never been Virginia," she spat. "My mother disowned me, my father used me as a plaything. I hated them both, and swore I would have my vengeance on them all. Grandparents, parents, all of them."

"When did you start killing everyone, Virginia? Was it with your brother, Chris, or was it your own father, burying him in that Eagle Rock backyard?"

"Ha! Chris! He didn't even remember he had a twin sister. No, long before that, Alan! That little asshole that came aboard the party boat and tried to screw every girl on board. My little half-brother, Teddy! He even came at me. I slashed his throat without a second thought, then cut him up. I guess I went half crazy.

Some of the girls got scared and ran off, but some of the others joined in. Strange how mob mentality takes over in certain situations. Grandpa White knew about Teddy; he just didn't want Regina or Grandma to know. That's why he insisted that the boat be pulled further out and burned the same day. He gave Regina some lame excuse that Teddy had run away. Ha! But I told her the truth just before I shot her!"

"Did you recruit Eric Betters and Sherri Foote, or how did that come about?"

Gina sank down on the sofa and continued her narration.

"Eric and Sherri had a good thing going long before I joined the staff. I agreed to join if I could write my own ticket. It worked well until Patti got involved. I could see the handwriting on the wall. Too weak. She was going to blow the whole thing. So she had to go.

Sharon began to suspect a problem and mentioned it to me. Said she was going to change the trust. I couldn't let her do that; we had a fight. She died. I'm sorry because she was my friend."

"So you cut her body up and brought it to the reunion to frame me."

"You seemed like the perfect patsy and we thought it would be an ironic gesture. We had forgotten that you weren't a participant twenty years ago, and we certainly didn't realize you aren't the wimp from that day either. Sherri told us after the fact."

"And Sherri. How on earth did she get involved in such criminal activity?"

"Ha! She told me Eric came to her one day and suggested she change one of the beneficiaries of a particular trust. So innocently, she did. Three months later she found herself the owner of four quarter-horses in Tennessee worth just under $2.5 million. She sold them within a week to a ready buyer. The trust owners were killed in a single car crash off Highway 1 just north of Santa Barbara. Sherri said Eric winked at her as he gave her the news.

The first few trusts she altered were, she

thought, simply tragic coincidences; soon she realized they were well-orchestrated events. By that time she was hooked. She owns properties in four or five states, including Hawaii."

"And you? What brought you to Gunn and Gunn?"

"Sherri hooked me up with Eric Betters on a date. He and I hit it off really well. He encouraged me to make application. Told me there would be perks galore. So I joined up. Everything worked great for more than ten years, Alan, until you stuck your nose in."

"Where is Sherri today, Gina?"

"No clue. We partied on Tom's boat over the weekend, then said our goodbyes."

"Why all the blood on the deck. It appears to be from all three of you."

"It is. To throw you off. With Eric Betters and Alex Graham dead and Jerry Ashcroft behind bars forever, we knew we were finished. Tom and I came here to pull our money out, Sherri split for parts unknown."

"So why did you deposit money in the bank when you first got here?"

"We had monies sent to Mexico. They had to be deposited here before we could access them. We had drawn up a $17 Million withdrawal for a *worthwhile cause* in the Arctic this afternoon. Then you come along and put a freeze on our funds! Damn you, Alan Garrett!"

"A phony cause in the Arctic, I presume."

She raised her eyebrows and rolled her eyes, "Is there any other kind?"

I shifted my revolver to my left hand and with my right I pulled my cell phone out of a pocket, along with the Belize Policeman's card. Punching in the numbers, I had only to wait two rings.

"Jose? Hi. You met me this morning . . . Yes, the private eye. Please be on the lookout for a . . . Sorry, say that again, please. . . . Is that right? . . . Oh, sorry to hear that. . . . Yes please, and check his black sedan. I'm looking for a list. It could be a ledger, a notebook or perhaps a computer. Okay, then. . . . No. I'm good. I will be joined by an FBI detachment shortly. . . . Would you do me a favor? . . . Ahh, Jose, you're way ahead of me. Great! Thanks. I'll call you later." I hung up.

"Seems your partner met up with the Belize police outside my hotel room. He tried to shoot it out with them. He's in a San Ignacio hospital pretty shot up. Probably won't make it."

"I'm surrounded by fools!" Gina exclaimed. "How about you and I fly to Mexico City, Alan? I have two tickets and a passport. You could put handcuffs on me. Once we're there we can disappear. I own a lovely château in Cozumel and enough money for us to live comfortably."

I laughed. "Oh, you'll be in handcuffs, Gina, but if you promise not to cause trouble I won't cuff you while we're waiting for the Feds. What's in your cases?"

"Just my clothes; what do you think?"

"Well, for one thing, the gun. For another, a ledger with your, shall we say, list of clients."

"I don't have a ledger, Alan."

"I don't believe you. Open them."

* * *

As it turns out, there was no ledger in her luggage. Along with her clothing, the gun was there; she put it, handle first, into my hands.

And so, we sat. Finally the call came through. The FBI was in San Ignacio. I directed them to the green bungalow; they were at the door within minutes.

After a discussion, I turned Gina over to the two Feds. They would hold her tonight but wanted me to dispatch her to LA tomorrow morning to meet an FBI detachment there. They would make the flight arrangements and escort us to Belize City tomorrow morning at 08:30 a.m. The flight would be at 09:28 a.m.

The bungalow was quiet. I searched it top to bottom for some kind of client list. Nothing. I walked back to my car. The little lady was sitting on her porch as I neared.

"You were in that house a long time, Sir. Your car is safe. I kept my eye on it for you."

"And I appreciate that. Can I reimburse you for doing that?"

"Oh no, Sir, but I saw another car park, and two men went in, and then they came back out with the old woman. I'm going to rest a few minutes here on the porch and have a cup of coffee. Would you join me? You can tell me about the people in the house."

Sure, why not? I asked myself . . . *leave out all the gore and details . . . just let her know that there was official police business on her block, including the FBI from the states. That should take care of many hours of gossip.* The coffee was strong.

I returned to my hotel, told them I would be leaving in the morning. The clerk handed me a message from Morris along with a laptop computer and a large manila package with an accompanying note from Jose Gallo: *Mr. Private Eye. Everything from the black sedan for you.*

The message from Morris was disturbing: *Sherri Foote's body was washed up near Laguna.* So much for honor among thieves . . . and murderers.

EIGHTY-TWO

Wednesday, October 1, the FBI contingent bade us goodbye in Belize City as we boarded a Delta direct flight to LAX. Gina sat sullenly almost all of the nearly six hour flight. Only once did she comment on the mistake I was making by bringing her to justice.

"Do you think your puny little office in Manhattan Beach will give you what I can give you, Alan? You'll be lucky to make $50 grand a year. I have well over ten times that much in legitimate savings accounts throughout the states. Take these cuffs off me. We'll disappear once we land in Los Angeles."

I simply looked at her and smiled. At the end of our flight we would be met by two federal agents who would take her off my hands. We arrived in Los Angeles at 1:14 p.m. As promised, Federal agents were there to meet us . . . along with sniffer dogs.

I took a cab to my office, immediately called Morris to let him know Gina was in the hands of the Feds, and invited him to the office after work for a drink. I made a pot of coffee, then sank into Liz' desk chair and breathed a long sigh of relief. It was finally over.

The messages on the desk phone answering machine were mostly robots telling me to support an impeachment petition or save the endangered polar bear population or take advantage of a government handout by going solar . . . but a few calls were of value.

One was from Peter Gunn, asking me to call him; another from Rachel, saying she missed me, where was I, and when could I join her for a drink, a dinner and a swim. The third was from Captain Albert for a progress report on Paul. I intended to return those calls.

A few new faxes were in the tray. I gathered them up, straightening the paper as I walked into my office. I sat for a few minutes, staring at the faces on my flip board. *So sad what greed does*, I thought.

The package officer Jose Gallo had given me sat on my desk. I was tempted to open it and go through it, but the phone calls beckoned me to respond. So, first things first.

I made the first call.

Peter Gunn sounded stressed. "Alan, I need your help. My firm could be in terminal jeopardy because of Eric Betters and his band of cronies. I've boxed up all of Eric's trust files since he joined the firm in 2002. I need someone to evaluate each one of them to determine which are legitimate, which are fraudulent. As you can understand, I cannot have it done *in-house*. Is your firm interested? I trust you to be discreet and thorough."

"Send the files, Peter. Of course, we'll help. How many files are we talking about?"

"Two hundred seventy-three. I'll have them there by 4:00 p.m. Thanks, Alan."

I called Pop. "Yeah, walked in about an hour ago. Everything wrapped up but for a couple of loose ends. You interested in a few weeks or months' work?"

Pop and I discussed the parameters: flag all trusts with the Roxanne DeVry Memorial Trust as secondary beneficiary, then follow up with phone calls, explain that those trusts would be redrawn at no charge to the client.

Pop was happy to take the assignment. "Is it a one-man gig or can I bring in some help?"

"Use discretion, Pop. Rita should be fine. I just don't want this to be a public spectacle. We need to hold the integrity of Gunn and Gunn intact."

"Understood, Son."

"Good. Do you have time this afternoon at 4:00 p.m.? Good. We'll meet here."

My next call was to Liz. "Yes, I'm home. Interesting short visit to Belize. "Now, what do you have for me?"

"You don't look at your emails, do you, Alan? Plus I sent you a long fax this morning--four pages worth. Now, what happened in Belize, Bossman?"

I filled her in. "Just a few loose ends to tie up. Gina even tried to seduce me on the way home," I laughed, "but the Feds have her now. So," I continued, "about you . . . how are you doing?"

"Oh no you don't, Gumshoe! Read my email to you. Then call me back. I'm just going for dinner. Call me after 4 p.m. your time. I'll be in my motel room."

I emailed Captain Albert, telling him I'd have information for him in the morning. Then I opened my email and began reading.

Gumshoe, We have a slight problem. Paul Maggorie is either a terrorist or in the hands of a terrorist organization. He's on an old fishing trawler off the Florida keys, or at least he was as of this afternoon. I'm staying at the Chelsea House in Key West.

Sitting in a nearby booth, I was able to hear a conversation at a cafe this morning. I used a listening device. Three rough-looking guys and a girl. They kept looking at me. Maybe I looked too interested. Nervous! Anyway, I'm attaching the audio here. it's a bit garbled but you'll get the gist. Call me for instructions. Fox

"Damn! Fox, don't go playing a hero, Girl!" I yelled aloud. "These people are dangerous!"

The front door closed. "Who's dangerous?"

I walked into the foyer to find Morris standing there. "My associate, Miss Betty-Anne McConnell, better known as Fox. Damn fool is trying to get as close to a fire as she can without getting burned."

"Why? Where is she?" Morris asked.

"Key West, Florida," I replied as I cracked a fresh

Martell, poured two fingers for each of us and offered Morris a chair. He sat, then pulled a fat envelope from an inside jacket pocket and handed it to me.

"From the families of the two Forensics officers, Alan. They won't take no for an answer. Take it and say thank you. Their addresses are inside the envelope."

"I can't take thi . . ." I tried to shove it back to him.

"Shut up and take it!" he demanded. "It's more blessed to give than to receive, but someone has to receive for someone else to be blessed, Gumshoe.

So," the Inspector continued, nodding his head, and pursing his lips, "it's over. And Gina is actually Virginia, the twin sister of that dead cop. Huh!" Morris shook his head. "We're sure all the players are accounted for?"

"Yes, but the final victim count isn't in yet. I'm meeting with Peter Gunn this afternoon. He's hired me to go through all the questionable files discreetly. Who knows how many were dumped at sea, buried in the desert, et cetera."

"Okay, Alan. This thing could blow up and destroy that attorney, Gunn and Gunn. Can you imagine the years of litigation! So far, we've released nothing to the press. Hustle with your investigation," he warned, draining his snifter. We shook hands; he bid me goodbye.

I poured myself another two fingers and prepared for my next call.

"Hi, Rachel . . . yeah, I'm back from a short trip . . . I'd love to have dinner and a swim, but I'm tied up until after 6 p.m. . . . no, Silly, not that kind of tied up . . . oh, well, that could be fun . . . I'll bring my handcuffs . . .

okay, I'll see you later." I decided to leave my cognac untouched . . . the day is young.

* * *

The four page fax was replete with pictures of the four Liz was sitting close to in the cafe. The note from Liz was brief: *I think he's being held for ransom. His captors look rough, but amateurish at best.*

Then there were pictures of the old trawler moored in Key West--a derelict craft for sure, named the Blue Moon, evidently where young Paul Maggorie was being held, Liz assumed, for a ransom. Sounded about right, but how the young man got mixed up with such hoodlums was a mystery.

The phone rang. It was Old Man Maggorie himself.

"Garrett, what the hell is going on with my son? Can you find him or not? Did I hire the wrong P.I.?"

"Florida, Sir," I stammered--*(I don't know why the old man still flusters me)*--he's in Florida. I've got my best person on it. We're concerned that he's been abducted, Sir."

"Abducted? Damn! Then the threat I received was genuine. Stay on it, Garrett. My son could be in real trouble with no small ramifications to me and further up the chain of command."

"Why, Sir? What does your son know?"

"It isn't what he knows. It's what he took from my office."

"And you're not going to share that with me, are you, Sir?"

"No, I'm not! Just find him, Garrett! Don't bring any lawmen in on this either. Bring him back to me."

"I thought I was only to locate his whereabouts, and let you know . . . now you want me to bring him back physically?"

"That's right. I'll bump up the fee; make it more worthwhile. Keep me informed, Garrett." He hung up, leaving me with a dead phone in my hand.

While I tried to absorb this increase in our assignment I heard the front door open and close. It was Pop. I looked at my cellphone; it was 3:50 p.m.

"Hi, Pop. Peter Gunn should be here any time, now. Care for a cognac? I poured one for myself, but things got in the way."

A minivan pulled up while Pop was having his last swallow. Peter Gunn walked through the door. I introduced him to Pop, then the three of us brought in box after box of files.

"Be sure we'll treat these files in the utmost confidence, Peter. Any discretionary funds or assets will be split between cancer, heart and homeless foundations. Hopefully, most of the clients have legitimate beneficiaries they can choose without being coerced into donating to the non-existent *Roxanne DeVry Memorial Trust*."

"Thanks, Alan. I feel relieved knowing you have it in your capable hands." He turned to Pop, "And of course, yours."

"Care for a cognac, Peter?" I asked.

"Can't. Picking the wife up. Going to a gala tonight celebrating thirty years in business. I'll drink my share at the dinner."

"You mean Gunn and Gunn?"

"Yes."

Pop left me alone to my own devices. I dialed Liz

in Key West. No answer. Now that's a surprise. She was supposed to be in her motel room by now.

I dragged the boxes of Gunn and Gunn files into my office and stacked them in a corner. There were fourteen boxes, and they were crammed full. What was it Peter had said? Two hundred seventy three files? They were certainly all here.

One more thing I must do. I opened the package from officer Gallo in Belize. I spied the notebook immediately. *Ahh, this is it! The client list!* I told myself. This will be a great assist for Pop and whomever we have going through the files. I put the notebook on top of the boxes.

I tried Liz again. Still no answer. Now I was getting worried. Where is that young lady? I stared at the flip-board and shook my head. Is it time to get involved in case #2?

I suppose it is, I said to myself, and erased the whiteboard clean. The photos and 4 x 6 notes on the cork side I stuck in a file folder and marked it <u>Case #1-- The Reunion.</u>

As Sergeant Preston used to say to his dog, *Well, King, guess this case is closed.*

* * *

I glanced at my cell phone. It was 6:12 p.m. Dinner and a swim really did sound great . . . I pointed my caddy toward Rachel's place

She met me at the door dressed in a smile . . . a smile and the bottom of a string bikini. One hand reached out with a snifter of cognac.

"You're right on time, Gumshoe," she laughed. "Looks like you could use a drink!"

Epilogue

Delightful! But a man's gotta do what a man's gotta do; I kissed a pouting Rachel goodnight and headed back to the office. It was well after 3 a.m.

I tried Liz one last time. Her phone rang six times. Still no answer. I hung up and called American Airlines, booked the first flight available for Key West: 8:14 a.m.

In my office I wrote on the white board in bold letters:

Paul Maggorie Case

Then using my notes from Liz, I jotted down the few things I knew:

•Tues. Sept. 30- Key West--Paul Maggorie accompanied by three males, one female boarding derelict fishboat _Blue Moon_.

•Wed. Oct. 1-   same group of four minus Paul last seen in cafe in Key West

On the cork-board side I tacked the pictures Liz had faxed to me: three photos of the rusted old fishing relic with the name _Blue Moon_ painted on her side in script . . . fading, but still legible . . . and the pock-marked faces of three young men and the girl.

Flipping the board back to the whiteboard side, I wrote in bold script for Pop to see:

Another Case to Solve, Pop ... I'll be back

I leaned back in my chair, set my feet and my fedora on my desk and closed my eyes. My luggage was already packed; I had nothing to do but go.

A Little About The Author

Singer, songwriter, author, poet is how Myron describes himself. Stir into this mix a conservative viewpoint and Christian ethic.

The youngest of four children, his beginnings were on a remote farm within a few miles of Lower Red Lake in northern Minnesota.

He recalls being bused twenty miles to a two-room schoolhouse--one room serving grades one through three, the other room grades four, five and six. During that time his teachers were a husband/wife team, followed by a mother/daughter duo.

Most of Myron's career was spent in the flat glass industry–from glass replacement on fishing boats in the Juan de Fuca Straits off Vancouver Island, British Columbia to designing and installing heavy glass systems for steam rooms in the San Francisco Diamond Heights District.

Since retirement, he has moved back to southern California, where he lives with his wife and two dogs. He has four grown children, and four grown grandchildren.

He began his writing career in 2015 with *A Lad From Sardinia.*

The Reunion is Myron's sixth book. Enjoy!